PENGUI

THE PORTAB

Each volume in The Viking Portable Library either presents a representative selection from the works of a single outstanding writer or offers a comprehensive anthology on a special subject. Averaging 700 pages in length and designed for compactness and readability, these books fill a need not met by other compilations. All are edited by distinguished authorities, who have written introductory essays and included much other helpful material.

"The Viking Portables have done more for good reading and good writers than anything that has come along since I can remember."
—Arthur Mizener

Some Volumes in
THE VIKING PORTABLE LIBRARY

SHAKESPEARE
015.008 0

POE
Edited by Philip Van Doren Stern. 015.012 9

OSCAR WILDE
Edited by Richard Aldington. 015.016 1

FAULKNER
Edited by Malcolm Cowley. Revised edition. 015.018 8

MARK TWAIN
Edited by Bernard DeVoto. 015.020 X

RABELAIS
Selected and translated by Samuel Putnam. 015.021 8

EMERSON
Edited by Mark Van Doren. 015.025 0

BLAKE
Edited by Alfred Kazin. 015.026 9

DANTE
Edited by Paolo Milano. 015.032 3

SWIFT
Edited by Carl Van Doren. 015.037 4

HAWTHORNE
Edited by Malcolm Cowley. Revised edition. 015.038 2

PLATO
Edited by Scott Buchanan. 015.040 4

VOLTAIRE
Edited by Ben Ray Redman. 015.041 2

MILTON
Edited by Douglas Bush. 015.044 7

MEDIEVAL READER
Edited by James Bruce Ross and Mary Martin McLaughlin. 015.046 3

COLERIDGE
Edited by I.A. Richards. 015.048 X

HENRY JAMES
Edited by Morton Dauwen Zabel. Revised by Lyall H. Powers. 015.055 2

CERVANTES
Translated and edited by Samuel Putnam. 015.057 9

MELVILLE
Edited by Jay Leyda. 015.058 7

GIBBON
Edited by Dero A. Saunders. 015.060 9

RENAISSANCE READER
Edited by James Bruce Ross and Mary Martin McLaughlin. 015.061 7

THE GREEK HISTORIANS
Edited by M. I. Finley. 015.065 X

VICTORIAN READER
Edited by Gordon S. Haight. 015.069 2

CHAUCER
Edited and translated by Theodore Morrison. Revised edition. 015.081 1

THE PORTABLE

Voltaire

EDITED, AND WITH AN INTRODUCTION, BY

Ben Ray Redman

PENGUIN BOOKS

Penguin Books Ltd, Harmondsworth,
Middlesex, England
Penguin Books, 625 Madison Avenue,
New York, New York 10022, U.S.A.
Penguin Books Australia Ltd, Ringwood,
Victoria, Australia
Penguin Books Canada Limited, 2801 John Street,
Markham, Ontario, Canada L3R 1B4
Penguin Books (N.Z.) Ltd, 182–190 Wairau Road,
Auckland 10, New Zealand

First published in the United States of America
by The Viking Press 1949
Paperbound edition published 1955
Expanded edition published 1968
Reprinted 1969 (twice), 1970, 1971, 1973, 1974, 1975, 1976
Published in Penguin Books 1977
Reprinted 1978, 1979

LIBRARY OF CONGRESS CATALOGING IN PUBLICATION DATA
Voltaire, François Marie Arouet de, 1694–1778.
The portable Voltaire.
I. Redman, Ben Ray, 1896– II. Title.
[PQ2075 1977] 848'.5'08 77-4746
ISBN 0 14 015.041 2

Printed in the United States of America
by Kingsport Press, Inc., Kingsport, Tennessee
Set in Caledonia

Contents

Editor's Introduction

ON THE twenty-first day of November, 1694, in the city of Paris, a fifth child was born to M. François Arouet, a prosperous lawyer long connected with the Department of Justice, and his wife Marie Marguerite, whose family name is variously recorded as Daumart, Daumard, and d'Aumard. On the very threshold of life this miserable male infant was so close to death that his survival was despaired of, and there is a tradition that he was hastily baptized at home; but there also exists a transcript from a register which states that he was carried to the font of Saint-André-des-Arts, church of the parish in which the Arouets then resided, and there quite properly named François Marie.

In any case, it was assumed that his stay on this corrupt earth would be of the utmost brevity, so it was a great surprise, even a miracle, to parents, doctors, nurses, godparents, and other adults interested in the feeble creature, when he defied fate by remaining alive for many weeks, and then for months that began to add up to a considerable total. Indeed, the miracle extended itself in a way that threatened to become monotonous, for if the notary's son spent his whole life—as we all do —in the act of dying, he was at it rather longer than most of us; since it was not until May 30, 1778, that the expectation aroused at his birth was finally realized. By that time, of course, all those who had surrounded his cradle had vanished from the earth, but there were still people to note his passing, for, when he finally did consent to die, the name which he had bestowed upon himself, that name with its eminently satisfying nobiliary particle—Arouet de Voltaire—had long been one of the most famous names in the world.

He had made it so by a lifetime of indefatigable effort in almost every branch of literature; by the exercise of a literary talent that was at once fine, robust, and amazingly adaptable; by a vigorous, extensive, and often embittered involvement with many of the great men of his age; by tireless pamphleteering against superstition, fanaticism, and oppression; and, in his later years, by an active and practical championship of several victims of the unjust forces he had so consistently opposed. His career divides itself into distinct phases, for the convenience of biographers, and his talent flowers in a succession of forms, but his most serious interests run like a continuous and unifying strand from his beginnings to his end. When the lord and patriarch of Ferney sharpened his quill for the defense of Calas, Sirven, and the Chevalier de la Barre, he was merely carrying to their logical conclusion the ideas of the young man who in his first play, *Oedipe*, had warned his hearers against the calculated deceptions and cruel tyrannies of the priestly craft. And if, in the course of his fight against the enemy which he called *l'infâme*, he began by using words that were only words, and then went on to give words the striking power of deeds, he was, in so doing, quite simply moving with the deepest ground swell or time spirit of his age. As historians have noted, the material for the battle of free thought was collected during the first half of the eighteenth century, while the battle itself was fought during the second half. But, if Voltaire moved with the times, he also moved with a degree of conspicuousness that was nearly unique; that caused men who came after him to speak of the century of Voltaire.

It is not, however, his underlying consistency that has impressed his admirers as much as his obvious versatility and his protean achievements. Charles Nodier was only slightly more eloquent than many others, when he declared: "There is something of the immense and the marvellous in the literary career of Voltaire. At eighteen, he was Aeschylus; at thirty, he was Sallust; at forty, Ariosto. He ended by joining to his scepter a jester's cap and bells, and the genius whose tragedies had evoked so many tears amused himself by eclipsing both Swift and Rabelais."

These are strong words, but they are at least matched by some of Goethe's, in a passage that takes off from the solid ground of *wahrheit* to soar in the free air of *dichtung*. Listen to Weimar's great ornament and oracle: "Depth, genius, imagination, taste, reason, sensibility, philosophy, elevation, originality, nature, intellect, fancy, rectitude, facility, flexibility, precision, art, abundance, variety, fertility, warmth, magic, charm, grace, force, an eagle's sweep of vision, vast understanding, rich instruction, excellent tone, urbanity, vivacity, delicacy, correctness, purity, clearness, elegance, harmony, brilliancy, rapidity, gaiety, pathos, sublimity, universality, perfection, indeed—behold Voltaire."

It would seem that just as Falstaff, who was himself witty, was the cause of wit in his companions, so Voltaire, who sometimes exaggerated, often caused others to do likewise. But if there are today few critics who would rank his tragedies with those of Aeschylus, and not many more who would salute him with all the eulogistic nouns that streamed from Goethe's pen, the warrants of his fame are still clear and genuine.

That his plays and nondramatic poems, with one or two exceptions, are now much read in France is improbable; and it is certain that they are even less often visited in their English versions. But one need go no further than the first of the dramas—in which the poet has rearranged classical elements with skill and power, while exhibiting both cultivated eloquence and a keen theatrical sense—to realize that Voltaire was a poet-playwright of high qualities. As for the history, running to many volumes, it is more praised than perused; and there is no reason why the case should be otherwise. It is praised because its author, following a lead of Fontenelle's, took for his object, not political or military history, but "the history of the arts, of commerce, of civilization, in a word of the human mind." It is praised for its original, innovating character; for its foreshadowing of a certain kind of history. But it need no longer be read, because the body of information which it offers has been rendered obsolete by historians who have practiced a type of scholarship and enjoyed advantages which were both unknown to Voltaire, and because no one of its component parts—neither the famous *Essay on Manners*, *Louis XIV*, *Charles XII*, nor the *Annals*—has the character of a self-sufficient literary masterpiece; the character by which some histories endure, even become what we call immortal, despite the supersession of their facts.

The excursions into science, the deistical treatises, the extensive and intensive Biblical criticism in which pioneer work was done, the dubious approaches to metaphysics? We should hardly say that it is for any one of these things that we value Voltaire today, that we read him, learn from him, enjoy him. And yet it is really for the sake of them all together, along with all his other interests and achievements that we turn to him; for it took the whole and many-sided man he was to write *Candide* and the other brilliant tales which express so pungently, so lucidly, and so amusingly his view of humanity and its predicament. It took the whole man to furnish the large and rambling structure of the *Philosophical Dictionary,* whose many chambers hold so much in the way of worldly wisdom, shrewd speculation, quaint history, and provocative argument. It took the whole man to write even the letters that reveal him so distinctly. And surely nothing less than the whole man could have made himself into the spokesman and embodiment that he became, that he is—the spokesman and representative of a great age that was heavy with the future; the embodiment of an intellectual position, courageously held in the midst of life's evils and mysteries.

Of course, it required many decades for him to become what he did, and, as has been said, the process appears to have divided itself into distinct phases which have proved a boon to tidy-minded biographers. Youth; the exile in England; the union with Madame du Châtelet; the visit to Frederick; the final avatar of Geneva and Ferney—these are the five periods into which the eighty-four years of Voltaire's life conveniently fall. We shall survey them, in a moment. But first, at this not inappropriate point, let us remind ourselves of the nature and extent of the ill-health which plagued Voltaire from birth to death, and let us try also to picture the face and figure of this extraordinary sufferer.

It seems most probable that the prime seat of his afflictions was tuberculosis, that he was the child of a tuberculous mother. Such, at least, is the conclusion of a physician who studied the case less than twenty years ago, and who wrote: "Intimate daily contact during infancy and early childhood with a mother evidently tuberculous may have much to do with Voltaire's perennial frailty. Such contact often leads to premature death, but occasionally as in Voltaire's case, confers a certain degree of immunity leaving a mummied crucible where the fires of genius may burn with an effulgence not often seen in the non-tuberculous." [1]

Whatever the seat of his maladies, they manifested themselves in a multitude of symptoms, reports of which swarm through his letters. At various times, and often with a concentration of ailments, we find him complaining that he is cursed by catarrh, dysentery, itch, smallpox, grippe, fever, chronic colic, erysipelas, gout, apoplexy, inflammation of the lungs, scurvy, herpes, rheumatism, strangury, deafness, indigestion, dropsy, falling teeth, loss of voice, neuritis, blindness, and paralysis. If he managed to be free from pain for two hours out of twelve, he counted himself fortunate. Distrusting and damning doctors, he was still an easy gull for novel remedies and was forever dosing himself, with a particularly heavy reliance on purges. He was always cold. No sun could be too hot for him, and he found no room comfortably furnished unless it included a blazing fire. Death stood always at his elbow, as he was fond of informing his correspondents. In 1746 he assured Frederick of Prussia: "I do not think my health will allow me to work much hereafter; I am fallen into a state where I think there is no help for me. I await death patiently." And eleven years later he informed the same royal friend: "I shall soon enter my sixty-fifth year; I was born sickly; I have but a moment to live . . ."

Indeed, he might well have borrowed a phrase from

[1] L. J. Moorman, M.D., "Tuberculosis and Genius: Voltaire," *Annals of Medical History*, New Series, Vol. III. 1931.

Pope—with whom he shared so many characteristics: wit, vanity, and venom among others—and spoken of "that long disease, my life." Yet one may suspect that, artist as he was in almost everything else, he was also something of an artist in complaint; that, wretched as his health really was, it amused him to depict it as being even more wretched. On one occasion, at least, we find him candidly confessing: "I am always complaining, in accordance with my custom, but by and large, I am quite comfortable."

The man who lived so long with death ended by looking rather like the conventional image of death itself, and even during youth and middle years his skin was stretched tight over bones that were nearly fleshless. But within this emaciated tenement the fire of life burned brightly, even dangerously, as everyone whose eyes ever met Voltaire's own eyes was forced to see at a glance. A police report, which describes him as he was in his twenties, says that he looked like a satyr. Baron Grimm, having mentioned his fleshless face, speaks of his witty, caustic expression, his sparkling, mischievous eyes, and declares that his behavior exhibits all the fire of his writings; that the brilliant play of his personality is dazzling in its intensity. And Grimm concludes: "A man so constituted could not help being a valetudinarian; the sword wears out the scabbard." Dr. John Moore, an Englishman, tells us that "an air of irony never entirely foresakes his face, but may always be observed lurking in his features, whether he frowns or smiles." And another physician, Dr. John Morgan of Philadelphia, who visited Ferney in 1764, reports that Voltaire "has a very sagacious but at the same time a comical look. Something satirical and very lively in his action . . ."

Witness after witness could be called, but the fiftieth would only confirm what the first few tell us: that Voltaire was a brilliant, fascinating creature, as lively and mischievous as a monkey; but with the difference that his liveliness and mischief were directed by one of the most agile brains ever housed in a human skull.

We know, with a knowledge abundantly and noisily documented, that he was even Whistler's superior in the gentle art of making enemies; but it is just as certain that his charm was irresistible when he wished it to be, and we may assume that this charm showed itself at a very tender age. Otherwise, the sprightly Abbé de Châteauneuf would hardly have bothered to act as little François's godfather, and amuse himself by teaching the child of three or four years to recite a string of irreverent verses from a poem called the *Moïsade*. Nor, if the budding charm had not flowered, would Châteauneuf have sponsored his precocious charge in the free-thinking society of the Temple, the house of the Grand Prior of Vendôme, where the Abbé de Chaulieu presided over an aristocratic circle of deists and libertines, whose boldness of speculation, and of wit, often threatened to spill over deistical frontiers into the bleak region of pure atheism. It was in this society that young Arouet's charm and other talents met their first important test; an encounter in which they scored a dashing triumph. Their possessor breathed deep of a heady atmosphere, and found it very pleasant indeed. It was nice, the notary's son discovered, to be able to look round a supper-table and declare, with easy assurance: "Here we are all either princes or poets." But this brings us to the first of those five famous Voltairean periods: Youth. And of this period, as of the others, certain features must be considered; even in an introduction that does not pretend to biographical adequacy.

At the outset, then, it is important to note that, health apart, François Marie Arouet got off to an excellent start in life, as the younger son of a rising family of the middle class; a class whose successful members were beginning to enjoy certain social, as well as merely financial, rewards; the class which, with the passing of a century, was destined to become dominant in France. On his father's side, the boy's ancestors were tradesmen, artisans, and farmers; on his mother's, they were much the same sort of folk, with a few small men of law in the immediate background; and, on both sides, the genealogical tree was deeply rooted in the soil of Poitou. But the residence of Arouet *père—ancien notaire au Châtelet de Paris,* prosperous official of the exchequer, whose friendly clients included such great noblemen as the dukes of Sully and Richelieu, and so glamorous a lady as Ninon de Lenclos—was not frequented by farmers and tradesmen. The society that met there was lively and often distinguished; the family's Jansenism, which seems to have been taken to heart only by the elder son, Armand, cast no pall over the household. Had it done so, Châteauneuf would not have made himself at home there; and, if the father had been as grave a Jansenist as some biographers would make him out, he would hardly have welcomed Châteauneuf, with his lessons from the *Moïsade,* or even Ninon's other dear friend, the ex-Jesuit, Abbé Nicholas Gédoyn. It is highly probable that the gay and attractive Mme. Arouet—dead at forty, when her younger son was seven—was the family's social magnet. In any case, the child who was nicknamed Zozo was familiar with polite company and conversation from the first moment that his ears could make sense of the sounds uttered by the huge creatures who surrounded him.

The Jesuits took care of his formal education, at the famous College of Louis-le-Grand, from his ninth to his seventeenth year; while his worldly education, as we have seen, was taken in hand by the entirely competent Châteauneuf. Some writers have made much of Voltaire's association with the Temple, and his participation in the legendary orgies of the Regency; but it is obvious that he had no more taste than physical fitness for the career of a debauchee. What he had a taste for was the business of rising in the world. He used the society of the Temple for his own purposes. At school he made fast friends with aristocrats who were destined for places of power, and in the circle of Chaulieu and the Grand Prior of Vendôme he acquired other valuable friends, while skillfully exploiting an audience whose approval could assure the fortune of a promising young poet. "A great man's friendship is the gift of heaven," declared Philoctetes in Voltaire's first play. It was a truth that he never forgot, a precept by which he continually profited. Frederick of Prussia was only the most exalted of his conquests. The Marquis de Saint-Ange, Sully, Richelieu, the Duchesse du Maine, Bolingbroke, the Maréchal and Maréchale de Villars, Madame de Pompadour—these, and many more, he cultivated and used along his way, expertly and with assiduity. But we must remember that it was no fault to cultivate the great in a society constituted as was the society of France and England in the eighteenth century; if, indeed, it is ever a fault. And we must remember, too, that in most cases Voltaire gave far more than he received; that in many instances, while accepting ephemeral favors, he bestowed a kind of secondary immortality upon those whose names he linked with his own.

The youth's father, who had little use for literature as a profession, most naturally wished his son to follow in his successful footsteps; and the son made some languid efforts to interest himself in the study of the law. But his clever, darting, curious, brilliant mind refused to be interested in that particular subject. Such dullness was not to be endured, when one could be a poet and sup with princes. The father exerted his authority by sending the poet to Caen for a few months, far from his princes: but the rebel returned from banishment with no greater liking for the law. And when young Arouet was sent to The Hague, in the suite of the Marquis de Châteauneuf, this corrective effort ended in his having to be called home because of a fiery, futile, and diplomatically embarrassing love affair with a Protestant young lady who endures in history under the nickname of Pimpette. Arouet *père* did not know it, of course, but he might as well have asked the moon to stand still, or the Pleiades to dance a quadrille, as ask his son to forgo the career towards which his powers inevitably urged him.

He aspired to be a great tragic poet, but he began by being a witty versifier, with a wit that was no respecter of persons. He composed lampoons against the Regent, which delighted the Duchesse du Maine's little court at Sceaux, and he was suspected of composing others; so it was natural, as things went in his day, that among the first rewards of his wit should be brief, monitory exiles from Paris, and a comfortable stay of some eleven months in the Bastille. He came out of prison with a finished draft of *Oedipe*, with much of the *Henriade* written, and with a new name; a name that was destined by its maker to serve as a patent of the nobility which birth had unkindly denied him. Monsieur Arouet de Voltaire. It sounded well, and it looked well. The young man assumed his new nobiliary particle, and his new surname, without fuss or fanfare; a few signatures to a few letters, a few words to friends, and the thing was done.

That anyone should have ever wondered why this

change was made is rather puzzling. The principal's own explanation to J. B. Rousseau, that he had been unhappy under the name of Arouet, is unacceptable; he remained Arouet, but with a delightful addition. Nor is there any sense in Saint-Simon's suggestion that the poet sought a disguise. Cardinal Dubois, the apothecary's son and favorite of the Duc d'Orleans, who knew all about the art of rising in the world, put his coarse thumb on the obvious truth when he accused Voltaire of wishing, quite simply, to ennoble himself in the eyes of society. There is no need to seek any other reason.

But whence came the name Voltaire? Here is a mystery that might well arouse curiosity, and it has done so to an extent that is probably disproportionate to the importance of the truth behind the mystery, whatever it may be. One popular explanation is that the name is an imperfect anagram of Arouet, *le jeune;* but there are cogent arguments against this theory. Another suggestion is that the name came from a family estate; but different writers favor different estates, on both the paternal and maternal sides, and careful research has been unable to transfer any one of these properties from the realm of imagination to that of reality. One writer derives the name from the phrase, "*Je vole ma terre.*" A second traces it back to Volterra, in Italy, birthplace of Persius, whose satires young Arouet read at Louis-le-Grand. A third would associate it with the schoolboy's nickname: *le volontaire.* But a recent and zealous student of the subject[1] rejects all these and other explanations, while presenting a novel solution of his own, which he supports learnedly and persuasively. According to this theory, Voltaire took his name from the town of Airvault, a place in which the Arouet clan did con-

[1] Ira Owen Wade, "Voltaire's Name," *Publication of Modern Language Association*, June 1929.

siderable business, and close to Saint-Loup, their place of origin. The poet merely transposed the syllables of Airvault, changed some letters without altering the basic pronunciation of his product, and the trick was done.

Wherever the name came from, its bearer remained sensitive to any questions regarding it, even decades after he had made it glorious. Only once, however, did his assumed nobility involve Voltaire in serious trouble —some seven years after the assumption—and then the upshot of the incident proved fortunate. The Chevalier de Rohan chose to pick up Voltaire's name as an instrument of insult; Voltaire replied in kind; the Chevalier had the impudent upstart beaten by lackeys; the bourgeois poet challenged the great aristocrat to a duel; the aristocrat had the bourgeois sent to the Bastille; after a fortnight, the prisoner was released on the condition that he go straight into exile in England; and the three years which Voltaire spent in England proved one of the important and fruitful experiences of his life.

Just how important it was is still the subject of controversy. One extreme view is that England was chiefly responsible for all that Voltaire became as a liberal thinker, as a foeman of fanaticism and intolerance, and as a defender of the rights of individual man; that in England he learned both to reason and to feel correctly; that, in Morley's famous phrase, he arrived a poet and returned home a philosopher. Excessive claims on one side of the Channel have evoked exaggerated counter-arguments from the other side. It is as foolish to say that Voltaire owed England practically nothing as it is to say that he owed England practically everything. The scholar[1] who argues that Voltaire did not have to cross

[1] Henry E. Haxo, "Pierre Bayle et Voltaire avant les lettres philosophiques," *Publication of Modern Language Association*, June 1931.

the water in order to become a deist is on firm ground. The child was already lisping deism when he recited the *Moïsade*. Châteauneuf was a deist; the Temple was alive with deism; all through France deistical currents were running strongly, often underground; and, above all, Pierre Bayle had been a deist. Was not the influence of Bayle dominant in Voltaire's thinking? Was not the pupil pleased to refer to his master as his spiritual father? And what was the *Henriade*, published more than a year before the fracas with Rohan, but a powerful deistical poem which violently attacked all organized religion, with a particular concentration of fire-power on that which stems from Rome?

So far so good. When the same scholar relegates Bolingbroke to a secondary position of influence, his argument still rests on fairly solid foundations. We may safely agree with him when he contends that it is always more or less the same Voltaire whom we meet in most of his works; that he was, even, very nearly "complete" in *Oedipe*. But when he refuses to credit Locke with as much influence as Voltaire himself attributed to the Englishman, he walks more shakily; and the danger is that, in his conscientious effort to arrive at the exact importance of the English sojourn, he may be encouraging readers to believe that it was less significant than it really was.

The truth would seem to be that Voltaire drank deep from two springs: from English freethinkers and scientific investigators, and from French sources that were similarly congenial to his intellect and temperament. An authority already drawn upon sees Voltaire's third period of development—what is known as the Cirey period, spent in the company of Madame du Châtelet—as one which he employed in harmonizing "the influences of the two preceding periods—in his assimilating writers interested in the same subjects, such as Pope and Fontenelle, Bolingbroke and Bayle, Woolston and Meslier. This assimilation is not exclusively characteristic of Voltaire, it is typical of the whole French movement in ideas from 1730 to 1750 . . . the French intellectual atmosphere of 1730-50 was subject to two influences—a strong traditional current and an equally strong English current. Voltaire merely breathed the same air which all intellectual Frenchmen were breathing." [1]

One estimate of the value of the English sojourn, which combines brevity with reasonable accuracy, is Lanson's: "England aroused, armed, and matured Voltaire: it did not make him." He came to England at the age of thirty-one—in the last year of George the First's reign—established as a brilliantly successful poet-playwright, destined to be a worthy successor to Corneille and Racine. Bolingbroke made him free of the highest Tory circles, while the ambassador of the government which had jailed him to oblige a Rohan was his sponsor with the Whigs. He was quickly acquainted with the leading writers and thinkers of the island, and soon friendly with a number of them. While enjoying the society of Pope and Swift, Gay, Young, and Thomson, he discovered the writings of Bacon, Locke, and Newton. He learned to read and write and think in English, and was presented at Court. He revised the *Henriade*, dedicated it to the Queen, and is said to have made two thousand or more pounds from the sale of subscriptions. He began his play *Brutus*, worked on his *History of Charles XII*, and soaked up the impressions and information which were to form the substance of the *English Letters* (*Lettres philosophiques sur les Anglais*)—in

[1] See Ira O. Wade, *Voltaire and Madame du Châtelet. An Essay on the Intellectual Activity at Cirey* (Princeton: Princeton University Press, 1941).

which he contrasted English political liberty, religious tolerance, and commercial enterprise with the prevailing spirit and actions of France, surveyed English poetry, and sketched the progress of English thought from Bacon to Newton.

The degree of religious tolerance prevailing in England could not fail to impress an author who was forced, at home, to write and print with cautious eyes fixed on powerful, fanatical churchmen. The degree of individual freedom was wonderful to a middle-class poet who had found himself at the mercy of an aristocracy which could use the Bastille as a kind of private jail. Wherever Voltaire looked in England, high or low, he found reasons for admiration. At the bottom of the scale there was the peasant, whose feet were not bruised by wooden shoes, who ate white bread, and whose clothes were not rags; while at the top of the scale, there was the philosopher, who was free to pursue his speculations, openly, as far as he had the wit to travel. On one side of the Channel, Voltaire thought that he saw the sunshine of day; on the other side, the darkness of night. When he returned home in 1729—with his skepticism and his deism strongly nourished by his English contacts, with a matured realization of his own intellectual position and a clear view of his direction—he was determined to uphold the torch of liberal thinking in France, and there make it blaze so that all Europe might learn to read by its light.

During the five years which elapsed between the end of the English exile and the beginning of the long liaison with Madame du Châtelet, Voltaire began to write the *Pucelle*, his notorious, bawdy, mock-heroic poem on the life of Joan of Arc; prepared *Charles XII* for a surreptitious printing, and had it smuggled into Paris; saw his *Brutus*, *Ériphyle*, and *Zaïre* acted with varying degrees of success; published his *Temple of Taste,* in which he sharpened his critical knives on several famous victims; and was forced to flee Paris in consequence of an unauthorized edition of the *English Letters.* For a while, during these years, he enjoyed the generous hospitality of a worldly, witty, and possibly wicked old lady, the Comtesse de Fontaine-Martel, in whose house he lived, whose horses he rode behind, and whose ample income he enjoyed having spent for his entertainment. When she died, he moved—but not too quickly—to the house of a wealthy corn merchant, named Demoulin, where he made himself at home. After the Comtesse's, this setting was comparatively mean, but it seems to have suited his convenience, and it is likely that he was engaged with Demoulin in an occupation to which he was quite as devoted as he was to literature: the business of making money. Any account of Voltaire's career and character would be sadly incomplete if it failed to take note of his financial talents; so let us take such note, at least briefly, at this point, even if it means that we must keep a most remarkable woman waiting for a moment or two.

Arouet *père* had been eager to buy his younger son a profitable legal post, to obviate the possibility of his starving in the lean paths of literature. He need never have worried. Voltaire wielded one of the most powerful pens of his or any age, but we may be sure that had he chosen, instead, to give all his strength to a pursuit that claimed no more than half of it, he would have met the greatest financiers on even terms, and probably outmaneuvered them into the bargain. He made himself not merely a remarkably rich writer, but a rich man by any standards. The sources of his wealth were various, for he did not live by words alone, and they were often dark and devious as well. The record is far from clear, authorities do not agree, but a few fairly certain facts may be cited.

Money began moving in his direction when he was still a child, when Ninon de Lenclos left him two thousand francs with which to buy books. The Regent gave him a pension of two thousand francs; a few years later another pension, from the Queen, amounted to fifteen hundred francs; when he was appointed historiographer-royal, due to the influence of Madame de Pompadour, the post paid two thousand francs annually; and while he was the guest of Frederick the Great he was paid twenty-odd thousand francs a year and his keep. The *Henriade,* as we have seen, brought him in a large amount of money; his plays were a steady, if not a great, source of revenue; and, despite the difficulties and subterfuges under which many of his books and pamphlets were published, he made them yield a considerable profit. When his father died, Voltaire fell heir to an income of four thousand francs a year, and he was annually enriched by another six thousand francs at his brother's death. But it was shrewd speculation that was chiefly responsible for the swelling of his capital. He is credited with one coup, in army contracts, which netted him six hundred thousand francs; a sum which, it is said, he promptly reinvested at a profit of thirty-three per cent.[1] Military uniforms, trading vessels, land, pictures, corn—these are a few of the items in which he speculated, while he made a pretty business of lending money to friends and acquaintances at high interest.

Through the years, it all added up enormously. At Ferney he went in for manufacturing on an ambitious scale: from the artisans, whose work he financed and whose products he distributed by means of high-power

[1] See Louis Nicolardot, *Ménage et Finances de Voltaire* (Paris: E. Dentu, 1854).

salesmanship, came silk stockings, cloth, lace, and the fine watches which he sold to distinguished purchasers throughout Europe; to Catherine of Russia, and to Catherine's enemy, Mustapha of Turkey. Towards the last, his annual income is calculated to have run between one hundred and sixty and two hundred and twenty thousand francs, while his household expenses amounted to less than forty thousand. He left his niece, Madame Denis, a yearly income of a hundred thousand francs, and six hundred thousand francs in cash and other assets. No, the good lawyer need never have worried about his younger son.

That Voltaire was extremely avaricious, there can be no doubt. Grimm declared that he worked less for reputation than for money, that he hungered and thirsted after wealth; and there is ample evidence that his fingers began to itch whenever he thought there were sous to be made; that he could not keep them out of shady deals, one of which embroiled him with his royal patron, Frederick, shortly after his arrival in Berlin. But Voltaire was no miser, nor was he even selfish. He was generous to his relatives, his friends, his tenants, the refugees who fled the rigors of Geneva to breathe the free air of Ferney, and men and women of all kinds who came within reach of his assistance. However much he might haggle over trifles, he could give with an open hand.

It was at Demoulin's that Voltaire met and fell in love with the Marquise du Châtelet; and it was at Cirey, the Châtelet manor on the border of Lorraine, that he found refuge shortly after the stir caused by the *English Letters* had made him hurriedly quit Paris to escape arrest and imprisonment. Gabrielle Émilie, daughter of the Baron de Breteuil, was twenty-six and her lover was thirty-eight when the famous liaison began. Married young to the Marquis du Châtelet, she had borne him three children and matched his infidelities with her own; the Duc de Richelieu being among Voltaire's predecessors in the field of her favors. A model of eighteenth-century husbandly decorum, the Marquis was quite content to have the famous author spend his money on rehabilitating Cirey, and settle down there with the Marquise in a union which embraced most of the values which man and woman have to offer each other. The union could be so complete because the lady was no mere *femme galante,* but also a *femme savante.* Having learned Italian and Latin at an early age, she was busy translating Virgil when she was fifteen, and she was to live to translate Newton's *Principia;* for the strict sciences of mathematics, physics, and astronomy excited her intelligence no less than did poetical flights, theatrical displays, historical researches, and excursions into Biblical criticism. An understanding reader of Leibnitz, she was friend and correspondent of the most learned men in Europe. Herself a tireless worker, she knew how to channel the powers of the man she loved and immeasurably admired. Indeed, in describing this union, we might well borrow Helen Waddell's fine phrase, descriptive of Abelard and Heloise, and speak of "the mating of eagles." In the Marquise du Châtelet, Voltaire found at first a passionate mistress, more enduringly a perfect intellectual companion, and the best friend of his whole, long life. That they could quarrel, even violently, merely completed the circle of their felicity.

The lady, like her lover, knew how to make enemies. Madame du Deffand, for example, whose claws were always sharp, has left a wicked physical portrait of Émilie, in which every feature—from head to feet, with all intermediate territory maliciously surveyed—is pictured as a masterpiece of ugliness. Such a portrait can have been inspired only by an intense personal dislike. Madame du Deffand is not borne out by the artists who have perpetuated Madame du Châtelet's likeness, nor by the record of her attractiveness to men. She was no great beauty, certainly, but she was a desirable woman; and it may be mentioned in passing that she was sure enough of her own good looks to bathe with aristocratic unconcern in the presence of a manservant.

Of course, the *ménage* at Cirey had its humorous aspects, which have been preserved by gossiping visitors and handed down from biographer to biographer. There are even those who have managed to find amusement in the spectacle of Émilie betraying her aging lover with a younger, lustier man, and seen high comedy in the old lover's devoted attendance at the childbed, which proved the deathbed, of a faithless mistress. The amusement of such persons is in direct proportion to their lack of understanding. The affair with Saint-Lambert began as a trivial incident; it happened to end fatally, as trivial incidents sometimes do. However much pain it may have caused Voltaire at the outset, the pain was fleeting, while the union with Émilie was above and beyond such intrusions. Indeed, Saint-Lambert could not really intrude in the relationship he destroyed. He could and did annihilate it, but only from without, and by accident.

The years spent at Cirey, and in frequent journeys with Madame du Châtelet to Brussels, Lunéville, Paris, Sceaux, and Versailles, were important in the history of Voltaire's intellectual development: they were years at once of consolidation and exploration. Hard work, regular work, was the rule of the household; interludes of gaiety and relaxation were well earned. Voltaire concerred himself more seriously than ever with moral philosophy, with the central problem of "happiness," and, striving to reach bedrock, he grappled with "the four traditional problems of the Paduan School: the proofs of the existence of God, the nature and immortality of the soul, free-will, and the origin of evil." [1] With his mistress he sought to thread the mazes of metaphysics, which he always approached with suspicion; and with her he followed, at a distance, in the experimental footsteps of Newton, fitting up a laboratory which they furnished with all the latest scientific instruments and gadgets procurable. Together they read Leibnitz, Madame taking the lead in a study which was naturally uncongenial to her distinguished companion. Together they tried to weigh fire. With Émilie's erudite assistance, Voltaire prepared his major scientific work, *Elements of Newton's Philosophy,* designed to acquaint France with the system of the great Englishman. Meanwhile, history was not abandoned: work went forward on the *Essay on the Manners and Spirit of Nations, The Century of Louis XIV,* and *The Century of Louis XV.* The Joan of Arc epic made ribald progress, by way of continual additions and revisions, providing its author with a constant means of diversion and refreshment.

During these same years, Voltaire won and lost favor at Court, was appointed royal historiographer, and was belatedly welcomed by the immortal company of the French Academy. With brilliantly successful productions of *Mahomet* and *Mérope,* he added new laurel leaves to his dramatist's crown; and, in the tale of *Zadig,* he proved himself master of a literary form which was to find its perfect flowering in *Candide.* His correspondence with Frederick of Prussia flourished. The prince sat at his feet for instruction, they spurred each other

[1] Wade, *Voltaire and Madame du Châtelet.*

on to hyperboles of mutual flattery, and the king wooed the man of letters by post, presents, and ambassador; but the pursued stood fast against all blandishments, refused to part from her whom the monarch called *"la sublime Émilie,"* and made Frederick content himself, for the time being, with only brief glimpses of his *"divin Voltaire."* Distinguished visitors came to Cirey, while correspondence linked the industrious household with a wide circle of famous and learned men. And, in addition to all these activities, there was another of prime importance that went steadily forward: a systematic, scholarly, textual demolishment of the Bible as the basis of an acceptable religion.

This sustained excursion into recently opened regions of criticism bore fruit in a number of works later published by Voltaire, and in a huge manuscript, *Examen de la Genèse,* sometimes attributed to him, but now pretty definitely proved [1] to be the product of Madame du Châtelet's industry; a product which, of course, came into existence assisted by endless conversational collaboration on the part of the lovers of Cirey. Biblical criticism, indeed, was to them as much an unfailing source of delight as it was an ever-present object of serious endeavor. They never tired of quoting the pioneer explorers in the field, chief among them Thomas Woolston, on whom they drew extensively; or of subjecting the scriptural *Commentaries* of Dom Calmet to the joint assault of their logic, their wit, and their historical knowledge. Verse by verse, chapter by chapter, book by book, they put Holy Writ under their rational microscope and found it a confused and confusing mass of incredible happenings, barbarous histories, contradictory testimony, and immoral anecdotes. Over their findings and conclusions there played the light of a

[1] See Wade, *Voltaire and Madame du Châtelet.*

lethal irony. They looked upon their work and found it good.

During this protracted study, Voltaire confirmed ideas which he had long held without thorough documentation, and stored an armory from which he was to draw, for purposes of offensive and defensive warfare, for the rest of his life. His rejection of the Bible, which of course meant the complete rejection of Christianity, was at the heart of his thinking, and was a powerful spring of action. Had he believed that the fanatical churchmen against whom he fought were merely corrupt or degenerate representatives of a true religion, he might have wielded his weapons less furiously than he did. But he was convinced that they were entrenched impostors who fattened on the exploitation of a false religion; one whose foundations could not be reasonably defended for an hour against the assaults of history and logic. So he fought to kill.

This brings us to the question of what Voltaire meant precisely by his famous term *l'infâme.* Some shrinking writers have refused to face his meaning squarely, and have identified *l'infâme* with superstition and fanaticism in general. Others have come closer to the truth, without closing their fists firmly upon the nettle.

"What was this famous thing?" asks one of Voltaire's popular biographers.[1] "A first rough answer to this question is easy. *L'infâme* was the accursed power that had bound Calas to a wheel and broken his limbs. It was the power that had tossed the spirited head of young De la Barre into the flames, and thrown the *Philosophical Dictionary* after it. It was the dark force, as stupid as it was cruel, that had robbed France of the hands and brains of half a million industrious Huguenots. It was a power with a venerable history behind it, yet still it

[1] H. N. Brailsford, *Voltaire* (New York: Henry Holt, 1935).

lived in this happy century of enlightenment, rabid in Toulouse, brutal in Abbeville, and firmly entrenched in the highest law court of the capital. Call it, as you please, intolerance or superstition, every philosopher knew what it meant. It had dogged him through all the years of his mental life. It burned his books. It imposed on him constant resort to humiliating subterfuges and disguises. It stood over him with the perpetual threat of exile or prison. The time had come, Voltaire felt, to make an end."

In another popular Life,[1] we read: "Friend and foe still remember him by that motto. [*Écrasez l'infâme.*] The one has idly forgotten, and the other carefully misunderstands, what it means and meant. To many Christians, '*Écrasez l'infâme*' is but the blasphemous outcry against the dearest and most sacred mysteries of their religion; and *l'infâme* means Christ. But to Voltaire, if it meant Christianity at all, it meant that which was taught in Rome in the eighteenth century, and not by the Sea of Galilee in the first. If it *was* Christianity at all, it was not the Christianity of Christ."

In such definitions as these, the nettle is indeed exposed, even seen for what it is; but it is dodged. No such evasive action is possible to those who read, without prejudice or fear, Voltaire's own words.

On January 5, 1767, he wrote to Frederick: "You are perfectly right, Sire. A wise and courageous prince, with money, troops, and laws, can perfectly well govern men without the aid of religion, which was made only to deceive them; but the stupid people would soon make one for themselves, and as long as there are fools and rascals there will be religions. Ours is assuredly the most ridiculous, the most absurd and the most bloody

[1] S. G. Tallentyre, *The Life of Voltaire* (3rd ed. London: Smith, Elder & Co., 1935).

which has ever infected this world." And Frederick replied, a month later: "The Englishman Woolston calculated that the *infamous* would last two hundred years; he could not calculate what has happened quite recently. The question is to destroy the prejudice which serves as foundation to this edifice. It is crumbling of itself, and its fall will be but the more rapid. Bayle began this; he was followed by a number of Englishmen, and you were reserved to complete it."

These passages are sufficient to show that when Voltaire and Frederick traded remarks regarding *l'infâme,* they meant not merely intolerance or fanaticism, but established Christianity; and that they understood each other perfectly. They also show that both men felt the need of striking at the roots which nourish all religions. But let us look at another letter, which disposes once and for all of the pious idea that, "If it *was* Christianity at all, it was not the Christianity of Christ" that Voltaire opposed. On April 6, 1767, he wrote to his royal friend at Potsdam: "You are right to say that the *infamous* will never be destroyed by force of arms, for it would be necessary to fight for another superstition which would be accepted only if it were more abominable. Arms can dethrone a Pope, dispossess an ecclesiastical Elector, but not dethrone a delusion. I cannot conceive why you did not take some good bishopric, for the cost of the war, in the last treaty; but I realize that you will destroy the Christ-worshipping superstition only by the arms of reason."

No, one cannot dodge. Whether one likes it or not —and multitudes have disliked it, and do, and will dislike it, with all their being—Voltaire's meaning is clear beyond argument. When he said, *Écrasez l'infâme,* he meant that Christianity must be wiped out root and branch; the whole structure—not only the Roman Catholic hierarchy with the Pope at its head, but the belief in Biblical revelation and "the Christ-worshipping superstition" (solace of millions) upon which organized Christianity was based, without which it would be nothing. To tear down the superstructure only, while leaving the foundations unassailed, would be an act of half-heartedness and folly.

This one particular religion was Voltaire's target because it was the one in power in the Europe of his day. Had another religion been dominant, he would have despised and attacked it with equal vigor. Of course, he did not condemn Christian morality, because he believed that the laws of right and wrong are known to all mankind, including Christians; a belief which he summed up in the statement, which may sound uninformed to a later generation, that there is only one morality just as there is only one geometry. Nor was he, according to his own thinking and that of his fellow deists, an atheist. He believed in the existence of God—a prime mover—for the homely reason that he found it impossible to conceive of a watch without a watchmaker. And did he not see the great watch of the universe, running marvelously, if not always beneficently as regarded mankind? The Church, quite naturally, could not distinguish for better or for worse between deism and atheism, any more than it can today; but this was hardly calculated to disturb a philosopher who looked upon the Church itself as a tower of falsehood, a fortress of superstition, while remaining comfortably sure that his own simple, if somewhat imprecise, belief in deity was the pure and inevitable product of self-sufficient reason.

Frederick's courtship of Voltaire had been long and ardent. The prince had offered himself unstintingly as a pupil and a friend; the king was able to offer far more as a powerful patron and protector. He would not be content until he had plucked from France this rare jewel among writers and set him down in Potsdam and Berlin as the brightest ornament of his very new Academy. If their words are to be believed, the admiration of the two men for each other was without bound, at least during the early stages of their intercourse. Voltaire, having addressed Frederick as a Horace, a Catullus, a Maecenas, an Alexander, a Socrates, a Trajan, an Augustus, and as the Solomon of the North; having, indeed, exhausted human comparisons, could only take leave of earth and salute his mighty friend by the supreme name of *Gott-Frederick.* The object of this eulogy returned the compliment by deferring to Voltaire as the wisest of men living or dead, and by declaring that the world could hope to look upon his like but once or twice in a thousand years. It was, of course, an age of gross flattery, but, after making all due allowances for the fashion of the day, we may still be fairly sure that the two men thought well of each other. Voltaire was genuinely tempted by what Frederick could give him, and Frederick yearned to stand before Europe as the patron of Voltaire. The victor of the Silesian Wars longed to be favored by the muses no less than by the god of battles. But, between the king's desire and its satisfaction, there was always the sublime Émilie. And then, suddenly, she died at Lunéville.

The road to Potsdam was open. Voltaire, at first crushed by grief, hating Lunéville and Cirey, ill at ease in Paris, was ready for a new way of life; ready to burn his French bridges behind him, even if it meant gravely displeasing his own lawful monarch. Within nine months of Madame du Châtelet's death, Frederick the Great of Prussia was ecstatically preparing to welcome his famous guest. "You will be received," wrote the king, "as the Virgil of this age; and the gentleman in ordinary to Louis XV will give place, if you please, to the great poet. Good-bye; may the rapid coursers of Achilles bring you, hilly roads flatten themselves before you! May the German inns change into palaces to receive you! May the winds of Aeolus be imprisoned in the vessels of Ulysses, may rainy Orion disappear, and our vegetable-garden Nymphs be changed into goddesses, so that your journey and your reception may be worthy of the author of the *Henriade*."

It all sounded wonderful; and perhaps it might have been, if only . . . But, no, there was not a chance. Disaster was inevitable when Voltaire's character and Frederick's power came together under the same roof, when they met daily at the same supper-table. The king was determined to be only a friend, but he could not help speaking and acting like a sovereign when his pet poet and philosopher provoked him; and perhaps on some other occasions as well. The poet took Frederick's money, food, and lodging, along with official and unofficial honors, but he was temperamentally incapable of being a good pensioner. He could not help getting into mischief himself, nor stirring up trouble for others. That a shady speculation might be intensely distasteful to the man on whose largesse he was living did not for an instant restrain him from fishing in dirty waters. That a witty pamphlet, designed to heap ridicule on the president of Frederick's precious Academy, might be hotly resented by Frederick himself did not keep Voltaire from writing it, or from continuing its circulation after he had assured his royal patron of its destruction. Voltaire equivocated, lied, cheated. Frederick became cold, harsh, contemptuous; and played the king. Grave differences were aggravated, without being dignified, by petty, despicable tricks and maneuvers on both sides. Both men felt sorry for themselves, saw themselves as the victims of cruel disillusionment. What had been intended to be an ideal, philosophical union of prince and poet; what had been meant to serve as model and lesson to an admiring world, was instead, quite simply, a sorry mess from beginning to end.

The story of this mess has been written many times. It is a mixture of low comedy, high comedy, and farce. It began with Voltaire's involvement with a Berlin usurer, reached its climax in the quarrel with Maupertuis, against whom Voltaire directed his deadly satire in the famous *Dr. Akakia* pamphlet which so outraged Frederick and so amused Europe, and ended with the arrest and release of Voltaire and his niece by the zealous Frankfort police. It all makes amusing reading for those who enjoy, as most of us do, the spectacle of great men making fools of themselves. But it need not be told again here. The Prussian sojourn of almost three years was a comparatively barren period of Voltaire's intellectual and literary life. During his stay with Frederick, he finally published his *Century of Louis XIV*, and made notes for the miscellany which was to be known as the *Philosophical Dictionary;* but the first had long been on the stocks, while the second, in one form or another, was to occupy him off and on for the rest of his life.

It is probably just as well that the Prussian episode was over and done with as quickly as it was. When it was finished, Voltaire was his own man again—perhaps really and completely his own man for the first time—and that is what he was fit to be. No verdict need be given on a quarrel in which both parties were culpable. If Frederick was goaded into playing the part of a royal boor, he was goaded by a malicious expert in the management of *pic* and *banderilla.* Even Voltaire's most uncritical admirers must agree that the great king was justified when he wrote to his difficult friend, some years after their parting: "Would that Heaven, which gave you so much wit, had given you judgment proportionately!"

For a time it seemed that he had really burned his bridges behind him. Barred from Paris, he spent half a year flitting from Mayence to Strasbourg to Colmar, where he began to write for the great *Encyclopedia* and corrected his *Annals of the Empire,* while his niece worked to open the doors that were shut against him. But his cause was rendered more hopeless than ever when his *Essay on Manners* was published in a mangled form at The Hague. This history, full of freethinking that was hateful at once to throne and church, could hardly endear him to the authorities he was seeking to propitiate. "Rome," it declared, "has always decided in favor of the opinion which most degraded the human mind, and most completely annihilated human reason." Exile stretched before him. But it was an exile which led to Geneva, to the house which he called Les Délices; and this was but one step from Ferney.

He had reached the last, long period of his long life; a period that was to be filled with ceaseless activity. During it he was to write *Candide,* that perfect thing, which will be read as long as men can read, even if some day every other line of its author's is utterly forgotten. He was to bombard *l'infâme* with deadly pamphlets, and wage tireless, tedious, expensive battles in behalf of its unfortunate victims: three years to win a declaration of innocence for Calas, brutally executed on charges of having murdered a son because he wished to turn Catholic; nine years to obtain the exculpation of the Sirvens, accused of murdering a daughter for a similar reason; twelve years to vindicate the Chevalier de la Barre, most horribly put to death for an offense against religion of which he had not been proved guilty! These are the famous cases which have forever linked Voltaire's name with the word, and concept, justice. But there were other cases only less notable, a series of them which began with his unsuccessful intervention in behalf of Admiral Byng, the unfortunate British officer who, as Voltaire ironically remarks in *Candide,* was shot "in order to encourage the others." The man of words, during what are the quiet and slippered years of most lives, was vigorously translating words into deeds.

He was busily engaged with other matters as well. That much-whispered-about delight of decades—*La Pucelle*—was pirated in 1755, and finally authorized seven years later. Work for the *Encyclopedia* continued. The *Philosophical Dictionary* began to make its appearance, charged with the essence of its author. *Natural Law* was published, and promptly burned at Paris. The influential *Treatise on Tolerance* made its way into the world, where it found one of its approving readers in Benjamin Franklin. There were numberless letters to be written, including those to Catherine of Russia, who acknowledged their worth by declaring that their writer had formed her mind; a responsibility, one may remark, of no mean proportions. There was a daughter to be adopted, furnished with a dowry, and properly married off. There were tales to be written that would be only a little less perfect than *Candide.* There was amusement to be found in a running battle with the Calvinistic fathers of Geneva; and what could be more stimulating to an aged invalid than an endless round of lively quarrels and controversies, notably one with Jean Jacques Rousseau, that child of nature who wished men to go on all fours? There was a biography of Peter the Great to be turned out on order. And, of course, one could not stop writing plays, producing plays, and acting in plays. A life from which the theater was excluded would have been no life at all to the man whose first love it had been and whose last love it would be.

At Ferney and the nearby estate of Tourney, the Lord and Count of Tourney—possessed at last of a legitimate if purchased title—cultivated his garden on a heroic scale and a diversified pattern. First of all, his chateau had to be practically torn down and rebuilt; marshes had to be drained, parks laid out, guest houses provided, a Catholic church solemnly erected by the most powerful anti-Christian in Europe (*Deo erexit Voltaire*), and trees planted—avenues of trees, miles and miles of trees. After that came the horse-breeding, the silkworm culture, the bee-keeping, the lace-making, the manufacture of silk and silk stockings, the watchmaking, and the care of one's workmen and peasants; a care which moved the patriarch of Ferney to fight for the mitigation of feudal rights and the decrease of taxes.

Then there were the guests, always the guests, scores and hundreds of them, of all nationalities, many famous and others obscure, some who came for an hour, some who made themselves comfortable for months on end; a steady tide that flowed in and out of Ferney, while the master dispensed a hospitality that entitled him to call himself the hotel keeper for all Europe. But he was less free with his time than with anything else that belonged to him. Ferney and Tourney might be filled to overflowing with visitors, and almost always were, but Voltaire remained inaccessible most of the day, working as uninterruptedly as if he were the tenant of a lonely tower.

So life went at Ferney, with a sanitative diminution

of guests during the final years, from the time that Voltaire was sixty-five until the time that he was eighty-three. As he grew older, the Lord and Count of Tourney lay longer and longer in bed, clung more closely to his dressing-gown and nightcap, and drank less and less coffee; but he had the trick of working in bed as well as anywhere else, and he learned to work without his cherished stimulant. He had reason to be well pleased with the Burgundian retreat that he had found and made for himself on the shore of Lake Leman, less than four miles from Geneva; an ideal haven for an author who might suddenly have urgent reasons for wishing to be in France one hour and in Switzerland the next. Everything had turned out very well, indeed, in what was after all, despite Leibnitz and Pope, not quite the best of all possible worlds. He might not live to finish his final deistical study, *La Bible enfin expliquée,* although there was really no reason why he should not, since he had lived so long already. But he could publish it tentatively, in an incomplete form. And, afterwards, he could get on with his play *Irène. That* he *would* finish, despite all the nonexistent devils in a nonexistent hell.

He was still correcting it, as he went into his eighty-fourth year, even after the tragedy had been read and accepted for production by the Comédie Française. Production in Paris. Eh? Well, why not? He would go to Paris himself, to the city which he had scarcely seen for twenty-eight years, along with his play. He would rehearse *Irène* as it should be rehearsed, and he would sit in triumph at its first night. Louis XV was dead: killed by smallpox almost four years ago. Of course, his successor would not welcome an author whom he feared as a dangerous and subversive force; but, through the long years of an exile which had never been formally decreed, Voltaire had acquired a prestige so formidable that a stronger king than Louis XVI might well have been willing to avoid an open clash with him. The mentor of Frederick of Prussia, Catherine of Russia, Gustavus of Sweden, Christian of Denmark, Joseph of Austria, and Stanislaus of Poland, was a king in his own right; one who knew his strength. It was almost certain that he could go to Paris, and return to Ferney, as he willed.

It all worked out very nearly as he had planned, excepting that he did not go back to Ferney.

Much eloquence has been spent on Voltaire's triumphant, magnificent, glorious, unparalleled return to the city of his birth, and the eloquence has been well spent. John Morley has called this last visit, this final blaze of a setting sun, one of the historic events of the eighteenth century. By the historical standards of which Voltaire himself was one of the first exponents, this description is just. The visit, which lasted for three and a half months, crowned one of the eighteenth century's most significant careers; the life of a man who had grown inextricably with the life of his age—a man who was at once an avid inbreather and a mighty trumpet of the *Zeitgeist*.

In the streets of Paris, Voltaire scored triumphs of a kind that are now known only to film stars. Receiving hundreds of callers in his apartment at the Marquis de Villette's, his audiences were regal. The Academy did homage to its greatest member, who had been barred for so long from the company that liked to think itself immortal. Voltaire did not sit in triumph at the first night of *Irène*, for on that night he was close to death; but, save for himself and the King, all Paris was present to applaud the poet who had left the Bastille with his first play ready for production some sixty years before. Cheating death for a little longer, and tasting immortality while he lived, Voltaire was on hand for the sixth performance, on the same day that he had been uniquely honored by the Academy. Submitting to an ovation that was literally overwhelming, and poetically and pertinaciously crowned with laurel—not once but twice—the incredible invalid cried out that they were killing him with glory. And he was right.

During these months in which Voltaire held court in Paris, an incident occurred which is of particular interest to Americans. It has been recounted often: how Benjamin Franklin called at the Hôtel Villette with his young grandson, how the two great men spoke English together until they were reminded that the rest of the company could not understand their conversation, how the American asked the Frenchman to give the boy his blessing, and how the old deist responded by placing his hands on the lad's head, while accompanying his gesture with three English words—"God and Liberty." But there was another meeting of the two philosophers, the first in public, of which we have an amusing account that should be better known than it is. The scene was the Academy of Sciences; the reporter was John Adams, writing in his *Diary*. When the two famous men were introduced, they merely bowed politely to each other, but this did not satisfy the assembled audience. So, going a step further, they clasped each other by the hand. But it was still not enough. Finally, they understood that they were expected to embrace *à la Française*. This they graciously consented to do, whereupon, writes Adams, "the cry immediately spread through the whole kingdom, and I suppose, all over Europe, *'Qu'il etait charmant de voir embrasser Solon et Sophocle!'* " ("How delightful to see Solon and Sophocles embrace!")[1]

Yes, they were killing him with glory. Having rallied

[1] See Mary-Margaret H. Barr, Voltaire in America, 1740-1800 (Baltimore: Johns Hopkins Press, 1941).

from a collapse which he had thought must prove fatal —during which he had tried to take out insurance against a dog's burial by signing a declaration that he was dying in the Catholic faith in which he was born —he sank again under the weight of his age and his exertions, still full of plans which included work on an Academy Dictionary of the French language, and the purchase of a Parisian residence. The end came on May 30, 1778, after two weeks of final struggle. The priests arrived to make sure of their old enemy, whose confession of faith they now held in their hands; but Voltaire had done all he proposed to do along that line—he had refused absolution and the last sacrament at the time of his recantation—or he was too weak and weary to play his part in what, at best, could have been only a farce. In any case, he waved the priests away, saying: "Let me die in peace."

That was how he died, at peace with the god of his watchmaker's universe, but in a state of sin so far as the Archbishop of Paris and all other strict ecclesiastics were concerned. The dog's ditch threatened, after all. However, thanks to his nephew, the Abbé Mignot, Voltaire's body was smuggled out of the city by night, and buried with proper rites in the chapel of the monastery at Scellières, in Champagne. Not until the Revolution was in spate were his bones to come back to Paris, to the Panthéon, but when they did come they were borne on the crest of a triumph which topped even the glory he had known alive.

We are sure that he was a great man—but what was the nature of his greatness? The superlatives of a Goethe or a Nodier are hardly helpful when it comes to answering this question. We must try to distinguish, define, and evaluate.

He was, obviously, not a great creative writer on the level of a Dante, a Milton, or a Shakespeare. Nor, in his prose, was he one on the level of a Tolstoy, a Balzac, a Dostoevski, a Dickens, or a Proust. He created no characters, he filled no scenes with bustling life, he explored no depths of human nature, he exposed and manipulated no psychological subtleties. In other words, he was not a great modern novelist, for the good and sufficient reason that in his day the modern novel had not yet been born; and he was no originator, no pioneer in literature. *Candide* is, indeed, a masterpiece, the origins and elements of which have been traced to *The Thousand and One Nights, Gulliver's Travels, The Persian Letters, Gil Blas,* and *Le Sopha.* It is a tale which, as Gustave Lanson has said, gathers and filters the traditions and formulas of all sorts of tales—philosophical, social, satirical, allegorical, fairy, and oriental. It is, in short, the tale at its highest level. But, even at its highest, this form is not one which is capable of bearing burdens that other literary forms can bear; not one in which the experience of life can find its fullest, most profound, and most affecting expression.

Voltaire was great neither as a lyric nor as a didactic poet. He was an admirable, witty, even brilliant playwright, who knew perfectly how to play the game in accordance with fashionable rules; but he was not a great dramatist, because his plays were never capable of crossing national and linguistic frontiers, and are hardly alive in France today. He was not a philosopher in the sense that Locke and Descartes were philosophers. He left no great history behind him, as did one of his visitors to Lausanne—Edward Gibbon by name—the first volume of whose majestic work was published two years before Voltaire's death. He was less successful than Benjamin Franklin in scientific experimentation, and he was much less of a naturalist than his colleague, d'Alembert. His Biblical studies, on which he lavished so much time, and which afforded him so much amusement, were soon superseded by the unremitting labors of gentlemen living on the other side of the Rhine. What, then, are we left with in the way of greatness?

The key to the matter, I think, is in the phrase which I used a little earlier, when I said that Voltaire was at once an avid inbreather and a mighty trumpet of the *Zeitgeist*. He was the perfect instrument of his century. His age—or as much of it as deserved to be called the age of enlightenment—spoke through him. As propagandist and publicist he has never been surpassed, for he was master of a style that was supremely capable of communicating ideas, that was devastating in controversy. Clarity, directness, simplicity, always the concrete expression, almost always the familiar word—but the familiar word incisively used—these were the characteristics which made it possible for Joubert to say that, "No more attention is required to read Voltaire than to listen to a man speak."

Commanding all degrees of irony and every shade of sarcasm, an adept in mock humility and the art of driving home opinion while pretending to beg for instruction, peerless in badinage and terrible in rage, unapproachable in wit, by turn subtle and brutal in persuasion, Voltaire was a teacher such as the world has seldom seen. For, in his eyes, the writer who did not teach was no writer at all. With Fontenelle he held that history should be a guide to rational conduct.[1] Moral philosophy and ethics were meaningless, he be-

[1] See H. Linn Edsall, *The Idea of Progress and History in Fontenelle and Voltaire,* Studies by Members of the French Department of Yale, 1941.

lieved, if they did not subserve the good of society by means of instruction. Even the poet's function was pedagogical. "Verses which do not teach men new and moving truths," he wrote to Frederick, "do not deserve to be read."

Because he was so effectively the spokesman of his age, so characteristically its representative, so completely its embodiment—its very type and symbol—Voltaire has been credited with originations and achievements that were not really his. To his own laurels have been added some that belong more properly to other men; laurels drawn to him by a power of attraction similar to that which causes famous wits, in every generation, to be credited with witticisms actually uttered by their less famous contemporaries. There is the matter of the *Encyclopedia*, for example.

Voltaire's name is inseverably linked with this arsenal of enlightenment, and he is popularly supposed, even by some of his biographers, to have played a far more important part than he did in this great collaborative effort, which was originally intended to produce a French version of, and an improvement upon, Chambers' *Cyclopedia.* One often comes on allusions and references which would indicate that his contribution must have eclipsed even that of Diderot himself, the editor-in-chief who, in George Saintsbury's words, "had perhaps the greatest faculty of any man that ever lived for the literary treatment in a workman-like manner of the most heterogeneous and in some cases rebellious subjects," and whose "untiring labour, not merely in writing original articles, but in editing the contributions of others, determined the character of the whole work."

The truth, according to one of the closest students of the subject, would seem to be that Voltaire was mistrustful of the undertaking from the outset, as having too official a flavor for his taste; that he was in disagreement with Diderot, whom he believed to be intent on mere compilation rather than propaganda; and that he never, despite certain valuable contributions, gave himself wholeheartedly to the work.[1] Certainly he did not stand fast during the crises of 1758 and 1760, when publication was suspended because of protests by Parliament, Jesuits, and Jansenists. If he did not withdraw from the enterprise completely, as did d'Alembert, he suddenly became remarkably discreet. Diderot and his staff, however, carried on to produce seventeen volumes by 1765. Summing up the relationship between Voltaire and the encyclopedists, Raymond Naves writes: "We have found a serious lack of understanding between them, and a parallelism rather than a convergence of efforts. Far from being the chief of the encyclopedists, Voltaire was only their *franc-tireur;* but it was in their service that he came to know himself completely, which is not the least interesting aspect of the story."

Then there is the matter of the Revolution. That Voltaire helped clear the ground for this cataclysmic event there can be no possible doubt; but it is erroneous to assume, as is often done, that he foresaw the Revolution or would have approved had he lived to witness it. He would have been shocked and horrified by the social overturn which was symbolized by the brutal stamping and whirling of the Carmagnole, in place of the stately minuet; by the disappearance of knee-breeches, in favor of trousers boldly striped in red and blue.

Voltaire believed in the dignity of the individual but he did not believe in mass-man. He was an aristocrat in all his fibers, by instinct and by conviction. Far from being a republican, he was a passionate monarchist, a de-

[1] See Raymond Naves, *Voltaire et l'Encyclopédie* (Paris, Les Éditions des presses modernes, 1938).

voted admirer of the *grand siècle,* whose ideal state was the kind of state that the old regime might have been, if only the great Louis had been greater than he was. Voltaire believed in political, administrative, legal, and moral reforms; but the only way he would have reformed the monarchy, had he been able, would have been by installing a philosopher king, worthy of absolute power. He believed neither in social equality, nor in unrestrained political liberty, nor in the extension of education to the lower classes. He wished and worked to alleviate the burdens of the people, to make their lives more worth living, but he could not imagine a time when an aristocracy would not be placed above them by the watchmaker of the universe. "Take but degree away, untune that string, and hark what discord follows!" He did, however, wish with all his heart for an aristocracy capable of tolerance and benevolence. He longed to see mankind happy and prosperous. "Yet, with all his faith in humanity, he never considered the people fit to govern themselves." [1] As late as 1768, he could declare: "As regards the people, they will always be stupid and barbarous. They are oxen which require a yoke, a goad, and some hay."

Those persons who have in their ignorance admired Voltaire for the wrong reasons may find it distressing to admit that he was so completely a creature of his intellectual milieu and his adopted class; that he did not ride the wave of the future more adventurously, that he did not look forward with shining hope to the century of the common man. The judicious, on the other hand, will be quite content to admire him for what he was and did, within the circle of his obvious limitations.

More distressing is the conspicuous, ugly vein of anti-

[1] Philip George Neserius, "The Political Ideas of Voltaire," *American Political Science Review,* February 1926.

Semitism which runs through much of his writing, particularly the *Philosophical Dictionary*. He almost never refers to a Jew, the Jewish people, or Jewish history, save in terms of contempt, contumely, and denigration; and such references are painfully numerous. One may argue that anti-Semitism was the rule in Europe, when Europe's Jews were still confined to ghettos and compelled to wear identifying badges. But should not the great soldier of tolerance have been superior to this detestable rule? What can we think, when the arch-foe of fanaticism himself fans the fires of one brand of fanaticism by writing of one particular people as if they were set apart from all the rest of mankind? We can only attempt to explain, I think, without apology or condonation.

Voltaire's anti-Semitism was of a special kind. He did not think of the Jews, as did so many of his contemporaries, as the murderers of Christ, or as an enduring threat to Christian children. He thought of them as the people who had made Christianity possible; as the seedbed of a religion which he despised, which he considered an affront to human intelligence. Their history, as related in the Old Testament, was to him barbarous, cruel, horrible, incredible; while the New Testament, built upon the Old, was the bulwark of *l'infâme*. So, when he poured out his hot lead upon the Jews, when he spat upon their gabardines, he was really striking through them at his mortal enemy. This is an explanation, as I have said; nothing more. It in no way alters a fact—or a complex of facts—which, however unpleasant, must be accepted.

If this evaluation is right, then, Voltaire's greatness consists in his having been so vigorously, so comprehensively, and so successfully the representative of his age

—the age of enlightenment—in which man, carrying the promises of the humanist Renaissance towards their logical conclusions, stood forth upon this earth in confidence and pride, reliant only on his own reason; when, in the words of a hostile historian, he "arrogated to himself the peculiarly divine privilege of absolute independence or self-sufficiency, which theologians term *aseitas*."[1] The rational man who is content to be nothing more than rational, who can perceive no need of being anything more, who finds reason equal to human problems, who looks forward to the continuing triumphs of reason over nature—this is the type of the eighteenth-century enlightenment; this is the type of which Voltaire is the supreme example.

Like Fontenelle, like many of his predecessors and contemporaries, Voltaire was a skeptic who believed in reason. But he believed, also, in the limitations of reason. Indeed, he trusted it only as far as he could see clearly with his own sharp eyes. Plato was incomprehensible to him, Aristotle baffling. As for his attitude toward scholastic philosophy, it is summed up in his reference to Occam as "a celebrated madman." The most profound mysteries and the highest truths were both, he was convinced, beyond reason's reach. In 1736, in his first letter to Frederick, he wrote: "I look upon metaphysical ideas as things which do honor to the human mind. They are flashes in the midst of a dark night; and that, I think, is all we can hope of metaphysics. It seems improbable that the first principles of things will ever be thoroughly known. The mice living in a few little holes of an immense building do not know if the building is eternal, who is the architect, or why the architect built it. They try to preserve their lives, to

[1] Jacques Maritain, *The Angelic Doctor* (New York: Sheed and Ward, 1931).

people their holes, and to escape the destructive animals which pursue them. We are the mice; and the divine architect who built this universe has not yet, so far as I know, told His secret to any of us."

We have traveled far since Voltaire's day. We have seen the age of enlightenment give rise to the age of progress; to a boundless optimism, a vast complacency, reared on a triple base—the theory of evolution, the business dynamism of the western world, and man's apparently unlimited power over nature. Then we have witnessed a failure of rational nerve; we have watched the prestige of reason decline, in many quarters, in direct proportion to the mounting achievements of science: an event caused partially, but not entirely, by the two most terrible wars in history and the threat of an even more terrible third. We have lived to hear our famous Renaissance, of which we were so proud, described not as a rebirth of human values, but as the beginning of a long period of human disintegration; while the road of science, on which we set out so bravely, is now seen by an ever increasing number of observers as the road to death.

Catholic thinkers and publicists have, of course, been most eloquent in analyzing a process which they believe to be a perfect justification of their unchanging historical and religious position. Christopher Dawson speaks brilliantly for them all, when he writes: "So we have the paradox that at the beginning of the Renaissance, when the conquest of nature and the creation of modern science are still unrealized, man appears in godlike freedom with a sense of unbounded power and greatness; while at the end of the nineteenth century, when nature has been conquered and there seem no limits to the powers of science, man is once more conscious of his misery and weakness as the slave of material circumstance and physical appetite and death. Instead of the heroic exaltation of humanity which was characteristic of the naturalism of the Renaissance, we see the humiliation of humanity in the anti-human naturalism of Zola. Man is stripped of his glory and freedom and left as a naked human animal shivering in an inhuman universe." [1]

The voice of Rome is not alone in proclaiming, to an unhappy and bewildered generation, the vanity of reason. A Toynbee looks up and down the long vistas of history, and persuades himself that we are in all probability moving toward the final triumph of Christianity. A Pitirim Sorokin can survey the periods of civilization, weigh their elements, chart tendencies, and decide that the western world is about to enter upon a new age of faith. Scientists, working at the highest levels, having reached the frontiers of empiricism, are finding it a comfort to supplement their knowledge with super-rational beliefs. Writers who were skeptical and uncompromising intellectuals only twenty years ago are now taking refuge in old religions of the West and even older Eastern mysteries. The fugitives from reason are following many paths, but their numbers are impressive, and the significance of their action is not to be ignored.

Whether or not this flight is a major movement in the intellectual history of man, whether or not the rational tide, after its long run, is destined to be borne backward by a rising tide of faith, remains to be demonstrated. But, whatever the upshot, Voltaire stands and will stand as a landmark and a symbol; toweringly identified with one notable stage of man's development; perfectly representing one of man's possible responses to the chal-

[1] Christopher Dawson, *Essays in Order* (New York: Macmillan, 1931).

lenge of life. And, for those of us who are incapable of finding supernatural solace, the rationalism of Voltaire —with all its limitations—must remain the best hope and the best instrument that man has on earth.

BEN RAY REDMAN

Some Dates in the Life of Voltaire

1694 November 21. François Marie Arouet is born in Paris.
1701 His mother dies.
1704 He enters Jesuit College of Louis-le-Grand.
1709 His mentor, the Abbé Châteauneuf, dies.
1711 He leaves Louis-le-Grand. During the next two years he frequents the society of the Temple, and is briefly exiled to Caen by his father.
1713 He goes to The Hague in the train of the Marquis de Châteauneuf, where he falls in love with Olympe Dunoyer, and is sent home in December.
1714 Pretends to study law in Paris, and later at the château of the Marquis de Saint-Ange, near Fontainbleau.
1715 Returns from Saint-Ange in August, as Louis XIV is dying, with manuscript of first play, *Oedipe.*
1716 Visits Saint-Ange at beginning of year; returns to Paris in May. Briefly exiled from capital because of a scurrilous epigram, and spends exile with Duke of Sully.
1717 Returns to Paris. Suspected of writing more libelous verse; sent to Bastille in May, where he revises *Oedipe,* begins the *Henriade,* and assumes the name of Voltaire.
1718 Released from Bastille, April 11. *Oedipe* produced in Paris (November): runs forty-five nights.
1719 Again informally exiled from capital. Returns in winter.

1720 *Artémire* produced: a failure.

1721 His father dies in December, leaving him 4,000 livres a year.

1722 Receives pension of 2,000 francs from king. Visits Holland with Mme. de Rupelmonde.

1723 Returns to Paris in February. Has *Henriade* printed at Rouen. Suffers from bad case of smallpox in November. Regent dies.

1724 Smuggles copies of *Henriade* into Paris. *Marianne* produced at Comédie Française: failure. Revises play, spends much time with Duc de Richelieu, and ingratiates himself at court.

1725 Revised version of *Marianne* produced along with *L'Indiscret.* He dedicates *Oedipe* and *Marianne* to Marie Leczinska, bride of Louis XV, and receives pension from her. Quarrels with Rohan in December.

1726 Sent to Bastille because of Rohan affair, April 17. Released April 29, on understanding he go to England. Lands at Greenwich first week in May (Whit-Monday).

1727 Presented at English court. Dedicates new edition of *Henriade* to queen. Begins *Brutus.* Writes most of *History of Charles XII.*

1728 *Henriade* published in England at great profit.

1729 He returns to France in spring, and soon afterwards wins huge amount in lottery. He begins the *Pucelle.* Completes *Charles XII* during this and beginning of next year. Works on *English Letters* (*Lettres philosophiques sur les Anglais*).

1730 *Brutus* acted with indifferent success. Ban on *Henriade* finally lifted in Paris.

1731 *Charles XII* surreptitiously printed at Rouen, where Voltaire spends five months, returning to Paris in August. *Charles XII* is smuggled into capital. While at Rouen, Voltaire works on *Ériphyle* and *Death of Caesar.* Moves in with Comtesse de Fontaine-Martel.

1732 *Ériphyle* acted with mild success. *Epistle to Uranie* printed without authorization. *Zaïre* produced in triumph.

1733 Comtesse de Fontaine-Martel dies, and Voltaire goes to live with Demoulin, where he meets Madame du Châtelet. *English Letters* and *Temple of Taste* printed.

1734 *Letters* condemned in June, and warrant issued against Voltaire. He goes to Cirey with Madame du Châtelet. Launches on the multiple activities characteristic of the Cirey period.

1735 Unauthorized printing of *Death of Caesar* in Paris.

1736 *Alzira* produced in Paris, with great success. Voltaire receives first letter from Frederick of Prussia (August). *The Prodigal Son* produced anonymously. At end of year leaves for Low Countries for three months, as result of new threats from authorities.

1737 Returns to Cirey in March. Quarrels with Desfontaines.

1738 *Elements of Newton's Philosophy* printed.

1739 Visits Paris and Brussels with Madame du Châtelet.

1740 Voltaire meets Frederick for the first time at Cleves, and later visits him at Remusberg.

1741 Brussels, Lille, Paris. *Mérope* and *Mahomet* are finished; latter is played at Lille.

1742 *Mahomet* produced with success in Paris (August).

1743 *Mérope* produced with overwhelming success (February). Makes bid for Academy seat and is rejected. Brief diplomatic mission to Frederick (September). Returns to Paris in November.

1744 Brussels, Cirey. During these years he composes much of the *Essay on the Manners and Spirit of Nations* (*Essai sur les moeurs*) and *Louis XIV*. He returns to court.

1745 Appointed royal historiographer, due to influence of Madame de Pompadour. His brother Armand dies (February), leaving Voltaire six thousand francs a year. *Temple of Glory* printed.

1746 He is elected to the Academy (April 25).

1747-48 Having lost favor at court, he takes refuge with Duchesse du Maine at Sceaux, and at King Stanislaus' court at Lunéville, where Madame du Châtelet is carrying on love affair with Saint-Lambert. Works on *Louis XV*. To Cirey in December.

1749 He and Madame du Châtelet go to Paris, where they resume their familiar life together. Then to Cirey, and on to Lunéville, where Madame dies on September 9, after giving birth to a girl.

1750 Voltaire arrives in Berlin, July 10, for a stay which lasts nearly three years, during which time he finishes and prints *Louis XIV* and begins *Philosophical Dictionary*.

1751 Voltaire hears that Frederick looks on him as a "used orange."

1752 The *Dr. Akakia* incident.

1753 Voltaire leaves Potsdam, March 26, and is arrested with his niece in Frankfort (May). Leaves Frankfort, July 7. Arrives in Colmar early in October, and settles down to finish *Annals of the Empire*.

1754 Pirated edition of *Essay on Manners* published (January) and Voltaire is barred from France, which really means only Paris. He goes to Plombières in the summer. Arrives in Geneva (December).

1755 He buys Les Délices (February). Pirated edition of *La Pucelle* printed. Lisbon destroyed by earthquake, November 1, and in his emotion on hearing the news he writes his poem *The Lisbon Earthquake*.

1757 Voltaire is active in Lausanne society, and acquires a winter house in the town. He tries to promote peace negotiations between France and Prussia.

1758 He arranges for the purchase of Ferney and Tourney, concluding the deals in February of the following year.

1759 Voltaire's *Natural Law* is burned by the hangman, and the *Encyclopedia* is suspended. *Candide* published. Voltaire finishes first volume of *History of*

Peter the Great. He coins the name, *L'infâme,* and dedicates himself to its extirpation.

1760 *The Scotch Girl* and *Tancred* produced in Paris.

1761 He builds a church—*Deo erexit Voltaire.* Writes *Olympie.*

1762 Jean Calas executed. Voltaire takes up his case. *La Pucelle* is finally published.

1763 *Treatise on Tolerance* written and surreptitiously distributed. Calas case is ordered retried.

1764 *Olympie* produced in Paris. First volume of *Philosophical Dictionary* published anonymously. New Calas trial begun.

1765 Calas is adjudged innocent. Voltaire comes to defense of Sirven family.

1766 La Barre executed. Voltaire attacks injustice of deed.

1767 La Harpe and his wife arrive at Ferney to stay for more than a year.

1768 *The Civil War of Geneva* completed. *The Man with Forty Crowns* written.

1770 A number of watchmakers leave Geneva to find refuge at Ferney. Voltaire backs their business, which by 1773 amounts to a half-million francs annually.

1771 The Sirvens are declared innocent.

1772 Lace-making industry begun at Ferney.

1774 Louis XV dies (May).

1777 Voltaire is busy with his last two plays, *Irène* and *Agathocle.*

1778 He arrives in Paris, February 10, where he enjoys a triumph. *Irène* produced (March). He dies during the night of May 30. His body is secretly removed from the city and hastily buried at the abbey of Scellières in Champagne.

A Brief Bibliography of Works by Voltaire

For the first time, Voltaire's *Philosophical Dictionary** has been translated in full—a well-documented two-volume edition by Peter Gay (New York and London, 1962). No complete version of the vast *Essai sur les Moeurs* is readily available in English; however, its many introductory chapters have been compiled under the title *The Philosophy of History,** with a preface by Thomas Kiernan (New York and London, 1965).

The *Philosophical Letters*—also called the *English Letters,* as in the present text—have been translated in their entirety by Ernest Dilworth (Indianapolis, Ind., and London, 1961); they are also contained in vol. XXIX of the *Harvard Classics.*

Voltaire is often regarded as the forerunner of modern historical writing, and his *Age of Louis XIV** continues to command interest. Translated by Martyn P. Pollack, it appears in Everyman's Library (New York and London, 1961). An abridged *Louis XIV,* together with excerpts from the *History of Charles XII* and related works, has been translated by J. H. Brumfitt: *Age of Louis XIV and Other Selected Writings** (New York, 1963; London, 1966).

Voltaire's neoclassical tragedies are no longer played, seldom read; but *Mahomet the Prophet or Fanaticism** has been published in a new prose translation by Robert L. Myers (New York, 1964). Voltaire's mock-heroic poem *La Pucelle,* condemned by the Church for licentiousness, exists in English as *The Virgin of Orleans* (Denver, Colo., 1965). Though Howard Nelson's translation is in prose it conveys the author's fiercely anticlerical tone. Another biting attack on organized religion and blind belief, the *Sermon of the Fifty,* has been rendered by J. A. R. Seguin (London, 1963).

A prolific correspondent, Voltaire wrote some twenty thousand letters. A compact compilation has been edited by Theodore Besterman: *Select Letters of Voltaire* (London and Camden, N.J., 1963). —James R. Hewitt

(See p. 570 for works about Voltaire.)

* Also available in paperback.

Philosophical Dictionary

Selections

ABBE

THE word *abbé,* let it be remembered, signifies father. If you become one you render a service to the state; you doubtless perform the best work that a man can perform; you give birth to a thinking being. In this action there is something divine. But if you are *Monsieur l'Abbé* only because you have had your head shaved, wear a clerical collar, and a short cloak, and are waiting for a fat benefice, you do not deserve the name of *abbé.*

The ancient monks gave this name to the superior whom they elected; the *abbé* was their spiritual father. What different things do the same words signify at different times! The spiritual father was a poor man at the head of others equally poor; but the poor spiritual fathers have since had incomes of two hundred or four hundred thousand livres, and there are poor spiritual fathers in Germany who have regiments of guards.

A poor man, making a vow of poverty, and in consequence becoming a sovereign? It has been said before. but it must be said a thousand times: this is intolerable.

The laws protest such an abuse; religion is shocked by it, and the really poor, who want food and clothing, appeal to heaven at the door of *Monsieur l'Abbé.*

But I hear the *abbés* of Italy, Germany, Flanders, and Burgundy ask: "Why are not we to accumulate wealth and honors? Why are we not to become princes? The bishops, who were originally poor, are like us; they have enriched and elevated themselves; one of them has become superior even to kings; let us imitate them as far as we are able."

Gentlemen, you are right. Invade the land; it belongs to him whose strength or skill obtains possession of it. You have made ample use of the times of ignorance, superstition, and infatuation, to strip us of our inheritances, and trample us under your feet, that you might fatten on the substance of the unfortunate. But tremble for fear that the day of reason will arrive!

ADAM

So much has been said and so much written concerning Adam, his wife, the pre-Adamites, etc., and the rabbis have put forth so many idle stories respecting Adam, and it is so dull to repeat what others have said before, that I shall here hazard a new idea, or one, at least, which is not to be found in any ancient author, father of the church, preacher, theologian, critic, or scholar with whom I am acquainted. I mean the profound *secrecy* with respect to Adam which was observed throughout the habitable earth, Palestine only excepted, until the time when the Jewish books began to be known in Alexandria, and were translated into Greek under one of the Ptolemies. Even then they were very little known; for large books were very rare and very dear. Besides, the Jews of Jerusalem were so incensed against those of

Alexandria, loaded them with so many reproaches for having translated their Bible into a profane tongue, called them so many ill names, and cried so loudly to the Lord, that the Alexandrian Jews concealed their translation as much as possible. It was so secret that no Greek or Roman author speaks of it before the time of the Emperor Aurelian.

The historian Josephus confesses, in his answer to Appian, that the Jews had only recently had any intercourse with other nations: "We inhabit," says he, "a country distant from the sea; we do not apply ourselves to commerce, nor have we any communication with other peoples. Is it to be wondered at that our nation, dwelling so far from the sea, and affecting never to write, have been so little known?"

Here it will probably be asked how Josephus could say that his nation affected *never to write anything*, when they had twenty-two canonical books, without reckoning the *Targum* by *Onkelos*. But it must be considered that twenty-two small volumes were not much when compared with the multitude of books preserved in the library of Alexandria, half of which were burned in Caesar's war.

It is certain that the Jews had written and read very little; that they were profoundly ignorant of astronomy, geometry, geography, and physics; that they knew nothing of the history of other nations; and that it was only in Alexandria that they at last began to acquire some learning. Their language was a barbarous mixture of ancient Phoenician and corrupted Chaldee; it was so poor that several moods were wanting in the conjugation of their verbs.

Moreover, as they communicated neither their books nor the titles of them to any foreigner, no one on earth except themselves had ever heard of Adam, or Eve, or

Abel, or Cain, or Noah. Abraham alone was, in course of time, known to the Oriental nations; but no ancient people admitted Abraham, or Ibrahim, was the root of the Jewish nation.

Such are the secrets of Providence, that the father and mother of the human race have ever been totally unknown to their descendants; so that the names of Adam and Eve are to be found in no ancient author, either of Greece, of Rome, of Persia, or of Syria, nor even among the Arabs, until near the time of Mohammed. It was God's pleasure that the origin of the great family of the world should be concealed from all but the smallest and most unfortunate part of that family.

How is it that Adam and Eve have been unknown to all their children? How could it be that neither in Egypt nor in Babylon was any trace—any tradition—of our first parents to be found? Why were they not mentioned by Orpheus, by Linus, or by Thamyris? For if they had said but one word of them, it would undoubtedly have been caught by Hesiod and even more surely by Homer, who speak of everything except the authors of the human race. Clement of Alexandria, who collected so many ancient records, would not have failed to quote any passage in which mention had been made of Adam and Eve. Eusebius, in his *Universal History,* has examined even the most doubtful testimonies, and would assuredly have made the most of the smallest allusion, or appearance of an allusion, to our first parents. It is, then, established that they were always utterly unknown to the nations.

We do not see the name of Noah or of Adam in any of the ancient dynasties of Egypt; they are not to be found among the Chaldaeans; in a word, the whole earth has been silent respecting them. It must be owned that such a silence is unparalleled. Every people has attributed to itself some imaginary origin, yet none has approached the true one. We cannot comprehend how the father of all nations has so long been unknown, while in the natural course of things his name should have been carried from mouth to mouth to the farthest corners of the earth.

Let us humble ourselves to the decrees of that Providence which has permitted so astonishing an oblivion. All was mysterious and concealed in the nation guided by God Himself, which prepared the way for Christianity, and was the wild olive on which the fruitful one has been grafted. That the names of the authors of mankind should be unknown to mankind is a mystery of the highest order.

I will venture to affirm that it has required a miracle thus to shut the eyes and ears of all nations—to destroy every monument, every memorial of their first father. What would Caesar, Antony, Crassus, Pompey, Cicero, Marcellus, or Metellus have thought, if a poor Jew, while selling them balm, had said, "We all descend from one father, named Adam." All the Roman senate would have cried, "Show us our genealogical tree." Then the Jew would have displayed his ten generations, down to the time of Noah, and the secret of the universal deluge. The senate would have asked him how many persons were in the ark to feed all the animals for ten whole months, and during the following year in which no food would be produced? The peddler would have said, "We were eight—Noah and his wife, their three sons, Shem, Ham, and Jauphet, and their wives. All this family descended in a direct line from Adam."

Cicero, would, doubtless, have inquired for the great monuments, the indisputable testimonies which Noah and his children had left of our common father. "After the deluge," he would have said, "the whole world would have resounded with the names of Adam and Noah, one the father, the other the restorer of every race. These names would have been in every mouth as soon as men could speak, on every parchment as soon as they could write, on the door of every house as soon as they could build, on every temple, on every statue. You mean to tell us that you knew so great a secret, yet concealed it from us?" The Jew would have answered: "It is because we are pure and you are impure." The Roman senate would have laughed and the Jew would have been whipped. So much are men attached to their prejudices!

ADULTERY

(*A memorial, written by a magistrate, about the year 1764.*)

A principal magistrate of a town in France is so unfortunate as to have a wife who was debauched by a priest before her marriage, and whose scandalous acts have since covered her with shame. He has, however, contented himself with a quiet separation. This man, who is forty years old, healthy, and of a pleasing appearance, needs a woman. He is too scrupulous to seek to seduce the wife of another; he even fears to contract an illicit intimacy with a girl or a widow. In this state of sorrow and perplexity he addresses the following complaints to the Church, of which he is a member:

"My wife is guilty, and it is I who am punished. A woman is necessary to the comfort of my life—nay, even to the preservation of my virtue; yet she is refused me by the Church, which forbids me to marry an honest woman. The civil law of the present day, which is, unhappily, founded on the canon law, deprives me of the rights of humanity. The Church compels me to seek either pleasures which it reprobates, or shameful consolations which it condemns; it would force me into guilt.

"If I survey the peoples of the earth, I see none except Roman Catholics who do not recognize divorce and second marriage as a natural right. What inversion of order, then, has made it a virtue in Catholics to suffer adultery and a duty to live without wives when their wives have thus shamefully injured them? Why is a cankered tie indissoluble, notwithstanding the great maxim adopted by the code, *Quicquid ligatur dissolubile est?* A separation of person and property is granted me, but not a divorce. The law takes from me my wife, and leaves something called *sacrament!* I no longer enjoy matrimony, but still I am married! What contradiction! What slavery! Under what laws have we been born!

"What makes it even stranger is that this law of the Church is directly contrary to the words which it believes to have been pronounced by Jesus Christ: 'Whosoever shall put away his wife, *except it be for fornication,* and shall marry another, committeth adultery.' (Matt. 19:9.)

"I have no wish here to inquire whether the pontiffs of Rome have a right to violate at pleasure the law of Him whom they regard as their Master, whether when a kingdom wants an heir, it is allowable to repudiate the woman who is incapable of giving one; nor whether a turbulent wife, one attacked by lunacy, or one guilty of murder, should not be divorced as well as an adulteress; I confine myself to what concerns my own sad situation. God permits me to marry again, but the bishop of Rome forbids me.

"Divorce was customary among Catholics under all the emperors, as well as in all the dismembered states of the Roman Empire. Almost all those kings of France who are called *of the first line,* repudiated their wives and took fresh ones. At length came one Gregory IX, an enemy to emperors and kings, who, by a decree, made the bonds of marriage indissoluble; and his *decretal* became the law of Europe. Hence, when a king wished to repudiate an adulterous wife, according to the law of Jesus Christ, he could not do so without seeking some ridiculous pretext. St. Louis was obliged, in order to effect his unfortunate divorce from Eleanora of Guienne, to allege a relationship which did not exist; and Henry IV, to repudiate Margaret of Valois, brought forward a still more unfounded pretence—a want of consent. Thus a lawful divorce could not be obtained without falsehood.

"What! may a sovereign abdicate his crown, and shall he not without the pope's permission abdicate his faithless wife? And is it possible that men, enlightened in other things, have so long submitted to this absurd and abject slavery?

"Let our priests and our monks abstain from women, if it must be so; they have my consent. It is detrimental to the progress of population and a misfortune for them; but they deserve that misfortune which they have contrived for themselves. They are the victims of the popes, who in them wish to possess slaves—soldiers without family or country, living for *the Church;* but I, a magistrate, who serve the state the whole day long, have need of a woman at night; and the Church has no right to deprive me of a possession allowed me by the Deity. The apostles were married, Joseph was married, and I wish to be married. If I, an Alsatian, am dependent on a priest who lives at Rome and has the barbarous power to deprive me of a wife, he may as well make me a eunuch to sing *Miserere* in his chapel."

ANCIENTS AND MODERNS

The great dispute between the ancients and the moderns is not yet settled; it has been on the table since the silver age succeeded the golden age. Mankind has always maintained that the good old times were much better than the present day. Nestor, in the *Iliad,* wishing to insinuate himself as a wise conciliator into the minds of Achilles and Agamemnon, starts by saying to them—"I lived formerly with better men than you; no, I have never seen and I shall never see such great personages as Dryas, Cenaeus, Exadius, Polyphemus, equals to the gods, etc."

Posterity has avenged Achilles for the poor compliment paid him by Nestor; now vainly praised by those who only praise antiquity. Nobody knows Dryas any longer; we have hardly heard of Exadius, or of Cenaeus; and as for Polyphemus, equal to the gods, he has not too good a reputation, unless the possession of a big eye in one's forehead, or the eating of men raw, partakes of divinity.

Lucretius does not hesitate to say that nature has degenerated (lib. II. v. 1159). Antiquity is full of eulogies of another more remote antiquity. Horace combats this prejudice with as much finesse as force in his beautiful Epistle to Augustus (Epist. I. liv. ii.). "Must our poems, then," he says, "be like our wines, of which the oldest are always preferred?"

The learned and ingenious Fontenelle expresses himself on this subject as follows:

"The whole question of pre-eminence as between the ancients and the moderns, once it is well understood, is reduced to knowing whether the trees which formerly were in our countryside were bigger than those of today.

In the event that they were, Homer, Plato, Demosthenes cannot be equaled in these latter centuries; but if our trees are as great as those of olden times, then we can equal Homer, Plato and Demosthenes.

"Let us throw light on this paradox. If the ancients had more intelligence than we have, it is because the brains of those times were better ordered, formed of firmer or more delicate fibers, filled with more animal spirits; but in what way were the brains of those times better ordered? The trees also would in that case have been bigger and more beautiful; for if nature was then younger and more vigorous, the trees, as well as men's brains, would have necessarily felt this vigor and this youth." ("Digression on the Ancients and the Moderns," vol. 4, 1742 edition.)

With the illustrious academician's permission, that is not at all the state of the question. It is not a matter of knowing whether nature has been able to produce in our day as great geniuses and as good works as those of Greek and Latin antiquity; but to know whether we have them in fact. Without a doubt it is not impossible for there to be as big oaks in the forest of Chantilli as in the forest of Dodona; but supposing that the oaks of Dodona had spoken, it would be quite clear that they had a great advantage over ours, which in all probability will never speak.

Nature is not bizarre; but it is possible that she gave the Athenians a country and a sky more suitable than Westphalia and the Limousin for forming certain geniuses. Further, it is possible that the government of Athens, by seconding the climate, put into Demosthenes' head something that the air of Climart and La Grenouillère and the government of Cardinal de Richelieu did not put into the heads of Omer Talon and Jerome Bignon.

This dispute is therefore a question of fact. Was antiquity more fecund in great monuments of all kinds, up to the time of Plutarch, than modern centuries have been from the century of the Medicis up to Louis XIV inclusive?

The Chinese, more than two hundred years before our era, constructed that great wall which was not able to save them from the invasion of the Tartars. The Egyptians, three thousand years before, had overloaded the earth with their astonishing pyramids, which had a base of about ninety thousand square feet. Nobody doubts that, if one wishes to undertake today these useless works, one could easily succeed by a lavish expenditure of money. The great wall of China is a monument to fear; the pyramids are monuments to vanity and superstition. Both bear witness to a great patience in the peoples, but to no superior genius. Neither the Chinese nor the Egyptians would have been able to make even a statue such as those which our sculptors form today.

Sir William Temple, who has made it his business to disparage all the moderns, claims that in architecture they have nothing comparable to the temples of Greece and Rome: but, English as he was, he must agree that the Church of St. Peter is incomparably more beautiful than was the Capitol.

It is curious with what assurance he maintains that there is nothing new in our astronomy, nothing in the knowledge of the human body, unless perhaps, he says, the circulation of the blood. Love of his own opinion, founded on his vast self-esteem, makes him forget the discovery of the satellites of Jupiter, the five moons and the ring of Saturn, the rotation of the sun on its axis, the calculated position of three thousand stars, the laws given by Kepler and Newton for the heavenly orbs, the causes of the precession of the equinoxes, and a hundred other pieces of knowledge of which the ancients did not suspect even the possibility.

The discoveries in anatomy are as great in number. A new universe in little, discovered by the microscope, was completely discounted by Sir William; he closed his eyes to the marvels of his contemporaries, and opened them only to admire ancient ignorance.

He goes so far as to pity us for having nothing left of the magic of the Indians, the Chaldeans, the Egyptians; and by this magic he understands a profound knowledge of nature, whereby they produced miracles: but he does not cite one miracle, because in fact there never were any. "What has become," he asks, "of the charms of that music which so often enchanted man and beast, the fishes, the birds, the snakes, and changed their nature?"

This enemy of his century really believes the fable of Orpheus, and has not apparently heard either the beautiful music of Italy, or even that of France, which in truth does not charm snakes, but does charm the ears of connoisseurs.

What is still more strange is that, having all his life cultivated belles-lettres, he does not reason better about our good authors than about our philosophers. He looks on Rabelais as a great man. He cites the "Amours des Gaules" as one of our best works. He was, however, a scholar, a courtier, a man of much wit, an ambassador, a man who had reflected profoundly on all he had seen. He possessed great knowledge: a prejudice sufficed to spoil all this merit.

Euripides has his beauties, and Sophocles has even more; but their defects are still greater. One dares say that the beautiful scenes of Corneille and the touching tragedies of Racine surpass the tragedies of Sophocles and Euripides as much as these two Greeks surpass Thespis. Racine was quite conscious of his great superiority over Euripides; but he praised the Greek poet in order to humiliate Perrault.

Molière, in his best plays, is as superior to the pure but cold Terence, and to the droll Aristophanes, as to Dancourt the buffoon.

There are therefore spheres in which the moderns are far superior to the ancients, and others, very few in number, in which we are their inferiors. It is to this that the whole dispute is reduced.

ANNALS

How many nations have long existed, and still exist, without annals. There were none in all America, that is, in one-half of our globe, excepting those of Mexico and Peru, which are not very ancient. Besides, knotted cords are a sort of books which cannot enter into very minute details. Three-fourths of Africa never had annals; and, at the present day, in the most learned nations, in those which have even used and abused the art of writing the most, ninety-nine out of a hundred persons may be regarded as not knowing anything that happened there further back than four generations, and as ignorant almost of the names of their great-grandfathers. Such is the case with nearly all the inhabitants of towns and villages, very few families holding titles of their possessions. When a litigation arises respecting the limits of a field or a meadow, the judges decide according to the testimony of the old men; and possession constitutes the title. Some great events are transmitted from father to son, and are entirely altered in passing from mouth to mouth. They have no other annals.

Look at all the villages of our Europe, so polished, so enlightened, so full of immense libraries, and which now seem to groan under the enormous mass of books. In each village two men at most, on an average, can read and write. Society loses nothing in consequence. All works are performed—building, planting, sowing, reaping—as they were in the remotest times. The laborer has not even leisure to regret that he has not been taught to consume some hours of the day in reading. This proves that mankind had no need of historical monuments to cultivate the arts really necessary to life.

It is astonishing, not that so many tribes of people are without annals, but that three or four nations have preserved them for five thousand years or thereabouts, through so many violent revolutions which the earth has undergone. Not a line remains of the ancient Egyptian, Chaldaean, or Persian annals, nor of those of the Latins and Etruscans. The only annals that can boast of a little antiquity are the Indian, the Chinese, and the Hebrew.

We cannot give the name of annals to vague and rude fragments of history without date, order, or connection. They are riddles proposed by antiquity to posterity, who understand nothing at all of them. We venture to affirm that Sanchoniathon, who is said to have lived before the time of Moses, composed annals. He probably limited his researches to cosmogony, as Hesiod afterwards did in Greece. We advance this latter opinion only as a doubt; for we write only to be informed, and not to teach.

But what deserves the greatest attention is that Sanchoniathon quotes the books of the Egyptian Thoth, who, he tells us, lived eight hundred years before him. Now Sanchoniathon probably wrote in the age in which we place Joseph's adventure in Egypt. We commonly place the epoch of the promotion of the Jew Joseph to the prime-ministry of Egypt at the year of the creation 2300.

If, then, the books of Thoth were written eight hundred years before, they were written in the year 1500 of the creation. Therefore, their date was a hundred and fifty-six years before the deluge. They must, then, have been engraved on stone, and preserved in the universal inundation. Another difficulty is that Sanchoniathon does not speak of the deluge, and that no Egyptian writer has ever been quoted who does speak of it. But these difficulties vanish before the Book of Genesis, inspired by the Holy Ghost.

We have no intention here to plunge into the chaos which eighty writers have sought to clear up, by inventing different chronologies; we always keep to the Old Testament. We only ask whether in the time of Thoth they wrote in hieroglyphics, or in alphabetical characters? whether stone and brick had yet been laid aside for vellum, or any other material? whether Thoth wrote annals, or only a cosmogony? whether there were some pyramids already built in the time of Thoth? whether Lower Egypt was already inhabited? whether canals had been constructed to receive the waters of the Nile? whether the Chaldaeans had already taught the arts of the Egyptians, and whether the Chaldaeans had received them from the Brahmins? There are persons who have resolved all these questions; which once occasioned a man of sense and wit to say of a grave doctor, "That man must be very ignorant, for he answers every question that is asked him."

ANTIQUITY

Have you ever, in some village, watched Pierre Aoudri and his wife Peronelle thrusting themselves ahead of their neighbors in a procession? "Our grandfathers," they say, "were bell-ringers before those who jostle us today owned even a pig-sty."

The vanity of Pierre, his wife and his neighbors, has nothing to go on; but their tempers rise. The quarrel is important; honor is in question. Proofs are necessary. A scholar who sings in the choir, discovers an old rusty iron pot, marked with an "A," first letter of the name of the potter who made the pot. Pierre Aoudri persuades himself that it was his ancestors' helmet. In this way was Caesar descended from a hero and from the goddess Venus. Such is the history of nations; such is, very nearly, our knowledge of antiquity.

The scholars of Armenia *demonstrate* that the terrestrial paradise was in their land. Some profound Swedes *demonstrate* that it was near Lake Vener which is visibly a remnant of it. Some Spaniards *demonstrate* also that it was in Castille; while the Japanese, the Chinese, the Indians, the Africans, the Americans are so unfortunate as not to know even that there was formerly a terrestrial paradise at the source of the Phison, the Gehon, the Tigris and the Euphrates, or, if you prefer it, at the source of the Guadalquivir, the Guadiana, the Douro and the Ebro; for from Phison one easily makes Phaetis, and from Phaetis one makes the Baetis which is the Guadalquivir. The Gehon is obviously the Guadiana, which begins with a "G." The Ebro, which is in Catalonia, is incontestably the Euphrates, of which the initial letter is "E."

But a Scotsman appears who *demonstrates* in his turn that the garden of Eden was at Edinburgh, which has retained its name; and it is to be believed that in a few centuries this opinion will make a fortune.

The whole globe was burned once upon a time, says a man versed in ancient and modern history; for I have read in a newspaper that some absolutely black charcoal has been found in Germany at a depth of a hundred feet, between mountains covered with wood. And one may even suspect that there were charcoal burners in this place.

Phaeton's adventure makes it clear that everything has boiled right down to the bottom of the sea. The sulphur of Mount Vesuvius proves invincibly that the banks of the Rhine, Danube, Ganges, Nile and the great Yellow River are merely sulphur, nitre and Guiac oil, which only await the moment of explosion to reduce the earth to the ashes that it has already been. The sand on which we walk is evident proof that the earth has been vitrified, and that our globe is really only a glass ball, just as are our ideas.

But if fire has changed our globe, water has produced still more remarkable revolutions. For you can clearly perceive that the sea, the tides of which mount as high as eight feet in our climate, has produced mountains of a height of sixteen to seventeen thousand feet. This is so true that some learned men who have never been in Switzerland have found a big ship with all its rigging petrified on Mount St. Gothard; or perhaps it was at the bottom of a precipice, or somewhere else. But it is quite certain that it was there. So men were originally fish: *quod erat demonstrandum.*

To descend to a less antique antiquity, let us speak of the times when most of the barbarous nations left their own countries, to seek others which were hardly better. It is true, if there be anything true in ancient history, that there were some Gaulish brigands who went to pillage Rome in the time of Camillus. Other Gaulish brigands had passed, it is said, through Illyria on their way toward Thrace, to hire out their services as murderers to other murderers. They exchanged their blood for bread, and later established themselves in Galatia. But who were these Gauls? were they Berichons and Angevins? They were without a doubt Gauls whom the Romans called Cisalpines, and whom we call Transalpines, famished mountaineers, neighbors of the Alps and the Apennines. The Gauls of the Seine and the Marne did not then know that Rome existed, and could not have thought of passing Mount Cenis, as Hannibal did later, in order to steal the wardrobes of Roman senators whose belongings at that time consisted only of a robe of poor gray material ornamented with an ox-blood band; two little knobs of ivory, or rather dog's bone, on the arms of a wooden chair; and a piece of rancid bacon in their kitchens.

The Gauls, dying of hunger, and finding nothing to eat in Rome, went off to seek their fortunes under more distant skies, as did the Romans later, when they ravaged so many countries one after the other; as did the peoples of the North when they destroyed the Roman Empire.

And what else is there to tell us even a little of these migrations? Only a few lines that the Romans wrote at hazard; for the Celts, the Velches and the Gauls—those men who are supposed to have been so eloquent—at that time knew neither how to read nor write; neither they nor their bards.

But to infer from such scanty evidence that the Gauls or Celts—afterward conquered by a few of Caesar's legions, and then by a horde of Bourguignons, and finally by a horde of Sicamores, under one Clodovic—had previously subjugated the whole world, and given their names and laws to Asia, seems to me a bit too much. The thing is not mathematically impossible, and if it be *demonstrated,* I will give way. It would be very uncivil to refuse to the Velches what one grants to the Tartars.

ARTS

(*That the Recent Birth of the Arts does not Prove the Recent Formation of the Globe.*)

All philosophers have thought matter eternal; but the arts appear to be new. Even the art of making bread is of recent origin. The first Romans ate pap; and those conquerors of so many nations had neither windmills nor watermills. This truth seems, at first sight, to contradict the doctrine of the antiquity of the globe as it now is, or to indicate that our earth has suffered terrible revolutions. Irruptions of barbarians can hardly annihilate arts which have become necessary. Suppose that an army of Negroes were to come upon us, like locusts, from the mountains of southern Africa, through Monomotapa, Monoemugi, etc., traversing Abyssinia, Nubia, Egypt, Syria, Asia Minor, and all Europe, ravaging and overturning everything in its way; there would still be a few bakers, tailors, shoemakers, and carpenters left; the necessary arts would revive; luxury alone would be annihilated. This was what happened at the fall of the Roman Empire; even the art of writing became very rare; nearly all those arts which contributed to render life agreeable were for a long time extinct. Now, we are inventing new ones every day.

From all this, no well-grounded inference can be drawn against the antiquity of the globe. For, supposing that a flood of barbarians had entirely swept away the arts of writing and making bread; supposing even that we had had bread, or pens, ink, and paper, only for ten years—the country which could exist for ten years without eating bread or writing down its thoughts could exist for an age, or a hundred thousand ages, without these resources.

It is quite clear that man and the other animals can very well subsist without bakers, without romance-writers, and without divines, as witness America, and as witness also three-fourths of our own continent. The recent birth of the arts among us does not prove the recent formation of the globe, as was pretended by Epicurus, one of our predecessors in speculation, who supposed that the eternal atoms in their declination one day formed our earth by pure chance. Pomponatius used to say: "*Se il mondo non e eterno, per tutti santi e molto vecchio*"—"If this world be not eternal, by all the saints, it is very old."

ASS

(*The Ass of Verona.*)

One must speak the truth, and not deceive one's readers. I am not positive that the Ass of Verona still exists in all his splendor, because I have not seen him, but the travelers who saw him forty or fifty years ago agree in saying that his relics were enclosed in the body of an artificial ass made for the purpose, which was in the keeping of forty monks of Our Lady of the Organs at Verona, and was carried in procession twice a year. This was one of the most ancient relics of the town. According to the tradition, this ass, having carried our Lord in his entry into Jerusalem, did not choose to abide any longer in that city, but trotted over the sea—which for that purpose became as hard as his hoof—by way of Cyprus, Rhodes, Candia, Malta, and Sicily. Thence he went to sojourn at Aquilea; and at last he settled at Verona, where he lived a long while.

This fable originated in the fact that most asses have a sort of black cross on their backs. There seems to have been an old ass in the neighborhood of Verona, on whose back the populace remarked a finer cross than his brethren could boast of; some good old woman was at hand to say that this was the ass on which Christ rode into Jerusalem; and the ass was honored with a magnificent funeral. The feast established at Verona passed into other countries, and was especially celebrated in France, where during the mass the ass's praise was sung:

Orientis partibus
Adventabit asinus,
Pulcher et fortissimus.

There was a long procession, headed by a young woman with a child in her arms, mounted on an ass, representing the Virgin Mary going into Egypt. At the end of the mass the priest, instead of saying *Ite missa est,* brayed three times with all his might, and the people answered in chorus.

We have books on the feast of the ass, and the feast of fools; they furnish material toward a universal history of the human mind.

ASTROLOGY

Astrology may rest on better foundations than Magic. For if no one has ever seen either goblins, or lemures, or goddesses, or peris, or demons, or cacodemons, the predictions of astrologers have often been seen to succeed. If, of two astrologers consulted on the life of a child and on the weather, one says that the child will live to manhood, the other not; if one announces rain, and the other fine weather, it is clear that one of them will be a prophet.

The prime misfortune of the astrologers is that the sky has changed since the rules of the art were established. The sun, which at the equinox was in Aries in the time of the Argonauts, is today in Taurus; and the astrologers, to the great hurt of their art, today attribute to one house of the sun what belongs visibly to another. This, however, is not a conclusive argument against astrology. The masters of the art deceive themselves; but it is not demonstrated that the art cannot exist.

There is no absurdity in saying: Such and such a child is born in the waxing of the moon, during stormy weather, at the rising of such and such star; his constitution has been feeble, and his life unhappy and short, which is the ordinary lot of poor constitutions: whereas this child, on the contrary, was born when the moon was full, the sun strong, the weather calm, at the rising of such and such star; his constitution has been good, his life long and happy. If these observations had been repeated, if they had been found accurate, experience would have been able after some thousands of centuries to form an art which it would have been difficult to doubt. One would have thought, with some reason, that men are like trees and vegetables which must be planted and sown only in certain seasons. It would have been of no avail against the astrologers to say: My son was born at a fortunate time, and nevertheless died in his cradle. The astrologer would have replied: It often happens that trees planted in the proper season perish; I answered to you for the stars, but I did not answer for the malformation you communicated to your child: Astrology operates only when no cause opposes itself to the good the stars can do.

One would have succeeded no better in discrediting the astrologer by saying: Of two children who were born in the same minute, one has been king, the other has been only churchwarden of his parish. For the astrologer could very well have defended himself by pointing out that the peasant made his fortune when he became churchwarden, as the prince when he became king.

And if one alleged that a bandit hanged by Sixtus V was born at the same time as Sixtus V himself, who from a pig-herd became Pope, the astrologers would say there had been a mistake of a few seconds, and that it is impossible, according to the rules, for the same star to bestow the triple crown and the gallows. Only because a host of experiences belied predictions, did men at last perceive that the art is illusory; but, before being undeceived, they were long credulous.

One of the most famous mathematicians in Europe, named Stoffler, who flourished in the fifteenth and sixteenth centuries, and who worked for a long time on the calendar reform which was proposed at the Council of Constance, foretold a universal flood for the year 1524. This flood was supposed to arrive in the month of February, and nothing was more plausible; for Saturn, Jupiter, and Mars were then in conjunction in the sign of Pisces. All the peoples of Europe, Asia and Africa, who heard of the prediction, were dismayed. Everyone expected the flood, rainbows to the contrary. Several contemporary authors record that the inhabitants of the maritime provinces of Germany hastened to sell their lands dirt cheap to those who had the most money, and who were less credulous than they. Everyone provided himself with a boat to serve as an ark. A Toulouse doctor, named Auriol, had a great ark made for himself, his family, and his friends; the same precautions were taken throughout a large part of Italy. At last the month of February arrived, and not a drop of water fell. Never was there a drier month, and never were the astrologers more embarrassed. Nevertheless they were neither discouraged nor neglected, and almost all princes continued to consult them.

I have not the honor of being a prince; but the celebrated Count of Boulainvilliers, and an Italian named Colonna, who was highly thought of in Paris, both foretold that I should most certainly die at the age of thirty-two. I have been malicious enough to outwit them by nearly thirty years already, wherefore I humbly beg their pardon.

ATOMS

The only question now at issue is, whether the author of nature has formed primordial parts unsusceptible of division, or if all is continually dividing and changing into other elements. The first system seems to account for everything, and the second, hitherto at least, for nothing.

If the first elements of things were not indestructible, one element might at last swallow up all the rest, and change them into its own substance. Hence, perhaps, it was that Empedocles imagined that everything came from fire, and would be destroyed by fire.

This question of atoms involves another famous question; that of the infinite divisibility of matter. The word *atom* signifies *without parts—not to be divided.* You divide it in thought only, for if you were to divide it in reality it would no longer be an atom.

You may divide a grain of gold into eighteen million visible parts; a grain of copper dissolved in spirit of sal ammoniac has exhibited upwards of twenty-two thousand parts; but when you have arrived at the last element the atom escapes the microscope, and you can divide no further except in imagination.

The infinite divisibility of atoms is like some propositions in geometry. You may pass an infinity of curves between a circle and its tangent, supposing the circle and the tangent to be lines without breadth; but there are no such lines in nature.

You likewise establish that asymptotes will approach one another without ever meeting; but it is under the supposition that they are lines having length without breadth—things which have only a speculative existence.

So, also, we represent unity by a line, and divide this line and this unity into as many fractions as you please; but this infinity of fractions will never be any other than our unity and our line.

It is not strictly demonstrated that atoms are indivisible, but it appears to be proved that they are undivided by the laws of nature.

AUTHORITY

Wretched human beings, whether you wear green robes, turbans, black robes or surplices, cloaks and clerical bands, never seek to use authority where it is only a question of reason, unless you wish to be scoffed at throughout the centuries as the most impertinent of men, and to suffer public hatred as the most unjust.

You have been spoken to a hundred times of the insolent absurdity with which you condemned Galileo, and I speak to you for the hundred and first, and I hope you will keep the anniversary of that event for ever. Would that there might be graved on the door of your Holy Office: "Here seven cardinals, assisted by minor brethren, had the finest thinker of Italy thrown into prison at the age of seventy; made him fast on bread and water because he instructed the human race, and because they were ignorant."

In the same place there was pronounced a sentence in favor of Aristotle's categories, and the penalty of the galleys was learnedly and equitably decreed for anyone who should be sufficiently daring as to hold an opinion different from those of the Stagyrite, whose books were formerly burned by two councils.

Still later a faculty—which was possessed of no great faculties—issued a decree condemning innate ideas, and later a decree in favor of innate ideas, without the said faculty being informed by its beadles what an idea is.

In the neighboring schools judicial proceedings were instituted against the circulation of the blood.

An action has been started against inoculation, and parties have been subpoenaed.

At the Customs of Thought twenty-one folio volumes were seized, in which it was treacherously and wickedly stated that triangles always have three angles; that a father is older than his son; that Rhea Silvia lost her virginity before giving birth to her child, and that flour is not an oak leaf.

On another occasion the action: *Utrum chimera bombinans in vacuo possit comedere secundas intentiones,* came up for judgment; and it was decided in the affirmative.

The result was that everyone thought himself far superior to Archimedes, Euclid, Cicero, and Pliny, and strutted proudly about the University quarter.

AUTHORS

Do you wish to be an author? Do you wish to make a book? Remember that it must be new and useful, or at least have great charm. Why from your provincial retreat should you slay me with another quarto, to teach me that a king ought to be just, and that Trajan was more virtuous than Caligula? You insist upon printing the sermons which have lulled your little obscure town to sleep, and you put all our histories under contributions to extract from them the life of a prince of whom you can say nothing new.

If you have written a history of your own time, doubt not but you will find some learned chronologist, or newspaper commentator, who will catch you up on a date, a Christian name, or a squadron which you have wrongly placed at the distance of three hundred paces from the place where it was really posted. Be grateful, and correct these important errors forthwith.

If an ignoramus, or an empty fool, pretend to criticize this thing or the other, you may properly confute him; but name him rarely, for fear of soiling your writings. If you are attacked on your style, never answer; your work alone should reply.

If you are said to be sick, content yourself that you are well, without wishing to prove to the people that you are in perfect health; and, above all, remember that the world cares very little whether you are well or ill.

A hundred authors compile to get their bread, and twenty fools extract, criticize, apologize, and satirize these compilations to get bread also, because they have no profession. All these people repair on Fridays to the lieutenant of the police at Paris to demand permission to sell their drugs. They have their audience immediately after the prostitutes, who pay no attention to them, because they know that they are poor customers.

They return with a tacit permission to sell and distribute throughout the kingdom their stories; their collection of bon-mots; the life of the blessed Regis; the translation of a German poem; new discoveries on eels; a new copy of verses; a treatise on the origin of bells, or on the loves of the toads. A bookseller buys their productions for ten crowns; they give five of them to a corner pamphleteer, on condition that he will speak well of them in his sheet. The scribbler takes their money, and says all the ill he can of their books. The aggrieved parties go to complain to the Jew, who is keeping the wife of the journalist, and the scene closes by the critic being carried to Fort-Evêque; and these are they who call themselves authors!

These poor people are divided into two or three bands, and go begging like mendicant friars; but not having taken vows, their society lasts only for a few days, for they betray one another like priests who run after the same benefice, though they have no benefice to hope for. But they still call themselves authors!

The misfortune of these men is that their fathers did not make them learn a trade, which is a great fault of our modern system. Every man of the people who can bring up his son in a useful art, and does not do so, merits punishment. The son of a mason becomes a Jesuit at seventeen; he is chased from society at four-and-twenty, because the looseness of his habits has become too notorious. Behold him without bread! He turns journalist, he cultivates the lowest kind of literature, and is scorned even by the mob. And such as these, again, call themselves authors!

The only authors are they who have succeeded in a genuine art, be it epic poetry, tragedy, comedy, history, or philosophy, and who teach or delight mankind. The others, of whom we have spoken, are, among men of letters, like bats among the birds.

BABEL

We will say nothing here of the confusion of tongues which took place during the construction of the tower of Babel. It is a miracle, related in the Holy Scriptures. We neither explain, nor even examine any miracles, and as the authors of that great work, the *Encyclopedia*, believed them, we also believe them with a lively and sincere faith.

We will simply affirm that the fall of the Roman Empire has produced more confusion and a greater number of new languages than that of the tower of Babel. From the reign of Augustus till the time of the Attilas, the Clovises, and the Gondiberts, during six ages, *terra erat unius labii*—the known earth was of one language. They spoke the same Latin on the Euphrates as at Mount Atlas. The laws which governed a hundred nations were written in Latin, while Greek served for amusement; and the barbarous provincial jargons were only for the lower classes. They pleaded in Latin in the tribunals of Africa as at Rome. An inhabitant of Cornwall could depart for Asia Minor sure of being understood everywhere along his route. It was at least one good effected by the rapacity of the Romans that people found themselves as well understood on the Danube as on the Guadalquivir. At the present time a citizen of Bergamo who travels into the small Swiss cantons, from which he is separated only by a mountain, has the same need of an interpreter as if he were in China. This is one of the greatest plagues of modern life.

BANKRUPTCY

Few bankruptcies were known in France before the sixteenth century. The great reason is that there were no bankers. Lombards and Jews lent on security at ten per cent: trade was conducted in cash. Exchange, remittances to foreign countries, was a secret unknown to all judges.

This does not mean that many people were not ruined —but it was not called *bankruptcy*. One said *discom-*

fiture; this word is sweeter to the ear. One used the word *rupture,* as did the Boulonnais, but rupture does not sound so well.

Bankruptcies came to us from Italy: *bancorotto, bancarotta, gambarotta e la giustizia non impicar.* Every merchant had his bench (*banco*) in the place of exchange; and when he had conducted his business badly, declared himself *fallito,* and abandoned his property to his creditors with the proviso that he retain a good part of it for himself, be free, and be reputed a very upright man. There was nothing to be said to him, his bench was broken, *banco rotto, banca rotta.* He could even, in certain towns, keep all his property and baulk his creditors, provided he seated himself bare-bottomed on a stone in the presence of all the merchants. This was a mild derivation of the old Roman proverb—*solvere aut in aere aut in cute*—to pay either with one's money or one's skin. But this custom no longer exists; creditors have preferred their money to a bankrupt's backside.

In England and in some other countries, one declares oneself bankrupt in the gazettes. Partners and creditors gather together by virtue of this announcement, which is read in the coffee-houses, and they come to an arrangement as best they can.

As there are many fraudulent cases in bankruptcy, it has been necessary to punish them. If they are taken to court, they are everywhere regarded as theft, and the guilty are condemned to ignominious penalties.

It is not true that in France the death penalty was decreed against bankrupts without distinction. Simple failures involved no penalty; fraudulent brankrupts suffered the penalty of death in the states of Orleans, under Charles IX, and in the states of Blois in 1576; but these edicts, renewed by Henry IV, were merely comminatory.

It is too difficult to prove that a man has dishonored himself deliberately, and has voluntarily ceded all his goods to his creditors in order to cheat them. When there has been a doubt, it has been deemed enough to put the unfortunate man in the pillory, or send him to the galleys, although ordinarily a banker makes a poor convict.

Bankrupts were very favorably treated in the last year of Louis XIV's reign, and during the Regency. The sad state to which the internal affairs of the kingdom were reduced, the multitude of merchants who could not or would not pay, the quantity of unsold or unsellable goods, the fear of halting all commerce, obliged the government in 1715, 1716, 1718, 1721, 1722, and 1726 to suspend all proceedings against all those who were in a state of insolvency. These actions were referred for decision to the judge-consuls; a jurisdiction of merchants very expert in these cases, and better constituted for going into these commercial details than the parliaments which have always been more occupied with the laws of the kingdom than with finance. As the state itself was at that time going bankrupt, it would have been too cruel to punish the poor middle-class bankrupts.

Since then we have had eminent men who have been fraudulent bankrupts, but they have not been punished.

BEAUTY

Ask a toad what beauty is, the *to kalon*? He will answer you that it is his toad wife with two great round eyes issuing from her little head, a wide, flat mouth, a yellow belly, a brown back. Interrogate a Guinea Negro. For him beauty is a black oily skin, deep set eyes, a flat nose. Interrogate the devil. He will tell you that beauty is a pair of horns, four claws and a tail. Finally, if you consult the philosophers, they will answer you with gibberish: they will insist on something conforming to the archtype of essential beauty, to the *to kalon.*

One day I was witnessing a tragic drama, a philosopher at my side. "How beautiful it is!" he said.

"What do you find beautiful about it?" I asked.

"It is beautiful," he answered, "because the author has done what he set out to do."

The following day he took some medicine which did him good. "The medicine has done what it set out to do," I said to him. "What a beautiful medicine!" He understood that one cannot call a medicine beautiful, and that to give the name of "beauty" to something, the thing must arouse in you both admiration and pleasure. He agreed that the tragedy had inspired these sentiments in him, and that it was in these that *to kalon,* beauty, resided.

We journey to England. The same piece, perfectly translated, was played there, but it made everybody in the audience yawn. "Ho, ho!" he said, "the *to kalon* is not the same for the English and the French." After much reflection he came to the conclusion that beauty is often very relative, just as what is decent in Japan is indecent in Rome, and what is fashionable in Paris, is not fashionable in Pekin; and he saved himself the trouble of composing a long treatise on beauty.

There are actions which the whole world finds beautiful. Two of Caesar's officers, who are mortal enemies, send each other a challenge, not as to who shall shed the other's blood with tierce and quarte behind a thicket as with us, but as to who shall best defend the Roman camp which the barbarians are about to attack. One of them, having repulsed the enemy, is near death, when the other flies to his aid, saves his life, and achieves the victory.

A friend gives his life for his friend, a son for his father. . . . Algonquin, Frenchman, Chinaman, will all agree that this is very *beautiful,* that these actions give them pleasure, that they admire them.

They will say as much of the great moral maxims—of Zoroaster's: "In doubt if an action be just, abstain . . ."; of Confucius's: "Forget injuries, never forget kindnesses."

The Negro with the round eyes and flat nose, who would never give the name of "beauty" to our court ladies, will unhesitatingly give it to the actions and maxims I have quoted. Even a wicked man will recognize the beauty of virtues which he cannot imitate. Beauty which strikes only the senses, the imagination, and what is called "intelligence," is therefore often uncertain. But not the beauty which speaks to the heart. You will find a host of people who will tell you that they have found nothing beautiful in three-quarters of the *Iliad;* but nobody will deny that Codrus's devotion to his people was very beautiful—supposing it to be true.

BEES

The bees may be regarded as superior to the human race in this, that from their own substance they produce another which is useful; while, of all our secretions, there is not one good for anything; nay, there is not one which does not render mankind disagreeable.

I have been charmed to find that the swarms which turn out of the hive are much milder than our sons when they leave school. The young bees sting no one; or at least but rarely and in extraordinary cases. They suffer themselves to be carried quietly in the bare hand to the hive which is destined for them. But no sooner have they learned in their new habitation to know their interests than they become like us and make war. I have seen bees go perfectly peaceably for six months to labor in a neighboring meadow covered with flowers which pleased them. When the mowers came they rushed furiously from their hive upon those who were about to steal their property and put them to flight.

We find in the Proverbs attributed to Solomon that "there are four things, the least upon earth, but which are wiser than the wise men—the ants, a little people who lay up food during the harvest; the hares, a weak people who lie on stones; the grasshoppers, who have no kings and who journey in flocks; and the lizards, which work with their hands and dwell in the palaces of kings." I do not know why Solomon forgot the bees, whose instinct seems very superior to that of hares, which do not lie on stone, unless it be the rocky soil of Palestine; or of lizards, with whose genius I am not acquainted. Moreover, I shall always prefer a bee to a grasshopper.

The bees have, in all ages, furnished the poet with descriptions, comparisons, allegories, and fables. Mandeville's celebrated *Fable of the Bees* made a great stir in England. Here is a short sketch of it:

> Once the bees, in worldly things,
>   Had a happy government;
> And their laborers and their kings
>   Made them wealthy and content;
> But some greedy drones at last
>   Found their way into their hive;
>   Those, in idleness to thrive,
> Told the bees they ought to fast.
>   Sermons were *their* only labors;
>   Work they preached unto their neighbors.
> In their language they would say,

"You shall surely go to heaven,
When to us you've freely given
Wax and honey all away."
Foolishly the bees believed,
Till by famine undeceived;
When their misery was complete,
All the strange delusion vanished!
Now the drones are killed or banished,
And the bees again may eat.

Mandeville goes much further; he asserts that bees cannot live at their ease in a great and powerful hive without many vices. "No kingdom, no state," says he, "can flourish without vices. Take away the vanity of ladies of quality, and there will be no more making of fine silk, no more employment for men and women in a thousand different branches; a great part of the nation will be reduced to beggary. Take away the avarice of our merchants, and the fleets of England will be annihilated. Deprive artists of envy, and emulation will cease; we shall sink back into primitive rudeness and ignorance."

He goes so far as to say that even crime has its uses, in that it helps to establish good laws. The highwayman is worth money to the man who denounces him, to those who arrest him, to the jailer who guards him, to the judge who condemns him, and to the hangman who executes him. In short, if there were no thieves, locksmiths would die of hunger.

It is quite true that a well-governed society turns every vice to account; but it is not true that these vices are necessary to the well-being of the world. Excellent remedies may be made from poisons, but it is not by poison that we live. By reducing the *Fable of the Bees* to its just value, it might be made a work of more utility.

BISHOP

Samuel Ornik, a native of Basel, was a very amiable young man, as you know, and one who had his New Testament by heart in both Greek and German. When he was twenty his parents sent him on a journey. He was commissioned to carry some books to the coadjutor of Paris, at the time of the Fronde. When he arrived at the door of the archbishop's residence, the Swiss servant told him that Monseigneur saw nobody. "Comrade," said Ornik, "you are very rude to your compatriots. The apostles let everyone approach them, and Jesus Christ desired that people should suffer all little children to come unto him. I have nothing to ask of your master; on the contrary, I have brought him something."

"Come inside, then," said the Swiss.

He waited for an hour in an outer chamber. As he was very naïve, he began a conversation with a servant who was very fond of telling all he knew of his master. "He must be extremely rich," said Ornik, "to have this crowd of pages and flunkeys whom I see running about the house."

"I don't know what his income is," answered the other, "but I heard it said that he is already two million in debt."

"But who is the lady who has just come out of that room?"

"That is Madame de Pomèreu, one of his mistresses."

"She is really very pretty; but I have not read that the apostles had any such company of a morning in their bedrooms. Ah! I think monsieur is going to give audience."

"Say 'His Highness, Monseigneur.'"

"Willingly." Ornik saluted His Highness, presented

his books, and was received with a very gracious smile. The archbishop said four words to him, then climbed into his coach, escorted by fifty horsemen. In climbing, Monseigneur let fall a sheath. Ornik was quite astonished that Monseigneur carried so large an ink-horn in his pocket. "Don't you see that's his dagger?" said the chatterbox. "Everyone carries a dagger when he goes to parliament."

"That's a nice way of officiating," said Ornik; and he went off very astonished.

He traversed France, learning as he went from town to town; and thence passed into Italy. When he was in the Pope's territory, he met one of those bishops whose income runs to a thousand crowns, walking on foot. Ornik was very polite; he offered him a place in his carriage. "You are doubtless on your way to comfort some sick man, Monseigneur?"

"Sir, I am on my way to my master's."

"Your master? I suppose you mean Jesus Christ?"

"Oh no, sir. I mean Cardinal Azolin. I am his almoner. He pays me very poorly, but he has promised to place me in the service of Donna Olimpia, the favorite sister-in-law *di nostro signore*."

"What! you are in the pay of a cardinal? But don't you know that there were no cardinals in the time of Jesus Christ and St. John?"

"Is it possible?" cried the Italian prelate.

"Nothing could be truer. You have read it in the Gospels."

"I have never read the Gospels," answered the bishop; "all I know is Our Lady's office."

"I tell you there were neither cardinals nor bishops, and when there were bishops, the priests were very nearly their equals; at least according to what Jerome says in several places."

"Holy Virgin," said the Italian. "I knew nothing about it: and the popes?"

"There were not any popes any more than cardinals."

The good bishop crossed himself; he thought he was with an evil spirit, and jumped out of the carriage.

BOOKS

You despise books, you whose whole life is devoted to the vanities of ambition and the search for pleasure, or plunged in idleness; but you should realize that the whole of the known world, with the exception of the savage races, is governed by books alone. The whole of Africa, including Ethiopia and Nigritia, obeys the Koran after having submitted to the Christian gospels. China is ruled by the moral book of Confucius; a greater part of India by the Vedas. Persia was governed for centuries by the books of one of the Zoroasters.

If you have a law suit, your goods, your honor, your very life depend on the interpretation of a book which you never read.

Robert the Devil, the *Four Sons of Aymon*, the *Imaginings of Mr. Oufle*, are books too. But it is with books as with men: the few play great parts, while the rest are lost in the crowd.

Who leads mankind in civilized countries? Those who know how to read and write. You do not know either Hippocrates, Boerhaave or Sydenham, but you put your body in the hands of those who have read them. You abandon your soul to those who are paid to read the Bible, although there are not fifty among them who have read it through with care.

To such an extent do books govern the world, that those who rule today in the city of the Scipios and the

Catos have willed that their books of law should be theirs alone. In these books is their power. They have made it a crime of *lèse-majesté* for their subjects to look into them without express permission. In other countries it has been forbidden to think in writing without letters patent.

There are nations among whom thought is regarded purely as an object of commerce. The operations of the human mind are valued there only at two sous the sheet. Whether the bookseller wishes a license for Rabelais or the Church Fathers, the magistrate grants the license without regard to the book's contents.

In another country, the liberty of explaining oneself by books is one of the most sacred prerogatives. Print all that you like, under pain of boring, or of being punished if you take too great an advantage of your natural right.

Before the admirable invention of printing, books were rarer and more expensive than precious stones. There were almost no books among the barbarian nations until Charlemagne, and from him to the French king Charles V, surnamed "the wise"—and from this Charles right down to François I—there was an extreme dearth.

The Arabs alone had books from the eighth century of our era to the thirteenth. China was filled with them when we did not know how to read or write.

Copyists were actively employed in the Roman Empire from the time of the Scipios down to the barbarians' invasions. The Greeks were great transcribers of books in the days of Amyntas, Philip, and Alexander; and they continued this practice extensively in Alexandria. The craft is rather unrewarding. The merchants always paid authors and copyists very badly. It took two years of assiduous labor for a copyist to transcribe the Bible fairly on vellum. What time and what trouble was spent in copying correctly, in Greek and Latin, the works of Origen, of Clement of Alexandria, and of all those other authors who are called "fathers."

The poems of Homer were so little known for so long a time that Pisistratus was the first who arranged, and had them transcribed in Athens, about five hundred years before the Christian era.

Today there are not perhaps a dozen copies of the Vedas or of the Zend-Avesta in the whole of the East.

You would not have found a single book in the whole of Russia in 1700, with the exception of some Missals and a few Bibles in the hand of brandy-drunken priests.

Today people complain of a surfeit of books. But it is not for readers to complain. The remedy is easy; nothing forces anyone to read. Nor have the authors any more reason to complain. Those who make up the crowd must not cry that they are being crushed. Despite the enormous quantity of books, how few people read! And if one read profitably, one would realize how much stupid stuff the vulgar herd is content to swallow every day.

What multiplies books, despite the law of not multiplying beings unnecessarily, is that books produce books. A new history of France or Spain is fabricated from several previously printed volumes, without anything new having been added. All dictionaries are made from dictionaries; almost all new geography books are repetitions of geography books. The *Summa* of St. Thomas has produced two thousand fat volumes of theology, and the same family of little worms that have fed upon the mother continue to feed upon the children.

CHARACTER

(*From the Greek word* impression, engraving. *It is what nature has graved in us.*)

Can one change one's character? Yes, if one changes one's body. It is possible for a man to be born a mischief-maker of tough and violent character, and, as a result of being stricken with apoplexy in his old age, to become a foolish, tearful child, timid and peaceable. His body has changed. But as long as his nerves, his blood and his marrow remain the same, his nature will not change any more than will a wolf's and a marten's instinct.

Our character is composed of our ideas and our feelings: and, since it has been proved that we give ourselves neither feelings nor ideas, our character does not depend on us.

If it did depend on us, there is nobody who would not be perfect.

We cannot give ourselves tastes or talents; why should we be able to give ourselves qualities?

If one does not reflect, one thinks oneself master of everything; but when one does reflect, one realizes that one is master of nothing.

Should you wish to change a man's character completely, purge him daily with diluents until you have killed him. Charles XII, in his suppurative fever on the road to Bender, was no longer the same man. He was as tractable as a child.

If I have a crooked nose and two cat's eyes, I can hide them with a mask. Can I do more with the character which nature has given me?

A man who was naturally violent and impetuous presented himself before François I, King of France, to complain of an injustice. The prince's countenance, the respectful bearing of the courtiers, the very place in which he found himself, made a powerful impression on this man. Mechanically he lowered his eyes, his rough voice softened, he presented his petition humbly; one would have thought him as gentle as were the courtiers themselves, whom he found so disconcerting. But François I understood physiognomy, he easily discovered in the lowered eyes, still burning with somber fire, in the strained facial muscles and the compressed lips, that this man was not as gentle as he was forced to appear. This man followed the king to Pavia, was captured with him, and put in the same prison in Madrid. François I's majesty no longer made the same impression on him; he grew familiar with the object of his respect. One day when he was pulling off the king's boots—and pulling them off badly—the king, embittered by his misfortune, became angry; whereupon my man sent the king about his business, and threw his boots out of the window.

Sixtus V was born petulant, stubborn, haughty, impetuous, vindictive, and arrogant. This character, however, seemed softened during the trials of his novitiate, and he began to enjoy a certain credit in his order. Then he flew into a passion with a guard, and battered him with his fist. As an inquisitor at Venice, he performed his duties insolently. Behold him a cardinal—he is possessed *dalla rabbia papale.* This passionate desire triumphs over his nature: he buries his person and his character in obscurity; he apes the humble and the dying man. Then he is elected Pope, and this moment gives back all its long-curbed elasticity to the spring which politics have bent. He is the haughtiest and most despotic of sovereigns.

Naturam expellas furca, tamen usque recurret.
(Horace, *Epistolae,* 1, 10)

Drive away nature, it returns at the gallop.
(Destouches, *Glorieux,* Act 3, Sc. 5)

Religion, morality put a brake on a nature's strength; they cannot destroy it. The drunkard in a cloister, reduced to a half-setier of cider at each meal, will no longer get drunk, but he will always like wine.

Age enfeebles character; it is a tree that produces only degenerate fruit, but the fruit is always of the same nature; the tree is knotted and covered with moss, it becomes worm-eaten, but it is always an oak or a pear tree. If one could change one's character, one would give oneself a character; one would be master of nature. But can one give oneself anything? Do we not receive everything? Try to arouse an indolent man to sustained activity; try to freeze with apathy the boiling soul of an impetuous fellow; or try to inspire someone who has neither ear nor taste with a taste for music and poetry, and you will no more succeed than if you undertook to give sight to a man born blind. We perfect, we soften, we conceal what nature has put in us, but we ourselves do not put in anything at all.

Someone says to a farmer: "You have too many fish in this pond, they will not prosper; there are too many cattle in your meadows, grass is lacking, and they will grow thin." After this exhortation it happens that the pike eat half my man's carp, and the wolves half of his sheep, while the rest grow fat. Will he not congratulate himself on his economy? This countryman is yourself: one of your passions has devoured the others, and you think that you have triumphed over yourself. Do not most of us resemble that old general of ninety who, having come on some young officers who were having a bit of fun with some girls, said to them angrily: "Gentlemen, is that the example I give you?"

CLIMATE

Climate influences religion in respect to ceremonies and usages. A legislator could have experienced no difficulty in inducing the Indians to bathe in the Ganges at certain phases of the moon; they find it a great pleasure. Had anyone proposed a like bath to the people who live on the banks of the Dwina, near Archangel, he would have been stoned. Forbid pork to an Arab, who after eating this species of animal food (the most miserable and disgusting in his own country) would be affected by leprosy, he will obey you with joy; prohibit it to a Westphalian, and he will be tempted to knock you down. Abstinence from wine is a good precept of religion in Arabia, where orange, lemon, and lime waters are necessary to health. Mahomet would not have forbidden wine in Switzerland, especially before going to battle.

There are usages that are merely fanciful. Why did the priests of Egypt devise circumcision? It was not for the sake of health. Cambyses, who treated as they deserved both them and their bull Apis, the courtiers of Cambyses, and his soldiers, enjoyed perfectly good health without having lost their foreskins. Climate does not affect a priest's genitals. One offered one's prepuce to Isis, probably on the same principle as the firstlings of the fruits of the earth were everywhere offered. It was typical of an offering of the first fruits of life.

Religions have always turned on two pivots—forms of observance and creed. Forms and ceremonies depend much on climate; faith not at all. A doctrine will be received with equal facility under the equator or near the pole. It will be afterwards equally rejected at Batavia and the Orcades, while it will be maintained, *unguibus et rostro*—with tooth and nail—at Salamanca. This depends not on sun and atmosphere, but solely upon opinion, that fickle empress of the world.

Certain libations of wine will naturally be enjoyed in a country abounding in vineyards; and it would never occur to any legislator to institute sacred mysteries, which could not be celebrated without wine, in such a country as Norway.

It will be expressly commanded to burn incense in the court of a temple where beasts are killed in honor of the Divinity, and for the priests' supper. This slaughterhouse, called a temple, would be a place of abominable infection, if it were not continually purified; and without the use of aromatics, the religion of the ancients would have introduced the plague. The interior of the temple was even festooned with flowers to sweeten the air.

The cow will not be sacrificed in the burning territory of the Indian peninsula, because it supplies the necessary article of milk, and is very rare in arid and barren districts, and because its flesh, being dry and tough, and yielding but little nourishment, would afford the Brahmins poor cheer. On the contrary, the cow will be considered sacred, in consequence of its rareness and utility.

The temple of Jupiter Ammon, where the heat is excessive, will be entered only with bare feet. To perform his devotions at Copenhagen, a man must be well shod.

It is not thus with doctrine. Polytheism has been believed in all climates; and it is equally easy for a Crim Tartar and an inhabitant of Mecca to acknowledge one single incommunicable God, neither begotten nor begetting. It is by doctrine, more than by rites, that a religion extends from one climate to another. The doctrine of the unity of God passed rapidly from Medina to Mount Caucasus. Climate, then, yields to opinion.

The Arabs said to the Turks: "We practiced the ceremony of circumcision in Arabia without very well knowing why. It was an ancient usage of the priests of Egypt to offer to Oshiret, or Osiris, a small portion of what they considered most valuable. We had adopted this custom three thousand years before we became Mahometans. You will become circumcised like us; you will bind yourself to sleep with one of your wives every Friday, and to give two and a half per cent of your income annually to the poor. We drink nothing but water and sherbet; all intoxicating liquors are forbidden us. In Arabia they are pernicious. You will embrace the same regimen, although you are passionately fond of wine, and although it is often a necessity on the banks of the Phasis and the Araxes. In short, if you wish to go to heaven, and to be well-placed there, you will take the road through Mecca."

The inhabitants of the northern Caucasus subject themselves to these laws, and adopt completely a religion which was never framed for them.

In Egypt the emblematical worship of animals succeeded to the doctrines of Thaut. The gods of the Romans afterwards shared Egypt with the dogs, the cats, and the crocodiles. To the Roman religion succeeded Christianity. That was completely banished by Mohammedanism, which will perhaps be superseded by some new religion.

In all these changes climate has effected nothing; government has done everything. We are here considering only secondary causes, without raising our unhallowed eyes to that Providence which directs them. The

Christian religion, which received its birth in Syria, and grew up towards its fullness of stature in Alexandria, now inhabits those countries where Teutat and Irminsul, Freya and Odin, were formerly adored.

There are some nations whose religion is the result neither of climate nor government. What cause detached the north of Germany, Denmark, three parts of Switzerland, Holland, England, Scotland, and Ireland, from the Romish communion? Poverty. Indulgences, and deliverance from purgatory for the souls of those whose bodies were at that time in possession of very little money, were sold too dear. The prelates and monks absorbed the whole revenue of a province. People adopted a cheaper religion. In short, after numerous civil wars, it was concluded that the pope's religion was a good one for nobles, and the reformed one for citizens. Time will show whether the religion of the Greeks or of the Turks will prevail on the coasts of the Euxine and Aegean seas.

CONCATENATION OF EVENTS

It is said that the present is pregnant with the future. Events are linked to each other by an invincible fatality: Homer puts Destiny above even Jupiter. This master of gods and men declares roundly that he cannot stop his son Sarpedon dying at his appointed time. Sarpedon was born at the moment when he had to be born, and could not be born at another moment; he could not die otherwise than before Troy; he could not be buried elsewhere than in Lycia; he had at the appointed time to produce vegetables which had to be changed into the substance of a few Lycians; his heirs had to establish a new order in his states; this new order had to exert an influence over the neighboring kingdoms; from it necessarily resulted a new arrangement of war and peace with the neighbors of the neighbors of Lycia: thus, step by step, the destiny of the whole world has been dependent on Sarpedon's death, which depended on Helen being carried off; and this carrying off was necessarily linked to Hecuba's marriage, which, when traced back to other events was linked to the origin of things.

If only one of these facts had been arranged differently, another universe would have resulted: but it was not possible for the present universe not to exist; therefore it was not possible for Jupiter to save his son's life, for all that he was Jupiter.

This system of necessity and fatality according to report has been invented in our time by Leibnitz, under the name of *self-sufficient reason.* It is, however, very ancient: that there is no effect without a cause and that often the smallest cause produces the greatest effects, is not a recent idea.

Lord Bolingbroke avows that the little quarrels of Madame Marlborough and Madame Masham gave birth to his chance of making Queen Anne's private treaty with Louis XIV; this treaty led to the Peace of Utrecht; this Peace of Utrecht established Philip V on the throne of Spain. Philip V took Naples and Sicily from the house of Austria; the Spanish prince who is today King of Naples clearly owes his kingdom to my lady Masham: and he would not have had it, he would not perhaps even have been born, if the Duchess of Marlborough had been more complaisant towards the Queen of England. His existence at Naples depended on one foolishness more or less at the court of London.

Examine the position of all the peoples of the universe. They are established like this on a sequence of facts which appear to be connected with nothing and which are connected with everything. Everything is cog, pulley, cord, spring, in this vast machine.

It is likewise in the physical sphere. A wind which blows from the depths of Africa and the southern seas brings with it a portion of the African atmosphere, which falls in rain in the valleys of the Alps. These rains fertilize our lands, while our north wind in its turn sends our vapors among the Negroes. We do good to Guinea, and Guinea does good to us. The chain stretches from one end of the universe to the other.

But it seems to me that the truth of this principle is strangely abused. From it some people conclude that there is not a sole minute atom whose movement has not exerted its influence in the present arrangement of the world; that there is not a single minute accident, among either men or animals, which is not an essential link in the great chain of fate.

Let us understand each other: every effect clearly has its cause, going back from cause to cause in the abyss of eternity; but every cause has not its effect going forward to the end of the centuries. All events are produced by each other, I admit; if the past is delivered of the present, the present is delivered of the future; every being has a father, but every being does not always have children. Here it is precisely as with a genealogical tree: each house goes back, as we say, to Adam; but in the family there are many persons who have died without issue.

There is a genealogical tree of the events of this world. It is incontestable that the inhabitants of Gaul and Spain are descended from Gomer, and the Russians from Magog, his younger brother: one finds this genealogy in so many fat books! On this basis one cannot deny that the Great Turk, who is also descended from Magog, was bound to be well beaten in 1769 by Catherine

II, Empress of Russia. This adventure is clearly connected with other great adventures. But that Magog spat to right or left, near Mount Caucasus, and that he made two circles in a well or three, that he slept on the left side or on the right, are matters which, in my opinion, had little influence on present affairs.

One must conclude that everything is not complete in nature, as Newton has demonstrated, and that every movement is not communicated step by step, until it makes a circuit of the world, as he has demonstrated still further. Throw into water a body of like density: You calculate easily that after a short time the movement of this body, and the movement it has communicated to the water, will be destroyed. The movement disappears and is effaced. In the same way, the movement that Magog might have produced by spitting in a well cannot influence what is passing today in Moldavia and Wallachia; therefore present events are not the children of *all* past events: they have their direct lines; but a thousand little collateral lines do not serve them at all. Once more, every being has a father, but every being does not have children.

DEMOCRACY

As a rule there is no comparison between the crimes of great men, who are always ambitious, and the crimes of the people, who always want, and can only want, liberty and equality. These two sentiments, Liberty and Equality, do not lead straight to calumny, rapine, assassination, poisoning, the devastation of one's neighbors' lands, etc. But ambitious might and the mania for power plunge men into all these crimes, whatever the time, whatever the place.

Popular government is in itself, therefore, less iniquitous, less abominable than despotic power.

The great vice of democracy is certainly not tyranny and cruelty. There have been mountain-dwelling republicans who were savage and ferocious; but it was not the republican spirit that made them so, it was nature.

The real vice of a civilized republic is expressed in the Turkish fable of the dragon with many heads and the dragon with many tails. The many heads injured one another, and the many tails obeyed a single head which sought to devour everything.

Democracy seems suitable only to a very little country, and one that is happily situated. However small it may be, it will make many mistakes, because it will be composed of men. Discord will reign there as in a monastery; but there will be no St. Bartholomew, no Irish massacres, no Sicilian vespers, no Inquisition, no condemnation to the galleys for having taken some water from the sea without paying for it—unless one assumes that this republic is composed of devils in a corner of hell.

Which is better—runs the endless question—a republic or a monarchy? The dispute always resolves itself into an agreement that it is a very difficult business to govern men. The Jews had God Himself for their master, and see what has happened to them as a result: nearly always have they been oppressed and enslaved and even today they do not appear to cut a very pretty figure.

DESTINY

Of all the books of the Occident which have come down to us, the most ancient is Homer. It is there that one finds the customs of profane antiquity, the gross heroes, the gross gods, made in the image of men; but it is there among dreams and inconsequentialities, that one finds too the seeds of philosophy, and above all the idea of that destiny which is master of the gods, as the gods are masters of the world.

When the magnanimous Hector is determined to fight the magnanimous Achilles, and with this object starts running away at top speed, thrice making the circuit of the city before fighting, in order to have more vigor; when Homer compares fleetfooted Achilles, who pursues him, to a sleeping man; when Madame Dacier goes into ecstasies of admiration over the art and mighty sense of this passage—then Jupiter wishes to save great Hector who has made so many sacrifices to him, and he consults the fates; he weighs the destinies of Hector and Achilles in the balance (*Iliad,* liv, xxii), and he finds that the Trojan must indubitably be killed by the Greek. He, Jupiter, cannot oppose it; and from this moment, Hector's guardian genius, Apollo, is forced to abandon his hero. The point is not that Homer is often prodigal —notably in this passage—of quite contradictory ideas, but that he is the first in whom one finds the notion of destiny. This notion, therefore, must have been much in vogue in his time.

The Pharisees, among the little Jewish people, did not adopt destiny until several centuries later; for these Pharisees, who were the first literates among the Jews, were very newfangled. In Alexandria they mixed a part of the Stoic dogmas with the old Jewish ideas. St. Jerome even claims that their sect is not much anterior to the Christian era.

The philosophers needed neither Homer nor the Pharisees to persuade themselves that everything happens through immutable laws, that everything is arranged, that everything is a necessary effect. This is how they argued. Either the world exists by its own nature, by its physical laws, or a supreme being has formed it according to his supreme laws: in both cases, these laws are immutable; in both cases everything is necessary; heavy bodies tend towards the center of the earth, without being able to rest in the air. Pear trees can never bear pineapples. A spaniel's instinct cannot be an ostrich's instinct; everything is arranged, geared, and controlled.

Man can have only a certain number of teeth, hair and ideas. There comes a time when he necessarily loses his teeth, his hair and his ideas.

If you could disturb the destiny of a fly, there would be nothing to stop you from controlling the destiny of all other flies, of all other animals, of all men, of all nature. You would find yourself in the end more powerful than God.

Imbeciles say: "My doctor has saved my aunt from a mortal malady; he has made her live ten years longer than she ought to have lived." Others who pretend to wisdom say: "The prudent man makes his own destiny."

But often the prudent, far from making their own destinies, succumb to them; it is destiny that makes them prudent.

Profound students of politics affirm that if Cromwell, Ludlow, Ireton and a dozen other parliamentarians had been assassinated a week before Charles I's head was cut off, this king might have lived longer and died in his bed. They are right. They might add that if the whole of England had been swallowed up in the sea, this monarch would not have perished on a scaffold near Whitehall; but things were so arranged that Charles had to have his neck severed.

Your doctor saved your aunt, but in doing so he assuredly did not contradict nature's order: he followed it. It is clear that your aunt could not stop herself being born in such and such a town, that she could not stop herself having a certain malady at a particular time, that the doctor could not be elsewhere than in the town where he was, that your aunt had to call him, that he had to prescribe for her the drugs which cured her, or which one thinks cured her, when nature was the only doctor.

A peasant thinks that it has hailed on his field by chance; but the philosopher knows that there is no chance, and that it was impossible, in the constitution of this world, for it not to hail on that day in that place.

There are persons who, frightened by this truth, admit only half of it—like debtors who offer half to their creditors, and ask respite for the rest. "There are," they say, "some events which are necessary, and others which are not." It would be laughable if one part of the world were arranged, and another part were not; if a part of what happens had to happen, and another part of what happens did not have to happen. If one looks closely at it, one sees that the doctrine opposed to that of destiny is absurd; but there are many people destined to reason badly, others not to reason at all, and others to persecute those who do reason.

Some say to you: "Do not believe in fatalism; for then, everything appearing inevitable, you will work at nothing, you will wallow in indifference, you will love neither riches, nor honors, nor glory; you will not wish to acquire anything, you will believe yourself as devoid of merit as of power; no talent will be cultivated, everything will perish through apathy."

Be not afraid, gentlemen, we shall always have passions and prejudices, since it is our destiny to be subjected to prejudices and passions: we shall know that it no more depends on us to have much merit and great talent, than to have a good head of hair and beautiful hands: we shall be convinced that we must not be vain about anything; and yet we shall always have vanity.

I necessarily have the urge to write this, and you have the itch to condemn me. Both of us are equally fools, equally the toys of destiny. Your nature is to do harm, mine is to love truth, and to make it public in spite of you.

The owl, which feeds on mice in its hovel, says to the nightingale: "Stop singing under your beautiful, shady trees. Come into my hole, that I may eat you." And the nightingale replies: "I was born to sing here —and to laugh at you."

You ask me what will become of liberty? I do not understand you. I do not know what this liberty is of which you speak; and you have been disputing about its nature for so long that you assuredly cannot be acquainted with it. If you wish—or rather, if you are able —to examine peaceably with me what it is, pass on to the letter "L."

DOG

It seems that nature has given the dog to man for his defense and pleasure; it is of all animals the most faithful; it is the best possible friend of man.

It appears that there are several species absolutely different. How can we believe that a greyhound comes originally from a spaniel? The one has neither the hair, legs, shape, ears, voice, scent, nor instinct of the other. A man who has never seen any dogs but barbets or spaniels, and who saw a greyhound for the first time, would take it rather for a dwarf horse than for an animal of the spaniel race. It is very likely that each race was always what it now is, with the exception of a few mongrel breeds.

It is astonishing that in the Jewish law the dog was considered unclean, as well as the griffin, the hare, the pig, and the eel; there must have been some moral or physical reason for it, which we have not yet discovered.

The tales that are told of the sagacity, obedience, friendship, and courage of dogs, are as extraordinary as they are true. The military philosopher, Ulloa, assures us that in Peru the Spanish dogs recognize the men of the Indian race, pursue them, and tear them to pieces; and that the Peruvian dogs do the same with the Spaniards. This would seem to prove that each species of dogs still retained the hatred which was inspired in it at the time of the conquest, and that each race always fought for its master with the same valor and attachment.

Why, then, has the word "dog" become a term of contempt? When we would be tender, we say my sparrow, my dove, my chicken; we even say my kitten, though this animal is famed for treachery; and, when we are angry, we call people dogs! The Turks, even when not angry, speak with horror and contempt of the Christian dogs. The English populace, when they see a man who, by his manner or dress, has the appearance of having been born on the banks of the Seine or of the Loire, commonly call him a French dog—a figure of speech which is neither just nor polite.

The fastidious Homer introduces the divine Achilles telling the divine Agamemnon that he is as impudent as a dog. This could excuse the English populace.

The most zealous friends of the dog must, however, confess that this animal has a bold eye; that some are snappish; that they often bite strangers whom they take for their master's enemies, as sentinels fire on passersby who approach too near the counterscarp. These are probably the reasons which have rendered the epithet "dog" insulting; but we dare not decide.

Why was the dog adored or revered—whichever you will—by the Egyptians? Because the dog is man's sentinel. Plutarch tells us that after Cambyses had killed their bull Apis, and had had it roasted, no animal except the dog dared to eat the remains of the feast, so profound was the respect for Apis; the dog, not so scrupulous, swallowed the god without hesitation. The Egyptians, as may be imagined, were exceedingly scandalized, and Anubis lost much of his credit.

The dog, however, still bears the honor of being always in the heavens, under the names of the great and little dog. We regularly record the dog days.

But of all dogs, Cerberus has had the greatest reputation; he had three heads. We have remarked that, anciently, all went by threes—Isis, Osiris, and Orus, the three first Egyptian divinities; the three brother gods of the Greek world—Jupiter, Neptune, and Pluto; the three Fates, the three Furies, the three Graces, the three judges of hell, and the three heads of this infernal dog.

We perceive here with grief that we have said nothing of cats. We will only remark that there are no cats in the heavens, as there are goats, crabs, bulls, rams, eagles, lions, fishes, hares, and dogs; but, in compensation, the cat has been consecrated, or revered, or adored, as partaking of saintliness, in several towns—and as altogether divine by no small number of women.

THE ECCLESIASTICAL MINISTRY

The institution of religion exists only to keep mankind in order, and to make men merit the goodness of God by their virtue. Everything in a religion which does not tend toward this goal must be considered alien or dangerous.

Instruction, exhortation, threats of torments to come, promises of immortal beatitude, prayers, counsels, spiritual help, are the only means ecclesiastics may use to try to make men virtuous here below, and happy for eternity. All other means are repugnant to the liberty of reason, to the nature of the soul, to the unalterable rights of conscience, to the essence of religion, to that of the ecclesiastical ministry, and to the rights of the sovereign.

Virtue supposes liberty, as the carrying of a burden supposes active force. Under coercion there is no virtue, and without virtue there is no religion. Make a slave of me, and I shall be no better for it. The sovereign, even, has no right to use coercion to lead men to religion, which in its nature presupposes choice and liberty. My thought is subject to authority no more than is sickness or health.

In order to disentangle all the contradictions with which books on canon law have been filled, and to clarify our ideas on the ecclesiastical ministry, let us investigate, amid a thousand equivocations, what the Church really is.

The Church is the assembly of all the faithful summoned on certain days to pray in common, and at all times to do good actions.

The priests are persons established under the authority of the sovereign to direct these prayers and all religious worship.

A numerous Church could not exist without ecclesiastics; but these ecclesiastics are not the Church.

It is no less evident that if the ecclesiastics, who are part of civil society, have acquired rights which might trouble or destroy society, these rights should be suppressed.

It is still more evident that, if God has attached to the Church prerogatives or rights, neither these rights nor these prerogatives should belong exclusively either to the chief of the Church or to the ecclesiastics, because they are not the Church, just as the magistrates are not the sovereign, in either a democratic state or in a monarchy.

Finally, it is quite evident that it is our souls which are under the clergy's care, solely in spiritual matters.

Our soul acts internally. Internal acts are thought, volition, inclinations, acquiescence in certain truths. All these acts are above coercion, and are within the ecclesiastical minister's sphere only in so far as he must instruct, but never command.

The soul also acts externally. External actions are under the civil law. Here coercion may have a place; temporal or corporal penalties maintain the law by punishing those who infringe it.

Obedience to ecclesiastical order must consequently always be free and voluntary: no other should be possible. Submission to civil order, on the other hand, may be compulsory and compelled.

For the same reason, ecclesiastical punishments, always spiritual, reach only those here below who are convinced inwardly of their fault. Civil pains, on the contrary, accompanied by physical ill, have their physical effects, whether or no the guilty person recognizes their justice.

From this it results, obviously, that the authority of the clergy is and can be spiritual only; that the clergy should not have any temporal power; that no coercive force is proper to its ministry, which would be destroyed by force.

It follows from this further that the sovereign, careful not to suffer any partition of his authority, must permit no enterprise which puts the members of society in external and civil dependence on an ecclesiastical body.

Such are the incontestable principles of real canon law, of which the rules and decisions should be judged at all times by the eternal and immutable truths which are founded on natural law and the necessary order of society.

EQUALITY

1. It is clear that men, in the enjoyment of their natural faculties, are equal: they are equal when they perform animal functions, and when they exercise their understanding. The King of China, the Great Mogul, the Padisha of Turkey, cannot say to the least of men: "I forbid you to digest, to go to the privy, or to think." All the animals of each species are equal among themselves. Animals, by nature, have over us the advantage of independence. If a bull which is wooing a heifer is driven away with the blows of the horns by a stronger bull, it goes in search of another mistress in another field, and lives free. A cock, beaten by a cock, consoles itself in another poultry-house. It is not so with us. A little vizier exiles a bostangi to Lemnos: the vizier Azem exiles the little vizier to Tenedos: the padisha exiles the vizier Azem to Rhodes: the Janissaries put the padisha in prison, and elect another who will exile good Mussulmans as he chooses; people will still be very obliged to him if he limits his sacred authority to this small exercise.

If this world were what it seems it should be, if man could find everywhere in it an easy subsistence, and a climate suitable to his nature, it is clear that it would be impossible for one man to enslave another. If this globe were covered with wholesome fruits; if the air, which should contribute to our life, gave us no diseases and no premature deaths; if man had no need of lodging and bed other than those of the buck and the deer; then the Gengis-Khans and the Tamerlanes would have no servants other than their children, who would be decent enough to help them in their old age.

In the natural state enjoyed by all untamed quadrupeds, birds and reptiles, man would be as happy as they. Domination would then be a chimera, an absurdity of which no one would think; for why seek servants when you have no need of their service?

If it came into the head of some individual of tyrannous mind and brawny arm to enslave a neighbor less strong than he, the thing would be impossible; the oppressed would be on the Danube before the oppressor had taken his measures on the Volga.

All men then would be necessarily equal, if they were without needs. It is the poverty connected with our species which subordinates one man to another. It is not the inequality which is the real misfortune, it is the dependence. It matters very little that So-and-so calls himself "His Highness," and So-and-so "His Holiness"; but to serve the one or the other is hard.

A big family has cultivated fruitful soil; two little families nearby have thankless and rebellious fields; the two poor families have to serve the opulent family, or slaughter it. There is no difficulty in that. But one of the two indigent families offers its arms to the rich family in exchange for bread, while the other attacks and is defeated. The subservient family is the origin of the servants and the workmen; the beaten family is the origin of the slaves.

In our unhappy world it is impossible for men living

in society not to be divided into two classes, the one the rich who command, the other the poor who serve; and these two classes are subdivided into a thousand, and these thousand still have different gradations.

When the lots are drawn you come to us and say: "I am a man like you. I have two hands and two feet, as much pride as you, nay more, a mind as disordered, at least, as inconsequent, as contradictory as yours. I am a citizen of San Marino, or of Ragusa, or Vaugirard: give me my share of the land. In our known hemisphere there are about fifty thousand million arpents to cultivate, some passable, some sterile. We are only about a thousand million featherless bipeds in this continent; that makes fifty arpents apiece: be just; give me my fifty arpents."

"Go and take them in the land of the Kaffirs," we answer, "or the Hottentots, or the Samoyedes; come to an amicable arrangement with them; here all the shares are taken. If you want to eat, be clothed, lodged, and warmed among us, work for us as your father did; serve us or amuse us, and you will be paid; otherwise you will be obliged to ask charity, which would be too degrading to your sublime nature, and would stop your being really the equal of kings, and even of country parsons, according to the pretensions of your noble pride."

II. All the poor are not unhappy. The majority were born in that state, and continual work keeps them from feeling their position too keenly; but when they do feel it, then one sees wars, like that of the popular party against the senate party in Rome, like those of the peasants in Germany, England, and France. All these wars finish sooner or later with the subjection of the people, because the powerful have money, and money is master of everything in a state. I say in a state, for it is not the same between nations. The nation which makes the best use of the sword will always subjugate the nation which has more gold and less courage.

All men are born with a sufficiently violent liking for domination, wealth, and pleasure, and with a strong taste for idleness; consequently, all men covet the money, the wives, or the daughters of other men; they wish to be their master, to subject them to all their caprices, and to do nothing, or at least to do only very agreeable things. You see clearly that with these fine inclinations it is as impossible for men to be equal as it is impossible for two preachers or two professors of theology not to be jealous of each other.

The human race, such as it is, cannot subsist unless there is an infinity of useful men who possess nothing at all; for it is certain that a man who is well off will not leave his own land to come to till yours, and if you have need of a pair of shoes, it is not the Secretary to the Privy Council who will make them for you. Equality, therefore, is at once the most natural thing and the most fantastic.

As men go to excess in everything when they can, this inequality has been exaggerated. It has been maintained in many countries that it was not permissible for a citizen to leave the country where chance has caused him to be born. The sense of this law is obviously: "This land is so bad and so badly governed, that we forbid any individual to leave it, for fear that everyone will leave it." Do better: make all your subjects wish to live in your country, and foreigners wish to come to it.

All men have the right in the bottom of their hearts to think themselves entirely equal to other men. It does not follow from this that the cardinal's cook should order his master to prepare him his dinner, but the cook can say: "I am a man like my master; like him I was born crying; like me he will die with the same pangs and the same ceremonies. Both of us perform the same animal functions. If the Turks take possession of Rome, and if then I am cardinal and my master cook, I shall take him into my service." This discourse is reasonable and just, but while waiting for the Great Turk to take possession of Rome, the cook must do his duty, or else all human society is disordered.

As regards a man who is neither a cardinal's cook, nor endowed with any other employment in the state; as regards a private person who is connected with nothing, but who is vexed at being received everywhere with an air of being patronized or scorned, who sees quite clearly that many monseigneurs have no more knowledge, wit, or virtue than he, and who at times is bored at waiting in their antechambers, what should he decide to do? Why, to take himself off.

EXPIATION

Perhaps the most beautiful institution of antiquity is that solemn ceremony which repressed crimes by the warning that they must be punished, and which calmed the despair of the guilty by permitting them to atone for their transgressions by various kinds of penitence. Remorse must necessarily have preceded expiation, for diseases are older than medicine, and all needs have existed before relief.

It was then, before all the creeds, a natural religion which troubled man's heart when in his ignorance or in his hastiness he had committed an inhuman action. A friend kills his friend in a quarrel, a brother kills his brother, a jealous and frantic lover even kills her without whom he cannot live. The head of a nation condemns a virtuous man, a useful citizen. These are men in despair, if they have sensibility. Their conscience harries them; nothing is realer; and it is the height of unhappiness. Only two choices remain: either reparation, or confirmed criminality. All sensitive souls choose the first, monsters choose the second.

As soon as religions were established, there were expiations; the ceremonies accompanying them were ridiculous: for what connection is there between the water of the Ganges and a murder? How could a man repair a homicide by bathing himself? We have already remarked this excess of aberration and absurdity, of imagining that he who washes his body washes his soul, and wipes away the stains of evil actions.

The water of the Nile had later the same virtue as the water of the Ganges, and to these purifications other ceremonies were added, which were even less to the point. The Egyptians took two goats, and drew lots for which of the two should be cast down, charged with the sins of the guilty. The name of "Hazazel," the expiator, was given to this goat. What connection, I ask you, is there between a goat and a man's crime?

It is true that God later permitted this ceremony to be sanctified among the Jews, our fathers, who took over so many Egyptian rites; but doubtless it was the repentance, and not the goat, which purified the Jewish souls.

We are told that Jason, having killed Absyrthe his stepbrother, came with Medea, more guilty than he, to have himself absolved by Circe, queen and priestess of Aea, who ever after passed for a great sorceress. Circe absolved them with a sucking-pig and salt cakes. This may be a fairly good dish, but it could hardly pay for

Absyrthe's blood or render Jason and Medea more respectable people, unless they avowed a sincere repentance while eating their sucking-pig.

Orestes' expiation (he had avenged his father by murdering his mother) was the task of stealing a statue from the Tartars of the Crimea. The statue must have been very badly made, and there was small profit in such a business. Since those days men have done better. They invented the mysteries, whereby the guilty might receive absolution by undergoing painful ordeals, and by swearing that they would lead a new life. It is from this oath that new members of any organization came to be called, among all nations, by a name which corresponds to initiates—*qui ineunt vitam novam,* those who began a new career, who entered into the path of virtue. The Christian catechumens were called *initiates* only when they were baptized.

It is certain that in these mysteries one was cleansed of one's sins only by the oath of virtue. The hierophant in all the Greek mysteries, when dismissing the assembly, pronounced two Egyptian words, "*Koth, ompheth,*" watch, be pure—which proves at once that the mysteries came originally from Egypt, and that they were invented only to make men better.

Sages in all times did what they could, then, to inspire virtue and keep human frailty from utter despair; but there are crimes so horrible that no mystery afforded expiation for them. Nero, although he was emperor, could not get himself initiated into the mysteries of Ceres. Constantine, according to Zosimus, could not obtain pardon for his crimes: he was stained with the blood of his wife, his son and all his kindred. It was in the interest of humanity that such great transgressions should remain without expiation, so that absolution should not encourage similar deeds, and so that universal horror might sometimes check villainy.

The Roman Catholics have expiations which are called "penances."

By the laws of the barbarians who destroyed the Roman Empire, crimes were expiated with money. This was called *compounding—componat cum decem, viginti, triginta solidis.* It cost two hundred sous of that time to kill a priest, and four hundred for killing a bishop; so that a bishop was worth precisely two priests.

Having thus compounded with men, one compounded with God, when confession was generally established. Finally, Pope John XXII, who made money out of everything, prepared a tariff of sins.

The absolution of incest cost four Tournois livres for a layman—*ab incestu pro laico in foro conscientiae turonenses quatuor.* For the man and the woman who have committed incest—eighteen livres four ducats and nine carlins. This is not just. If one person paid only four livres, the two owed only eight livres.

Sodomy and bestiality are put at the same rate, with the inhibitory clause to title XLIII: this amounts to ninety Tournois livres twelve ducats and six carlins: *cum inhibitione turnonenses* 90, *ducatos* 12, *carlinos* 6, etc.

It is very difficult to believe that Leo X was so imprudent as to have this impost printed in 1514, as has been asserted; but it must be considered that at that time no spark was visible of the conflagration which reformers kindled later, that the court of Rome slumbered on the people's credulity, and neglected to cover its exactions with the lightest veil. The public sale of indulgences, which followed soon after, makes it clear that this court took no precaution to hide the turpitudes to which so many nations were accustomed. As soon as complaints against the Church's abuses burst forth, the court did what it could to suppress the book; but it could not succeed.

If I dare give my opinion of this impost, I must say that the various editions are not reliable; the prices are not at all proportionate: and these prices do not agree with those which are given by d'Aubigné, grandfather of Madame de Maintenon, in the *Confession de Sanci.* He rates virginity at six *gros,* and incest with a mother or sister at five *gros*—a scale which is obviously ridiculous. I think that there was in fact a tariff established in the Datary's office, for those who came to Rome to be absolved, or to bargain for dispensations; but that the enemies of Rome added a good deal to it in order to render the tariff more odious.

What is quite certain is that these imposts were never authorized by any council; that it was an enormous abuse invented by avarice, and respected by those whose interest it was not to abolish it. The buyers and the sellers were equally satisfied, so hardly anyone protested, until the troubled days of the reformation. It must be admitted that an exact knowledge of all these imposts would be of great service to the history of the human mind.

FAITH

(*We have long been uncertain whether or not we should print this article, which we found in an old book. Our respect for St. Peter's see restrained us. But some pious men having convinced us that Pope Alexander VI had nothing in common with St. Peter, we at last decided to bring this little piece into the light, without scruple.*)

One day Prince Pico della Mirandola met Pope Alexander VI at the house of the courtesan Emilia, while

Lucretia, the holy father's daughter, was in childbed. No one in Rome knew who the child's father was—the Pope, or his son the Duke of Valentinois, or Lucretia's husband, Alphonse of Aragon, who was supposed to be impotent. The conversation was at first very sprightly. Cardinal Bembo records a part of it.

"Little Pic," said the Pope, "who do you think is my grandson's father?"

"Your son-in-law, I imagine," answered Pic.

"Eh! how can you believe such nonsense?"

"I believe it through faith."

"But don't you know that an impotent man cannot have children?"

"Faith consists," returned Pic, "in believing things because they are impossible. And, besides, the honor of your house demands that Lucretia's son shall not be considered the fruit of incest. You make me believe even more incomprehensible mysteries. Do I not have to believe that a serpent spoke—since when all men have been damned—that Balaam's she-ass also spoke very eloquently, and that the walls of Jericho fell at the sound of trumpets?" Pic then ran through a litany of all the admirable things he believed.

Alexander collapsed with laughter on his sofa.

"I believe all that stuff, just as you do," he said, "for I know that only by faith can I be saved, and that I shall not be saved by my works."

"Ah! Holy Father," said Pic, "you have need of neither works nor faith. They are good for poor profane people like us, but you who are God's regent on earth can believe and do whatever you choose. You have the keys of heaven, and there is no chance of St. Peter shutting the door in your face. But for myself, who am only a poor prince, I admit that I should need potent protection if I had slept with my daughter, and if I had used the stiletto and the cantarella as often as your Holiness."

Alexander could take a joke. "Let us talk seriously," he said to Prince della Mirandola. "Tell me what merit one can have in telling God that one is persuaded of things of which in fact one cannot be persuaded? What pleasure can that give God? Between ourselves, saying that one believes what is impossible to believe is lying."

Pico della Mirandola made a great sign of the cross. "Eh! God the father!" he cried. "May your Holiness pardon me, but you are not a Christian."

"No, by my faith," said the Pope.

"I thought as much," said Pico della Mirandola.

FATHERLAND

A young journeyman pastrycook who had been to college, and who still knew a few of Cicero's phrases, boasted one day of loving his fatherland. "What do you mean by your fatherland?" a neighbor asked him. "Is it your oven? Is it the village where you were born and which you have never seen since? Is it the street in which dwelt your father and mother, who have been ruined with the result that you are reduced to baking little pies for a living? Is it the town hall where you will never be the police superintendent's clerk? Is it the church of Our Lady where you have not been able to become a choirboy, while a stupid man is archbishop and duke with an income of twenty thousand golden louis?"

The journeyman pastrycook did not know what to answer. A philosopher, who was listening to this conversation, concluded that in a fatherland of any extent there must often be several million men who have no fatherland.

You, pleasure-loving Parisians, who have never traveled farther than Dieppe to eat fresh fish; who know nothing but your brilliant town house, your pretty country house, and your box at an Opera where the rest of Europe persists in being bored; who speak your own language well enough because you know no other—you love all these things, and you love the girls you keep, the champagne which comes to you from Rheims, the dividends which the Hotel-de-Ville pays you every six months; and you say you love your fatherland!

Now, in all conscience, does a financier sincerely love his fatherland?

The officer and the soldier who pillage their winter quarters, if one lets them—have they a very warm love for the peasants they ruin?

Where was the fatherland of the scarred Duc de Guise, was it in Nancy, Paris, Madrid, Rome? What fatherland have you, Cardinals de La Balue, Duprat, Lorraine, Mazarin? Where was the fatherland of Attila, and of a hundred other heroes of his type? I would like someone to tell me which was Abraham's fatherland.

The first man to write that one's fatherland is wherever one feels comfortable was, I believe, Euripides in his *Phaeton*. But the first man who left his birthplace to seek his comfort elsewhere had said it before him.

What, then, is a fatherland? Is it not a good field, whose owner, lodged in a well-kept house, can say: "This field that I till, this house that I have built, are mine. I live here protected by laws which no tyrant can infringe. When those who own fields and houses, like myself, meet in their common interest, I have my voice in the assembly; I am a part of everything, a part of the community, a part of the dominion—there is my fatherland"?

Very well. But is it better for your fatherland to be

a monarchy or a republic? For four thousand years has this question been debated. Ask the rich for an answer, they all prefer aristocracy; question the people, they want democracy: only kings prefer royalty. How then is it that nearly the whole world is governed by monarchs? Ask the rats who proposed to hang a bell round the cat's neck. But in truth, the real reason is, as has been said, that men are very rarely worthy of governing themselves.

It is sad that in order to be a good patriot one often has to be the enemy of the rest of mankind. Whenever old Cato, that excellent citizen, spoke before the Roman senate, he always used to say: "Such is my opinion, and Carthage must be destroyed." To be a good patriot is to wish that one's city may be enriched by trade, and be powerful by arms. It is clear that one country cannot gain without another's losing, and that one cannot conquer without bringing misery to another. Such then is the human state, that to wish greatness for one's country is to wish harm to one's neighbors. He who wished that his fatherland might never be greater, smaller, richer, or poorer, would be a citizen of the world.

FREE WILL

Ever since men have been able to reason, philosophers have obscured the question of free will; but the theologians have rendered it unintelligible by absurd subtleties about grace. Locke was perhaps the first man to find a thread in the labyrinth, for he was the first who, instead of arrogantly setting out from a general principle, examined human nature by analysis. For three thousand years people have disputed whether or not the will is free. In the *Essay on the Human Understanding,* Locke shows that the question is fundamentally absurd, and that liberty can no more belong to the will than can color and movement.

What is the meaning of this phrase "to be free"? It means "to be able," or else it has no meaning. To say that the will "can" is as ridiculous at bottom as to say that the will is yellow or blue, round or square. Will is wish, and liberty is power. Let us examine step by step the chain of our inner processes without befuddling our minds with scholastic terms or antecedent principles.

It is proposed to you that you mount a horse. You must absolutely make a choice, for it is quite clear that you either will go or that you will not go. There is no middle way. You must wish yes or no. Up to this point it is clear that the will is not free. You wish to mount the horse. Why? An ignoramus will say: "Because I wish it." This answer is idiotic. Nothing happens or can happen without a reason, a cause; so there must be one for your wish. What is it? It is the agreeable idea of going on horseback, which presents itself in your brain as the dominant idea, the determinant idea. But, you will say, can I not resist an idea which dominates me? No, for what would be the cause of your resistance? None. Your will could "resist" only by obeying a still more despotic idea.

Now you receive all your ideas; therefore you receive your "wish," you "wish" by necessity. The word "liberty" does not therefore belong in any way to your will.

You ask me how thought and wish are formed in us. I answer you that I have not the remotest idea. I do not know how ideas are made any more than how the world was made. All we can do is to grope in darkness for the springs of our incomprehensible machine.

Will, therefore, is not a faculty that can be called free. A free will is an expression absolutely void of sense, and what the scholastics have called "will of indifference," that is to say, willing without cause, is a chimera unworthy of being combated.

In what, then does liberty consist? In the power to do what one wills. I wish to leave my study, the door is open, I am free to leave it.

But, you say, suppose the door is closed, and I wish to stay where I am. Then I stay there freely. Let us be explicit. In this case you exercise the power that you have of staying; for you have this power, but not that of going out.

Liberty, then, about which so many volumes have been written is, when accurately defined, only the power of acting.

In what sense then must one utter the phrase: "Man is free"? In the same sense that one uses the words, "health," "strength," and "happiness." Man is not always strong, always healthy, nor always happy. A great passion, a great obstacle, may deprive him of his liberty, his power of action.

The words "liberty," and "free will," are therefore abstract words, general words, like beauty, goodness, justice. These terms do not signify that all men are always beautiful, good, and just; similarly, they are not always free.

Let us go further. If liberty is only the power of acting, what is this power? It is the effect of the constitution and the actual state of our organs. Leibnitz wishes to solve a geometrical problem, but he has an apoplectic fit, and in this condition he certainly is not free to solve his problem. Is a vigorous young man, madly in love, who holds his willing mistress in his arms, free to tame his passion? Undoubtedly not. He has the power of enjoying, and has not the power of refraining. Locke, then, is quite right when he calls liberty "power." When can this young man refrain despite the violence of his passion? Only when a stronger, contradictory idea determines the activity of his body and his soul.

But does this mean that the other animals have the same liberty, the same power? Why not? They have senses, memory, feeling, perceptions, as we have. They act with spontaneity as we act. They must also have, as we have, the power of acting by virtue of their perceptions, by virtue of the play of their organs.

Someone cries: "If all this is true, all things are only machines, everything in the universe is subjected to eternal laws." Well, would you have everything subject to a million blind caprices? Either everything is a necessary consequence of the nature of things, or everything is the effect of the eternal order of an absolute master. In either case we are only cogs in the machine of the world.

It is a foolish commonplace to assert that without the pretended liberty of the will, all pains and rewards are useless. Reason, and you will come to a quite contrary conclusion.

If, when a brigand is executed, his accomplice who sees him expire has the liberty of not being frightened at the punishment; if his will is determined by itself, he will go from the foot of the scaffold to commit murder on the broad highway. But if his organs, stricken with horror, make him experience an unconquerable terror, he will abandon crime. His companion's punishment becomes useful to him, and an insurance for society, only so long as his will is not free.

Liberty, then, is only and can be only the power to do what one wills. This is what philosophy teaches us. But if one considers liberty in the theological sense, it is a matter so sublime that profane eyes dare not look so high.

FRIENDSHIP

Friendship is the marriage of souls, and this marriage is subject to divorce. It is a tacit contract between two sensitive and virtuous persons. I say sensitive, because a monk, a recluse, can be innocent of evil and still live without knowing the meaning of friendship. I say virtuous, because the wicked have only accomplices; voluptuaries have companions in debauch, self-seekers have partners, politicians attract partisans; the generality of idle men have attachments; princes have courtiers; while virtuous men alone have friends. Cethegus was the accomplice of Catiline, and Maecenas the courtier of Octavius; but Cicero was the friend of Atticus.

GLORY

In 1723, a Chinese visited Holland. This Chinese was a man of letters and a merchant; which two professions ought not to be incompatible, but which have become so among us, thanks to the extreme regard which is paid to money, and the little consideration which mankind has ever shown, and will ever show, for merit.

This Chinese, who spoke a little Dutch, was once in a bookseller's shop with some men of learning. He asked for a book, and Bossuet's *Universal History*, badly translated, was suggested to him. "Ah!" said he, "how fortunate! I shall now see what is said of our great empire—of our nation, which has existed as one people for more than fifty thousand years—of that succession of emperors who have governed us for so many ages. I shall now see what is thought of the religion of the literate—of that simple worship which we render to the Supreme Being. How pleasing to see what is said in Europe of our arts, many of which are more ancient among us than all the kingdoms of Europe. I suppose the author will have made many mistakes in the history of the war which we had twenty-two thousand five hundred and fifty-two years ago, with the warlike nations of Tonkin and Japan, and of that solemn embassy which the mighty emperor of the Moguls sent to ask laws from us, in the year of the world 500,000,000,000,079,123,450,000." "Alas!" said one of the learned men to him, "you are not even mentioned in that book; you are not important enough; it is almost all about the first nation in the world—the only nation, the great Jewish people!"

"The Jewish people!" exclaimed the Chinese. "Are they, then, masters of at least three-quarters of the earth?" "They flatter themselves that they shall one day be so," was the answer; "until which time they have the honor of being our old-clothesmen, and, now and then, clippers of our coin."—"You jest," said the Chinese; "had these people ever a vast empire?" "They had as their own for some years," said I, "a small country; but it is not by the extent of their states that a people are to be judged; as it is not by his riches that we are to estimate a man."

"But is no other people spoken of in this book?" asked the man of letters. "Certainly," returned a learned man who stood next me, and who took it upon himself to do the talking, "there is a deal said in it of a small country sixty leagues broad, called Egypt, where it is asserted that there was a lake a hundred and fifty leagues round, cut by the hands of men."—"Zounds!" said the Chinese; "a lake a hundred and fifty leagues round in a country only sixty broad! That is fine, indeed!"—"Everybody was wise in that country," added the doctor. "Oh! those must have been happy days!" said the Chinese. "But is that all?"—"No," replied the European; "there is also mention of that celebrated people, the Greeks." "Who are these Greeks?" asked the man of letters. "Ah!" continued the other, "they inhabited a province about a two-hundredth part as large as China, but which has been famous throughout the world." "I have never heard of these people, neither in Mogul nor in Japan, nor in Great Tartary," said the Chinese, with an ingenuous look.

"Oh, ignorant, barbarous man!" politely exclaimed our scholar. "Know you not, then, the Theban Epaminondas, nor the harbor of Piraeus, nor the name of the two horses of Achilles, nor that of Silenus's ass? Have you not heard of Jupiter, nor of Diogenes, nor of Lais, nor of Cybele, nor—"

"I am much afraid," replied the Chinese man of letters, "that you know nothing at all of the ever memorable adventure of the celebrated Xixofou Concochigramki, nor of the mysteries of the great Fi Psi Hi Hi. But pray, what are the other unknown things of which this universal history treats?" The scholar then spoke for a quarter of an hour on the Roman commonwealth: but when he came to Julius Caesar, the Chinese interrupted him, saying, "As for him, I think I know him: was he not a Turk?"

"What!" said the scholar, somewhat warm, "do you not at least know the difference between Pagans, Christians, and Mussulmans? Do you not know Constantine, and the history of the popes?" "We have vaguely heard," answered the Asiatic, "of one Mohammed."

"It is impossible," returned the other, "that you should not, at least, be acquainted with Luther, Zuinglius, Bellarmin, Oecolampadius." "I shall never remember those names," said the Chinese.

He then went away to sell a considerable parcel of tea and fine grogram, with which he bought two fine girls and a cabin-boy, whom he took back to his own country, adoring Tien, and commending himself to Confucius.

For myself, who was present at this conversation, I clearly saw what glory is. And I said: since Caesar and Jupiter are unknown in the finest, the most ancient, the most extensive, the most populous and well-regulated kingdom upon earth, it beseems you, ye governors of some little country, ye preachers in some little parish, or some little town—ye doctors of Salamanca and of Bourges, ye flimsy authors, and ye ponderous commentators—it beseems you to make pretensions to renown!

GOVERNMENT

What, then, is the destiny of mankind? Scarcely any great people is governed by itself. Begin from the east, and take the circuit of the world. Japan closed its ports against foreigners from the well-founded apprehension of a dreadful revolution. China actually experienced such a revolution; she obeys Tartars of a mixed race, half Manchu and half Hun. India obeys Mogul Tartars. The Nile, the Orontes, Greece, and Epirus are still under the yoke of the Turks. It is not an English race that reigns in England; it is a German family which succeeded to a Dutch prince, as the latter succeeded a Scotch family which had succeeded an Angevin family, that had replaced a Norman family, which had expelled a family of usurping Saxons. Spain obeys a French family, which succeeded to an Austrasian race; that Austrasian race had succeeded families that boasted of Visigoth extraction; these Visigoths had long before been driven out by the Arabs, after having succeeded to the Romans, who had expelled the Carthaginians. Gaul obeys Franks, after having obeyed Roman prefects.

The same banks of the Danube have belonged to Germans, Romans, Arabs, Slavonians, Bulgarians, and Huns, to twenty different families, and almost all of them foreigners.

And what greater wonder has Rome had to exhibit than so many emperors who were born in the barbarous provinces, and so many popes born in provinces no less barbarous? Let him govern who can. And when anyone has made himself master, he governs as best he can.

INCUBUS

Have there ever been incubi or succubi? Our learned juriconsults and demonologists admit both the one and the other.

It is pretended that Satan, always on the alert, inspires young ladies and gentlemen with lascivious dreams, that he gathers the result common to such masculine dreams, and that he carries it neatly and still warm to the feminine reservoir for which it is destined by nature. It is this process which produced so many heroes and demigods in the days of antiquity.

The devil took a great deal of superfluous trouble in this matter; he had only to leave the young people alone, and the world would have been sufficiently supplied with heroes without any assistance from him.

An idea may be formed of incubi by this explanation of the great Delrio, of Boguets, and other writers learned in sorcery; but they do not account for succubi. A female might pretend to believe that she had communicated with and was pregnant by a god, the explication of Delrio being very favorable to the assumption. The devil in this case has deposited in her the essential substance taken from a young man's dream; she is pregnant, and gives birth without reproach; the devil has been her incubus. But if the devil wishes to be a succubus, it is quite another matter. He has then to become a she-devil, and a man's seed must enter her. It is this she-devil who is then bewitched by a man, and she who bears the child. The gods and goddesses of antiquity acted much more nobly and decorously; Jupiter in person, was the incubus of Alcmena and Semele; Thetis in person, the succubus of Peleus, and Venus of Anchises, without having recourse to the various contrivances of our extraordinary demonism.

Let us simply observe, that the gods frequently disguised themselves, in their pursuit of our girls, sometimes as an eagle, sometimes as a pigeon, a swan, a horse. a shower of gold; but the goddesses assumed no disguise: they had only to show themselves, to please. It must however be presumed, that whatever shapes the gods assumed to steal a march, they consummated their loves in the form of men. Jupiter could not take his pleasure of Danae while he was only gold, and he would have been very much embarrassed with Leda—as she would have been also—had he been only a swan; but he became a god again, that is to say, a handsome young man, and all was well.

As to the new manner of rendering girls pregnant by the ministry of the devil, it is not to be doubted, for the Sorbonne decided the point in the year 1318.

"*Per tales artes et ritus impios et invocationes et demonum, nullus unquam sequatur effectus ministerio demonum, error.*"—"It is an error to believe, that these magic arts and invocations of the devils are without effect."

This decision has never been revoked. Thus we are bound to believe in succubi and incubi, because our teachers have always believed in them.

There have been many other sages in this science, as

well as the Sorbonne. Bodin, in his book concerning sorcerers, dedicated to Christopher de Thou, first president of the Parliament of Paris, relates that John Hervilier, a native of Verberie, was condemned by that parliament to be burned alive for having prostituted his daughter to the devil, a great black man, whose semen was icy cold. This would seem contrary to the devil's nature, but our jurisprudence has always admitted that the devil's sperm is cold, and the prodigious number of sorcerers which it has burned in consequence will always remain a proof of its accuracy.

The celebrated Picus of Mirandola—a prince never lies—says he knew an old man of the age of eighty years who had slept half his life with a female devil, and another of seventy who enjoyed a similar felicity. Both were buried at Rome, but nothing is said of the fate of their children. Thus is the existence of incubi and succubi demonstrated.

It is impossible, at least, to prove to the contrary; for if we are called on to believe that devils can enter our bodies, who can prevent them from taking kindred liberties with our wives and our daughters? And if there are devils, there are probably she-devils; for to be consistent, if the demons beget children on our females, it must follow that we do the same thing on the bodies of the female demons. Never has there been a more universal empire than that of the devil. What has dethroned him? Reason.

INTOLERANCE

Read the article on *Intolerance* in the great *Encyclopedia.* Read the treatise on *Toleration* composed on occasion of the dreadful assassination of Jean Calas, a citizen of Toulouse; and if, after that, you allow of persecution in matters of religion, compare yourself at once to Ravaillac. Ravaillac, you know, was highly intolerant. The following is the substance of all the discourses ever delivered by the intolerant:

You monster: who will be burned to all eternity in the next world, and whom I will myself burn as soon as ever I can in this, you really have the insolence to read de Thou and Bayle, who have been put on the index at Rome! When I was preaching to you in the name of God, how Samson had killed a thousand men with the jawbone of an ass, your head, still harder than the arsenal from which Samson obtained his arms, showed me by a slight movement from left to right that you believed nothing of what I said. And when I stated that the devil Asmodeus, who out of jealousy twisted the necks of the seven husbands of Sarah among the Medes, was put in chains in upper Egypt, I saw a small contraction of your lips, in Latin called *cachinnus* (a grin), which plainly indicated to me that in the privacy of your mind you hold the history of Asmodeus in derision.

And as for you, Isaac Newton; Frederick the Great, king of Prussia and elector of Brandenburg; John Locke; Catherine, empress of Russia, victorious over the Ottomans; John Milton; the beneficent sovereign of Denmark; Shakespeare; the wise king of Sweden; Leibnitz; the august house of Brunswick; Tillotson; the emperor of China; the Parliament of England; the Council of the great Mogul; in short, all you who do not believe one word which I have taught in my courses on divinity, I declare to you, that I regard you all as pagans and publicans, as, in order to engrave it on your unimpressible brains, I have often told you before. You are a set of callous miscreants; you will all go to gehenna, where the worm dies not and the fire is not quenched; for I am right, and you are all wrong; and I have grace, and you have none. I regularly confess three devout ladies of my neighborhood, while you do not confess a single one; I have executed the mandates of bishops, as you have never done; I have abused philosophers in the language of the fishmarket, while you have protected, imitated, or equaled them; I have composed pious defamatory libels, stuffed with infamous calumnies, and you have never so much as read them. I say mass every day in Latin for fourteen sous, and you are never even so much as present at it, any more than Cicero, Cato, Pompey, Caesar, Horace, or Virgil, were ever present at it—consequently you deserve each of you to have your right hand cut off, your tongue cut out, to be put to the torture, and at last burned at a slow fire; for God is merciful.

Such, without the slightest abridgment, are the maxims of the intolerant, and the sum and substance of all their books. How delightful to live with such amiable people!

KISSING

The young people of both sexes must forgive me, for they may not find here what they will probably seek. This article is only for scholars and serious persons, to whom it might seem hardly suitable at first blush.

There is but too much business of kissing in the comedies of Molière's day. Champagne, in *La Mère Coquette* by Quinault, asks Laurette to kiss him; whereupon she says, "You are not satisfied? Really, I am ashamed of you! I have already kissed you twice." And Champagne answers her: "What! you kiss by count?" The valets were always begging kisses of the lady's maids; people were busy kissing all over the stage. It was usually very dull and boring, particularly in the case of ugly actors, who were positively nauseating.

If the reader wants kisses, let him look for them in *Pastor Fido,* which has one entire chorus devoted to nothing but kisses while the whole play is based solely on a kiss that Mirtillo gave one fine day to beautiful Amarilli, during a game of blind man's buff—*un bacio molto saporito.*

Everyone knows the chapter on kisses, in which Jean de la Casa, Archbishop of Benevento, says that people may kiss each other from head to foot. He pities people with big noses who can approach each other only with difficulty; and he advises long-nosed ladies to have flat-nosed lovers.

The kiss was a very ordinary form of salutation throughout ancient times. Plutarch recalls that the conspirators, before killing Caesar, kissed his face, hand, and breast. Tacitus says that when Agricola, his father-in-law, returned from Rome, Domitian received him with a coid kiss, said nothing to him, and left him confounded in the crowd. The inferior who could not aspire to greet his superior by kissing him, put his mouth to his own hand, and threw him a kiss which the other returned in the same way, if he so desired.

This salutation was used even for worshiping the gods. Job, in his parable, which is perhaps the oldest of known books, says that he has not worshiped the sun and the moon like the other Arabs, that he has not carried his hand to his mouth as he looked at these heavenly bodies.

In our Occident nothing remains of this ancient custom but the puerile and genteel civility that is still taught to children in some small towns, of kissing their right hands when someone has given them some sweets.

It was a horrible thing to betray with a kiss; it was

this which made Caesar's assassination still more hateful. We know all about Judas's kisses; they have become proverbial.

Joab, one of David's captains, being very jealous of Amasa, another captain, said to him: "Art thou in health, my brother? And Joab took Amasa by the beard with the right hand to kiss him." While with his other hand he drew his sword and "smote him therewith in the fifth rib, and shed out his bowels to the ground."

No other kiss is to be found connected with the other fairly frequent murders which were committed among the Jews, unless it be perhaps the kisses which Judith gave to the captain Holophernes, before cutting off his head, while he was in bed asleep; but no mention is made of them, and the thing is merely probable.

In one of Shakespeare's tragedies called *Othello*, this Othello, who is a Negro, kisses his wife twice before strangling her. This may seem abominable to decent people; but Shakespeare's partisans say it is beautifully natural, particularly in the case of a Negro.

When Giovanni Galeas Sforza was assassinated in Milan Cathedral, on St. Stephen's day; when the two Medici were killed in the Reparata church; when Admiral Coligny, the Prince of Orange, the Maréchal d'Ancre, the brothers Witt, and so many others were murdered, at least they were not kissed.

The ancients must have considered the kiss as somehow symbolic and sacred, since they kissed the statues of their gods, and the beards of the statues, when the sculptors had given them beards. Initiates kissed each other at the mysteries of Ceres, as a sign of concord.

The early Christians, men and women, kissed each other on the mouth in their *agapae*. This word signified "love-feast." They gave each other the holy kiss, the kiss of peace, the kiss of brother and sister. This custom lasted for more than four centuries, and was abolished at last on account of its consequences. It was these kisses of peace, these *agapae* of love, these names of "brotner" and "sister," that long drew down upon the little-known Christians those imputations of debauchery with which the priests of Jupiter and the priestesses of Vesta charged them. You may see in Petronius, and in other profane authors, that libertines called themselves "brother" and "sister." It was thought that among the Christians the same names signified the same infamies. They were innocent accomplices in spreading these accusations over the Roman empire.

There were in the beginning seventeen different Christian societies, just as there were nine among the Jews, including the two kinds of Samaritans. The societies which flattered themselves on being the most orthodox accused the others of the most inconceivable obscenities. The term of "gnostic," which was at first so honorable, signifying "learned," "enlightened," "pure," became a term of horror and scorn, a reproach of heresy. Saint Epiphanius, in the third century, claimed that the men and women of this sect began by tickling each other, that they then exchanged very immodest kisses, and that they judged the degree of their faith by the voluptuousness of these kisses. When a husband presented a young initiate to his wife, he said to her: "Have an *agape* with my brother." And they had an *agape*.

We do not dare repeat here, in the chaste French tongue, what Saint Epiphanius adds in Greek (Epiphanius, *contra haeres,* lib. I, vol. ii). We will say merely that perhaps this saint was somewhat imposed upon, that he allowed himself to be carried away by zeal, and that all heretics are not hideous debauchees.

The sect of Pietists, in imitation of the early Christians, give each other kisses of peace on leaving the assembly, calling each other "my brother" or "my sister"; or so, at least, I was told some twenty years ago, by a very pretty and very human Pietist lady. The ancient custom was to kiss on the mouth; the Pietists have carefully preserved it.

There was no other manner of greeting ladies in France, Germany, Italy, England; it was the right of cardinals to kiss queens on the mouth, even in Spain. What is odd is that they did not have the same prerogative in France, where ladies always enjoyed more liberty than anywhere else; but "every country has its ceremonies," and there is no usage so general that chance and custom have not provided exceptions. It would have been an incivility, an affront, for a respectable woman, when she received a nobleman's first visit, not to have kissed him, despite his mustaches. "It is a displeasing custom," says Montaigne, "and offensive to ladies, to have to lend their lips to anyone who has three serving-men in his suite, disagreeable though he be." Yet this custom was the oldest in the world.

If it is disagreeable for a young and pretty mouth to yield itself out of courtesy to an old and ugly mouth, there is considerable danger when fresh, red mouths of twenty to twenty-five years of age are involved; and this is what finally brought about the abolition of the ceremony of kissing in the mysteries and the *agapae*. This is what caused women to be confined among the Orientals, so that they might kiss only their fathers and their brothers; a custom long ago introduced into Spain by the Arabs.

Here is the danger: there is one nerve, of the fifth pair, which goes from the mouth to the heart, and thence even lower. With what delicate industry has nature prepared everything! The little glands of the lips, their spongy tissue, their velvety paps, their fine, ticklish skin, produce in them an exquisite and voluptuous sensation, which is not without analogy to a still more hidden and still more sensitive part. Modesty may suffer from a lengthily savored kiss collaborated in by two Pietists of eighteen.

It should be noted that only men, turtle-doves, and pigeons, are acquainted with kisses; thence came the Latin word *columbatim,* which our language has not been able to translate. There is nothing which has not been abused. The kiss, designed by nature for the mouth, has often been prostituted to membranes which do not seem made for this usage. One knows of what the Templars were accused.

We cannot honestly treat this interesting subject at greater length, although Montaigne says: "One should speak of it shamelessly. We boldly talk of killing, wounding, and betraying; but of this one thing we dare speak only in whispers."

LAWS

Sheep live very placidly together, and they are considered very easygoing, because we do not see the prodigious quantity of animals they devour. It is possible, of course, that they eat them innocently and without knowing it, as we do when we eat a Sassenage cheese. The republic of the sheep is a faithful representation of the golden age.

A chicken-run is obviously the most perfect monarchic state. There is no king comparable to a cock. If he marches proudly in the midst of his people, it is not out of vanity. If an enemy approaches, he does not order his subjects to go forth to kill themselves for his sake, by virtue of his infallible wisdom and plenary power; he goes to battle himself, ranges his chickens behind him and fights to the death. If he is the victor, he himself sings the *Te Deum*. In civil life there is no one so gallant, so honest, so disinterested. The cock has all the virtues. If his royal beak holds a grain of corn, or a grub, he gives it to the first lady among his subjects who presents herself. Solomon in his harem did not even approach a barnyard cock.

If it is true that bees are governed by a queen to whom all her subjects make love, then the bees enjoy a still more perfect government.

Ants are considered to be excellent democrats. Democracy is above all the other states, because in a democracy everyone is equal, and each individual works for the good of all. The republic of the beavers is superior to even that of the ants, at least if we judge by their masonry work. As for the monkeys, they resemble strolling players rather than a civilized people; and they do not appear to be united under fixed, fundamental laws, as are the species previously mentioned.

We resemble the monkeys more than any other animal, by virtue of our gift of mimicry, the frivolity of our ideas, and the inconstancy which has never permitted us to establish uniform and durable laws.

When nature formed our species, she gave us certain instincts: self-esteem for our preservation, benevolence for the preservation of others, love which is common to all species, and the inexplicable gift of combining more ideas than all the animals together. Then, having given us our portion, she said to us: "Do as you can."

No country has a good code of laws. The reason for this is evident: the laws have been made according to the time, the place, the need, etc.

When the needs have changed, the laws which have remained have become ridiculous. Thus the law which forbade the eating of pig and the drinking of wine was very reasonable in Arabia, where pig and wine are injurious. But it is absurd at Constantinople.

The law which gives the whole estate to the eldest son is very good in times of anarchy and pillage. Then the eldest son is the captain of the castle which the brigands will attack sooner or later; the younger sons will be his chief officers, the husbandmen his soldiers. The only danger is that the younger son may assassinate or poison the Salian lord, his elder brother, in order to become in his turn the master of the hovel; but these cases are rare, because nature has so combined our instincts and our passions that our horror of assassinating our elder brother is stronger than our envy of his position. But this law, suitable for the owners of dungeons in Chilperic's time, is detestable when it is a question of sharing revenues in a city.

To the shame of mankind, it is well known that the laws which govern our games are the only ones which are completely just, clear, inviolable and enforced. Why is the Indian who gave us the rules of the game of chess willingly obeyed all over the world, and why are the popes' decretals, for example, today an object of horror and scorn? The reason is that the inventor of chess arranged everything with precision for the satisfaction of the players, while the popes, in their decretals, had nothing in view but their own interest. The Indian wished to exercise men's minds equally, and give them pleasure; the popes wished to besot men's minds. Also, the essence of the game of chess has remained the same for five thousand years, it is common to all the inhabitants of the earth; and the decretals are known only at Spoletto, Orvieto, Loretto, where the shallowest lawyer secretly hates and despises them.

Full of all these reflections, I like to think that there is a natural law independent of all human conventions.

the fruit of my work must belong to me; I must honor my father and my mother; I have no right over my fellow's life, and my fellow has none over mine, etc. But when I reflect that from the days of Chedorlaomer to those of Mentzel[1] everyone has gone about loyally killing and pillaging his neighbors, with a license in his pocket, I am very sad.

I am told that there are laws among thieves, and also laws of war. I ask what are these laws of war. I learn that they mean hanging a brave officer who has stood fast in a bad post without cannon against a royal army; that they mean having a prisoner hanged, if the enemy has hanged one of yours; that they mean putting to fire and sword villages which have not made their required contributions on an appointed day, according to the orders of the gracious sovereign of the district. "Good," say I, "this is the *Spirit of the Laws.*"

It seems to me that almost everyone has received from nature enough common sense to make laws, but that no one is just enough to make good laws.

LENT

I. Our questions on Lent will concern only police regulation. It appeared useful to have a season in the year when we should eat fewer oxen, calves, lambs, and poultry. Young fowls and pigeons are not ready in February and March, the time in which Lent falls; and it is good to cease the carnage for some weeks in countries in which pastures are not so rich as those of England and Holland.

[1] Chedorlaomer was king of the Elamites, and contemporary with Abraham. See Genesis 14.

Mentzel was a famous chief of Austrian partisans in the war of 1741. At the head of five thousand men, he made Munich capitulate on February 13, 1742.

The police magistrates have very wisely ordered that meat should be a little dearer at Paris during this time, and that the profit should be given to the hospitals. It is an almost insensible tribute paid by luxury and gluttony to indigence; for it is the rich who are not able to keep Lent—the poor fast all the year.

There are very few farming men who eat meat once a month. If they ate of it every day, there would not be enough for the most flourishing kingdom. Twenty millions of pounds of meat a day would make seven thousand three hundred millions of pounds a year. This calculation is appalling.

The small number of the rich, financiers, prelates, principal magistrates, great lords, and great ladies who condescend to have Lenten fare served at their tables, fast during six weeks on sole, salmon, turbot, and sturgeon.

One of our most famous financiers had couriers, who for a hundred crowns brought him fresh sea fish every day to Paris. This expense supported the couriers, the dealers who sold the horses, the fishermen who furnished the fish, the makers of nets, the boatbuilders, and the druggists from whom came the refined spices which give a fish a taste superior to that of meat. Lucullus could not have kept Lent more voluptuously.

It should further be remarked that fresh sea fish, in coming to Paris, pays a considerable tax. The secretaries of the rich, their valets, ladies' maids, and stewards, partake of the dessert of Croesus, and fast as deliciously as he.

It is not the same with the poor; not only if for four sous they partake of a small portion of tough mutton do they commit a great sin, but they seek in vain for this miserable aliment. What, then, do they eat? Chestnuts, rye bread, cheeses which they have pressed from the milk of their cows, goats or sheep, and a few eggs from their hens.

There are churches which forbid them eggs and milk. What then remains for them to eat? Nothing. They consent to fast; but they do not consent to die. It is absolutely necessary that they should live, if it be only to cultivate the lands of the fat rectors and lazy monks.

We therefore ask, if it is not the business of the magistrates of the police of the kingdom, charged with watching over the health of the inhabitants, to give them permission to eat the cheeses which their own hands have formed, and the eggs which their fowls have laid?

It appears that milk, eggs, cheese, and all which can nourish the farmer, are regulated by the police, and not by a religious rule.

We are not told that Jesus Christ forbade omelets to His apostles; on the contrary He said to them: "Eat such things as are set before you."

The Holy Church has ordained Lent, but in its quality of Church it commands only the heart; it can inflict spiritual pains alone; it cannot as formerly burn a poor man, who, having only some rusty bacon, put a slice of it on a piece of black bread the day after Shrove Tuesday.

Sometimes in the provinces the pastors go beyond their duty, and forgetting the rights of the magistracy, undertake to go among the innkeepers and cooks, to see if they have not some ounces of meat in their saucepans, some old fowls on their hooks, or some eggs in a cupboard; for eggs are forbidden in Lent. They intimidate the poor people, and even use violence against these unfortunates, who do not know that this police duty is the business of the magistrates alone. It is an odious and punishable inquisition.

Only the magistrates can be accurately informed as to

the quantity of provisions available to feed the poor people of the provinces. The clergy have more sublime occupations. Should it not therefore belong to the magistrates to regulate what the people eat in Lent? Who should inspect the food supply of a country if not the police of that country?

II. Did the first man who decided to fast adopt this regimen by order of a physician, because of indigestion? The want of appetite which we feel in grief—was this the origin of fast-days prescribed in melancholy religions?

Did the Jews take the custom of fasting from the Egyptians, all of whose rites they imitated, including flagellation and the scapegoat? Why did Jesus fast for forty days in the desert, where He was taken by the devil? St. Matthew remarks that after this Lent He was hungry. Does this mean that He was not hungry during the fast?

Why, on days of abstinence, does the Roman Church consider it a sin to eat terrestrial animals, and a good work to be served with sole and salmon? The rich Papist who has five hundred francs' worth of fish on his table shall be saved, and the poor wretch dying with hunger, who has eaten four sous' worth of salt pork, shall be damned.

Why must we ask permission of our bishop to eat eggs? If a king ordered his people never to eat eggs, would he not be thought the most ridiculous of tyrants? How strange the aversion of bishops to omelets!

Can we believe that among Papists there have been tribunals imbecile, dull, and barbarous enough to condemn to death poor citizens, who had committed no other crime than that of having eaten horseflesh in Lent? The fact is but too true; I have in my hands a judgment of this kind. What renders it still stranger is that the judges who passed such sentences believed themselves superior to the Iroquois.

Foolish and cruel priests, for whom do you order Lent? Is it for the rich? They take good care to observe it. Is it for the poor? They keep Lent all the year. The unhappy peasant scarcely ever eats meat, and has not the wherewithal to buy fish. Fools that you are, when will you correct your absurd laws?

LIBERTY

Either I am very much mistaken, or that great definer, Locke, has well defined liberty as "power." I am mistaken again, or Collins, the celebrated London magistrate, is the only philosopher who has really sifted this idea; and Clark's answer to him was merely that of a theologian. But of all that has been written in France on liberty, the following little dialogue seems to me the clearest.

A: There is a battery of guns firing in your ears. Have you the liberty to hear them or not to hear them?

B: Obviously, I can't help hearing them.

A: Do you want this cannon to carry away your head and the heads of your wife and daughter, who are walking with you?

B: What are you talking about? As long as I am of sound mind, I cannot want such a thing; it is impossible.

A: Good. You hear this gun necessarily, and you wish necessarily that neither you nor your family shall die from a cannon shot while you are out for a walk. You have not the power either of not hearing or of wishing to remain here?

B: Clearly.

A: You have consequently taken some thirty steps in order to be sheltered from the gun; you have had the power to walk these few steps with me?

B: Again very clearly.

A: And if you had been a paralytic, you could not have avoided being exposed to this battery, you would necessarily have heard and received a gun shot; and you would be dead necessarily?

B: Nothing could be truer.

A: In what then does your liberty consist, unless it be in the power that you have exercised in performing what your will required of absolute necessity?

B: You embarrass me. Do you mean that liberty is nothing but the power of doing what I want to do?

A: Think about it, and see if liberty can be understood otherwise.

B: In that case my hunting dog is as free as I am; he has necessarily the will to run when he sees a hare, and the power of running if he has not a pain in his legs. In that case, I am in no way superior to my dog; you reduce me to the state of the beasts.

A: What poor sophistry from the poor sophists who have taught you! You are certainly in a bad way if you are merely free like your dog! Do you not eat, sleep, and propagate like him, almost in the same positions? Would you smell other than through your nose? Why do you wish to be free in a way that your dog is not?

B: But I have a soul which reasons a great deal, while my dog reasons hardly at all. He has only the simplest of ideas, and I have a thousand metaphysical ideas.

A: Very well, then, you are a thousand times freer than he is; that is, you have a thousand times more power of thinking than he has. But you do not think otherwise than he does.

B: What! I am not free to wish what I wish?

A: What do you mean by that?

B: I mean what everyone means. Isn't it a proverb that wishes are free?

A: A proverb is not a reason; explain yourself more clearly.

B: I mean that I am free to wish as I please.

A: Begging your pardon, that is nonsense. Don't you see that it is ridiculous to say, I wish to wish? You wish necessarily, as a result of the ideas that have offered themselves to you. Do you wish to be married? Yes or no?

B: But what if I tell you that I wish neither the one nor the other?

A: You will be answering like someone who says: "Some believe Cardinal Mazarin to be dead, others believe him to be alive, but as for me I believe neither the one nor the other."

B: Well, I wish to be married.

A: Ah! that is an answer. Why do you wish to be married?

B: Because I am in love with a beautiful, sweet, well-bred young girl, who is fairly rich and sings very well, whose parents are very nice people, and because I flatter myself I am loved by her, and very welcome to her family.

A: That is a reason. You see that you cannot wish without reason. I declare to you that you are free to marry; that is, that you have the power to sign the contract, have your nuptials, and sleep with your wife.

B: What! I cannot wish without reason? And what will become of that other proverb: *Sit pro ratione voluntas;* my will is my reason, I wish because I wish?

A: That is absurd, my dear fellow. In that case, there would be an effect without a cause.

B: What! When I play at odds and evens, I have a reason for choosing evens rather than odds?

A: Yes, undoubtedly.

B: And what is the reason, if you please?

A: The reason is that the idea of even rather than the opposite idea presents itself to your mind. It would be absurd if there were cases in which you wished because there was a cause of wishing, and cases in which you wished without any cause. When you wish to be married, you are obviously conscious of the dominating reason. You are not conscious of it when you are playing at odds and evens, and yet there certainly must be one.

B: But, I repeat, this means that I am not free.

A: Your will is not free, but your actions are. You are free to act, when you have the power to act.

B: But all the books I have read on "the liberty of indifference . . ."

A: What do you mean by "the liberty of indifference?"

B: I mean the liberty of spitting to the right or to the left, of sleeping on my right side or on my left, of taking a walk of four turns or five.

A: That would certainly be a wonderful sort of liberty! God would have given you a fine gift! It would really be something to boast of! Of what use to you would be a power which was exercised only on such futile occasions? But the fact is that it is ridiculous to assume the will to wish to spit to the right. Not only is this will to wish absurd, but it is certain that several trifling circumstances determine you in these acts that you call "indifferent." You are no more free in these acts than in the others. But, I repeat, you are free at all time, in all places—as soon as you do what you wish to do.

B: I suspect you are right. I will think about it.[1]

[1] See "Free Will."

LIBERTY OF THE PRESS

What harm can the prediction of Jean-Jacques[1] do to Russia? None. He is free to explain it in a mystical, typical, allegorical sense, according to custom. The nations which will destroy the Russians will be belles-lettres, mathematics, wit, and social graces which degrade man and pervert nature.

From five to six thousand pamphlets have been printed in Holland against Louis XIV, none of which helped to make him lose the battles of Blenheim, Turin, and Ramillies.

In general, we have as natural a right to make use of our pens as of our tongue, at our peril, risk, and hazard. I know many books which have bored their readers, but I know of none which has done real evil. Theologians, or pretended politicians, cry: "Religion is destroyed, the government is lost, if you print certain truths or certain paradoxes. Never dare to think, till you have asked permission from a monk or a clerk. It is against the public welfare for a man to think for himself. Homer, Plato, Cicero, Virgil, Pliny, Horace, never published anything but with the approbation of the doctors of the Sorbonne and of the holy Inquisition.

"See into what horrible decadence the liberty of the press has brought England and Holland. It is true that they possess the commerce of the whole world, and that England is victorious on sea and land; but it is merely a false greatness, a false opulence: they are hastening to their ruin. An enlightened people cannot exist."

No one could reason more justly, my friends; but let

[1] Rousseau had predicted the imminent destruction of the Russian empire; his chief reason being that Peter I had sought to disseminate the arts and sciences.

us see, if you please, what state has been ruined by a book. The most dangerous, the most pernicious book of all, is that of Spinoza. Not only in the character of a Jew does he attack the New Testament, but in the character of a scholar he ruins the Old. His system of atheism is a thousand times better constructed and reasoned than those of Straton and of Epicurus. It requires the most profound sagacity to answer to the arguments by which he endeavors to prove that one substance cannot form another.

Like yourself, I detest this book, which I perhaps understand better than you, and to which you have replied very badly. But have you discovered that it has changed the face of the world? Has any preacher lost a florin of his income by the publication of the works of Spinoza? Is there a bishop whose rents have diminished? On the contrary, their revenues have doubled since his time: all the ill is limited to a small number of peaceable readers, who have examined Spinoza's arguments in their studies, and who have written for or against them in works that are little known.

For ourselves, you have hardly been consistent in having printed, *ad usum Delphini,* the atheism of Lucretius—as you have already been reproached with doing. No trouble, no scandal, has ensued from it; so Spinoza might be left to live in peace in Holland, as was Lucretius in Rome.

But if there appears among you any new book, the ideas of which shock your own—supposing you have any—or of which the author may be of a party contrary to yours—or what is worse, of which the author may not be of any party at all—then you cry out "Fire!" and all is noise, scandal, and uproar in your small corner of the earth. There is an abominable man who has declared in print that if we had no hands we would not be able to make shoes nor stockings. The devout cry out, furred doctors assemble, alarms multiply from college to college, from house to house, whole communities are disturbed. And why? For five or six pages, about which no one will give a fig at the end of three months. Does a book displease you? Refute it. Does it bore you? Don't read it.

Oh! you say to me, the books of Luther and Calvin have destroyed the Roman Catholic religion in one-half of Europe? Why not say also, that the books of the patriarch Photius have destroyed this Roman religion in Asia, Africa, Greece, and Russia?

You deceive yourself grossly, when you think that you have been ruined by books. The empire of Russia is two thousand leagues in extent, and there are not six men who are aware of the points disputed by the Greek and Latin Church. If the monk Luther, John Calvin, and the vicar Zuinglius had been content with writing, Rome would still hold in subjugation all the states that it has lost; but these people and their adherents ran from town to town, from house to house, exciting the women, and they were supported by princes. The fury, which tormented Amata, and which, according to Virgil, whipped her like a top, was not more turbulent. Be assured that one enthusiastic, factious, ignorant, supple, vehement Capuchin—the emissary of some ambitious monks—who goes about preaching, confessing, communicating, and caballing, will much sooner overthrow a province than a hundred authors can enlighten it. It was not the Koran which made Mohammed succeed: it was Mohammed who caused the success of the Koran.

No! Rome has not been vanquished by books. It has been vanquished because it revolted Europe by its rapacity, by the public sale of indulgences, by insulting men and wishing to govern them like domestic animals, for having abused its power to such an extent that it is astonishing a single village remains to it. Henry VIII. Elizabeth, the duke of Saxony, the landgrave of Hesse, the princes of Orange, the Condes and Colignys, have done all, and books nothing. Trumpets have never gained battles, nor caused any walls to fall except those of Jericho.

You fear books, as certain small cantons fear violins. Let men read, and let men dance—these two amusements will never do any harm to the world.

LOVE

There are so many sorts of love that one does not know where to seek a definition of it. The name of "love" is given boldly to a caprice of a few days' duration; to a sentiment devoid of esteem; to a casual liaison; to the affectations of a cicisbeo; to a frigid habit; to a romantic fantasy; to relish followed by prompt disrelish: —yes, people give this name to a thousand chimeras.

If philosophers wish to probe to the bottom this hardly philosophical matter, let them meditate on Plato's *Symposium,* in which Socrates, the honorable lover of Alcibiades and Agathon, converses with them on the metaphysics of love.

Lucretius deals with it more from the point of view of a natural philosopher: Virgil follows in the steps of Lucretius; *amor omnibus idem.*

It is the stuff of nature embroidered by imagination. Do you want an idea of love? look at the sparrows in your garden; look at your pigeons; look at the bull which is brought to the heifer. Look at this proud horse which two of your grooms lead to the quiet mare awaiting him; she draws aside her tail to welcome him; see how her eyes sparkle; hark to the neighing; watch the prancing, the curvetting, the ears pricked, the mouth opening with little convulsions, the swelling nostrils, the fiery breath, the manes rising and floating, the impetuous movement with which he hurls himself on the object which nature has destined for him. But do not be jealous of him. Think of the advantages of the human species; love compensates them for all those qualities that nature has given to the animals—strength, beauty, nimbleness, and speed.

There are even animals who do not know the joy of intercourse. Scale fish are deprived of this delight: the female throws millions of eggs on the mud; the male who encounters them swims over them, and fertilizes them with his seed, without troubling about the female to whom they belong.

Most animals that couple, taste pleasure only by a single sense, and as soon as the appetite is satisfied, everything is extinguished. You are the only animal who knows what kissing is. The whole of your body is sensitive, but your lips especially are capable of a pleasure that is tireless; and this pleasure belongs to no species but yours. You can give yourself up to love at any time, and the animals have but a fixed time. If you reflect on these superiorities, you will say with the earl of Rochester: "In a country of atheists, love would cause the Deity to be worshiped."

As men have received the gift of perfecting all the gifts of nature, they have perfected love. Cleanliness and the care of oneself, by making the skin more delicate, increase the pleasure of contact; and attention to one's health renders the organs of pleasure more sensitive. All the other sentiments enter into that of love, just like metals which amalgamate with gold: friendship and esteem come to help; the faculties of mind and body are still further chains.

Self-love, above all, tightens all these bonds. One applauds oneself for one's choice, and a crowd of illusions form the decoration of the building of which nature has laid the foundations.

There are the advantages you have over the animals. But if you taste so many pleasures unknown to them, how many sorrows, too, are there of which the beasts have no idea! How terrible for you that over three-fourths of the earth nature has poisoned the pleasures of love and the sources of life with an appalling disease to which man alone is subject, and by which only man's organs of generation are infected!

This plague is not like so many other maladies which are caused by our excesses. It was not debauch that introduced it into the world. Phryne, Lais, Flora, Messalina and those like them, were not attacked by it. It was born in some islands where men lived in innocence, and thence spread itself over the ancient world.

If ever one could accuse nature of despising her work, of contradicting her plans, of acting against her designs, it is in this detestable scourge which has soiled the earth with horror and filth. Is this the best of all possible worlds? Even if Caesar, Antony, Octavius never had this disease, might it not have been possible for it to spare François I? "No," people say, "things were ordered thus for the best." I should like to think so; but it is sad for those to whom Rabelais dedicated his book.

Erotic philosophers have often debated the question of whether Heloise could still really love Abelard when he was both a monk and a eunuch. One of these qualities did great harm to the other. But console yourself, Abelard, you were loved. The root of the hewn tree still retains a remnant of sap; the imagination aids the heart. One can still be happy at table even though one eats no longer. Is it love? Is it simply a memory? Is it friendship? It is an indefinable complex of all these elements. It is an obscure feeling resembling the fantastic passions retained by the dead in the Elysian fields. The heroes who, during their lifetime, shone in the chariot races, drove imaginary chariots when they were dead. Heloise lived with you on illusions and memories. She kissed you sometimes, and with all the more pleasure because she had taken a vow at the Paraclete to love you no longer, which made her kisses thereby more precious as they were more culpable. A woman can hardly be seized with a passion for a eunuch: but she can keep her passion for a lover who has become a eunuch, provided that he remains lovable.

It is not the same, ladies, for a lover who has grown old in service. The externals no longer remain the same. The wrinkles horrify, the white eyebrows shock, the lost teeth disgust, the infirmities estrange. All that one can do is to enjoy the virtue of playing nurse, and of tolerating what one once loved. It is burying a dead man.

LOVE OF GOD

The disputes that have occurred over the love of God have kindled as much hatred as any theological quarrel. Jesuits and Jansenists have been contending for a hundred years as to which party loved God in the most correct manner, and which should at the same time most completely discomfit the other.

When the author of *Telemachus*, who was in high repute at the court of Louis XIV, recommended men to love God in a manner which did not happen to coincide with that of the author of the *Funeral Orations*, the latter, who was a complete master of the weapons of controversy, declared open war against him, and procured his condemnation in the ancient city of Romulus, where God was the one object most loved—after domination, ease, luxury, pleasure, and money.

LOVE PHILTERS

These were for the young. They were sold by the Jews at Rome and Alexandria, and are at the present day sold in Asia. You will find some of their secrets in the *Petit Albert;* and will become further initiated by reading the plea composed by Apuleius when he was accused by a Christian, whose daughter he had married, of having bewitched her by philters. Emilian, his father-in-law, alleged that he had made use of certain fishes, since, Venus having been born of the sea, fishes must necessarily have prodigious influence in exciting women to love.

The usual mixture consisted of vervain, tenia, and hippomanes—or a small portion of the placenta of a mare that had just foaled, together with a little bird called wagtail; in Latin *motacilla.*

But Apuleius was chiefly accused of having employed shellfish, lobster patties, she-hedgehogs, spiced oysters, and cuttlefish, which were celebrated for their fecundity.

Apuleius clearly explains the real philter, or charm, which had made Pudentilla give herself to him. He undoubtedly admits, in his defense, that his wife had called him a magician. "But what," says he, "if she had called me a consul, would that have made me one?"

The plant satyrion was considered both among the Greeks and Romans as the most powerful of philters. It was called *plante aphrodisia,* the plant of Venus. That called by the Latins *eruca* is now often added to the former. *Et venerem revocans eruca morantem.*

A little essence of amber is frequently used. Mandragora has gone out of fashion. Some exhausted debauchees have employed cantharides, which strongly affects the genitals, and often produces severe and painful consequences.

Youth and health are the only genuine philters. Chocolate was for a long time in great celebrity with our debilitated *petits-maitres.* But a man may take twenty cups of chocolate without inspiring any attachment to his person. "*. . . ut amoris amabilis esto.*" "Wouldst thou be loved, be lovable."

MAN, GENERAL REFLECTION ON

It requires twenty years for man to rise from the vegetable state in which he is within his mother's womb, and from the pure animal state which is the lot of his early childhood, to the state when the maturity of reason begins to appear. It has required thirty centuries to learn a little about his structure. It would need eternity to learn something about his soul. It takes an instant to kill him.

MARRIAGE

I came across a logician who said: "Make your subjects marry as soon as possible; let them be exempt from taxes the first year, and let their tax be distributed among those who at the same age are celibate.

"The more married men you have, the less crime there will be. Look at the frightful records of your criminal registers; you will find there a hundred bachelors hanged or broken on the wheel for one father of a family.

"Marriage makes man wiser and more virtuous. The father of a family, who is on the verge of committing a crime, is often stopped by his wife whose blood, less feverish than his, makes her gentler, more compassionate, more fearful of theft and murder, more timorous, more religious.

"The father of a family does not want to blush before his children. He fears to leave them a heritage of shame.

"Marry your soldiers, they will not desert any more. Bound to their families, they will be bound also to their fatherland. A bachelor soldier is often nothing but a vagabond, to whom it is indifferent whether he serves the king of Naples or the king of Morocco."

The Roman warriors were married; they fought for their wives and children; and they enslaved the wives and children of other nations.

A great Italian politician, who was also very learned in oriental languages—a very rare thing among our politicians—said to me in my youth: "*Caro figlio,* remember that the Jews have never had more than one good institution: a horror of virginity." If this little race of superstitious middlemen had not considered marriage as the first law of man, if there had been convents of nuns in their midst, they would have been irreparably lost.

MEN OF LETTERS

In our barbarous ages, when the Franks, the Germans, the Bretons, the Lombards, and the Spanish Muzarabs, could neither read nor write, there were established schools and universities, composed almost entirely of ecclesiastics who, knowing nothing but their own jargon, taught this jargon to those who wished to learn it. The academies did not come until much later; they despised the foolishness of the schools, but did not always dare to rise against them, because there are follies that are respected provided they concern respectable things.

The men of letters who have rendered the greatest services to the small number of thinking beings spread over the world are the isolated writers, the true scholars shut in their studies, who have neither argued on the benches of the universities, nor told half-truths in the academies; and almost all of them have been persecuted. Our wretched species is so made that those who walk on the well-trodden path always throw stones at those who are opening a new road.

Montesquieu says that the Scythians pierced their slaves' eyes, so that they might be less subject to distraction when they were churning their butter. This is exactly how the Inquisition functions, and in the land where this monster reigns almost everyone is blind. In England people have had two eyes for more than two hundred years; the French are starting to open one eye; but sometimes there are men in power who do not want the people to have even this one eye open.

These poor persons in power are like Doctor Balouard of the Italian Comedy, who does not want to be served by anyone but the dolt Harlequin, and who is afraid of having too shrewd a valet.

Compose some odes in praise of My Lord Superbus Fadus, some madrigals for his mistress; dedicate a book on geography to his doorkeeper, and you will be well received; enlighten mankind, and you will be exterminated.

Descartes was forced to leave his country, Gassendi was calumniated, Arnauld dragged out his days in exile; every philosopher is treated as the prophets were among the Jews.

Who would believe that in the eighteenth century a philosopher was dragged before a secular tribunal, and accused of impiety for having said that men could not practice the arts if they had no hands? I should not be surprised if the first person so insolent as to say that men could not think if they had no heads were immediately condemned to the galleys. "For," some young graduate will say to him, "the soul is a pure spirit, the head is only matter; God can put the soul in the heel, as well as in the brain; therefore I denounce you as impious."

Perhaps the greatest misfortune of a man of letters is not in being the object of his confreres' jealousy, the victim of a cabal, or despised by men in power; but in being judged by fools. Fools go far sometimes, particularly when bigotry is added to ineptitude, and to ineptitude the spirit of vengeance. Another great misfortune of a man of letters is that ordinarily he stands alone. A bourgeois buys himself a small position, and in it he is backed by his colleagues. If he suffers an injustice, he finds defenders at once. The man of letters is unsuccored; he resembles a flying-fish; if he rises a little, the birds devour him; if he dives, the fish eat him.

Every public man pays tribute to malignity, but he is repaid in honors and gold.

MOHAMMEDANS

I tell you again, you ignorant imbeciles, whom other ignoramuses have convinced that the Mohammedan religion is voluptuous and sensual, that there is not a word of truth in it. You have been deceived on this point, as on so many others.

Canons, monks, vicars even, if a law were imposed on you not to eat or drink from four in the morning till ten at night, during the month of July, when Lent came at this period; if you were forbidden to play at any game of chance under pain of damnation; if wine were forbidden you under the same penalty; if you had to make a pilgrimage into the burning desert; if you were compelled to give at least two and a half per cent of your income to the poor; if, accustomed to enjoy possession of eighteen women, the number were cut down suddenly by fourteen—honestly, would you dare call that religion sensual?

The Latin Christians have so many advantages over the Mussulmans, I do not say in the matter of war, but in the matter of doctrines, and the Greek Christians have beaten them so thoroughly from 1769 to 1773, that spreading unjust charges against Islam is hardly worth the trouble.

Try, if you will, to retake from the Mohammedans all that they usurped. But it is easier to calumniate them.

I hate calumny so much that I do not wish to accuse even the Turks of foolishness although I detest them as tyrants over women and enemies of the arts.

I do not know why the historian of the Lower Empire maintains that Mohammed speaks in his Koran of his journey into the sky: Mohammed does not say a word about it; we have proved it.

But one must fight on ceaselessly. When one has destroyed an error, there is always someone to resuscitate it.

MOUNTAIN

It is a very old, universal fable that tells of the mountain which, having frightened all the countryside by its outcry that it was in labor, was hissed by all present when it brought into the world a mere mouse. The people in the pit were not philosophers. Those who hissed should have admired. It was as remarkable for the mountain to give birth to a mouse, as for the mouse to give birth to a mountain. A rock which produces a rat is a very prodigious thing; and never has the world seen anything approaching this miracle. All the globes of the universe could not call a fly into existence. Where the vulgar laugh, the philosopher admires; and he laughs where the vulgar open their big, stupid eyes in astonishment.

NAKEDNESS

Why should we lock up a man or a woman who chooses to walk stark naked in the street? And why is no one shocked by absolutely nude statues, by pictures of the Madonna and of Jesus that may be seen in some churches?

It is quite probable that the human race lived for a long time without clothes. People unacquainted with clothing have been found in more than one island and on the American continent. The most civilized, however, hide the organs of generation with leaves, woven rushes, or feathers. Whence comes this form of modesty? Is it the instinct to arouse desire by hiding what gives pleasure when discovered?

Is it really true that among slightly more civilized nations, such as the Jews and half-Jews, there have been entire sects who would not worship God save by stripping themselves of all their clothes? Such, we are told, were the Adamites and the Abelians. They gathered quite naked to sing the praises of God: St. Epiphanius and St. Augustine say so. It is true that they were not contemporary, and that they were very far from these peoples' country. But, at all events, this madness is possible: it is no more extraordinary, no more mad than a hundred other follies which have traveled round the world one after the other.

We have said elsewhere that even today the Mohammedans still have saints who are madmen, and who go naked like monkeys. It is very possible that some fanatics thought it was better to present themselves to the Deity in the state in which He formed them, than in the disguise invented by man. It *is* possible that they showed all out of piety. There are so few well-made persons of both sexes, that nakedness might have inspired chastity, or rather disgust, instead of increasing desire.

It is said particularly that the Abelians renounced marriage. If there were any fine lads and pretty lasses among them, they were at least comparable to St. Adhelme and to blessed Robert d'Arbisselle, who slept with the most attractive girls, so that their continence might triumph the more.

But I admit that it must have been very entertaining to see a hundred Helens and Parises singing anthems, giving each other the kiss of peace, and making *agapae.*

All of which shows that there is no singularity, no extravagance, no superstition which has not passed through the heads of mankind. Happy the day when these superstitions cease to trouble society and make it a scene of disorder, hatred, and fury! It is better, no doubt, to pray God stark naked than to stain His altars and the public places with human blood.

NATURAL LAW

B: What is natural law?

A: The instinct which makes us feel justice.

B: What do you call just and unjust?

A: What appears so to the entire universe.

B: The universe is composed of many heads. It is said that Sparta applauded thefts for which Athenians were condemned to the mines.

A: Abuse of words, logomachy, equivocation; theft

could not be committed in Sparta, when everything was common property. What you call theft was the punishment for avarice.

B: It was forbidden to marry one's sister in Rome. It was allowed among the Egyptians, the Athenians and even among the Jews, to marry one's sister on the father's side. It is with regret that I cite that wretched little Jewish people, who should certainly not serve as a model for anyone, and who (putting religion aside) were never anything but a race of ignorant and fanatic brigands. But still, according to their books, the young Tamar, before being ravished by her brother Amnon, says to him: "Nay, my brother, do not thou this folly, but speak unto the king; for he will not withhold me from thee."

A: All that is conventional law, arbitrary customs, passing fashions; the essential remains always. Show me a country where it was honorable to rob me of the fruit of my toil, to break one's promise, to lie in order to hurt, to calumniate, to assassinate, to poison, to be ungrateful toward a benefactor, to beat one's father and one's mother when they offer you food.

B: Have you forgotten that Jean Jacques, one of the fathers of the modern Church, has said that "the first man who dared enclose and cultivate a piece of land" was the enemy "of the human race," that he should have been exterminated, and that "the fruits of the earth are for all, and the land belongs to none"? Have we not already examined together this lovely proposition which is so useful to society?

A: Who is this Jean Jacques? He is certainly not either John the Baptist, nor John the Evangelist, nor James the Greater, nor James the Less; it must be some Hunnish wit who wrote that abominable impertinence or some mischievous wag who wanted to laugh at what the whole world regards most seriously. For instead of going to spoil the land of a wise and industrious neighbor, he had only to imitate him; and when every father of a family followed this example, it did not take long to establish a very pretty village. The author of this passage seems to me a very unsociable animal.

B: You think then that by outraging and robbing the good man who has surrounded his garden and chicken-run with a hedge, he has been wanting in respect toward the requirements of natural law?

A: Yes, yes. There is a natural law, and it does not consist either in doing harm to others or in rejoicing thereat.

B: I imagine that man likes and does harm only for his own advantage. But so many people are led to look for their own interest in the misfortune of others, vengeance is so violent a passion, there are such disastrous examples of it; ambition, still more fatal, has inundated the world with so much blood, that when I retrace for myself the horrible picture, I am tempted to avow that man is very diabolical. In vain do I carry the notion of justice and injustice in my heart. An Attila courted by St. Leo; a Phocas flattered by St. Gregory with the most cowardly baseness; an Alexander VI sullied with so many incests, so many murders, so many poisonings, with whom weak Louis XII (called "the good") makes the most infamous and intimate alliance; a Cromwell whose protection is sought by Cardinal Mazarin, and for whose sake the cardinal drives out of France the heirs of Charles I, Louis XIV's first cousins—a hundred examples of this sort upset my ideas completely and I no longer know where I am.

A: Well, do storms stop our enjoyment of today's beautiful sun? Did the earthquake which destroyed half the city of Lisbon stop your traveling very comfortably to Madrid? If Attila was a brigand and Cardinal Mazarin a rogue, are there not princes and ministers who are honest people? Has it not been remarked that in the war of 1701, Louis XIV's council was composed of the most virtuous men? The Duc de Beauvilliers, the Marquis de Torci, the Maréchal de Villars, and last of all Chamillart, who was supposed to be incompetent, but never dishonest. Does not the idea of justice subsist always? It is upon justice that all laws are founded. The Greeks called laws "daughters of heaven," which means only daughters of nature. Have you no laws in your country?

B: Yes, some good, some bad.

A: Where, if not in the notion of natural law, did you obtain the idea that is natural to every man when his mind is well made? You must have obtained it there, or nowhere.

B: You are right, there is a natural law; but it is still more natural to many people to forget it.

A: It is natural also to be one-eyed, hump-backed, lame, deformed, unhealthy; but one prefers people who are well made and healthy.

B: Why are there so many one-eyed and deformed minds?

A: Pax! But turn to the article on "Power."

NATURE

(Dialogue between the Philosopher and Nature.)

THE PHILOSOPHER: Who are you, Nature? I live in you; for fifty years I have been seeking you, and I have not found you yet.

NATURE: The ancient Egyptians, who it is said lived some twelve hundred years, reproached me on the same grounds. They called me Isis; they put a great veil on my head, and they said that nobody could lift it.

THE PHILOSOPHER: That is why I am appealing to you. I have been able to measure some of your globes, know their paths, assign the laws of motion; but I have not been able to learn who you are. Are you always active? Are you always passive? Did your elements arrange themselves, as water deposits itself on sand, oil on water, air on oil? Have you a mind which directs all your operations, as councils are inspired as soon as they are assembled, although their members are sometimes fools? Please tell me the answer to your riddle.

NATURE: I am the great everything. I know no more about it. I am not a mathematician; and everything in my world is arranged according to mathematical laws. Guess, if you can, how it is all done.

THE PHILOSOPHER: Certainly, since your great everything does not know mathematics, and since all your laws are most profoundly geometrical, there must be an eternal geometer who directs you, a supreme intelligence who presides over your operations.

NATURE: You are right. I am water, earth, fire, atmosphere, metal, mineral, stone, vegetable, and animal. I am quite sure that I possess an intelligence. You have an intelligence, but you do not see it. I do not see mine either. I feel this invisible power but I cannot know it. Why should you, who are but a small part of me, want to know what I do not know?

THE PHILOSOPHER: We are curious. I should like to know why you are so unsubtle in your mountains, your deserts, and your seas, when you exhibit such ingenuity in your animals and in your vegetables?

NATURE: My poor child, do you wish me to tell you the truth? The fact is that I have been given a name which does not suit me. They call me Nature, when I am all art.

THE PHILOSOPHER: That word upsets all my ideas. Do you mean to say that nature is only art?

NATURE: Yes, without doubt. Do you not realize that there is an infinity of art in those seas and those mountains that you find so unsubtly made? Do you not realize that all those waters gravitate toward the center of the earth, and rise only by immutable laws; that those mountains which crown the earth are the immense reservoirs of the eternal snows which unceasingly produce those fountains, lakes, and rivers without which my animal species and my vegetable species would perish? And as for what are called my animal kingdom, my vegetable kingdom, and my mineral kingdom, you see here only three; but you should realize that I have millions of kingdoms. If you consider only the creation of an insect, of an ear of corn, of gold, or of copper, everything will appear as a marvel of art.

THE PHILOSOPHER: It is true. The more I think about it, the more I see that you are only the art of some superlatively potent and ingenious mighty being, who hides himself while he makes you appear. All thinkers since Thales, and probably long before him, have played at blind man's buff with you. They have said: "I have you!" And they had nothing. We all resemble Ixion: he thought he was kissing Juno, and he was embracing only a cloud.

NATURE: Since I am all that there is, how can a being such as you, so small a part of myself, comprehend me? Be content, atoms who are my children, with understanding a few atoms that surround you, with drinking a few drops of my milk, with nourishing yourself briefly on my breast, and with dying without having known your mother or your nurse.

THE PHILOSOPHER: My dear mother, tell me something of why you exist, of why there is anything.

NATURE: I will answer you as, for so many centuries, I have answered all those who have asked me about first principles: I Know Nothing About Them.

THE PHILOSOPHER: Would not nothingness be better than this multitude of existences made only for continual dissolution, this host of animals born only to devour and to be devoured, this host of sentient beings created to endure so much pain, and that other crowd of rational beings by whom reason is so rarely heard? Tell me, Nature, what good is there in all that?

NATURE: Oh! go and ask Him who made me.

NEW NOVELTIES

It seems that the first words of Ovid's *Metamorphoses, In nova fert animus,* are the motto of the human race. Nobody is moved by the wonderful spectacle of the sun which rises, or rather appears to rise, every day; everybody runs to see the tiniest meteor which flames for an instant in that accumulation of vapors, called the sky, which surrounds the earth.

An itinerant bookseller does not burden himself with a Virgil, with a Horace, but with a new book, even though it be detestable. He draws you aside and says to you: "Sir, do you want some books from Holland?"

From the beginning of time, women have complained that men have been unfaithful to them for the sake of novelty, for the sake of other women whose novelty was their only merit. Many ladies (it must be confessed, despite the infinite respect we have for them) have treated men as they complain they have themselves been treated; and the story of Gioconda is much older than Ariosto.

Perhaps this universal taste for novelty is one of nature's blessings. People cry to us: "Be content with what you have, desire nothing that is above your station, restrain your curiosity, curb your intellectual activity." These are excellent maxims, but if we had always followed them, we should still be eating acorns, we should still be sleeping in the open air, and we should not have had Corneille, Racine, Molière, Poussin, Lebrun, Lemoine, or Pigalle.

POWER, OMNIPOTENCE

I suppose that anyone who reads this article is convinced that this world has been created by an intelligence, and that a little knowledge of astronomy and anatomy is enough to make this universal and supreme intelligence admired. But can he know by himself that this intelligence is omnipotent, that is to say, infinitely powerful? Has he the least notion of the infinite, or the ability to understand what is an infinite power?

The celebrated historian philosopher, David Hume, says: "A weight of ten ounces is lifted in a balance by another weight; therefore this other weight is of more than ten ounces; but one can adduce no reason why it should weigh a hundred ounces."

One can argue likewise: You recognize a supreme intelligence strong enough to create you, to preserve you for a limited time, to reward you, to punish you. Do you know enough of this intelligence to demonstrate that it can do still more?

How can you prove by your reason that this being can do more than he has done?

The life of all animals is short. Could he make it longer?

All animals are the prey of one another; everything is born to be devoured. Could he create without destroying?

You do not know what nature is. You cannot therefore know if nature has not forced the supreme intelligence to do only the things it has done.

This globe is only a vast field of destruction and carnage. Either the great Being has been able to make of it an eternal abode of delight for all sentient beings, or He has not been able. If He has been able, and if He has not done so, He must be regarded as malevolent; but if He has not been able, do not hesitate to look on Him as a very great power, circumscribed by Nature.

Whether or not His power is infinite is nothing to you. It is a matter of indifference to a subject whether his master possesses five hundred leagues of land or five thousand; he is subject, neither more nor less, in either case.

Which would be the greater insult to this ineffable Being? To say, "He has made men miserable without being able to do anything about it," or, "He has made them for His pleasure"?

Many sects represent Him as cruel; others, for fear of admitting a wicked God, have the audacity to deny His existence. Is it not probably better to say that the necessity of His nature and the necessity of things have determined everything?

The world is the theater of moral ill and physical ill: We are all only too aware of it, and the "Everything is for the best" of Shaftesbury, Bolingbroke, and Pope, is only a witty paradox, a rather poor joke.

The two principles of Zoroaster and Manes, so carefully scrutinized by Bayle, are a still poorer joke. They are, as has been remarked already, Molière's two doctors, one of whom says to the other: "Grant me the emetic, and I will grant you the bleeding." Manichaeism is absurd; and that is why it has had so many supporters.

I admit that I have not been enlightened by all that Bayle says about the Manichaeans and the Paulicans. That is controversy, and I would have preferred pure philosophy. Why discuss our mysteries in relation to Zoroaster's? As soon as you dare to examine our mysteries, which require only faith and no reason, you walk on the edge of a precipice.

The trash in our scholastic theology has nothing to do with the trash in Zoroaster's ravings.

Why debate original sin with Zoroaster? There was never any question of such a thing until St. Augustine's time. Neither Zoroaster nor any legislator of antiquity had ever heard of it.

If you dispute with Zoroaster, put under lock and key the Old and the New Testaments with which he was unacquainted, and which one must revere without desiring to explain them.

What, then, should I say to Zoroaster? My reason cannot admit two gods who are opposed to each other; such an idea is fit only for a poem where Minerva quarrels with Mars. My feeble reason is much more satisfied with a single great Being, whose essence was to create, and who has created as much as nature would permit, rather than with the conception of two great Beings, one of whom spoils all the works of the other. Your bad principle, Ahriman, has not been able to upset a single one of the astronomical and physical laws of the good principle, Ormuzd; everything progresses in the heavens with the greatest regularity. Why should the wicked Ahriman have had power over this little globe of the world?

If I had been Ahriman, I should have attacked Ormuzd in his fine vast provinces of multitudinous suns and stars. I should not have limited myself to making war on him in a little village.

There is much evil in this village: but how do you know that this evil is not inevitable?

You are forced to admit an intelligence operating throughout the universe. But do you know, for instance, if this power is able to foresee the future? You have asserted it a thousand times, but you have never been able either to prove it, or to understand it. You cannot know how any being whatever sees what is not. Well, the future is not; therefore no being can see it. You are reduced to saying that He foresees it; but foreseeing is conjecturing. This is the opinion of the Socinians.

Well, a God who, according to you, conjectures, can be mistaken. In your system He is really mistaken, for if He had foreseen that His enemy would poison all His works here below, He would not have produced them, He would not have arranged matters so that He would have to suffer the shame of continual defeat.

Do I not do Him much more honor by saying that He has made everything by the necessity of His nature, than you do Him by raising an enemy who disfigures, soils, and destroys all His works here below?

One does not have an unworthy idea of God when one says that, after He had formed thousands of millions of worlds where death and evil do not dwell, it was necessary that evil and death should dwell in this world.

One does not disparage God when one says that He could not form man without giving him self-esteem; that this self-esteem could not lead him without misleading him most of the time; that his passions are necessary, but that they are disastrous; that propagation cannot be executed without desire; that desire cannot animate man without resulting in quarrels; that these quarrels necessarily bring wars in their train, etc.

When we see even a part of the operations of the animal, vegetable, and mineral kingdoms, and contemplate this globe of ours which is a perfect sieve, from which innumerable exhalations are constantly escaping, what philosopher among us will be bold enough, what scholastic foolish enough, to believe that nature could stop the effects of volcanoes, the abrupt changes of the atmosphere, the violence of the winds, plagues, and all destructive scourges?

One must be very powerful, very strong, very ingenious, to have created lions which devour bulls, and to have created men capable of inventing weapons which can, at a blow, kill not only bulls and lions, but other men. One must be very powerful to have created spiders which spin webs to catch flies—but this does not mean that one has to be omnipotent, infinitely powerful.

If the great Being had been infinitely powerful, there is no reason why He should not have made sentient animals infinitely happy. He has not done so; therefore He was unable to do so.

All the philosophical sects have stranded on the reef of moral and physical ill. We can only conclude and avow that God, having acted for the best, has not been able to act better.

This necessity settles all the difficulties and finishes all the disputes. We are not impudent enough to say: "All is good." We say: "All is as little bad as possible."

Why does a child often die in its mother's womb? Why is another who has had the misfortune to be born, reserved for lifelong torments terminated by a frightful death?

Why has the source of life been poisoned all over the world since the discovery of America? Why, since the seventh century of our era, has smallpox carried off the eighth part of the human race? Why since the beginning of time have bladders been subject to becoming stone quarries? Why the plague, war, famine, the Inquisition?

Try as you will, you can arrive at no other solution than that everything has been necessary.

I speak here to philosophers only, not to theologians. We well know that faith is the thread in the labyrinth. We know that the fall of Adam and Eve, original sin, the immense power given to the devil, the predilection accorded by the great Being to the Jewish people, and the baptism substituted for the amputation of the prepuce, are the answers which explain everything. We have argued only against Zoroaster, and not against the university of Conimbre or Coimbre, to which we submit in our articles.

PRAYERS

We do not know of any religion without prayers; even the Jews prayed, although they had no public formula, until they began to sing canticles in their synagogues, which was very late in their history.

All men, in desire and fear, have invoked the aid of a deity. Some philosophers, more respectful to the Supreme Being, and less condescending to human frailty, would have no prayer but resignation. It is, indeed, what seems proper as between creature and creator. But philosophy is not made to govern the world; she rises above the common herd; she speaks a language that the crowd cannot understand. It would be like telling fishwives to study conic sections.

Even among the philosophers, I do not believe that anyone apart from Maximus of Tyre has treated of this matter. This is the substance of Maximus's ideas.

The Eternal has His intentions from all eternity. If prayer accords with His immutable wishes, it is quite useless to ask of Him what He has resolved to do. If one prays Him to do the contrary of what He has resolved, it is praying that He be weak, frivolous, inconstant; it is believing that He is all these things; it is to mock Him. Either you ask Him a just thing, in which case He must do it, and the thing will be done without your praying Him for it—entreating Him is even to distrust Him: or the thing is unjust, in which case you insult Him. You are worthy or unworthy of the grace you implore: if worthy, He knows it better than you; if unworthy, you commit one more crime by asking for what you do not deserve.

In a word, we pray to God only because we have made Him in our own image. We treat Him like a pasha, like a sultan whom one may provoke and appease. In short, all nations pray to God: wise men resign themselves and obey Him. Let us pray with the people, and resign ourselves with the wise men.

PREJUDICES

Prejudice is an opinion without judgment. Thus, all over the world, people inspire children with as many opinions as they choose to, before the children can judge.

There are some universal, necessary prejudices, which are even virtuous. In all countries children are taught to recognize a rewarding and revenging God, to respect and love their father and their mother, to look on theft as a crime and selfish lying as a vice, before they can guess what is a vice and what a virtue.

There are, then, some very good prejudices; they are those which are ratified by judgment when one comes to reason.

Sentiment is not simply prejudice; it is something much stronger. A mother does not love her son because she has been told she must love him; she cherishes him happily in spite of herself. It is not through prejudice that you run to the help of an unknown child about to fall from a precipice, or be eaten by a beast.

But it is through prejudice that you will respect a man clad in certain clothes, walking gravely, speaking likewise. Your parents have told you that you should bow before this man; you respect him before knowing whether or not he merits your respect. You grow in years and in knowledge, and you perceive that this man is a charlatan steeped in arrogance, self-interest, and artifice. You despise what you revered, and prejudice cedes to judgment. Through prejudice you have believed the fables with which your childhood was cradled. You have been told that the Titans made war on the gods, that Venus was amorous of Adonis; when you are twelve you accept these fables as truths; when you are twenty you look on them as ingenious allegories.

Let us examine briefly the different sorts of prejudices, so as to set our affairs in order. Perhaps we shall find ourselves like those who, at the time of the Mississippi Bubble, discovered that they had been dealing in imaginary riches.

PREJUDICES OF THE SENSES

Is it not strange that our eyes always deceive us, even when we have excellent sight, and that on the contrary our ears do not deceive us? Let your well-informed ear hear, "You are beautiful, I love you," and it is quite certain that someone has not said, "I hate you, you are ugly." But you see a smooth mirror, when the fact is that you are mistaken, that it has a very uneven surface. You see the sun as about two feet in diameter, when in truth it is a million times bigger than the earth.

It seems that God has put truth in your ears, and error in your eyes; but study optics, and you will see that God has not deceived you, and that it is impossible for objects to appear to you otherwise than you see them in the present state of things.

PREJUDICES, PHYSICAL

The sun rises, the moon also, the earth is motionless: these are natural physical prejudices. But that lobsters are good for the blood, because when cooked they are red; that eels cure paralysis because they wriggle; that the moon affects our maladies because one day someone observed that a sick man had an increase of fever during the waning of the moon—these ideas and a thousand others are the errors of ancient charlatans who judged without reasoning, and who, being deceived, deceived others.

PREJUDICES, HISTORICAL

Most historical stories have been believed without examination, and this belief is a prejudice. Fabius Pictor relates that many centuries before his time, a vestal of the town of Alba, going to draw water in her pitcher, was ravished, that she gave birth to Romulus and Remus, that they were fed by a she-wolf, etc. The Roman people believed this fable; they did not inquire whether or not there were vestals in Latium, at that time, whether it was probable that a king's daughter would leave her convent with her pitcher, or whether it was likely that a she-wolf would suckle two children instead of eating them. The prejudice established itself.

A monk writes that Clovis, being in great danger at the battle of Tolbiac, made a vow to turn Christian if he escaped; but is it natural to address oneself to a foreign god on such an occasion? Is it not then that the religion in which one was born acts most potently? What Christian, in battle against the Turks, will not address himself to the Holy Virgin rather than to Mohammed? It is added that a pigeon brought the holy phial in its beak to anoint Clovis, and that an angel brought the oriflamme to lead him; prejudice believed all the little tales of this kind. Those who understand human nature know perfectly well that Clovis the usurper, and Rolon (or Rol) the usurper, turned Christian in order to govern the Christians more securely, just as the Turkish usurpers turned Mussulman in order to govern the Mussulmans more securely.

PREJUDICES, RELIGIOUS

If your nurse has told you that Ceres rules over the crops, or that Vistnou and Xaca made themselves men several times, or that Sammonocodom came to cut down a forest, or that Odin awaits you in his hall near Jutland, or that Mohammed or somebody else made a journey into the sky; if, lastly, your tutor comes to drive into your brain what your nurse has imprinted on it, you keep it for life. If your judgment wishes to rise against these prejudices, your neighbors and, above all, your neighbors' wives cry out: "Impious reprobate," and dismay you. Your dervish, fearing to see his income diminish, accuses you to the cadi, and this cadi has you impaled if he can, because he likes ruling over fools, and thinks that fools obey better than those who are not fools. And all this will go on until your neighbors and the dervish and the cadi begin to understand that foolishness is good for nothing, and that persecution is abominable.

RARE

Rare, in natural philosophy, is the opposite of dense. In moral philosophy, it is the opposite of common. This second variety of rare is what excites admiration. One never admires what is common; one enjoys it.

An eccentric thinks himself superior to the rest of wretched mankind when he has in his study a rare medal that is good for nothing, a rare book that nobody has the courage to read, an old engraving by Albrecht Durer, badly designed and badly printed. He triumphs if his garden contains a stunted tree from America. This eccentric has no taste; he has only vanity. He has heard that the beautiful is rare; but he should know that all that is rare is not beautiful.

Beauty is rare in all nature's works, and in all works of art.

Whatever ill things have been said of women, I maintain that it is rarer to find women perfectly beautiful than tolerably good. In the country you will meet ten thousand women attached to their homes, who are laborious and sober, and busy feeding, rearing, and teaching their children; but you will find hardly one whom you could exhibit in the theaters of Paris, London, and Naples, or in the public gardens, and who would be considered a beauty.

Similarly, in works of art you have ten thousand daubs and scrawls to one masterpiece.

If everything were beautiful and good, it is clear that one would no longer admire anything; one would only enjoy. But would one have pleasure in enjoying? That is a big question.

Why have the beautiful passages in *The Cid* and

Cinna had such a prodigious success? Because in the profound night in which people were plunged, they suddenly saw a burst of new light which they had not expected. It was because this kind of beauty was the rarest thing in the world.

The groves of Versailles were a beauty unique in the world, as were certain passages of Corneille. St. Peter's, in Rome, is unique. But let us suppose that all the churches of Europe were equal to St. Peter's, that all statues were Venus de Medici, that all tragedies were as beautiful as Racine's *Iphigénie,* all works of poetry as well written as Boileau's *Art Poétique,* all comedies as good as *Tartufe,* and so on in every sphere. Would you then have as much pleasure in enjoying masterpieces that had become common as you did when they were rare? I say boldly: "No!" And I believe that the ancient school, which so rarely was right, was right when it said: *Ab assuetis non fit passio*—habit does not make passion.

But, my dear reader, will it be the same with the works of nature? Will you be disgusted if all the maids are as beautiful as Helen; and you, ladies, if all the lads are like Paris? Let us suppose that all wines are excellent, will you have less desire to drink? If partridges, pheasants, pullets were common at all seasons, would you have less appetite? I say boldly again: "No!" despite the axiom of the schools—"Habit does not make passion"—and the reason, as you know, is that all the pleasures which nature gives us are always recurring needs, necessary enjoyments, while the pleasures of the arts are not necessary. It is not necessary for a man to have groves where water gushes to a height of a hundred feet from the mouth of a marble face, and on leaving these groves to go to see a fine tragedy. But the two sexes are always necessary to each other. The table and the bed are necessities. The habit of being alternately on these two thrones will never disgust you.

In Paris a few years ago people admired a rhinoceros. If there were in one province ten thousand rhinoceroses, men would run after them only to kill them. But let there be a hundred thousand beautiful women men will always run after them to—honor them.

REASON

At the time when all France was mad over the Mississippi Bubble, and John Law was controller-general, there came to him a man who was always right, who always had reason on his side. Said he to Law, in the presence of a large crowd:

"Sir, you are the biggest madman, the biggest fool, or the biggest rogue who has yet appeared among us, and that is saying a great deal. This is how I prove it. You have imagined that a state's wealth can be increased tenfold with paper, but as this paper can represent only the money that is representative of true wealth—the products of the land and industry—you should have begun by giving us ten times more corn, wine, cloth, canvas, etc. That is not enough, you must be sure of your market. But you make ten times as many notes as we have of silver and commodities, therefore you are ten times more extravagant, or more inept, or more of a rogue than all the comptrollers who have preceded you. Now this is how I prove the major term of my thesis."

But he had hardly started his major when he was led off to a lunatic asylum.

When he came out of the asylum, where he studied hard and strengthened his reason, he went to Rome, where he asked for a public audience with the Pope, on condition that he would not be interrupted in his harangue. And he spoke to the Pope in these terms: "Holy Father, you are an antichrist and this is how I prove it to Your Holiness. I call antichrist the man who does the contrary to what Christ did and commanded. Now Christ was poor, and you are very rich; he paid tribute, and you exact tribute; he submitted to the powers that were, and you have become a power yourself; he walked on foot, and you go to Castel-Gandolfo in a sumptuous equipage; he ate whatever anyone was good enough to give him, and you want us to eat fish on Friday and Saturday, when we live far from sea and river; he forbade Simon Barjona to use a sword, and you have swords in your service, etc., etc., etc. Therefore in this sense Your Holiness is antichrist. In every other sense I hold you in great veneration, and I ask you for an indulgence *in articulo mortis.*"

My man was put in the Castello St. Angelo.

When he came out of the Castello St. Angelo, he rushed to Venice, and asked to speak to the doge.

"Your Serenity," he said, "must be a very extravagant person to marry the sea every year: for, in the first place, one only marries the same person once; secondly, your marriage resembles Harlequin's which was half made, seeing that it lacked but the consent of the bride; thirdly, how do you know that other maritime powers will not one day declare you incapable of consummating the marriage?"

Having spoken, he was shut up in the Tower of St. Mark's.

When he came out of the Tower of St. Mark's, he went to Constantinople, where he had an audience with the mufti, and spoke to him in these terms: "Your religion, although it has some good points, such as worship of a supreme Being, and the rule of being just and charitable, is otherwise nothing but a rehash of Judaism and a tedious collection of fairy tales. If the archangel Gabriel had brought the leaves of the Koran to Mohammed from some planet, all Arabia would have seen Gabriel come down; but nobody saw him. Therefore Mohammed was a brazen impostor who deceived imbeciles."

Hardly had he pronounced these words than he was run through with a sword. Nevertheless he had always been right, and had always had reason on his side.

RELIGION

Tonight I was in a meditative mood. I was absorbed in the contemplation of nature; I admired the immensity, the movements, the harmony of those infinite globes which the vulgar do not know how to admire.

I admired still more the intelligence which directs these vast forces. I said to myself: "One must be blind not to be dazzled by this spectacle; one must be stupid not to recognize the author of it; one must be mad not to worship Him. What tribute of worship should I render Him? Should not this tribute be the same in the whole of space, since it is the same supreme power which reigns equally in all space? Should not a thinking being who dwells in a star in the Milky Way offer Him the same homage as the thinking being on this little globe where we are? Light is uniform for the star Sirius and for us; moral philosophy must be uniform. If a sentient, thinking animal in Sirius is born of a tender father and mother who have been occupied with his happiness, he owes them as much love and care as we owe to our parents. If someone in the Milky Way sees a needy cripple, if he can help him, and if he does not do so, he is guilty in the sight of all globes. Everywhere the heart has the same duties: on the steps of the throne of God, if He has a throne; and in the depth of the abyss, if He is an abyss."

I was plunged in these ideas when one of those genii who throng the interplanetary spaces came down to me. I recognized this aerial creature as one who had appeared to me on another occasion, to teach me how different God's judgments were from our own, and how a good action is preferable to an argument.

He transported me into a desert, covered with piles of bones; and between these heaps of dead men there were walks of evergreen trees, and at the end of each walk there was a tall man of august mien, who regarded these sad remains with pity.

"Alas! my archangel," said I, "where have you brought me?"

"To desolation," he answered.

"And who are these fine patriarchs whom I see sad and motionless at the end of these green walks? They seem to be weeping over this countless crowd of dead."

"You shall know, poor human creature," answered the genie from the interplanetary spaces. "But first of all you must weep."

He began with the first pile. "These," he said, "are the twenty-three thousand Jews who danced before a calf, with the twenty-four thousand who were killed while lying with Midianitish women. The number of those massacred for such errors and offenses amounts to nearly three hundred thousand.

"In the other walks are the bones of the Christians slaughtered by each other in metaphysical quarrels. They are divided into several heaps of four centuries each. One heap would have mounted right to the sky, so they had to be divided."

"What!" I cried. "Brothers have treated their brothers

like this, and I have the misfortune to be of this brotherhood!"

"Here," said the spirit, "are the twelve million Americans killed in their native land because they had not been baptized."

"My God! why did you not leave these frightful bones to dry in the hemisphere where their bodies were born, and where they were consigned to so many different deaths? Why assemble here all these abominable monuments to barbarism and fanaticism?"

"To instruct you."

"Since you wish to instruct me," I said to the genie, "tell me if there have been peoples other than the Christians and the Jews in whom zeal and religion wretchedly transformed into fanaticism have inspired so many horrible cruelties."

"Yes," he said. "The Mohammedans were sullied with the same inhumanities, but rarely; and when one asked *amman*, pity, of them and offered them tribute, they were merciful. As for the other nations, there has not been a single one, from the beginning of the world, which has ever made a purely religious war. Follow me now." I followed him.

A little beyond these piles of dead men, we found other piles; they were composed of sacks of gold and silver, and each had its label: "Substance of the heretics massacred in the eighteenth century, the seventeenth, and the sixteenth." And so on in going back: "Gold and silver of Americans slaughtered," etc., etc. And all these piles were surmounted with crosses, mitres, croziers, and triple crowns studded with precious stones.

"What, my genie! Do you mean that these dead were piled up for the sake of their wealth?"

"Yes, my son."

I wept. And when, by my grief, I was worthy of being led to the end of the green walks, he led me there.

"Contemplate," he said, "the heroes of humanity who were the world's benefactors, and who were all united in banishing from the world, as far as they were able, violence and rapine. Question them."

I ran to the first of the band. He had a crown on his head, and a little censer in his hand. I humbly asked him his name. "I am Numa Pompilius," he said to me. "I succeeded a brigand, and I had to govern brigands. I taught them virtue and the worship of God, but after me they forgot both more than once. I forbade that there should be any image in the temples, because the Deity which animates nature cannot be represented. During my reign the Romans had neither wars nor seditions, and my religion did nothing but good. All the neighboring peoples came to honor me at my funeral; and a unique honor it was."

I kissed his hand, and I went to the second. He was a fine old man about a hundred years old, clad in a white robe. He put his middle finger on his mouth, and with the other hand he cast some beans behind him. I recognized Pythagoras. He assured me he had never had a golden thigh, and that he had never been a cock; but that he had governed the Crotoniates with as much justice as Numa governed the Romans, almost at the same time; and that this justice was the rarest and most necessary thing in the world. I learned that the Pythagoreans examined their consciences twice a day. The honest people! How far we are from them! But we, who have been nothing but assassins for thirteen hundred years, we call these wise men arrogant.

In order to please Pythagoras, I did not say a word to him, and I passed on to Zoroaster, who was occupied in concentrating the celestial fire in the focus of a concave mirror, in the middle of a hall with a hundred doors which all led to wisdom. (Zoroaster's precepts are called *doors,* and are a hundred in number.) Over the principal door I read these words which are the sum of all moral philosophy, and which cut short all the disputes of the casuists: "When in doubt if an action is good or bad, refrain."

"Certainly," I said to my genie, "the barbarians who immolated all these victims had never read these beautiful words."

We then saw Zaleucus, Thales, Anaximandor, and all the sages who had sought truth and practiced virtue.

When we came to Socrates, I recognized him very quickly by his flat nose. "Well," I said to him, "so you are one of the Almighty's confidants! All the inhabitants of Europe, except the Turks and the Tartars of the Crimea, who know nothing, pronounce your name with respect. It is revered, loved, this great name, to the point that people have wanted to know those of your persecutors. Melitus and Anitus are known because of you, just as Ravaillac is known because of Henry IV; but I know only this name of Anitus. I do not know precisely who was the scoundrel who calumniated you, and who succeeded in having you condemned to drink hemlock."

"Since my adventure," replied Socrates, "I have never thought about that man, but seeing that you make me remember it, I pity him. He was a wicked priest who secretly conducted a business in hides, a trade reputed shameful among us. He sent his two children to my school. The other disciples taunted them with having a father who was a currier, and they were obliged to leave. The irritated father did not rest until he had stirred up all the priests and all the sophists against me. They persuaded the council of five hundred that I was an impious fellow who did not believe that the Moon,

Mercury, and Mars were gods. Indeed, I used to think, as I think now, that there is only one God, master of all nature. The judges handed me over to the poisoner of the republic. He cut short my life by a few days: I died peacefully at the age of seventy, and since that time I have led a happy life with all these great men whom you see, and of whom I am the least."

After enjoying some time in conversation with Socrates, I went forward with my guide into a grove situated above the thickets where all the sages of antiquity seemed to be tasting sweet repose.

I saw a man of gentle, simple countenance, who seemed to me to be about thirty-five years old. From afar he cast compassionate glances on these piles of whitened bones, across which I had had to pass to reach the sages' abode. I was astonished to find his feet swollen and bleeding, his hands likewise, his side pierced, and his ribs flayed with whip cuts. "Good Heavens!" I said to him, "is it possible for a just man, a sage, to be in this state? I have just seen one who was treated in a very hateful way, but there is no comparison between his torture and yours. Wicked priests and wicked judges poisoned him. Were priests and judges your torturers?"

He answered with much courtesy: "Yes."

"And who were these monsters?"

"They were hypocrites."

"Ah! that says everything. I understand by this single word that they must have condemned you to death. Had you proved to them then, as Socrates did, that the Moon was not a goddess, and that Mercury was not a god?"

"No, these planets were not in question. My compatriots did not know what a planet is; they were all arrant ignoramuses. Their superstitions were quite different from those of the Greeks."

"You wanted to teach them a new religion, then?"

"Not at all. I said to them simply: 'Love God with all your heart and your fellow creature as yourself, for that is man's whole duty.' Judge if this precept is not as old as the universe; judge if I brought them a new religion. I did not stop telling them that I had come not to destroy the law but to fulfill it. I observed all their rites; circumcized as they all were, baptized as were the most zealous among them. Like them I paid the Corban; I observed the Passover as they did, eating, standing up, a lamb cooked with lettuce. I and my friends went to pray in the temple; my friends even frequented this temple after my death. In a word, I fulfilled all their laws without a single exception."

"What! these wretches could not even reproach you with swerving from their laws?"

"Not, not possibly."

"Why then did they reduce you to the condition in which I now see you?"

"What do you expect me to say! They were very arrogant and selfish. They saw that I knew them for what they were; they knew that I was making the citizens acquainted with them; they were the stronger; they took away my life: and people like them will always do as much, if they can, to anyone who does them too much justice."

"But did you say nothing, do nothing that could serve them as a pretext?"

"To the wicked everything serves as pretext."

"Did you not say once that you were come not to bring peace, but a sword?"

"It is a copyist's error. I told them that I brought peace and not a sword. I never wrote anything; what I said may have been changed without evil intention."

"You therefore contributed in no way by your speeches, badly reported, badly interpreted, to these frightful piles of bones which I saw on my road in coming to consult you?"

"It is with horror only that I have seen those who have made themselves guilty of these murders."

"And these monuments of power and wealth, of pride and avarice, these treasures, these ornaments, these signs of grandeur, which I have seen piled up on the road while I was seeking wisdom, do they come from you?"

"That is impossible. I and my followers lived in poverty and meanness: my grandeur was in virtue only."

I was about to beg him to be so good as to tell me just who he was. My guide warned me to do nothing of the sort. He told me that I was not made to understand these sublime mysteries. But I did implore him to tell me in what true religion consisted.

"Have I not already told you? Love God and your fellow creature as yourself."

"What! If one loves God, one can eat meat on Friday?"

"I always ate what was given me, for I was too poor to give anyone food."

"In loving God, in being just, should one not be rather cautious not to confide all the adventures of one's life to an unknown being?"

"That was always my practice."

"Can I not, by doing good, dispense with making a pilgrimage to St. James of Compostella?"

"I have never been in that region."

"Is it necessary for me to imprison myself in a retreat with fools?"

"As for me, I was always making little journeys from town to town."

"Is it necessary for me to take sides either for the Greek Church or the Latin?"

"When I was in the world, I never differentiated between the Jew and the Samaritan."

"Well, if that is so, I take you for my only master." Then he made me a sign with his head which filled me with consolation. The vision disappeared, and a clear conscience stayed with me.

SECT

Every sect, of every kind, is a rallying-point for doubt and error. Scotist, Thomist, Realist, Nominalist, Papist, Calvinist, Molinist, and Jansenist, are only pseudonyms.

There are no sects in geometry. One does not speak of a Euclidean, an Archimedean. When the truth is evident, it is impossible for parties and factions to arise. There has never been a dispute as to whether there is daylight at noon. The branch of astronomy which determines the course of the stars and the return of eclipses being once known, there is no dispute among astronomers.

In England one does not say: "I am a Newtonian, a Lockian, a Halleyan." Why? Those who have read cannot refuse their assent to the truths taught by these three great men. The more Newton is revered, the less do people style themselves Newtonians; this word supposes that there are anti-Newtonians in England. Maybe we still have a few Cartesians in France, but only because Descartes' system is a tissue of erroneous and ridiculous speculations.

It is the same with the small number of matters of fact which are well established. The records of the Tower of London having been authentically gathered by Rymer, there are no Rymerians, because it occurs to no one to assail this collection. In it one finds neither contradictions, absurdities, nor prodigies; nothing which revolts the reason, nothing, consequently, which sectarians strive to maintain or upset by absurd arguments. Everyone agrees, therefore, that Rymer's records are worthy of belief.

You are a Mohammedan; therefore there are people who are not; therefore you might well be wrong.

What would be the true religion if Christianity did not exist? The religion in which there were no sects, the religion in which all minds were necessarily in agreement.

Well, to what dogma do all minds agree? To the worship of a God, and to honesty. All the philosophers of the world who have had a religion have said in all ages: "There is a God, and one must be just." There, then, is the universal religion established in all ages and throughout mankind. The point in which they all agree is therefore true, and the systems through which they differ are therefore false.

"My sect is the best," says a Brahmin to me. But, my friend, if your sect is good, it is necessary; for if it were not absolutely necessary you would admit to me that it was useless. If it is absolutely necessary, it is for all men. How, then, can it be that all men have not what is absolutely necessary to them? How is it possible for the rest of the world to laugh at you and your Brahma?

When Zoroaster, Hermes, Orpheus, Minos, and all the great men say: "Let us worship God, and let us be just," nobody laughs. But everyone hisses the man who claims that one cannot please God unless one is holding a cow's tail when one dies; or the man who wants one to have the end of one's prepuce cut off; or the man who consecrates crocodiles and onions; or the man who attaches eternal salvation to dead men's bones carried under one's shirt, or to a plenary indulgence which may be bought at Rome for two and a half sous.

Whence comes this universal competition in hisses and derision from one end of the world to the other? It is clear that the things at which everyone sneers are not very evidently true. What would we say of one of Sejan's secretaries who dedicated to Petronius a bombastic book entitled: "The Truths of the Sibylline Oracles, Proved by the Facts"?

This secretary proves to you, first, that it was necessary for God to send on earth several sibyls one after the other; for He had no other means of teaching mankind. It is demonstrated that God spoke to these sibyls, for the word sibyl signifies *God's counsel.* They had to live a long time, for persons to whom God speaks should have this privilege, at the very least. They were twelve in number, for this number is sacred. They had certainly predicted all the events in the world, for Tarquinius Superbus bought three of their books from an old woman for a hundred crowns. "What incredulous fellow," adds the secretary, "will dare deny all these obvious facts which happened in a corner in the sight of the whole world? Who can deny the fulfillment of their prophecies? Has not Virgil himself quoted the predictions of the sibyls? If we have no first editions of the Sibylline Books, written at a time when people did not know how to read or write, have we not authentic copies? Impiety must be silent before such proofs." Thus did Houttevillus speak to Sejan. He hoped to have a position as augur which would be worth an income of fifty thousand francs, and he had nothing.

"What my sect teaches is obscure, I admit it," says a fanatic; and it is because of this obscurity that it must be believed; for the sect itself says it is full of obscurities. My sect is extravagant, therefore it is divine; for how should what appears so mad have been embraced by so many peoples, if it were not divine?" It is precisely like the Koran which the Sonnites say has an angel's face and an animal's snout. Be not scandalized by the animal's snout, and worship the angel's face. Thus speaks this mad fellow. But a fanatic of another sect answers: "It is you who are the animal, and I who am the angel."

Well, who shall judge the case? Who shall decide between these two fanatics? Why, the reasonable, impartial man who is learned in a knowledge that is not that of words; the man free from prejudice and the lover of truth and justice—in short, the man who is not the foolish animal, and who does not think he is the angel.

Sect and *error* are synonymous. You are a Peripatetic and I a Platonist; we are therefore both wrong; for you combat Plato only because his fantasies have revolted you, while I am alienated from Aristotle only because it seems to me that he does not know what he is talking about. If one or the other had demonstrated the truth, there would be a sect no longer. To declare oneself for the opinion of one or the other is to take sides in a civil war. There are no sects in mathematics, in experimental physics. A man who examines the relations between a cone and a sphere is not of the sect of Archimedes: he who sees that the square of the hypotenuse of a right-angled triangle is equal to the square of the two other sides is not of the sect of Pythagoras.

When you say that the blood circulates, that the air is heavy, that the sun's rays are pencils of seven refrangible rays, you are not either of the sect of Harvey, or the sect of Torricelli, or the sect of Newton; you merely agree with the truth as demonstrated by them, and the entire world will always be of your opinion.

This is the character of truth: it is of all time, it is for all men, it has only to show itself to be recognized, and one cannot argue against it. A long dispute means that *both parties are wrong.*

SELF-LOVE

Nicole in his *Essais de Morale*—written on top of two or three thousand other volumes of ethics—says that "by means of the wheels and gibbets which people erect in common, the tyrannous thoughts and designs of each individual's self-love are repressed."

I shall not inquire whether or not people have gibbets in common, as they have meadows and woods in common, and a common purse, or if one represses ideas with wheels; but it seems very strange to me that Nicole should take highway robbery and assassination for self-love. One should distinguish shades of difference a little better. The man who said that Nero had his mother assassinated through self-love, and that Cartouche had an excess of self-love, would not be expressing himself very correctly. Self-love is not wickedness, it is a sentiment that is natural to all men; it is much nearer vanity than crime.

A beggar in the suburbs of Madrid was nobly begging charity. A passer-by said to him: "Are you not ashamed to practice this infamous calling when you are able to work?"

"Sir," answered the beggar, "I ask for money, not advice." And he turned on his heel with full Castilian dignity.

This gentleman was a proud beggar, his vanity was wounded by a trifle. He asked charity out of love for himself, and could not tolerate the reprimand out of further love for himself.

A missionary traveling in India met a fakir laden with chains, naked as a monkey, lying on his stomach, who was having himself whipped for the sins of his compatriots, the Indians, who gave him a few farthings.

"What self-denial!" said one of the spectators.

"Self-denial!" answered the fakir. "I have myself flogged in this world in order to give this flogging back to you in the next world, when you will be horses and I a horseman."

Those who have said that love of ourselves is the basis of all our opinions and all our actions, have therefore been quite right in India, Spain, and all the habitable world: and as one does not write to prove to men that they have faces, it is not necessary to prove to them that they have self-love. Self-love is our instrument of preservation; it resembles the instrument which perpetuates the species. It is necessary, it is dear to us, it gives us pleasure, and it has to be hidden.

SOCRATES

One day, two citizens of Athens, returning from the temple of Mercury, perceived Socrates in the public square. One said to the other: "Is not that the rascal who says that one can be virtuous without going every day to offer up sheep and geese?" "Yes," said the other, "that is the sage who has no religion; that is the atheist who says there is only one God." Socrates approached them with his simple air, his daemon, and his irony, which Madame Dacier has so highly extolled. "My friends," said he to them, "one word, if you please: a man who prays to God, who adores Him, who seeks to resemble Him as much as human weakness can do, and who does all the good which lies in his power, what would you call him?" "A very religious soul," said they. "Very well; we may therefore adore the Supreme Being, and have a great deal of religion?" "Granted," said the two Athenians. "But do you believe," pursued Socrates, "that when the Divine Architect of the world arranged all the spheres which revolve above our heads, when He gave motion and life to so many different beings, He made use of the arm of Hercules, the lyre of Apollo, or the flute of Pan?" "It is not probable," said they. "But if it is not probable that He called in the aid of others to construct that which we see, it is not credible that He preserves it through others rather than through Himself. If Neptune were the absolute master of the sea, Juno of the air, Aeolus of the winds, Ceres of harvests—and if one desired a calm, when another wanted wind and rain—you see clearly, that the order of nature could not exist as it is. You will confess, that all depends upon Him who has made all. You attribute four white horses to the sun, and four black ones to the moon; but is it not more likely, that day and night are the effect of the motion given to the stars by their Master, than that they were produced by eight horses?" The two citizens looked at him, but answered nothing. In short, Socrates concluded by proving to them that they might have harvests without giving money to the priests of Ceres; go to the chase without offering little silver statues to the temple of Diana; that Pomona gave not fruits; that Neptune gave not horses; and that they should thank the Sovereign who had made all.

His discourse was most exactly logical. Xenophon, his disciple, a man who knew the world, and who afterwards sacrificed to the wind, during the retreat of the ten thousand, took Socrates by the sleeve, and said to him: "Your discourse is admirable; you have spoken better than an oracle; and you are lost. One of these good people to whom you speak is a butcher, who sells sheep and geese for sacrifices; and the other a goldsmith, who profits by making little gods of silver and brass for women. They will accuse you of being a blasphemer, who would diminish their trade. They will depose against you to Melitus and Anitus, your enemies, who have resolved upon your ruin. Have a care of hemlock; your familiar spirit should have warned you not to say to a butcher and a goldsmith what you should say only to Plato and Xenophon."

Some time after, the enemies of Socrates caused him to be condemned by the council of five hundred. He had two hundred and twenty voices in his favor, by which it may be presumed that there were two hundred and twenty philosophers in this tribunal; but it shows that, in all companies, the number of philosophers is always the minority.

Socrates therefore drank hemlock, for having spoken in favor of the unity of God; and the Athenians afterward consecrated a temple to Socrates—to him who disputed against all temples dedicated to inferior beings.

STATES, GOVERNMENT

The details of all forms of government have recently been subjected to close study. Tell me then, you who have traveled, in what state, under what sort of government would you choose to be born. I imagine that a great land-owning lord in France would not be vexed if he were to be born in Germany; for there he would be sovereign instead of subject. A peer of France would be happy to have the privileges of the English peerage; for then he would be a legislator. The lawyer and the financier, however, are better off in France than elsewhere.

But what country would a wise, free man, a man of moderate fortune, and without prejudices, choose?

A member of the government of Pondicherry, a fairly

learned man, returned to Europe overland with a Brahmin better educated than the ordinary Brahmin. "What do you think of the government of the Great Mogul?" asked the councilor.

"I think it abominable," answered the Brahmin. "How can you expect a state to be happily governed by the Tartars? Our rajahs, our omrahs, our nabobs, are well enough pleased, but the citizens are quite the contrary, and millions of citizens are not to be ignored."

Discoursing philosophically, the councilor and the Brahmin traversed the whole of Upper Asia. "I notice," said the Brahmin, "that there is not one republic in all this vast part of the world."

"Formerly there was the republic of Tyre," said the councilor, "but it did not last long; and there was still another in the direction of Arabia Petrea, in a little corner called Palestine—if one can honor with the name of republic a horde of thieves and usurers, who sometimes governed by judges, sometimes by a species of kings, sometimes by grand-pontiffs; a people who were enslaved seven or eight times, and finally driven out of the country which they had usurped."

"I imagine," said the Brahmin, "that one is likely to find very few republics on the earth. Men are rarely worthy of governing themselves. This happiness to be enjoyed only by little peoples who hide themselves in islands, or among the mountains, like rabbits who shun carnivorous beasts. But, in the long run, they are bound to be discovered and devoured."

When the two travelers reached Asia Minor, the councilor said to the Brahmin: "Would you believe that a republic was once established in a corner of Italy, which lasted more than five hundred years, and which ruled over Asia Minor, Asia, Africa, Greece, Gaul, Spain, and the whole of Italy?"

"She soon became a monarchy, then," said the Brahmin.

"You have guessed right," said the other. "But this monarchy fell, and we busy ourselves composing fine dissertations in order to explain the cause of its decadence and downfall."

"You take needless trouble," said the Indian. "This empire fell because it existed. Everything has to fall. I hope as much will happen to the Grand Mogul's empire."

"By the way," said the European, "do you think that there is more honor in a despotic state, and more virtue in a republic?"

The Indian, having had explained to him what we mean by honor, answered that honor was more necessary in a republic, and that virtue was more needed in a monarchy. "For," said he, "a man who is elected by the people, will not be elected if he is dishonored; whereas at court he could easily obtain a place, in accordance with a great prince's maxim, that in order to succeed a courtier should have neither honor nor character. As regards virtue, one must be prodigiously virtuous to dare to speak the truth. The virtuous man is much more at his ease in a republic; he does not have to flatter anyone."

"Do you think," said the European, "that laws and religions are made for climates, just as one has to have furs in Moscow, and thin stuffs in Delhi?"

"Without a doubt," answered the Brahmin. "All the laws which concern material things are calculated for the meridian one lives in. A German needs only one wife, and a Persian three or four.

"The rites of religion are of the same nature. How, if I were Christian, should I say mass in my province where there is neither bread nor wine? As regards dogmas, that is another matter; the climate has nothing to do with them. Did not your religion begin in Asia, whence it was driven out? Does it not exist near the Baltic Sea, where it was unknown?"

"In what state, under what rule, would you like best to live?" asked the councilor.

"Anywhere but where I do live," answered his companion. "And I have met many Siamese, Tonkinese, Persians, and Turks who said the same thing."

"But," persisted the European, "what state would you choose?"

The Brahmin answered, "The state where only the laws are obeyed."

"That is an old answer," said the councilor.

"It is none the worse for that," said the Brahmin.

"Where is that country?" asked the councilor.

"We must look for it," answered the Brahmin.

SUPERSTITION

The superstitious man is to the rogue what the slave is to the tyrant. Further, the superstitious man is governed by the fanatic and becomes a fanatic. Superstition born in paganism, and adopted by Judaism, invested the Christian Church from the earliest times. All the fathers of the Church, without exception, believed in the power of magic. The Church always condemned magic, but she always believed in it: she did not excommunicate sorcerers as madmen who were mistaken, but as men who were really in communication with the devil.

Today one half of Europe thinks that the other half has long been and still is superstitious. The Protestants regard the relics, the indulgences, the mortifications, the prayers for the dead, the holy water, and almost all the rites of the Roman Church, as evidences of superstitious dementia. Superstition, according to them, consists in taking useless practices for necessary practices. Among the Roman Catholics there are some more enlightened than their ancestors, who have renounced many of these usages formerly considered sacred; and they defend themselves against the others who have retained them, by saying: "They are unimportant, and what is merely unimportant cannot be an evil."

It is difficult to set the limits of superstition. A Frenchman traveling in Italy finds almost everything superstitious, and he is right. The Archbishop of Canterbury maintains that the Archbishop of Paris is superstitious; the Presbyterians direct the same reproach against His Grace of Canterbury, and are in their turn treated as superstitious by the Quakers, who are the most superstitious of all in the eyes of other Christians.

In Christian societies, therefore, no one agrees as to what superstition is. The sect which seems to be the least attacked by this malady of the intelligence is that which has the fewest rites. But if, with few ceremonies, it is still strongly attached to an absurd belief, this absurd belief is equivalent alone to all the superstitious practices observed from the time of Simon the magician to that of Father Gauffridi.

It is therefore clear that it is the fundamentals of the religion of one sect which are considered as superstition by another sect.

The Moslems accuse all Christian societies of it, and are themselves accused. Who will judge this great matter? Will it be reason? But each sect claims to have reason on its side. It will therefore be force which will judge, while awaiting the time when reason can penetrate a sufficient number of heads to disarm force.

Up to what point can statecraft permit superstition

to be destroyed? This is a very thorny question. It is like asking to what depth should one make an incision in a dropsical person, who may die under the operation. It is a matter for the doctor's discretion.

Can there exist a people free from all superstitious prejudices? This is equivalent to asking: Can there exist a nation of philosophers? It is said that there is no superstition in the magistracy of China. It is probable that some day none will remain in the magistracy of a few towns of Europe.

Then the magistrates will stop the superstition of the people from being dangerous. These magistrates' example will not enlighten the mob, but the leading citizens of the middle class will hold the mob in check. There is perhaps not a single riot, a single religious outrage in which the middle classes were not once involved; because these same middle classes were then the mob. But reason and time will have changed them. Their softened manners will soften those of the lowest and most savage populace. We have had striking examples of this in more than one country. In a word, less superstition, less fanaticism; and less fanaticism, less misery.

THEIST

The theist is a man firmly persuaded of the existence of a Supreme Being, as good as He is powerful, who has created all beings that are extensive, vegetative, sentient, and reflective; who perpetuates their species, who punishes crimes without cruelty, and rewards virtuous actions with kindness.

The theist does not know how God punishes, how he protects, how he pardons, for he is not bold enough to flatter himself that he knows how God acts, but he knows that God acts and that He is just. Arguments against Providence do not shake him in his faith, because they are merely great arguments, and not proofs. He submits to this Providence, although he perceives only a few effects and a few signs of this Providence: and—judging of the things he does not see by the things he does see—he considers that this Providence extends to all time and space.

United by this principle with the rest of the universe, he does not embrace any of the sects, all of which contradict one another. His religion is the most ancient and the most widespread, for the simple worship of a God has preceded all the systems of the world. He speaks a language that all peoples understand, while they do not understand one another. He has brothers from Pekin to Cayenne, and he counts all wise men as his brethren. He believes that religion does not consist either in the opinions of an unintelligible metaphysic, or in vain display, but in worship and justice. The doing of good, there is his service; being submissive to God, there is his doctrine. The Mohammedan cries to him: "Have a care if you do not make the pilgrimage to Mecca!" "Woe unto you," says a Recollet, "if you do not make a journey to Our Lady of Loretto!" He laughs at Loretto and at Mecca; but he succors the needy and he defends the oppressed.

TESTICLES

1. This word is scientific, and a trifle obscene: it signifies *little witnesses*. Sixtus V, a Cordelier become pope, declared, by his letter of June 25, 1587, to his nuncio in Spain, that he must unmarry all those who were not possessed of testicles. It seems by this order, which was executed by Philip II, that there were many husbands in Spain deprived of these two organs. But

how could a man, who had been a Cordelier, be ignorant of the fact that the testicles of men are often hidden in the abdomen, and that in that situation they are even more fit for conjugal action? We have beheld in France three brothers of the highest rank, one of whom possessed three, the other only one, while the third possessed no appearance of any, and yet was the most vigorous of the three.

The angelic doctor, who was simply a Jacobin, decides that two testicles are *de essentia matrimonii* (of the essence of marriage): in which opinion he is followed by Ricardus, Scotus, Durandus, and Sylvius. If you are not able to obtain a sight of the pleadings of the advocate Sebastian Rouillard, in 1600, in favor of the testicles of his client, concealed in his abdomen, at least consult the dictionary of Bayle, at the article "Quellenec." You will there discover that the wicked wife of the client of Sebastian Rouillard wished to render her marriage void, on the plea that her husband could not exhibit testicles. The defendant replied, that he had perfectly fulfilled his matrimonial duties. He specified intromission and ejaculation, and offered a repeat performance in the presence of witnesses. The jade replied that this trial was too offensive to her modesty, and was, moreover, superfluous, since the defendant was visibly deprived of testicles, and the gentlemen of the assembly were fully aware that testicles are essential to ejaculation.

I am unacquainted with the result of this process, but I suspect that her husband was non-suited and lost his cause. What induces me to think so is that the same Parliament of Paris, on January 8, 1665, issued a decree, asserting the necessity of two visible testicles, without which marriage was not to be contracted. Had there been any member in the assembly in the situation described, and reduced to the necessity of being a witness, he might have convinced the assembly that it decided without a due knowledge of circumstances. Pontas may be profitably consulted on testicles, as well as upon any other subject. He was a sub-penitentiary, who decided every sort of case, and who sometimes came near to Sanchez.

II. A word or two on hermaphrodites. A prejudice has for a long time crept into the Russian Church, that it is not lawful to say mass without testicles; or, at least, they must be hid in the officiator's pocket. This ancient idea was based on the Council of Nicea which forbade the admission into orders of those who mutilated themselves. The example of Origen, and of certain enthusiasts, was the cause of this prohibition, which was confirmed at the second Council of Arles.

The Greek Church did not exclude from the altar those who had endured the operation of Origen against their own consent. The patriarchs of Constantinople, Nicetas, Ignatius, Photius, and Methodius, were eunuchs. At present this point of discipline seems undecided in the Catholic Church. The most general opinion, however, is that a recognized eunuch who wishes to be ordained must receive a dispensation.

The banishment of eunuchs from the service of the altar appears contrary to the purity and chastity which the service exacts; and certainly eunuchs who confessed pretty boys and girls would be exposed to less temptation. But other reasons of convenience and decorum have determined those who make these laws.

In Leviticus, all corporeal defects are excluded from the service of the altar—the blind, the crooked, the maimed, the lame, the one-eyed, the leper, the scabby, long noses, and short noses. Eunuchs are not spoken of, as there were none among the Jews. Those who acted as eunuchs in the service of their kings were foreigners.

It has been demanded whether an animal, a man for example, can possess at once testicles and ovaries, or the glands which are taken for ovaries, a penis and a clitoris, a foreskin and a vagina; whether, in a word, nature can form true hermaphrodites, and whether or not a hermaphrodite may beget a child upon a woman or be made pregnant by a man. I answer, as usual, that I know nothing about it, nor the ten-thousandth part of what is within the operation of nature. I believe, however, that Europe has never witnessed a genuine hermaphrodite, nor has it indeed produced elephants, zebras, giraffes, ostriches, and many more of the animals which inhabit Asia, Africa, and America. It is hazardous to assert, that because we never beheld a thing, it does not exist.

Examine Cheselden's *Anatomy*, page 34, and you will behold there a very good delineation of an animal man and woman—a Negro man and woman of Angola, which was brought to London in its infancy, and carefully examined by this celebrated surgeon, as much distinguished for his probity as his wisdom. The plate is entitled "Members of an Hermaphrodite Negro, of both Sexes, Aged Twenty-six Years." They are not absolutely perfect, but they exhibit an astonishing mixture of the one and the other.

Cheselden has frequently attested the truth of this prodigy, which, however, may not be so remarkable in some of the countries of Africa. The two sexes are not perfect in this instance; but who can assure us, that other Negroes, or yellow or red natives, are not absolutely male and female? It would be as reasonable to assert that a perfect statue cannot exist, because we have witnessed none without defects. There are insects which possess both sexes; why may there not be human beings similarly endowed? I affirm nothing; God keep me from doing so. I only doubt.

How many things belong to the animal man, in respect to which he must doubt, from his pineal gland to his spleen, the use of which is unknown; and from the principle of his thoughts and sensations to his animal spirits, of which everybody speaks, and which nobody has ever seen.

TOLERANCE

What is tolerance? It is the natural attribute of humanity. We are all formed of weakness and error: let us pardon reciprocally each other's folly. That is the first law of nature.

It is clear that the individual who persecutes a man, his brother, because he is not of the same opinion, is a monster. There is no difficulty here. But the government! But the magistrates! But the princes! How do they treat those whose religion is other than theirs? If they are powerful foreigners, it is certain that a prince will make an alliance with them. François I, most Christian, will unite with Mussulmans against Charles V, most Catholic. François I will give money to the Lutherans of Germany to support them in their revolt against the Emperor; but, in accordance with custom, he will start by having Lutherans burned at home. For political reasons he pays them in Saxony; for political reasons he burns them in Paris. But what happens? Persecutions make proselytes. Soon France will be full of new Protestants. At first they will let themselves be hanged, later they in their turn will hang. There will be civil wars, then will come St. Bartholomew's Eve, and this corner of the world will be worse than all that the ancients and moderns have ever told of hell.

Madmen, who have never been able to worship the God who made you! Miscreants, whom the examples of the learned Chinese, the Parsees, and all the sages have never been able to lead! Monsters, who need superstitions as crows' gizzards need carrion! It has been said before, and it must be said again: if you have two religions in your land, the two will cut each other's throats; but if you have thirty religions, they will dwell in peace. Look at the Great Turk. He governs Guebres, Banians, Greek Christians, Nestorians, Romans. The first who tried to stir up tumult would be impaled; and everyone is at peace.

Of all religions, the Christian is without doubt the one which should inspire tolerance most, although up to now the Christians have been the most intolerant of all men. The Christian Church was divided in its cradle, and was divided even in the persecutions which it sometimes endured under the first emperors. Often the martyr was regarded as an apostate by his brethren, and the Carpocratian Christian expired beneath the sword of the Roman executioners, excommunicated by the Ebionite Christian, while the Ebionite was anathema to the Sabellian.

This horrible discord, which has lasted for so many centuries, is a very striking lesson that we should pardon each other's errors. Discord is the great ill of mankind, and tolerance is the only remedy for it.

There is nobody who does not agree with this truth, whether he meditates soberly in his study, or peaceably examines the truth with his friends. Why then do the same men who in private advocate indulgence, kindness, and justice, rise in public with so much fury against these virtues? Why? Can it be that their own interest is their god, and that they sacrifice everything to this monster which they worship?

I possess a dignity and a power founded on ignorance and credulity; I walk on the heads of the men who lie prostrate at my feet; if they should rise and look me in the face, I am lost; I must bind them to the ground, therefore, with iron chains. Thus have reasoned the men whom centuries of bigotry have made powerful. They have other powerful men beneath them, and these have still others, who all enrich themselves with the spoils of the poor, grow fat on their blood, and laugh at their stupidity. They all detest tolerance, as partisans grown rich at the public expense fear to render their accounts, and as tyrants dread the word liberty. And then, to crown everything, they hire fanatics to cry at the top of their voices: "Respect my master's absurdities, tremble, pay, and keep your mouths shut."

It is thus that a great part of the world was long treated; but today when so many sects make a balance of power, what course shall we take with them? Every sect, as one knows, is a ground of error; there are no sects of geometers, algebraists, arithmeticians, because all the propositions of geometry, algebra, and arithmetic are true. In every other field of knoweldge one may be deceived. What Thomist or Scotist theologian would dare say seriously that he is sure of his case?

If it were permitted to reason consistently in religious matters, it would be clear that we all ought to become Jews, because Jesus Christ our Savior was born a Jew, lived a Jew, died a Jew, and said expressly that he was accomplishing, that he was fulfilling the Jewish religion. But it is clearer still that we ought to be tolerant of one another, because we are all weak, inconsistent, liable to fickleness and error. Shall a reed laid low in the mud by the wind say to a fellow reed fallen in the opposite direction: "Crawl! as I crawl, wretch, or I shall petition that you be torn up by the roots and burned"?

TRUTH

"Pilate therefore said unto him, Art thou a king then? Jesus answered, Thou sayest that I am a king. To this end was I born, and for this cause came I into the world, that I should bear witness unto the truth. Everyone that is of the truth heareth my voice.

"Pilate saith unto Him, What is truth? And when he had said this he went out, etc."

It is a sad thing for the human race that Pilate went out without waiting for the answer; we should know what truth is. Pilate had very little curiosity. The accused led before him says he is king, that he was born to be king; and Pilate does not inquire how these things can be. He is supreme judge in Caesar's name, he has power of life and death; his duty is to probe the sense of these words. He ought to say: "Tell me what you understand by being king. How were you born to be king and to bear witness to the truth? It is maintained that it is hard for truth to reach the ears of kings. I am a judge, and I have always had great trouble in finding it. While your enemies are howling against you outside, give me some information on the point; you will be doing me the greatest service that has ever been done a judge; and I much prefer to learn to recognize truth, than to accede to the Jews' clamorous demand to have you hanged."

Of course, we cannot dare to imagine what the author of all truth would have been able to reply to Pilate.

Would he have said: "Truth is an abstract word which most men use indifferently, in their books and judgments, for error and falsehood?" This definition would have been marvelously appropriate to all makers of systems. Similarly the word "wisdom" is often taken for folly, and "wit" for nonsense.

Humanly speaking, let us define truth, while waiting for a better definition, as *a statement of the facts as they are.*

I suppose that if one had given only six months to teaching Pilate the truths of logic, he would assuredly have made this conclusive syllogism: One must not take away a man's life for simply good morality. Well, the accused man has, even on the showing of his enemies, often preached excellent morality. Therefore he should not be punished with death.

He might have drawn this further argument. My duty is to disperse the riotous assemblage of a seditious people who demand a man's death, unreasonably and without legal form. Very well. This is the exact position of the Jews in this instance; therefore I must drive them away and break up their meeting.

We suppose that Pilate knew arithmetic; hence we will not speak of those forms of truth.

As regards mathematical truths, I think it would have taken at least three years before he could have learned higher geometry. The truths of physics combined with those of geometry would have demanded more than four years. We spend six, ordinarily, in studying theology; but I ask twelve for Pilate, seeing that he was pagan; on the ground that six years would not have been too much for eradicating all his old errors, and six years more would be required to fit him to receive a doctor's hood.

If Pilate had had a well-balanced mind, I should have asked only two years to teach him metaphysical truth; and as metaphysical truth is necessarily allied to moral truth, I flatter myself that in less than nine years he would have become a real scholar and a perfectly virtuous man.

I should then have said to Pilate: Historical truths are merely probabilities. If you fought at the battle of Philippi, that is for you a truth which you know by intuition, by perception. But for us who dwell near the Syrian desert, it is merely a very probable thing, which we know by hearsay. How much hearsay is necessary to form a conviction equal to that of a man who, having seen the thing, can flatter himself that he has a sort of certainty?

He who has heard the thing told by twelve thousand eye-witnesses, has only twelve thousand probabilities, equal to one strong probability, which is not equal to certainty. If you have the thing from only one of these witnesses, you know nothing; you should be skeptical. If the witness is dead, you should be still more skeptical, for you cannot enlighten yourself. If from several witnesses who are dead, you are in the same plight. If from those to whom the witnesses have spoken, your skepticism should increase still more.

From generation to generation skepticism increases, and probability diminishes; and soon probability is reduced to zero.

TYRANNY

One gives the name of tyrant to the sovereign who knows no laws but those of his caprice, who takes his subjects' property, and then mobilizes them to take the property of his neighbors. There are none of these tyrants in Europe.

One distinguishes between the tyranny of one man and that of many. The tyranny of one man is comparable to that of a body which has invaded the rights of other bodies, and which exercises despotism under cover of laws which it has itself corrupted. Nor are there any tyrants of this sort in Europe.

Under which tyranny would you like to live? Under neither, but if I had to choose, I should detest the tyranny of one man less than that of many. A despot always has his good moments; an assembly of despots never. If a tyrant does me an injustice, I can disarm him through his mistress, his confessor, or his page; but a company of solemn tyrants is inaccessible to all seductions. When it is not unjust, it is at the least harsh, and never does it bestow favors.

If I have only one despot, I am quit of him by drawing myself up against a wall when I see him pass, or by bowing low, or by striking the ground with my forehead, according to the custom of the country. But if there is a company of a hundred despots, I may have to repeat this ceremony a hundred times a day, which in the long run can be very annoying if one's hams are not supple. If I have a farm in the neighborhood of one of our nobles, I am wiped out. If I plead against a relation of the relations of one of our noblemen, I am ruined. What is to be done? I fear that in this world one must be either hammer or anvil; for it is indeed a lucky man who escapes these alternatives!

Miscellany

One of our great Italian theologians, named Piazza, in his *Dissertation on Paradise*, informs us that the elect will forever sing and play the guitar. "They will have," says he, "three privileges, three advantages: gratification without titillation, caresses without laxity, and voluptuousness without excess." St. Thomas assures us that the smell of the glorified bodies will be perfect, and will not be tainted by perspiration. This question has been profoundly treated by many other doctors.

The art of versifying is, indeed, prodigiously difficult, especially in our language where alexandrines follow one another two by two, where it is rare to avoid monotony, where it is absolutely necessary to rhyme, where noble and pleasing rhymes are too limited in number, and where a misplaced word or a harsh syllable is sufficient to spoil a happy thought. It is like dancing in fetters on a rope: but the greatest success in this part of the art is, by itself, nothing.

If none but true and useful things were recorded, our immense historical libraries would be reduced to a very narrow compass; but we should know more and know it better.

Aristophanes—he whom commentators admire because he was a Greek, forgetting that Socrates was also a Greek—Aristophanes was the first who accustomed the Athenians to regard Socrates as an atheist. This comic poet, who is neither comic nor poetical, would not among us have been permitted to exhibit his farces at St. Lawrence's fair. He appears to me to be much lower than Plutarch represents him. Let us see what the wise Plutarch says of this buffoon. "The language of Aristophanes bespeaks his miserable quackery; it is made up of the lowest and most disgusting puns; he is not even pleasing to the people, and to men of judgment and honor he is insupportable; his arrogance is intolerable, and all good men detest his malignity." This, then, is the jack-pudding whom Madame Dacier, an admirer of Socrates, ventures to admire! Such was the man who, indirectly, prepared the poison by which infamous judges put to death the most virtuous man in Greece.

Atheism and fanaticism are two monsters which may tear society in pieces; but the atheist preserves his reason, which checks his propensity to mischief, while the fanatic is under the influence of a madness which is constantly goading him on.

The government of Augustus is still admired, because under him Rome tasted peace, pleasure, and abundance. Seneca says of him: *Clementium non voco lassam crudelitatem*—I do not call exhausted cruelty clemency.

Dedications are often only offerings from interested baseness to disdainful vanity.

Every country where begging, where mendacity, is a profession, is ill-governed.

An almost infallible means of saving yourself from the desire of self-destruction is always to have something to do. Creech, the commentator on Lucretius, marked upon his manuscripts: "N.B. Must hang myself when I have finished." He kept his word with himself, that he might have the pleasure of ending like his author. Had he undertaken a commentary upon Ovid, he would have lived longer.

Money is always to be found when men are to be sent to the frontiers to be destroyed, but when the object is to preserve them it is no longer so.

To succeed in chaining the multitude, you must seem to wear the same fetters.

We shall not extend our views into the depths of theology. God preserve us from such presumption. Humble faith is enough for us. We never assume any other part than that of a mere historian.

Pliny, the naturalist—relying, evidently, on the authority of Flavius Josephus—calls the Essenes, *gens aeterna in quo nemo nascitur*—a perpetual family in which no one is ever born—because the Essenes very rarely married. The description has been since applied to our monks.

History supplies little beyond a list of those who have accommodated themselves with the property of others.

The most beautiful of all emblems is that of God, whom Timaeus of Locris describes under the image of "A circle whose center is everywhere and circumference nowhere."

In metaphysics and in morals, the ancients have said everything. We always encounter or repeat them.

Reasonable enthusiasm is the patrimony of great poets.

Homer never produces tears. The true poet, according to my idea, is he who touches the soul and softens it; others are only fine speakers. I am far from proposing this opinion as a rule. "I give my opinion," says Montaigne, "not as being good, but as being my own."

We will take this opportunity to observe that neither the Jews nor any other people ever thought of fixing persons to the cross by nails; and that there is not even a single instance of it. It is the fiction of some painter, built upon an opinion completely erroneous.

It is very likely that the more ancient fables, in the style of those attributed to Aesop, were invented by the first subjugated people. Free men would not have had occasion to disguise the truth; a tyrant can scarcely be spoken to except in parables; and at present, even this is a dangerous liberty.

What is faith? Is it to believe that which is evident? No. It is perfectly evident to my mind that there exists a necessary, eternal, supreme, and intelligent being. This is no matter of faith, but of reason. I have no merit in thinking that this eternal and infinite being, whom I consider as virtue, as goodness itself, is desirous that I should be good and virtuous. Faith consists in believing not what seems true, but what seems false to our understanding.

Let us ever discriminate between fable and truth, and keep our minds in the same subjection with respect to whatever surprises and astonishes us, as with respect to whatever appears perfectly conformable to their circumscribed and narrow views.

It is a great evil to be a heretic; but is it a great good to maintain orthodoxy by soldiers and executioners? Would it not be better that every man should eat his bread in peace under the shade of his own fig tree? I suggest so bold a proposition with fear and trembling.

If you are desirous to prevent the overrunning of a state by any sect, show it toleration.

Enthusiasm is not always the companion of total ignorance, it is often that of erroneous information.

What would constitute useful history? That which should teach us our duties and our rights, without appearing to teach them.

All certainty which does not consist in mathematical demonstration is nothing more than the highest probability; there is no other historical certainty.

But we may say with respect to rules for writing history, as of those for all the intellectual arts—there are many precepts, but few masters.

If you are desirous of obtaining a great name, of becoming the founder of a sect or establishment, be completely mad; but be sure that your madness corresponds with the turn and temper of your age. Have in your madness reason enough to guide your extravagances; and do not forget to be excessively opinionated and obstinate. It is certainly possible that you may get hanged; but if you escape hanging, you will have altars erected to you.

It is far better to be silent than merely to increase the quantity of bad books.

I never was in Judaea, thank God! and I never will go there. I have met with men of all nations who have returned from it, and they have all of them told me that the situation of Jerusalem is horrible; that all the land round it is stony; that the mountains are bare; that the famous river Jordan is not more than forty feet wide; that the only good spot in the country is Jericho; in short, they all spoke of it as St. Jerome did, who resided a long time in Bethlehem, and describes the country as the refuse and rubbish of nature.

From Titus Livius to de Thou, inclusively, all historians have been infected with prodigies.

But where are the men to be found who will dare to speak out?

Laws have proceeded, in almost every state, from the interest of the legislator, from the urgency of the moment, from ignorance, and from superstition, and have accordingly been made at random, and irregularly, just as cities have been built. . . . It was only after London had been reduced to ashes that it became fit to live in. The streets, after that catastrophe, were widened and straightened. If you are desirous of having good laws, burn those which you have at present, and make fresh ones.

We have seen that man in general, one with another, or (as it is expressed) on the average, does not live above two-and-twenty years; and during these two-and-twenty years he is liable to two-and-twenty thousand evils, many of which are incurable. Yet even in this dreadful state men still strut and pose on the stage of life; they make love at the risk of destruction, intrigue, carry on war, and form projects, just as if they were to live in luxury and happiness for a thousand ages.

More than half the habitable world is still peopled with two-footed animals, who live in the horrible state approaching pure nature, existing and clothing themselves with difficulty, scarcely enjoying the gift of speech, scarcely perceiving that they are unfortunate, and living and dying almost without knowing it.

Define your terms, you will permit me again to say, or we shall never understand one another.

After being extricated from one slough for a time, mankind is soon plunged into another. To ages of civilization succeed ages of barbarism; that barbarism is again expelled and again reappears: it is the regular alternation of day and night.

In general, the art of government consists in taking as much money as possible from one part of the citizens to give it to the other.

Let each of us boldly and honestly say: How little it is that I really know!

There is but one morality, as there is but one geometry.

It requires ages to destroy a popular opinion.

The origin of evil has always been an abyss, the depth of which no one has been able to sound.

Let us place at the end of every chapter of metaphysics the two letters used by the Roman judges when they did not understand a pleading. N L.—*non liquet*—it is not clear.

Nothing is so common as to imitate the practice of enemies, and to use their weapons.

St. Augustine was the first who brought this strange notion [original sin] into credit: a notion worthy of the warm and romantic brain of an African debauchee and penitent, a Manichaean and Christian, tolerant and a persecutor—who passed his life in perpetual self-contradiction.

The Epistles of St. Paul are so sublime that it is often difficult to understand them.

I believe that there never was a creator of a philosophical system who did not confess at the end of his life that he had wasted his time. It must be admitted that the inventors of the mechanical arts have been much more useful to men than the inventors of syllogisms. He who imagined a ship, towers considerably above him who imagined innate ideas.

One merit of poetry few persons will deny: it says more, and in fewer words, than prose.

In every author let us distinguish the man from his works. Racine wrote like Virgil, but he became a Jansenist through weakness; and he died as the result of no less remarkable a weakness—because a man, passing through a gallery, did not give him a glance. I am very sorry for all this; but it does not make the part of Phaedra any the less admirable.

When a country possesses a great number of idlers, you may be sure that it is well populated; for these idlers are lodged, clothed, fed, amused, and respected by those who work. The principal object, however, is not to possess a superfluity of men, but to render such as we have as little unhappy as possible.

Pleasantry when it requires explanation ceases to be pleasantry, and a commentator on *bon mots* is seldom capable of conveying them.

Dr. Swift is Rabelais sober, and living in good company.

It is with books as with the fires in our grates: everybody borrows a light from his neighbor to kindle his own, which is in turn communicated to others, and each partakes of all.

Every chief of a philosophical sect has been something of a quack, but the greatest of all have been those who have aspired to govern. Cromwell was the most terrible of all quacks, and appeared precisely at the time when he could succeed. Under Elizabeth he would have been hanged; under Charles II, laughed at. Fortunately for himself he came at a time when people were disgusted with kings; his son followed, when they were weary of protectors.

The progress of rivers to the sea is not as rapid as that of man to error.

I have taken St. Thomas of Didymus for my patron saint, who always insisted on an examination with his own hands.

The necessity of saying something, the embarrassment produced by the consciousness of having nothing to say.

and the desire to exhibit ability, are three things sufficient to render even a great man ridiculous.

We hold the Jews in horror, and we insist that all which has been written by them, and collected by us, bears the stamp of Divinity. There never was so palpable a contradiction.

Sors tua mortalis, non est mortale quod optas.—Mortal thy fate, thy wishes those of gods.

I will say, in the spirit of the wise Locke: Philosophy consists in stopping when the torch of physical science fails us.

Thus goes the world under the empire of fortune, which is nothing but necessity, insurmountable fatality. *Fortuna saevo laeta negatio.* She makes us blindly play her terrible game, and we never see beneath the cards.

The true charter of liberty is independence, maintained by force.

We should say to every individual: "Remember thy dignity as a man."

Man is not born wicked: he becomes so, as he becomes sick.

We learn more from the single experiments of the Abbé Nollet than from all the philosophical works of antiquity.

Translation by H. I. Woolf

Candide

CHAPTER I

How Candide Was Brought Up in a Noble Castle and How He Was Expelled from the Same

IN THE castle of Baron Thunder-ten-tronckh in Westphalia there lived a youth, endowed by Nature with the most gentle character. His face was the expression of his soul. His judgment was quite honest and he was extremely simple-minded; and this was the reason, I think, that he was named Candide. Old servants in the house suspected that he was the son of the Baron's sister and a decent honest gentleman of the neighborhood, whom this young lady would never marry because he could only prove seventy-one quarterings, and the rest of his genealogical tree was lost, owing to the injuries of time. The Baron was one of the most powerful lords in Westphalia, for his castle possessed a door and windows. His Great Hall was even decorated with a piece of tapestry. The dogs in his stableyards formed a pack of hounds when necessary; his grooms were his huntsmen; the village curate was his Grand Almoner. They all called him "My Lord," and laughed heartily at his stories. The Baroness weighed about three hundred and fifty pounds, was therefore greatly respected, and did the honors of the house with a dignity which rendered her still more respectable. Her daughter Cunegonde, aged seventeen, was rosy-cheeked, fresh, plump and tempting. The Baron's son appeared in every respect worthy of his father. The tutor Pangloss was the oracle of the house, and little Candide followed his lessons with all the candor of his age and character. Pangloss taught metaphysico-theologo-cosmolonigology. He proved admirably that there is no effect without a cause and that in this best of all possible worlds, My Lord the Baron's castle was the best of castles and his wife the best of all possible Baronesses. " 'Tis demonstrated," said he, "that things cannot be otherwise; for, since everything is made for an end, everything is necessarily for the best end. Observe that noses were made to wear spectacles; and so we have spectacles. Legs were visibly instituted to be breeched, and we have breeches. Stones were formed to be quarried and to build castles; and My Lord has a very noble castle; the greatest Baron in the province should have the best house; and as pigs were made to be eaten, we eat pork all the year round; consequently, those who have asserted that all is well talk nonsense; they ought to have said that all is for the best." Candide listened attentively and believed innocently; for he thought Mademoiselle Cunegonde extremely beautiful, although he was never bold enough to tell her so. He decided that after the happiness of being born Baron of Thunder-ten-tronckh, the second degree of happiness was to be Mademoiselle Cunegonde; the third, to see her every day; and the fourth to listen to Doctor Pangloss, the greatest philosopher of the province and therefore of the whole world. One day when Cunegonde was walking near the castle, in a little wood which was called The Park, she observed Doctor Pangloss in the bushes, giving a lesson in experimental physics to her mother's waiting-maid, a very pretty and docile brunette. Mademoiselle Cunegonde had a great inclination for science and watched breathlessly the reiterated experiments she witnessed; she observed clearly the Doctor's sufficient reason, the effects and the causes, and returned home very much excited, pensive, filled with the desire of learning, reflecting that she might be the sufficient reason of young Candide and that he might be hers. On her way back to the castle she met Candide and blushed; Candide also blushed. She bade him good morning in a hesitating voice; Candide replied without knowing what he was saying. Next day, when they left the table after dinner, Cunegonde and Candide found themselves behind a screen; Cunegonde dropped her handkerchief, Candide picked it up; she innocently held his hand; the young man innocently kissed the young lady's hand with remarkable vivacity, tenderness and grace; their lips met, their eyes sparkled, their knees trembled, their hands wandered. Baron Thunder-ten-tronckh passed near the screen, and, observing this cause and effect, expelled Candide from the castle by kicking him in the backside frequently and hard. Cunegonde swooned; when she recovered her senses, the Baroness slapped her in the face; and all was in consternation in the noblest and most agreeable of all possible castles.

CHAPTER II

What Happened to Candide Among the Bulgarians

Candide, expelled from the earthly paradise, wandered for a long time without knowing where he was going, turning up his eyes to Heaven, gazing back frequently at the noblest of castles which held the most beautiful of young Baronesses; he lay down to sleep supperless between two furrows in the open fields; it snowed heavily in large flakes. The next morning the shivering Candide, penniless, dying of cold and exhaustion, dragged himself toward the neighboring town, which was called Waldberghoff-trarbk-dikdorff. He halted sadly at the door of an inn. Two men dressed in blue noticed him. "Comrade," said one, "there's a well-built young man of the right height." They went up to Candide and very civilly invited him to dinner. "Gentlemen," said Candide with charming modesty, "you do me a great honor, but I have no money to pay my share." "Ah, sir," said one of the men in blue, "persons of your figure and merit never pay anything; are you not five feet five tall?" "Yes, gentlemen," said he, bowing, "that is my height." "Ah, sir, come to table; we will not only pay your expenses, we will never allow a man like you to be short of money; men were only made to help each other." "You are in the right," said Candide, "that is what Doctor Pangloss was always telling me, and I see that everything is for the best." They begged him to accept a few crowns, he took them and wished to give them an I O U; they refused to take it and all sat down to table. "Do you not love tenderly . . ." "Oh, yes," said he. "I love Mademoiselle Cunegonde tenderly." "No," said one of the gentlemen. "We were asking if you do not tenderly love the King of the Bulgarians." "Not a bit," said he, "for I have never seen him." "What! He is the most charming of Kings, and you must drink his health." "Oh, gladly, gentlemen." And he drank. "That is sufficient," he was told. "You are now the support, the aid, the defender, the hero of the Bulgarians; your fortune is made and your glory assured." They immediately put irons on his legs and took him to a regiment. He was made to turn to the right and left, to raise the ramrod and return the ramrod, to take aim, to fire, to double up, and he was given thirty strokes with a stick; the next day he drilled not quite so badly, and received only twenty strokes; the day after, he only had ten and was looked on as a prodigy by his comrades. Candide was completely mystified and could not make out how he was a hero. One fine spring day he thought he would take a walk, going straight ahead, in the belief that to use his legs as he pleased was a privilege of the human species as well as of animals. He had not gone two leagues when four other heroes, each six feet tall, fell upon him, bound him and dragged him back to a cell. He was asked by his judges whether he would rather be thrashed thirty-six times by the whole regiment or receive a dozen lead bullets at once in his brain. Although he protested that men's wills are free and that he wanted neither one nor the other, he had to make a choice; by virtue of that gift of God which is called *liberty,* he determined to run the gauntlet thirty-six times and actually did so twice. There were two thousand men in the regiment. That made four thousand strokes which laid bare the muscles and nerves from his neck to his backside. As they were about to proceed to a third turn, Candide, utterly exhausted, begged as a favor that they would be so kind as to smash his head; he obtained this favor; they bound his eyes and he was made to kneel down. At that moment the King of the Bulgarians came by and inquired the victim's crime; and as this King was possessed of a vast genius, he perceived from what he learned about Candide that he was a young metaphysician very ignorant in worldly matters, and therefore pardoned him with a clemency which will be praised in all newspapers and all ages. An honest surgeon healed Candide in three weeks with the ointments recommended by Dioscorides.

He had already regained a little skin and could walk when the King of the Bulgarians went to war with the King of the Abares.

CHAPTER III

How Candide Escaped from the Bulgarians and What Became of Him

Nothing could be smarter, more splendid, more brilliant, better drawn up than the two armies. Trumpets, fifes, hautboys, drums, cannons, formed a harmony such as has never been heard even in hell. The cannons first of all laid flat about six thousand men on each side; then the musketry removed from the best of worlds some nine or ten thousand blackguards who infested its surface. The bayonet also was the sufficient reason for the death of some thousands of men. The whole might amount to thirty thousand souls. Candide, who trembled like a philosopher, hid himself as well as he could during this heroic butchery. At last, while the two Kings each commanded a Te Deum in his camp, Candide decided to go elsewhere to reason about effects and causes. He clambered over heaps of dead and dying men and reached a neighboring village, which was in ashes; it was an Abare village which the Bulgarians had burned in accordance with international law. Here, old men dazed with blows watched the dying agonies of their murdered wives who clutched their children to their bleeding breasts; there, disemboweled girls who had been made to satisfy the natural appetites of heroes gasped their last sighs; others, half-burned, begged to be put to death. Brains were scattered on the ground among dismembered arms and legs. Candide fled to another village as fast as he could; it belonged to the Bulgarians, and Abarian heroes had treated it in the same way. Candide, stumbling over quivering limbs or across ruins, at last escaped from the theater of war, carrying a little food in his knapsack, and never forgetting Mademoiselle Cunegonde. His provisions were all gone when he reached Holland; but, having heard that everyone in that country was rich and a Christian, he had no doubt at all but that he would be as well treated as he had been in the Baron's castle before he had been expelled on account of Mademoiselle Cunegonde's pretty eyes. He asked an alms of several grave persons, who all replied that if he continued in that way he would be shut up in a house of correction to teach him how to live. He then addressed himself to a man who had been discoursing on charity in a large assembly for an hour on end. This orator, glancing at him askance, said: "What are you doing here? Are you for a good cause?" "There is no effect without a cause," said Candide modestly. "Everything is necessarily linked up and arranged for the best. It was necessary that I should be expelled from the company of Mademoiselle Cunegonde, that I ran the gauntlet, and that I beg my bread until I can earn it; all this could not have happened differently." "My friend," said the orator, "do you believe that the Pope is Anti-Christ?" "I had never heard so before," said Candide, "but whether he is or isn't, I am starving." "You don't deserve to eat," said the other. "Hence, rascal; hence, you wretch; and never come near me again." The orator's wife thrust her head out of the window and seeing a man who did not believe that the Pope was Anti-Christ, she poured on his head a full . . . O Heavens! To what excess religious zeal is carried by ladies! A man who had not been baptized, an honest Anabaptist named Jacques, saw the cruel and ignominious treatment of one of his brothers, a featherless two-legged creature with a soul; he took him home, cleaned him up, gave him bread and beer, presented him with two florins, and even offered to teach him to work at the manufacture of Persian stuffs which are made in Holland. Candide threw himself at the man's feet, exclaiming: "Doctor Pangloss was right in telling me that all is for the best in this world, for I am vastly more touched by your extreme generosity than by the harshness of the gentleman in the black cloak and his good lady." The next day when he walked out he met a beggar covered with sores, dull-eyed, with the end of his nose fallen away, his mouth awry, his teeth black, who talked huskily, was tormented with a violent cough and spat out a tooth at every cough.

CHAPTER IV

How Candide Met His Old Master in Philosophy, Doctor Pangloss, and What Happened

Candide, moved even more by compassion than by horror, gave this horrible beggar the two florins he had received from the honest Anabaptist, Jacques. The phantom gazed fixedly at him, shed tears and threw its arms round his neck. Candide recoiled in terror. "Alas!" said the wretch to the other wretch, "don't you recognize your dear Pangloss?" "What do I hear? You, my dear master! You, in this horrible state! What misfortune has happened to you? Why are you no longer in the noblest of castles? What has become of Mademoiselle Cunegonde, the pearl of young ladies, the masterpiece of Nature?" "I am exhausted," said Pangloss. Candide immediately took him to the Anabaptist's stable where he gave him a little bread to eat; and when Pangloss had recovered: "Well!" said he, "Cunegonde?" "Dead," replied the other. At this word Candide swooned; his friend restored him to his senses with a little bad vinegar which happened to be in the stable. Candide opened his eyes. "Cunegonde dead! Ah! best of worlds, where are you? But what illness did she die of? Was it because she saw me kicked out of her father's noble castle?" "No," said Pangloss. "She was disemboweled by Bulgarian soldiers, after having been raped to the limit of possibility; they broke the Baron's head when he tried to defend her; the Baroness was cut to pieces; my poor pupil was treated exactly like his sister; and as to the castle, there is not one stone standing on another, not a barn, not a sheep, not a duck, not a tree; but we were well avenged, for the Abares did exactly the same to a neighboring barony which belonged to a Bulgarian Lord." At this, Candide swooned again; but, having recovered and having said all that he ought to say, he inquired the cause and effect, the sufficient reason which had reduced Pangloss to so piteous a state. "Alas!" said Pangloss, " 'tis love; love, the consoler of the human race, the preserver of the universe, the soul of all tender creatures, gentle love." "Alas!" said Candide, "I am acquainted with this love, this sovereign of hearts, this soul of our soul; it has never brought me anything but one kiss and twenty kicks in the backside. How could this beautiful cause produce in you so abominable an effect?" Pangloss replied as follows: "My dear Candide! You remember Paquette, the maid-servant of our august Baroness; in her arms I enjoyed the delights of Paradise which have produced the tortures of Hell by which you see I am devoured; she was infected and perhaps is dead. Paquette received this present from a most learned monk, who had it from the source; for he received it from an old countess, who had it from a cavalry captain, who owed it to a marchioness, who derived it from a page, who had received it from a Jesuit, who, when a novice, had it in a direct line from one of the companions of Christopher Columbus. For my part, I shall not give it to anyone, for I am dying." "O Pangloss!" exclaimed Candide, "this is a strange genealogy! Wasn't the devil at the root of it?" "Not at all," replied that great man. "It was something indispensable in this best of worlds, a necessary ingredient; for, if Columbus in an island of America had not caught this disease, which poisons the source of generation, and often indeed prevents generation, we should not have chocolate and cochineal; it must also be noticed that hitherto in our continent this disease is peculiar to us, like theological disputes. The Turks, the Indians, the Persians, the Chinese, the Siamese and the Japanese are not yet familiar with it; but there is a sufficient reason why they in their turn should become familiar with it in a few centuries. Meanwhile, it has made marvelous progress among us, and especially in those large armies composed of honest, well-bred stipendiaries who decide the destiny of States; it may be asserted that when thirty thousand men fight a pitched battle against an equal number of troops, there are about twenty thousand with the pox on either side." "Admirable!" said Candide. "But you must get cured." "How can I?" said Pangloss. "I haven't a sou, my friend, and in the whole extent of this globe, you cannot be bled or receive an enema without paying or without someone paying for you." This last speech determined Candide; he went and threw himself at the feet of his charitable Anabaptist, Jacques, and drew so touching a picture of the state to which his friend was reduced that the good easy man did not hesitate to succor Pangloss; he had him cured at his own expense. In this cure Pangloss only lost one eye and one ear. He could write well and knew arithmetic perfectly. The Anabaptist made him his bookkeeper. At the end of two months he was compelled to go to Lisbon on business and took his two philosophers on the boat with him. Pangloss explained to him how everything was for the best. Jacques was not of this opinion. "Men," said he, "must have corrupted nature a little, for they were not born wolves, and they have become wolves. God did not give them twenty-four-pounder cannons or bayonets, and they have made bayonets and cannons to destroy each other. I might bring bankruptcies into the account and Justice which seizes the goods of bankrupts in order to deprive the creditors of them." "It was all indispensable," replied the one-eyed doctor, "and private misfortunes make the public good, so that the more private misfortunes there are, the more everything is well." While he was reasoning, the air grew dark, the winds blew from the four quarters of the globe and the ship was attacked by the most horrible tempest in sight of the port of Lisbon.

CHAPTER V

Storm, Shipwreck, Earthquake, and What Happened to Dr. Pangloss, to Candide and the Anabaptist Jacques

Half the enfeebled passengers, suffering from that inconceivable anguish which the rolling of a ship causes in the nerves and in all the humors of bodies shaken in contrary directions, did not retain strength enough even to trouble about the danger. The other half screamed and prayed; the sails were torn, the masts broken, the vessel leaking. Those worked who could, no one cooperated, no one commanded. The Anabaptist tried to help the crew a little; he was on the main deck; a furious sailor struck him violently and stretched him on the deck; but the blow he delivered gave him so violent a shock that he fell head-first out of the ship. He remained hanging and clinging to part of the broken mast. The good Jacques ran to his aid, helped him to climb back, and from the effort he made was flung into the sea in full view of the sailor, who allowed him to drown without condescending even to look at him. Candide came up, saw his benefactor reappear for a moment and then be engulfed for ever. He tried to throw himself after him into the sea; he was prevented by the philosopher Pangloss, who proved to him that the Lisbon roads had been expressly created for the Anabaptist to be drowned in them. While he was proving this *a priori,* the vessel sank, and everyone perished except Pangloss, Candide and the brutal sailor who had drowned the virtuous Anabaptist; the blackguard swam successfully to the shore and Pangloss and Candide were carried there on a plank. When they had recovered a little, they walked toward Lisbon; they had a little money by the help of which they hoped to be saved from hunger after having escaped the storm. Weeping the death of their benefactor, they had scarcely set foot in the town when they felt the earth tremble under their feet; the sea rose in foaming masses in the port and smashed the ships which rode at anchor. Whirlwinds of flame and ashes covered the streets and squares; the houses collapsed, the roofs were thrown upon the foundations, and the foundations were scattered; thirty thousand inhabitants of every age and both sexes were crushed under the ruins. Whistling and swearing, the sailor said: "There'll be something to pick up here." "What can be the sufficient reason for this phenomenon?" said Pangloss. "It is the last day!" cried Candide. The sailor immediately ran among the debris, dared death to find money, found it, seized it, got drunk, and having slept off his wine, purchased the favors of the first woman of good-will he met on the ruins of the houses and among the dead and dying. Pangloss, however, pulled him by the sleeve. "My friend," said he, "this is not well, you are disregarding universal reason, you choose the wrong time." "Blood and 'ounds!" he retorted, "I am a sailor and I was born in Batavia; four times have I stamped on the crucifix during four voyages to Japan; you have found the right man for your universal reason!" Candide had been hurt by some falling stones; he lay in the street covered with debris. He said to Pangloss: "Alas! Get me a little wine and oil; I am dying." "This earthquake is not a new thing," replied Pangloss. "The town of Lima felt the same shocks in America last year; similar causes produce similar effects; there must certainly be a train of sulphur underground from Lima to Lisbon." "Nothing is more probable," replied Candide; "but, for God's sake, a little oil and wine." "What do you mean, probable?" replied the philosopher; "I maintain that it is proved." Candide lost consciousness, and Pangloss brought him a little water from a neighboring fountain. Next day they found a little food as they wandered among the ruins and regained a little strength. Afterward they worked like others to help the inhabitants who had escaped death. Some citizens they had assisted gave them as good a dinner as could be expected in such a disaster; true, it was a dreary meal; the hosts watered their bread with their tears, but Pangloss consoled them by assuring them that things could not be otherwise. "For," said he, "all this is for the best; for, if there is a volcano at Lisbon, it cannot be anywhere else; for it is impossible that things should not be where they are; for all is well." A little, dark man, a familiar of the Inquisition, who sat beside him, politely took up the conversation, and said: "Apparently, you do not believe in original sin; for, if everything is for the best, there was neither fall nor punishment." "I most humbly beg your excellency's pardon," replied Pangloss still more politely, "for the fall of man and the curse necessarily entered into the best of all possible worlds." "Then you do not believe in free-will?" said the familiar. "Your excellency will pardon me," said Pangloss; "free-will can exist with absolute necessity; for it was necessary that we should be free; for in short, limited will . . ." Pangloss was in the middle of his phrase when the familiar nodded to his armed attendant who was pouring out port or Oporto wine for him.

CHAPTER VI

How a Splendid Auto-da-Fé Was Held to Prevent Earthquakes, and How Candide Was Flogged

After the earthquake which destroyed three-quarters of Lisbon, the wise men of that country could discover no more efficacious way of preventing a total ruin than by giving the people a splendid *auto-da-fé*. It was decided by the university of Coimbre that the sight of several persons being slowly burned in great ceremony is an infallible secret for preventing earthquakes. Consequently they had arrested a Biscayan convicted of having married his fellow-godmother, and two Portuguese who, when eating a chicken, had thrown away the bacon; after dinner they came and bound Dr. Pangloss and his disciple Candide, one because he had spoken and the other because he had listened with an air of approbation; they were both carried separately to extremely cool apartments, where there was never any discomfort from the sun; a week afterward each was dressed in a sanbenito and their heads were ornamented with paper mitres; Candide's mitre and sanbenito were painted with flames upside down and with devils who had neither tails nor claws; but Pangloss's devils had claws and tails, and his flames were upright. Dressed in this manner they marched in procession and listened to a most pathetic sermon, followed by lovely plain-song music. Candide was flogged in time to the music, while the singing went on; the Biscayan and the two men who had not wanted to eat bacon were burned, and Pangloss was hanged, although this is not the custom. The very same day, the earth shook again with a terrible clamour. Candide, terrified, dumbfounded, bewildered, covered with blood, quivering from head to foot, said to himself: "If this is the best of all possible worlds, what are the others? Let it pass that I was flogged, for I was flogged by the Bulgarians, but, O my dear Pangloss! The greatest of philosophers! Must I see you hanged without knowing why! O my dear Anabaptist! The best of men! Was it necessary that you should be drowned in port! O Mademoiselle Cunegonde! The pearl of women! Was it necessary that your belly should be slit!" He was returning, scarcely able to support himself, preached at, flogged, absolved and blessed, when an old woman accosted him and said: "Courage, my son, follow me."

CHAPTER VII

How an Old Woman Took Care of Candide and How He Regained That Which he Loved

Candide did not take courage, but he followed the old woman to a hovel; she gave him a pot of ointment to rub on, and left him food and drink; she pointed out a fairly clean bed; near the bed there was a suit of clothes. "Eat, drink, sleep," said she, "and may our Lady of Atocha, my Lord Saint Anthony of Padua and my Lord Saint James of Compostella take care of you; I shall come back tomorrow." Candide, still amazed by all he had seen, by all he had suffered, and still more by the old woman's charity, tried to kiss her hand. " 'Tis not my hand you should kiss," said the old woman, "I shall come back tomorrow. Rub on the ointment, eat and sleep." In spite of all his misfortune, Candide ate and went to sleep. Next day the old woman brought him breakfast, examined his back and smeared him with another ointment; later she brought him dinner, and returned in the evening with supper. The next day she went through the same ceremony. "Who are you?" Candide kept asking her. "Who has inspired you with so much kindness? How can I thank you?" The good woman never made any reply; she returned in the evening without any supper. "Come with me," said she, "and do not speak a word." She took him by the arm and walked into the country with him for about a quarter of a mile; they came to an isolated house, surrounded with gardens and canals. The old woman knocked at a little door. It was opened; she led Candide up a back stairway into a gilded apartment, left him on a brocaded sofa, shut the door, and went away. Candide thought he was dreaming, and felt that his whole life was a bad dream and the present moment an agreeable dream. The old woman soon reappeared; she was supporting with some difficulty a trembling woman of majestic stature, glittering with precious stones and covered with a veil. "Remove the veil," said the old woman to Candide. The young man advanced and lifted the veil with a timid hand. What a moment! What a surprise! He thought he saw Mademoiselle Cunegonde, in fact he was looking at her, it was she herself. His strength failed him, he could not utter a word and fell at her feet. Cunegonde fell on the sofa. The old woman dosed them with distilled waters; they recovered their senses and began to speak: at first they uttered only broken words, questions and answers at cross purposes, sighs, tears, exclamations. The old woman advised them to make less noise and left them alone. "What! Is it you?" said Candide. "You are alive, and I find you here in Portugal! Then you were not raped? Your belly was not slit, as the philosopher Pangloss assured me?" "Yes, indeed," said the fair Cunegonde; "but those two accidents are not always fatal." "But your father and mother were killed?" " 'Tis only too true," said Cunegonde, weeping. "And your brother?" "My brother was killed too." "And why are you in Portugal? And how did you know I was here? And by what strange adventure have you brought me to this house?" "I will tell you everything," replied the lady, "but first of all you must tell me everything that has happened to you since the innocent kiss you gave me and the kicks you received." Candide obeyed with profound respect; and, although he was bewildered, although his voice was weak and trembling, although his back was still a little painful, he related in the most natural manner all he had endured since the moment of their separation. Cunegonde raised her eyes to heaven; she shed tears at the death of the good Anabaptist and Pangloss, after which she spoke as follows to Candide, who did not miss a word and devoured her with his eyes.

CHAPTER VIII

Cunegonde's Story

"I was fast asleep in bed when it pleased Heaven to send the Bulgarians to our noble castle of Thunder-ten-tronckh; they murdered my father and brother and cut my mother to pieces. A large Bulgarian six feet tall, seeing that I had swooned at the spectacle, began to rape me; this brought me to, I recovered my senses, I screamed, I struggled, I bit, I scratched, I tried to tear out the big Bulgarian's eyes, not knowing that what was happening in my father's castle was a matter of custom; the brute stabbed me with a knife in the left side where I still have the scar." "Alas! I hope I shall see it," said the naïve Candide. "You shall see it," said Cunegonde, "but let me go on." "Go on," said Candide. She took up the thread of her story as follows: "A Bulgarian captain came in, saw me covered with blood, and the soldier did not disturb himself. The captain was angry at the brute's lack of respect to him, and killed him on my body. Afterwards, he had me bandaged and took me to his billet as a prisoner of war. I washed the few shirts he had and did the cooking; I must admit he thought me very pretty; and I will not deny that he was very well built and that his skin was white and soft; otherwise he had little wit and little philosophy; it was plain that he had not been brought up by Dr. Pangloss. At the end of three months he lost all his money and got tired of me; he sold me to a Jew named Don Issachar, who traded in Holland and Portugal and had a passion for women. This Jew devoted himself to my person but he could not triumph over it; I resisted him better than the Bulgarian soldier; a lady of honor may be raped once, but it strengthens her virtue. In order to subdue me, the Jew brought me to this country house. Up till then I believed that there was nothing on earth so splendid as the castle of Thunder-ten-tronckh; I was undeceived. One day the Grand Inquisitor noticed me at Mass; he ogled me continually and sent a message that he wished to speak to me on secret affairs. I was taken to his palace; I informed him of my birth; he pointed out how much it was beneath my rank to belong to an Israelite. A proposition was made on his behalf to Don Issachar to give me up to His Lordship. Don Issachar, who is the court banker and a man of influence, would not agree. The Inquisitor threatened him with an *auto-da-fé*. At last the Jew was frightened and made a bargain whereby the house and I belong to both in common. The Jew has Mondays, Wednesdays and the Sabbath day, and the Inquisitor has the other days of the week. This arrangement has lasted for six months. It has not been without quarrels; for it has often been debated whether the night between Saturday and Sunday belonged to the old law or the new. For my part, I have hitherto resisted them both; and I think that is the reason why they still love me. At last My Lord the Inquisitor was pleased to arrange an *auto-da-fé* to remove the scourge of earthquakes and to intimidate Don Issachar. He honored me with an invitation. I had an excellent seat; and refreshments were served to the ladies between the Mass and the execution. I was indeed horror-stricken when I saw the burning of the two Jews and the honest Biscayan who had married his fellow-godmother; but what was my surprise, my terror, my anguish, when I saw in a sanbenito and under a mitre a face which resembled Pangloss's! I rubbed my eyes, I looked carefully, I saw him hanged; and I fainted.

I had scarcely recovered my senses when I saw you stripped naked; that was the height of horror, of consternation, of grief and despair. I will frankly tell you that your skin is even whiter and of a more perfect tint than that of my Bulgarian captain. This spectacle redoubled all the feelings which crushed and devoured me. I exclaimed, I tried to say: 'Stop, Barbarians!' but my voice failed and my cries would have been useless. When you had been well flogged, I said to myself: 'How does it happen that the charming Candide and the wise Pangloss are in Lisbon, the one to receive a hundred lashes, and the other to be hanged, by order of My Lord the Inquisitor, whose darling I am? Pangloss deceived me cruelly when he said that all is for the best in the world.' I was agitated, distracted, sometimes beside myself and sometimes ready to die of faintness, and my head was filled with the massacre of my father, of my mother, of my brother, the insolence of my horrid Bulgarian soldier, the gash he gave me, my slavery, my life as a kitchen-wench, my Bulgarian captain, my horrid Don Issachar, my abominable Inquisitor, the hanging of Dr. Pangloss, that long plain-song *miserere* during which you were flogged, and above all the kiss I gave you behind the screen that day when I saw you for the last time. I praised God for bringing you back to me through so many trials, I ordered my old woman to take care of you and to bring you here as soon as she could. She has carried out my commission very well; I have enjoyed the inexpressible pleasure of seeing you again, of listening to you, and of speaking to you. You must be very hungry; I have a good appetite; let us begin by having supper." Both sat down to supper; and after supper they returned to the handsome sofa we have already mentioned; they were still there when Signor Don Issachar, one of the masters of the house, arrived. It was the day of the Sabbath. He came to enjoy his rights and to express his tender love.

CHAPTER IX

What Happened to Cunegonde, to Candide, to the Grand Inquisitor and to a Jew

This Issachar was the most choleric Hebrew who had been seen in Israel since the Babylonian captivity. "What!" said he. "Bitch of a Galilean, isn't it enough to have the Inquisitor? Must this scoundrel share with me too?" So saying, he drew a long dagger which he always carried and, thinking that his adversary was unarmed, threw himself upon Candide; but our good Westphalian had received an excellent sword from the old woman along with his suit of clothes. He drew his sword, and although he had a most gentle character, laid the Israelite stone-dead on the floor at the feet of the fair Cunegonde. "Holy Virgin!" she exclaimed, "what will become of us? A man killed in my house! If the police come we are lost." "If Pangloss had not been hanged," said Candide, "he would have given us good advice in this extremity, for he was a great philosopher. In default of him, let us consult the old woman." She was extremely prudent and was beginning to give her advice when another little door opened. It was an hour after midnight, and Sunday was beginning. This day belonged to My Lord the Inquisitor. He came in and saw the flogged Candide sword in hand, a corpse lying on the ground, Cunegonde in terror, and the old woman giving advice. At this moment, here is what happened in Candide's soul and the manner of his reasoning: "If this holy man calls for help, he will infallibly have me burned; he might do as much to Cunegonde; he had me pitilessly lashed; he is my rival; I am in the mood to kill, there is no room for hesitation." His reasoning was clear and swift; and, without giving the Inquisitor time to recover from his surprise, he pierced him through and through and cast him beside the Jew. "Here's another," said Cunegonde, "there is no chance of mercy; we are excommunicated, our last hour has come. How does it happen that you, who were born so mild, should kill a Jew and a prelate in two minutes?" "My dear young lady," replied Candide, "when a man is in love, jealous, and has been flogged by the Inquisition, he is beside himself." The old woman then spoke up and said: "In the stable are three Andalusian horses, with their saddles and bridles; let the brave Candide prepare them; mademoiselle has moidores and diamonds; let us mount quickly, although I can only sit on one buttock, and go to Cadiz; the weather is beautifully fine, and it is most pleasant to travel in the coolness of the night." Candide immediately saddled the three horses. Cunegonde, the old woman and he rode thirty miles without stopping. While they were riding away, the Holy Hermandad arrived at the house; My Lord was buried in a splendid church and Issachar was thrown into a sewer. Candide, Cunegonde and the old woman had already reached the little town of Avacena in the midst of the mountains of the Sierra Morena; and they talked in their inn as follows.

CHAPTER X

How Candide, Cunegonde and the Old Woman Arrived at Cadiz in Great Distress, and How They Embarked

"Who can have stolen my pistoles and my diamonds?" said Cunegonde, weeping. "How shall we live? What shall we do? Where shall we find Inquisitors and Jews to give me others?" "Alas!" said the old woman, "I strongly suspect a reverend Franciscan father who slept in the same inn at Badajoz with us; Heaven forbid that I should judge rashly! But he twice came into our room and left long before we did." "Alas!" said Candide, "the good Pangloss often proved to me that this world's goods are common to all men and that everyone has an equal right to them. According to these principles the monk should have left us enough to continue our journey. Have you nothing left then, my fair Cunegonde?" "Not a maravedi," said she. "What are we to do?" said Candide. "Sell one of the horses," said the old woman. "I will ride postillion behind Mademoiselle Cunegonde, although I can only sit on one buttock, and we will get to Cadiz." In the same hotel there was a Benedictine friar. He bought the horse very cheap. Candide, Cunegonde and the old woman passed through Lucena, Chillas, Lebrixa, and at last reached Cadiz. A fleet was there being equipped and troops were being raised to bring to reason the reverend Jesuit fathers of Paraguay, who were accused of causing the revolt of one of their tribes against the kings of Spain and Portugal near the town of Sacramento. Candide, having served with the Bulgarians, went through the Bulgarian drill before the general of the little army with so much grace, celerity, skill, pride and agility, that he was given the command of an infantry company. He was now a captain; he embarked with Mademoiselle Cunegonde, the old woman, two servants, and the two Andalusian horses which had belonged to the Grand Inquisitor of Portugal. During the voyage they had many discussions about the philosophy of poor Pangloss. "We are going to a new world," said Candide, "and no doubt it is there that everything is for the best; for it must be admitted that one might lament a little over the physical and moral happenings in our own world." "I love you with all my heart," said Cunegonde, "but my soul is still shocked by what I have seen and undergone." "All will be well," replied Candide; "the sea in this new world already is better than the seas of our Europe; it is calmer and the winds are more constant. It is certainly the new world which is the best of all possible worlds." "God grant it!" said Cunegonde, "but I have been so horribly unhappy in mine that my heart is nearly closed to hope." "You complain," said the old woman to them. "Alas! you have not endured such misfortunes as mine." Cunegonde almost laughed and thought it most amusing of the old woman to assert that she was more unfortunate. "Alas! my dear," said she, "unless you have been raped by two Bulgarians, stabbed twice in the belly, have had two castles destroyed, two fathers and mothers murdered before your eyes, and have seen two of your lovers flogged in an *auto-da-fé,* I do not see how you can surpass me; moreover, I was born a Baroness with seventy-two quarterings and I have been a kitchen wench." "You do not know my birth," said the old woman, "and if I showed you my backside you would not talk as you do and you would suspend your judgment." This speech aroused intense curiosity in the minds of Cunegonde and Candide. And the old woman spoke as follows.

CHAPTER XI

The Old Woman's Story

"My eyes were not always bloodshot and red-rimmed; my nose did not always touch my chin and I was not always a servant. I am the daughter of Pope Urban X and the Princess of Palestrina. Until I was fourteen I was brought up in a palace to which all the castles of your German Barons would not have served as stables; and one of my dresses cost more than all the magnificence of Westphalia. I increased in beauty, in grace, in talents, among pleasures, respect and hopes; already I inspired love, my breasts were forming; and what breasts! White, firm, carved like those of the Venus de' Medici. And what eyes! What eyelids! What black eyebrows! What fire shone from my two eyeballs, and dimmed the glitter of the stars, as the local poets pointed out to me. The women who dressed and undressed me fell into ecstasy when they beheld me in front and behind; and all the men would have liked to be in their place. I was betrothed to a ruling prince of Massa-Carrara. What a prince! As beautiful as I was, formed of gentleness and charms, brilliantly witty and burning with love; I loved him with a first love, idolatrously and extravagantly. The marriage ceremonies were arranged with unheard-of pomp and magnificence; there were continual fêtes, revels, and comic operas; all Italy wrote sonnets for me and not a good one among them. I touched the moment of my happiness when an old marchioness who had been my prince's mistress invited him to take chocolate with her; less than two hours afterwards he died in horrible convulsions; but that is only a trifle. My mother was in despair, though less distressed than I, and wished to absent herself for a time from a place so disastrous. She had a most beautiful estate near Gaeta; we embarked on a galley, gilded like the altar of St. Peter's at Rome. A Salle pirate swooped down and boarded us; our soldiers defended us like soldiers of the Pope; they threw down their arms, fell on their knees and asked the pirates for absolution *in articulo mortis.* They were immediately stripped as naked as monkeys and my mother, our ladies of honor, and myself as well. The diligence with which these gentlemen strip people is truly admirable but I was still more surprised by their inserting a finger in a place belonging to all of us where we women usually only allow the end of a syringe. This appeared to me a very strange ceremony; but that is how we judge everything when we leave our own country. I soon learned that it was to find out if we had hidden any diamonds there; 'tis a custom established from time immemorial among the civilized nations who roam the seas. I have learned that the religious Knights of Malta never fail in it when they capture Turks and Turkish women; this is an international law which has never been broken. I will not tell you how hard it is for a young princess to be taken with her mother as a slave to Morocco; you will also guess all we had to endure in the pirates' ship. My mother was still very beautiful; our ladies of honor, even our waiting-maids, possessed more charms than could be found in all Africa; and I was ravishing, I was beauty, grace itself, and I was a virgin; I did not remain so long; the flower which had been reserved for the handsome prince of Massa-Carrara was ravished from me by a pirate captain; he was an abominable Negro who thought he was doing me a great honor. The Princess of Palestrina and I must indeed have been strong to bear up against all we endured before our arrival in Morocco! But let that pass; these things are so common that they are not worth mentioning. Morocco was swimming in blood when we arrived. The fifty sons of the Emperor Muley Ismael had each a faction; and this produced fifty civil wars, of blacks against blacks, browns against browns, mulattoes against mulattoes. There was continual carnage throughout the whole extent of the empire. Scarcely had we landed when the blacks of a party hostile to that of my pirate arrived with the purpose of depriving him of his booty. After the diamonds and the gold, we were the most valuable possessions. I witnessed a fight such as is never seen in your European climates. The blood of the northern peoples is not sufficiently ardent; their madness for women does not reach the point which is common in Africa. The Europeans seem to have milk in their veins; but vitriol and fire flow in the veins of the inhabitants of Mount Atlas and the neighboring countries. They fought with the fury of the lions, tigers and serpents of the country to determine who should have us. A Moor grasped my mother by the right arm, my captain's lieutenant held her by the left arm; a Moorish soldier held one leg and one of our pirates seized the other. In a moment nearly all our women were seized in the same way by four soldiers. My captain kept me hidden behind him; he had a scimitar in his hand and killed everybody who opposed his fury. I saw my mother and all our Italian women torn in pieces, gashed, massacred by the monsters who disputed them. The prisoners, my companions, those who had captured them, soldiers, sailors, blacks, browns, whites, mulattoes and finally my captain were all killed and I remained expiring on a heap of corpses. As everyone knows, such scenes go on in an area of more than three hundred square leagues and yet no one ever fails to recite the five daily prayers ordered by Mohammed. With great difficulty I extricated myself from the bloody heaps of corpses and dragged myself to the foot of a large orange-tree on the bank of a stream; there I fell down with terror, weariness, horror, despair and hunger. Soon afterward, my exhausted senses fell into a sleep which was more like a swoon than repose. I was in this state of weakness and insensibility between life and death when I felt myself oppressed by something which moved on my body. I opened my eyes and saw a white man of good appearance who was sighing and muttering between his teeth: *O che sciagura d'essere senza coglioni!*

CHAPTER XII

Continuation of the Old Woman's Misfortunes

"Amazed and delighted to hear my native language, and not less surprised at the words spoken by this man, I replied that there were greater misfortunes than that of which he complained. In a few words I informed him of the horrors I had undergone and then swooned again. He carried me to a neighboring house, had me put to bed, gave me food, waited on me, consoled me, flattered me, told me he had never seen anyone so beautiful as I, and that he had never so much regretted that which no one could give back to him. 'I was born at Naples,' he said, 'and every year they make two or three thousand children there into capons; some die of it, others acquire voices more beautiful than women's, and others become the governors of States. This operation was performed upon me with very great success and I was a musician in the chapel of the Princess of Palestrina.' 'Of my mother,' I exclaimed. 'Of your mother!' cried he, weeping. 'What! Are you that young princess I brought up to the age of six and who even then gave promise of being as beautiful as you are?' 'I am! my mother is four hundred yards from here, cut into quarters under a heap of corpses . . .' I related all that had happened to me; he also told me his adventures and informed me how he had been sent to the King of Morocco by a Christian power to make a treaty with that monarch whereby he was supplied with powder, cannons, and ships to help to exterminate the commerce of other Christians. 'My mission is accomplished,' said this honest eunuch, 'I am about to embark at Ceuta and I will take you back to Italy. *Ma che sciagura d'essere senza coglioni!*' I thanked him with tears of gratitude; and instead of taking me back to Italy he conducted me to Algiers and sold me to the Dey. I had scarcely been sold when the plague which had gone through Africa, Asia and Europe, broke out furiously in Algiers. You have seen earthquakes; but have you ever seen the plague?" "Never," replied the Baroness. "If you had," replied the old woman, "you would admit that it is much worse than an earthquake. It is very common in Africa; I caught it. Imagine the situation of a Pope's daughter aged fifteen, who in three months had undergone poverty and slavery, had been raped nearly every day, had seen her mother cut into four pieces, had undergone hunger and war, and was now dying of the plague in Algiers. However, I did not die; but my eunuch and the Dey and almost all the seraglio of Algiers perished. When the first ravages of this frightful plague were over, the Dey's slaves were sold. A merchant bought me and carried me to Tunis; he sold me to another merchant who resold me at Tripoli; from Tripoli I was resold to Alexandria, from Alexandria resold to Smyrna, from Smyrna to Constantinople. I was finally bought by an Aga of the Janizaries, who was soon ordered to defend Azov against the Russians who were besieging it. The Aga, who was a man of great gallantry, took his whole seraglio with him, and lodged us in a little fort on the Islands of Palus-Maeotis, guarded by two black eunuchs and twenty soldiers. He killed a prodigious number of Russians but they returned the compliment as well. Azov was given up to fire and blood, neither sex nor age was pardoned; only our little fort remained; and the enemy tried to reduce it by starving us. The twenty Janizaries had sworn never to surrender us. The extremities of hunger to which they were reduced forced them to eat our two eunuchs for fear of breaking their oaths. Some days later they resolved to eat the women. We had with us a most pious and compassionate Imam who delivered a fine sermon to them by which he persuaded them not to kill us altogether. 'Cut,' said he, 'only one buttock from each of these ladies and you will make very good cheer; if you have to return, there will still be as much left in a few days; Heaven will be pleased at so charitable an action and you will be saved.' He was very eloquent and persuaded them. This horrible operation was performed upon us; the Imam anointed us with the same balm that is used for children who have just been circumcized; we were all at the point of death. Scarcely had the Janizaries finished the meal we had supplied when the Russians arrived in flat-bottomed boats; not a Janizary escaped. The Russians paid no attention to the state we were in. There are French doctors everywhere; one of them who was very skillful took care of us; he healed us and I shall remember all my life that, when my wounds were cured, he made propositions to me. For the rest, he told us all to cheer up; he told us that the same thing had happened in several sieges and that it was a law of war. As soon as my companions could walk they were sent to Moscow. I fell to the lot of a Boyar who made me his gardener and gave me twenty lashes a day. But at the end of two years this lord was broken on the wheel with thirty other Boyars owing to some court disturbance, and I profited by this adventure; I fled; I crossed all Russia; for a long time I was servant in an inn at Riga, then at Rostock, at Wismar, at Leipzig, at Cassel, at Utrecht, at Leyden, at The Hague, at Rotterdam; I have grown old in misery and in shame, with only half a backside, always remembering that I was the daughter of a Pope; a hundred times I wanted to kill myself but I still loved life. This ridiculous weakness is perhaps the most disastrous of our inclinations; for is there anything sillier than to desire to bear continually a burden one always wishes to throw on the ground; to look upon oneself with horror and yet to cling to oneself; in short, to caress the serpent which devours us until he has eaten our heart? In the countries it has been my fate to traverse and in the inns where I have served I have seen a prodigious number of people who hated their lives; but I have only seen twelve who voluntarily put an end to their misery: three Negroes, four Englishmen, four Genevans and a German professor named Robeck. I ended up as servant to the Jew, Don Issachar; he placed me in your service, my fair young lady; I attached myself to your fate and have been more occupied with your adventures than with my own. I should never even have spoken of my misfortunes, if you had not piqued me a little and if it had not been the custom on board ship to tell stories to pass the time. In short, Mademoiselle, I have had experience, I know the world; provide yourself with an entertainment, make each passenger tell you his story; and if there is one who has not often cursed his life, who has not often said to himself that he was the most unfortunate of men, throw me head-first into the sea."

CHAPTER XIII

How Candide Was Obliged to Separate from the Fair Cunegonde and the Old Woman

The fair Cunegonde, having heard the old woman's story, treated her with all the politeness due to a person of her rank and merit. She accepted the proposition and persuaded all the passengers one after the other to tell her their adventures. She and Candide admitted that the old woman was right. "It was most unfortunate," said Candide, "that the wise Pangloss was hanged contrary to custom at an *auto-da-fé;* he would have said admirable things about the physical and moral evils which cover the earth and the sea, and I should feel myself strong enough to urge a few objections with all due respect." While each of the passengers was telling his story the ship proceeded on its way. They arrived at Buenos Aires. Cunegonde, Captain Candide and the old woman went to call on the governor, Don Fernando d'Ibaraa y Figueora y Mascarenes y Lampourdos y Souza. This gentleman had the pride befitting a man who owned so many names. He talked to men with a most noble disdain, turning his nose up so far, raising his voice so pitilessly, assuming so imposing a tone, affecting so lofty a carriage, that all who addressed him were tempted to give him a thrashing. He had a furious passion for women. Cunegonde seemed to him the most beautiful woman he had ever seen. The first thing he did was to ask if she were the Captain's wife. The air with which he asked this question alarmed Candide; he did not dare say that she was his wife, because as a matter of fact she was not; he dared not say she was his sister, because she was not that either; and though this official lie was formerly extremely fashionable among the ancients, and might be useful to the moderns, his soul was too pure to depart from truth. "Mademoiselle Cunegonde," said he, "is about to do me the honor of marrying me, and we beg your excellency to be present at the wedding." Don Fernando d'Ibaraa y Figuerora y Mascarenes y Lampourdos y Souza twisted his mustache, smiled bitterly, and ordered Captain Candide to go and inspect his company. Candide obeyed; the governor remained with Mademoiselle Cunegonde. He declared his passion, vowed that the next day he would marry her publicly, or otherwise, as it might please her charms. Cunegonde asked for a quarter of an hour to collect herself, to consult the old woman and to make up her mind. The old woman said to Cunegonde: "You have seventy-two quarterings and you haven't a shilling; it is in your power to be the wife of the greatest Lord in South America, who has an exceedingly fine mustache; is it for you to pride yourself on a rigid fidelity? You have been raped by Bulgarians, a Jew and an Inquisitor have enjoyed your good graces; misfortunes confer certain rights. If I were in your place, I confess I should not have the least scruple in marrying the governor and making Captain Candide's fortune." While the old woman was speaking with all that prudence which comes from age and experience, they saw a small ship come into the harbor; an Alcayde and some Alguazils were on board, and this is what had happened. The old woman had guessed correctly that it was a long-sleeved monk who stole Cunegonde's money and jewels at Badajoz, when she was flying in all haste with Candide. The monk tried to sell some of the gems to a jeweler. The merchant recognized them as the property of the Grand Inquisitor. Before the monk was hanged he confessed that he had stolen them; he described the persons and the direction they were taking. The flight of Cunegonde and Candide was already known. They were followed to Cadiz; without any waste of time a vessel was sent in pursuit of them. The vessel was already in the harbor at Buenos Aires. The rumor spread that an Alcayde was about to land and that he was in pursuit of the murderers of His Lordship the Grand Inquisitor. The prudent old woman saw in a moment what was to be done. "You cannot escape," she said to Cunegonde, "and you have nothing to fear; you did not kill His Lordship; moreover, the governor is in love with you and will not allow you to be maltreated; stay here." She ran to Candide at once. "Fly," said she, "or in an hour's time you will be burned." There was not a moment to lose; but how could he leave Cunegonde and where could he take refuge?

CHAPTER XIV

How Candide and Cacambo Were Received by the Jesuits in Paraguay

Candide had brought from Cadiz a valet of a sort which is very common on the coasts of Spain and in colonies. He was one-quarter Spanish, the child of a half-breed in Tucuman; he had been a choir-boy, a sacristan, a sailor, a monk, a postman, a soldier and a lackey. His name was Cacambo and he loved his master because his master was a very good man. He saddled the two Andalusian horses with all speed. "Come, master, we must follow the old woman's advice; let us be off and ride without looking behind us." Candide shed tears. "O my dear Cunegonde! Must I abandon you just when the governor was about to marry us! Cunegonde, brought here from such a distant land, what will become of you?" "She will become what she can," said Cacambo. "Women never trouble about themselves; God will see to her; let us be off." "Where are you taking me? Where are we going? What shall we do without Cunegonde?" said Candide. "By St. James of Compostella," said Cacambo, "you were going to fight the Jesuits; let us go and fight for them; I know the roads, I will take you to their kingdom, they will be charmed to have a captain who can drill in the Bulgarian fashion; you will make a prodigious fortune; when a man fails in one world, he succeeds in another. 'Tis a very great pleasure to see and do new things." "Then you have been in Paraguay?" said Candide. "Yes, indeed," said Cacambo. "I was servitor in the College of the Assumption, and I know the government of *Los Padres* as well as I know the streets of Cadiz. Their government is a most admirable thing. The kingdom is already more than three hundred leagues in diameter and is divided into thirty provinces. *Los Padres* have everything and the people have nothing; 'tis the masterpiece of reason and justice. For my part, I know nothing so divine as *Los Padres* who here make war on the Kings of Spain and Portugal and in Europe act as their confessors; who here kill Spaniards and at Madrid send them to Heaven; all this delights me; come on; you will be the happiest of men. What a pleasure it will be to *Los Padres* when they know there is coming to them a captain who can drill in the Bulgarian manner!" As soon as they reached the first barrier, Cacambo told the picket that a captain wished to speak to the

Commandant. This information was carried to the main guard. A Paraguayan officer ran to the feet of the Commandant to tell him the news. Candide and Cacambo were disarmed and their two Andalusian horses were taken from them. The two strangers were brought in between two ranks of soldiers; the Commandant was at the end, with a three-cornered hat on his head, his gown tucked up, a sword at his side and a spontoon in his hand. He made a sign and immediately the two newcomers were surrounded by twenty-four soldiers. A sergeant told them that they must wait, that the Commandant could not speak to them, that the reverend provincial father did not allow any Spaniard to open his mouth in his presence or to remain more than three hours in the country. "And where is the reverend provincial father?" said Cacambo. "He is on parade after having said Mass, and you will have to wait three hours before you will be allowed to kiss his spurs." "But," said Cacambo, "the captain who is dying of hunger just as I am, is not a Spaniard but a German; can we not break our fast while we are waiting for his reverence?" The sergeant went at once to inform the Commandant of this. "Blessed be God!" said that lord. "Since he is a German I can speak to him; bring him to my arbor." Candide was immediately taken to a leafy summerhouse decorated with a very pretty colonnade of green marble and gold, and lattices enclosing parrots, hummingbirds, colibris, guinea-hens and many other rare birds. An excellent breakfast stood ready in gold dishes; and while the Paraguayans were eating maize from wooden bowls, out of doors and in the heat of the sun, the reverend father Commandant entered the arbor. He was a very handsome young man, with a full face, a fairly white skin, red cheeks, arched eyebrows, keen eyes, red ears, vermilion lips, a haughty air, but a haughtiness which was neither that of a Spaniard nor of a Jesuit. Candide and Cacambo were given back the arms which had been taken from them and their two Andalusian horses; Cacambo fed them with oats near the arbor, and kept his eye on them for fear of a surprise. Candide first kissed the hem of the Commandant's gown and then they sat down to table. "So you are a German?" said the Jesuit in that language. "Yes, reverend father," said Candide. As they spoke these words they gazed at each other with extreme surprise and an emotion they could not control. "And what part of Germany do you come from?" said the Jesuit. "From the filthy province of Westphalia," said Candide; "I was born in the castle of Thunder-ten-tronckh." "Heavens! Is it possible!" cried the Commandant. "What a miracle!" cried Candide. "Can it be you?" said the Commandant. "'Tis impossible!" said Candide. They both fell over backwards, embraced and shed rivers of tears. "What! Can it be you, reverend father? You, the fair Cunegonde's brother! You, who were killed by the Bulgarians! You, the son of My Lord the Baron! You, a Jesuit in Paraguay! The world is indeed a strange place! O Pangloss! Pangloss! How happy you would have been if you had not been hanged!" The Commandant sent away the Negro slaves and the Paraguayans who were serving wine in goblets of rock-crystal. A thousand times did he thank God and St. Ignatius; he clasped Candide in his arms; their faces were wet with tears. "You would be still more surprised, more touched, more beside yourself," said Candide, "if I were to tell you that Mademoiselle Cunegonde, your sister, whom you thought disemboweled, is in the best of health." "Where?" "In your neighborhood, with the governor of Buenos Aires; and I came to make war on you." Every word they spoke in this long conversation piled marvel on marvel. Their whole souls flew from their tongues, listened in their ears and sparkled in their eyes. As they were Germans, they sat at table for a long time, waiting for the reverend provincial father; and the Commandant spoke as follows to his dear Candide.

CHAPTER XV

How Candide Killed His Dear Cunegonde's Brother

"I shall remember all my life the horrible day when I saw my father and mother killed and my sister raped. When the Bulgarians had gone, my adorable sister could not be found, and my mother, my father and I, two maid-servants and three little murdered boys were placed in a cart to be buried in a Jesuit chapel two leagues from the castle of my fathers. A Jesuit sprinkled us with holy water; it was horribly salt; a few drops fell in my eyes; the father noticed that my eyelids trembled, he put his hand on my heart and felt that it was still beating; I was attended to and at the end of three weeks was as well as if nothing had happened. You know, my dear Candide, that I was a very pretty youth, and I became still prettier; and so the Reverend Father Croust, the Superior of the house, was inspired with a most tender friendship for me; he gave me the dress of a novice and some time afterwards I was sent to Rome. The Father General wished to recruit some young German Jesuits. The sovereigns of Paraguay take as few Spanish Jesuits as they can; they prefer foreigners, whom they think they can control better. The Reverend Father General thought me apt to labor in his vineyard. I set off with a Pole and a Tyrolese. When I arrived I was honored with a subdeaconship and a lieutenancy;

I am now colonel and priest. We shall give the King of Spain's troops a warm reception; I guarantee they will be excommunicated and beaten. Providence has sent you to help us. But is it really true that my dear sister Cunegonde is in the neighborhood with the governor of Buenos Aires?" Candide assured him on oath that nothing could be truer. Their tears began to flow once more. The Baron seemed never to grow tired of embracing Candide; he called him his brother, his savior. "Ah! My dear Candide," said he, "perhaps we shall enter the town together as conquerors and regain my sister Cunegonde." "I desire it above all things," said Candide, "for I meant to marry her and I still hope to do so." "You, insolent wretch!" replied the Baron. "Would you have the impudence to marry my sister who has seventy-two quarterings! I consider you extremely impudent to dare to speak to me of such a foolhardy intention!" Candide, petrified at this speech, replied: "Reverend Father, all the quarterings in the world are of no importance; I rescued your sister from the arms of a Jew and an Inquisitor; she is under considerable obligation to me and wishes to marry me. Dr. Pangloss always said that men are equal and I shall certainly marry her." "We shall see about that, scoundrel!" said the Jesuit Baron of Thunder-ten-tronckh, at the same time hitting him violently in the face with the flat of his sword. Candide promptly drew his own and stuck it up to the hilt in the Jesuit Baron's belly; but, as he drew it forth smoking, he began to weep. "Alas! My God," said he, "I have killed my old master, my friend, my brother-in-law; I am the mildest man in the world and I have already killed three men, two of them priests." Cacambo, who was acting as sentry at the door of the arbor, ran in. "There is nothing left for us but to sell our lives dearly," said his master. "Somebody will certainly come into the arbor and we must die weapon in hand." Cacambo, who had seen this sort of thing before, did not lose his head; he took off the Baron's Jesuit gown, put it on Candide, gave him the dead man's square bonnet, and made him mount a horse. All this was done in the twinkling of an eye. "Let us gallop, master; everyone will take you for a Jesuit carrying orders and we shall have passed the frontiers before they can pursue us." As he spoke these words he started off at full speed and shouted in Spanish: "Way, way for the Reverend Father Colonel . . ."

CHAPTER XVI

What Happened to the Two Travelers with Two Girls, Two Monkeys, and the Savages Called Oreillons

Candide and his valet were past the barriers before anybody in the camp knew of the death of the German Jesuit. The vigilant Cacambo had taken care to fill his saddlebag with bread, chocolate, ham, fruit, and several bottles of wine. On their Andalusian horses they plunged into an unknown country where they found no road. At last a beautiful plain traversed by streams met their eyes. Our two travelers put their horses to grass. Cacambo suggested to his master that they should eat and set the example. "How can you expect me to eat ham," said Candide, "when I have killed the son of My Lord the Baron and find myself condemned never to see the fair Cunegonde again in my life? What is the use of prolonging my miserable days since I must drag them out far from her in remorse and despair? And what will the Journal de Trévoux say?" Speaking thus, he began to eat. The sun was setting. The two wanderers heard faint cries which seemed to be uttered by women.

They could not tell whether these were cries of pain or of joy; but they rose hastily with that alarm and uneasiness caused by everything in an unknown country. These cries came from two completely naked girls who were running gently along the edge of the plain, while two monkeys pursued them and bit their buttocks. Candide was moved to pity; he had learned to shoot among the Bulgarians and could have brought down a nut from a tree without touching the leaves. He raised his double-barreled Spanish gun, fired, and killed the two monkeys. "God be praised, my dear Cacambo, I have delivered these two poor creatures from a great danger; if I committed a sin by killing an Inquisitor and a Jesuit, I have atoned for it by saving the lives of these two girls. Perhaps they are young ladies of quality and this adventure may be of great advantage to us in this country." He was going on, but his tongue clove to the roof of his mouth when he saw the two girls tenderly kissing the two monkeys, shedding tears on their bodies and filling the air with the most piteous cries. "I did not expect so much human kindliness," he said at last to Cacambo, who replied: "You have performed a wonderful masterpiece; you have killed the two lovers of these young ladies." "Their lovers! Can it be possible? You are jesting at me, Cacambo; how can I believe you?" "My dear master," replied Cacambo, "you are always surprised by everything; why should you think it so strange that in some countries there should be monkeys who obtain ladies' favors? They are quarter men, as I am a quarter Spaniard." "Alas!" replied Candide, "I remember to have heard Dr. Pangloss say that similar accidents occurred in the past and that these mixtures produce Aigypans, fauns, and satyrs; that several eminent persons of antiquity have seen them; but I thought they were fables." "You ought now to be convinced that it is true," said Cacambo, "and you see how people behave when they have not received a proper education; the only thing I fear is that these ladies may get us into difficulty." These wise reflections persuaded Candide to leave the plain and to plunge into the woods. He ate supper there with Cacambo and, after having cursed the Inquisitor of Portugal, the governor of Buenos Aires and the Baron, they went to sleep on the moss. When they woke up they found they could not move; the reason was that during the night the Oreillons, the inhabitants of the country, to whom they had been denounced by the two ladies, had bound them with ropes made of bark. They were surrounded by fifty naked Oreillons, armed with arrows, clubs, and stone hatchets. Some were boiling a large cauldron, others were preparing spits and they were all shouting: "Here's a Jesuit, here's a Jesuit! We shall be revenged and have a good dinner; let us eat the Jesuit, let us eat the Jesuit!" "I told you so, my dear master," said Cacambo sadly. "I knew those two girls would play us a dirty trick." Candide perceived the cauldron and the spits and exclaimed: "We are certainly going to be roasted or boiled. Ah! What would Dr. Pangloss say if he saw what the pure state of nature is? All is well, granted; but I confess it is very cruel to have lost Mademoiselle Cunegonde and to be spitted by the Oreillons." Cacambo never lost his head. "Do not despair," he said to the wretched Candide. "I understand a little of their dialect and I will speak to them." "Do not fail," said Candide, "to point out to them the dreadful inhumanity of cooking men and how very unchristian it is." "Gentlemen," said Cacambo, "you mean to eat a Jesuit today? 'Tis a good deed; nothing could be more just than to treat one's enemies in this fashion. Indeed the law of nature teaches us to kill our neighbor and this is how people behave all over the world. If we do not exert the right of eating our neighbor, it is because we have other means of making good cheer; but you have not the same resources as we, and it is certainly better to eat our enemies than to abandon the fruits of victory to ravens and crows. But, gentlemen, you would not wish to eat your friends. You believe you are about to place a Jesuit on the spit, and 'tis your defender, the enemy of your enemies you are about to roast. I was born in your country; the gentleman you see here is my master and, far from being a Jesuit, he has just killed a Jesuit and is wearing his clothes; which is the cause of your mistake. To verify what I say, take his gown, carry it to the first barrier of the kingdom of *Los Padres* and inquire whether my master has not killed a Jesuit officer. It will not take you long and you will have plenty of time to eat us if you find I have lied. But if I have told the truth, you are too well acquainted with the principles of public law, good morals and discipline, not to pardon us." The Oreillons thought this a very reasonable speech; they deputed two of their notables to go with all diligence and find out the truth. The two deputies acquitted themselves of their task like intelligent men and soon returned with the good news. The Oreillons unbound their two prisoners, overwhelmed them with civilities, offered them girls, gave them refreshment, and accompanied them to the frontiers of their dominions, shouting joyfully: "He is not a Jesuit, he is not a Jesuit!" Candide could not cease from wondering at the cause of his deliverance. "What a nation," said he. "What men! What manners! If I had not been so lucky as to stick my sword through the body of Mademoiselle Cunegonde's brother I should infallibly have been eaten. But, after all, there is something good in the pure state of nature, since these people, instead of eating me, offered me a thousand civilities as soon as they knew I was not a Jesuit."

CHAPTER XVII

Arrival of Candide and His Valet in the Country of Eldorado and What They Saw There

When they reached the frontiers of the Oreillons, Cacambo said to Candide: "You see this hemisphere is no better than the other; take my advice, let us go back to Europe by the shortest road." "How can we go back," said Candide, "and where can we go? If I go to my own country, the Bulgarians and the Abares are murdering everybody; if I return to Portugal I shall be burned; if we stay here, we run the risk of being spitted at any moment. But how can I make up my mind to leave that part of the world where Mademoiselle Cunegonde is living?" "Let us go to Cayenne," said Cacambo, "we shall find Frenchmen there, for they go all over the world; they might help us. Perhaps God will have pity on us." It was not easy to go to Cayenne. They knew roughly the direction to take, but mountains, rivers, precipices, brigands, and savages were everywhere terrible obstacles. Their horses died of fatigue; their provisions were exhausted; for a whole month they lived on wild fruits and at last found themselves near a little river fringed with cocoanut-trees which supported their lives and their hopes. Cacambo, who always gave advice as prudent as the old woman's, said to Candide: "We can go no farther, we have walked far enough; I can see an empty canoe in the bank, let us fill it with cocoanuts, get into the little boat and drift with the current; a river always leads to some inhabited place. If we do not find anything pleasant, we shall at least find something new." "Come on then," said Candide, "and let us trust to Providence." They drifted for some leagues between banks which were sometimes flowery, sometimes bare, sometimes flat, sometimes steep. The river continually became wider; finally it disappeared under an arch of frightful rocks which towered up to the very sky. The two travelers were bold enough to trust themselves to the current under this arch. The stream, narrowed between walls, carried them with horrible rapidity and noise. After twenty-four hours they saw daylight again; but their canoe was wrecked on reefs; they had to crawl from rock to rock for a whole league and at last they discovered an immense horizon, bordered by inaccessible mountains. The country was cultivated for pleasure as well as for necessity; everywhere the useful was agreeable. The roads were covered or rather ornamented with carriages of brilliant material and shape, carrying men and women of singular beauty, who were rapidly drawn along by large red sheep whose swiftness surpassed that of the finest horses of Andalusia, Tetuan, and Mequinez. "This country," said Candide, "is better than Westphalia." He landed with Cacambo near the first village he came to. Several children of the village, dressed in torn gold brocade, were playing quoits outside the village. Our two men from the other world amused themselves by looking on; their quoits were large round pieces, yellow, red, and green which shone with peculiar luster. The travelers were curious enough to pick up some of them; they were of gold, emeralds, and rubies, the least of which would have been the greatest ornament in the Mogul's throne. "No doubt," said Cacambo, "these children are the sons of the King of this country playing at quoits." At that moment the village schoolmaster appeared to call them into school. "This," said Candide, "is the tutor of the Royal Family."

The little beggars immediately left their game, abandoning their quoits and everything with which they had been playing. Candide picked them up, ran to the tutor, and presented them to him humbly, giving him to understand by signs that their Royal Highnesses had forgotten their gold and their precious stones. The village schoolmaster smiled, threw them on the ground, gazed for a moment at Candide's face with much surprise and continued on his way. The travelers did not fail to pick up the gold, the rubies and the emeralds. "Where are we?" cried Candide. "The children of the King must be well brought up, since they are taught to despise gold and precious stones." Cacambo was as much surprised as Candide. At last they reached the first house in the village, which was built like a European palace. There were crowds of people round the door and still more inside; very pleasant music could be heard and there was a delicious smell of cooking. Cacambo went up to the door and heard them speaking Peruvian; it was his maternal tongue, for everyone knows that Cacambo was born in a village of Tucuman where nothing else is spoken. "I will act as your interpreter," he said to Candide, "this is an inn, let us enter." Immediately two boys and two girls of the inn, dressed in cloth of gold, whose hair was bound up with ribbons, invited them to sit down to the table d'hôte. They served four soups each garnished with two parrots, a boiled condor which weighed two hundred pounds, two roast monkeys of excellent flavor, three hundred colibris in one dish and six hundred hummingbirds in another, exquisite ragouts and delicious pastries, all in dishes of a sort of rock-crystal. The boys and girls brought several sorts of drinks made of sugar-cane. Most of the guests were merchants and coachmen, all extremely polite, who asked Cacambo a few questions with the most delicate discretion and answered his in a satisfactory manner. When the meal was over, Cacambo, like Candide, thought he could pay the reckoning by throwing on the table two of the large pieces of gold he had picked up; the host and hostess laughed until they had to hold their sides. At last they recovered themselves. "Gentlemen," said the host, "we perceive you are strangers; we are not accustomed to seeing them. Forgive us if we began to laugh when you offered us in payment the stones from our highways. No doubt you have none of the money of this country, but you do not need any to dine here. All the hotels established for the utility of commerce are paid for by the government. You have been ill-entertained here because this is a poor village; but everywhere else you will be received as you deserve to be." Cacambo explained to Candide all that the host had said, and Candide listened in the same admiration and disorder with which his friend Cacambo interpreted. "What can this country be," they said to each other, "which is unknown to the rest of the world and where all nature is so different from ours? Probably it is the country where everything is for the best; for there must be one country of that sort. And, in spite of what Dr. Pangloss said, I often noticed that everything went very ill in Westphalia."

CHAPTER XVIII

What They Saw in the Land of Eldorado

Cacambo informed the host of his curiosity, and the host said: "I am a very ignorant man and am all the better for it; but we have here an old man who has retired from the court and who is the most learned and most communicative man in the kingdom." And he at once took Cacambo to the old man. Candide now played only the second part and accompanied his valet. They entered a very simple house, for the door was only of silver and the paneling of the apartments in gold, but so tastefully carved that the richest decorations did not surpass it. The antechamber indeed was only encrusted with rubies and emeralds; but the order with which everything was arranged atoned for this extreme simplicity. The old man received the two strangers on a sofa padded with colibri feathers, and presented them with drinks in diamond cups; after which he satisfied their curiosity in these words: "I am a hundred and seventy-two years old and I heard from my late father, the King's equerry, the astonishing revolutions of Peru of which he had been on eye-witness. The kingdom where we now are is the ancient country of the Incas, who most imprudently left it to conquer part of the world and were at last destroyed by the Spaniards. The princes of their family who remained in their native country had more wisdom; with the consent of the nation, they ordered that no inhabitants should ever leave our little kingdom, and this it is that has preserved our innocence and our felicity. The Spaniards had some vague knowledge of this country, which they called Eldorado, and about a hundred years ago an Englishman named Raleigh came very near to it; but, since we are surrounded by inaccessible rocks and precipices, we have hitherto been exempt from the rapacity of the nations of Europe who have an inconceivable lust for the pebbles and mud of our land and would kill us to the last man to get possession of them." The conversation was long; it touched upon the form of the government, manners, women, public spectacles and the arts. Finally Candide, who was always interested in metaphysics, asked through Cacambo whether the country had a religion. The old man blushed a little. "How can you doubt it?" said he. "Do you think we are ingrates?" Cacambo humbly asked what was the religion of Eldorado. The old man blushed again. "Can there be two religions?" said he. "We have, I think, the religion of everyone else; we adore God from evening until morning." "Do you adore only one God?" said Cacambo, who continued to act as the interpreter of Candide's doubts. "Manifestly," said the old man, "there are not two or three or four. I must confess that the people of your world ask very extraordinary questions." Candide continued to press the old man with questions; he wished to know how they prayed to God in Eldorado. "We do not pray," said the good and respectable sage, "we have nothing to ask from him; he has given us everything necessary and we continually give him thanks." Candide was curious to see the priests; and asked where they were. The good old man smiled. "My friends," said he, "we are all priests; the King and all the heads of families solemnly sing praises every morning, accompanied by five or six thousand musicians." "What! Have you no monks to teach, to dispute, to govern, to intrigue and to burn people who do not agree with them?" "For that, we should have to become fools," said the old man; "here we are all of the same opinion and do not understand what you mean with your monks." At all this Candide was in an ecstasy and said to himself: "This is very different from Westphalia and the castle of His Lordship the Baron; if our friend Pangloss had seen Eldorado, he would not have said that the castle of Thunder-ten-tronckh was the best of all that exists on the earth; certainly, a man should travel." After this long conversation the good old man ordered a carriage to be harnessed with six sheep and gave the two travelers twelve of his servants to take them to court. "You will excuse me," he said, "if my age deprives me of the honor of accompanying you. The King will receive you in a manner which will not displease you and doubtless you will pardon the customs of the country if any of them disconcert you." Candide and Cacambo entered the carriage; the six sheep galloped off and in less than four hours they reached the King's palace, which was situated at one end of the capital. The portal was two hundred and twenty feet high and a hundred feet wide; it is impossible to describe its material. Anyone can see the prodigious superiority it must have over the pebbles and sand we call *gold* and *gems.* Twenty beautiful maidens of the guard received Candide and Cacambo as they alighted from the carriage, conducted them to the baths and dressed them in robes woven from the down of colibris; after which the principal male and female officers of the Crown led them to his Majesty's apartment through two files of a thousand musicians each, according to the usual custom. As they approached the throne-room, Cacambo asked one of the chief officers how they should behave in his Majesty's presence; whether they should fall on their knees or flat on their faces, whether they should put their hands on their heads or on their backsides; whether they should lick the dust of the throne-room; in a word, what was the ceremony? "The custom," said the chief officer, "is to embrace the King and to kiss him on either cheek." Candide and Cacambo threw their arms round his Majesty's neck; he received them with all imaginable favor and politely asked them to supper. Meanwhile they were carried to see the town, the public buildings rising to the very skies, the marketplaces ornamented with thousands of columns, the fountains of rose-water and of liquors distilled from sugar-cane, which played continually in the public squares paved with precious stones which emitted a perfume like that of cloves and cinnamon. Candide asked to see the law courts; he was told there were none, and that nobody ever went to law. He asked if there were prisons and was told there were none. He was still more surprised and pleased by the palace of sciences, where he saw a gallery two thousand feet long, filled with instruments of mathematics and physics. After they had explored all the afternoon about a thousandth part of the town, they were taken back to the King. Candide sat down to table with his Majesty, his valet Cacambo and several ladies. Never was better cheer, and never was anyone wittier at supper than His Majesty. Cacambo explained the Kings' witty remarks to Candide and even when translated they still appeared witty. Among all the things which amazed Candide, this did not amaze him the least. They enjoyed this hospitality for a month. Candide repeatedly said to Cacambo: "Once again, my friend, it is quite true that the castle where I was born cannot be compared with this country; but then Mademoiselle Cunegonde is not here and you probably have a mistress in Europe. If we remain here, we shall only be like everyone else; but if we return to our own world with only twelve sheep laden with Eldorado pebbles, we shall be richer than all the kings put together; we shall have no more Inquisitors to fear and we can easily regain Mademoiselle Cunegonde." Cacambo agreed with this; it is so pleasant to be on the move, to show off before friends, to make a parade of the things seen on one's travels, that these two happy men resolved to be so no longer and to ask his Majesty's permission to depart. "You are doing a very silly thing," said the King. "I know my country is small; but when we are comfortable anywhere we should stay there; I certainly have not the right to detain foreigners, that is a tyranny which does not exist either in our manners or our laws; all men are free, leave when you please, but the way out is very difficult. It is impossible to ascend the rapid river by which you miraculously came here and which flows under arches of rock. The mountains which surround the whole of my kingdom are ten thousand feet high and are perpendicular like walls; they are more than ten leagues broad, and you can only get down from them by way of precipices. However, since you must go, I will give orders to the directors of machinery to make a machine which will carry you comfortably. When you have been taken to the other side of the mountains, nobody can proceed any farther with you; for my subjects have sworn never to pass this boundary and they are too wise to break their oath. Ask anything else of me you wish." "We ask nothing of your Majesty," said Cacambo, "except a few sheep laden with provisions, pebbles, and the mud of this country." The King laughed. "I cannot understand," said he, "the taste you people of Europe have for our yellow mud; but take as much as you wish, and much good may it do you." He immediately ordered his engineers to make a machine to hoist these two extraordinary men out of his kingdom. Three thousand learned scientists worked at it; it was ready in a fortnight and only cost about twenty million pounds sterling in the money of that country. Candide and Cacambo were placed on the machine; there were two large red sheep saddled and bridled for them to ride on when they had passed the mountains, twenty sumpter sheep laden with provisions, thirty carrying presents of the most curious productions of the country, and fifty laden with gold, precious stones, and diamonds. The King embraced the two vagabonds tenderly. Their departure was a splendid sight and so was the ingenious manner in which they and their sheep were hoisted onto the top of the mountains. The scientists took leave of them after having landed them safely, and Candide's only desire and object was to go and present Mademoiselle Cunegonde with his sheep. "We have sufficient to pay the governor of Buenos Aires," said he, "if Mademoiselle Cunegonde can be bought. Let us go to Cayenne, and take ship, and then we will see what kingdom we will buy."

CHAPTER XIX

What Happened to Them at Surinam and How Candide Made the Acquaintance of Martin

Our two travelers' first day was quite pleasant. They were encouraged by the idea of possessing more treasures than all Asia, Europe, and Africa could collect. Candide in transport carved the name of Cunegonde on the trees. On the second day two of the sheep stuck in a marsh and were swallowed up with their loads; two other sheep died of fatigue a few days later; then seven or eight died of hunger in a desert; several days afterwards others fell off precipices. Finally, after they had traveled for a hundred days, they had only two sheep left. Candide said to Cacambo: "My friend, you see how perishable are the riches of this world; nothing is steadfast but virtue and the happiness of seeing Mademoiselle Cunegonde again." "I admit it," said Cacambo, "but we still have two sheep with more treasures than ever the King of Spain will have, and in the distance I see a town I suspect is Surinam, which belongs to the Dutch. We are at the end of our troubles and the beginning of our happiness." As they drew near the town they came upon a Negro lying on the ground wearing only half his clothes, that is to say, a pair of blue cotton drawers; this poor man had no left leg and no right hand.

"Good heavens!" said Candide to him in Dutch, "what are you doing there, my friend, in that horrible state?" "I am waiting for my master, the famous merchant Monsieur Vanderdendur." "Was it Monsieur Vanderdendur," said Candide, "who treated you in that way?" "Yes, sir," said the Negro, "it is the custom. We are given a pair of cotton drawers twice a year as clothing. When we work in the sugar mills and the grindstone catches our fingers, they cut off the hand; when we try to run away, they cut off a leg. Both these things happened to me. This is the price paid for the sugar you eat in Europe. But when my mother sold me for ten patagons on the coast of Guinea, she said to me: 'My dear child, give thanks to our fetishes, always worship them, and they will make you happy; you have the honor to be a slave of our lords the white men and thereby you have made the fortune of your father and mother.' Alas! I do not know whether I made their fortune, but they certainly did not make mine. Dogs, monkeys, and parrots are a thousand times less miserable than we are; the Dutch fetishes who converted me tell me that we are all of us, whites and blacks, the children of Adam. I am not a genealogist, but if these preachers tell the truth, we are all second cousins. Now, you will admit that no one could treat his relatives in a more horrible way." "O Pangloss!" cried Candide. "This is an abomination you had not guessed; this is too much, in the end I shall have to renounce optimism." "What is optimism?" said Cacambo. "Alas!" said Candide, "it is the mania of maintaining that everything is well when we are wretched." And he shed tears as he looked at his Negro; and he entered Surinam weeping. The first thing they inquired was whether there was any ship in the port which could be sent to Buenos Aires. The person they addressed happened to be a Spanish captain, who offered to strike an honest bargain with them. He arranged to meet them at an inn. Candide and the faithful Cacambo went and waited for him with their two sheep. Candide, who blurted everything out, told the Spaniard all his adventures and confessed that he wanted to elope with Mademoiselle Cunegonde. "I shall certainly not take you to Buenos Aires," said the captain. "I should be hanged and you would, too. The fair Cunegonde is his Lordship's favorite mistress." Candide was thunderstruck; he sobbed for a long time; then he took Cacambo aside. "My dear friend," said he, "this is what you must do. We have each of us in our pockets five or six millions worth of diamonds; you are more skillful than I am; go to Buenos Aires and get Mademoiselle Cunegonde. If the governor makes any difficulties give him a million; if he is still obstinate give him two; you have not killed an Inquisitor so they will not suspect you. I will fit out another ship, I will go and wait for you at Venice; it is a free country where there is nothing to fear from Bulgarians, Abares, Jews, or Inquisitors." Cacambo applauded this wise resolution; he was in despair at leaving a good master who had become his intimate friend; but the pleasure of being useful to him overcame the grief of leaving him. They embraced with tears. Candide urged him not to forget the good old woman. Cacambo set off that very same day; he was a very good man, this Cacambo. Candide remained some time longer at Surinam waiting for another captain to take him to Italy with the two sheep he had left. He engaged servants and bought everything necessary for a long voyage. At last Monsieur Vanderdendur, the owner of a large ship, came to see him. "How much do you want," he asked this man, "to take me straight to Venice with my servants, my baggage, and these two sheep?" The captain asked for ten thousand piastres. Candide did not hesitate. "Oh! Ho!" said the prudent Vanderdendur to himself, "this foreigner gives ten thousand piastres immediately! He must be very rich." He returned a moment afterwards and said he could not sail for less than twenty thousand. "Very well, you shall have them," said Candide. "Whew!" said the merchant to himself, "this man gives twenty thousand piastres as easily as ten thousand." He came back again, and said he could not take him to Venice for less than thirty thousand piastres. "Then you shall have thirty thousand," replied Candide. "Oho!" said the Dutch merchant to himself again, "thirty thousand piastres is nothing to this man; obviously the two sheep are laden with immense treasures; I will not insist any further; first let me make him pay the thirty thousand piastres, and then we will see." Candide sold two little diamonds, the smaller of which was worth more than all the money the captain asked. He paid him in advance. The two sheep were taken on board. Candide followed in a little boat to join the ship which rode at anchor; the captain watched his time, set his sails, and weighed anchor; the wind was favorable. Candide, bewildered and stupefied, soon lost sight of him. "Alas!" he cried, "this is a trick worthy of the old world." He returned to shore, in grief; for he had lost enough to make the fortunes of twenty kings. He went to the Dutch judge; and, as he was rather disturbed, he knocked loudly at the door; he went in, related what had happened, and talked a little louder than he ought to have done. The judge began by fining him ten thousand piastres for the noise he had made; he then listened patiently to him, promised to look into his affair as soon as the merchant returned, and charged him another ten thousand piastres for the expenses of the audience. This behavior reduced Candide to despair; he had indeed endured misfortunes a thousand times more painful; but the calmness of the judge and of the captain who had robbed him, stirred up his bile and plunged him into a black melancholy. The malevolence of men revealed itself to his mind in all its ugliness; he entertained only gloomy ideas. At last a French ship was about to leave for Bordeaux and, since he no longer had any sheep laden with diamonds to put on board, he hired a cabin at a reasonable price and announced throughout the town that he would give the passage, food and two thousand piastres to an honest man who would make the journey with him, on condition that this man was the most unfortunate and the most disgusted with his condition in the whole province. Such a crowd of applicants arrived that a fleet would not have contained them. Candide, wishing to choose among the most likely, picked out twenty persons who seemed reasonably sociable and who all claimed to deserve his preference. He collected them in a tavern and gave them supper, on condition that each took an oath to relate truthfully the story of his life, promising that he would choose the man who seemed to him the most deserving of pity and to have the most cause for being discontented with his condition, and that he would give the others a little money. The sitting lasted until four o'clock in the morning. As Candide listened to their adventures he remembered what the old woman had said on the voyage to Buenos Aires and how she had wagered that there was nobody on the boat who had not experienced very great misfortunes. At each story which was told him, he thought of Pangloss. "This Pangloss," said he, "would have some difficulty in supporting his system. I wish he were here. Certainly, if everything is well, it is only in Eldorado and not in the rest of the world." He finally determined in favor of a poor man of letters who had worked ten years for the booksellers at Amsterdam. He judged that there was no occupation in the world which could more disgust a man. This man of letters, who was also a good man, had been robbed by his wife, beaten by his son, and abandoned by his daughter, who had eloped with a Portuguese. He had just been deprived of a small post on which he depended and the preachers of Surinam were persecuting him because they thought he was a Socinian. It must be admitted that the others were at least as unfortunate as he was; but Candide hoped that this learned man would help to pass the time during the voyage. All his other rivals considered that Candide was doing them a great injustice; but he soothed them down by giving each of them a hundred piastres.

CHAPTER XX

What Happened to Candide and Martin at Sea

So the old man, who was called Martin, embarked with Candide for Bordeaux. Both had seen and suffered much; and if the ship had been sailing from Surinam to Japan by way of the Cape of Good Hope they would have been able to discuss moral and physical evil during the whole voyage. However, Candide had one great advantage over Martin, because he still hoped to see Mademoiselle Cunegonde again, and Martin had nothing to hope for; moreover, he possessed gold and diamonds; and, although he had lost a hundred large red sheep laden with the greatest treasures on earth, although he was still enraged at being robbed by the Dutch captain, yet when he thought of what he still had left in his pockets and when he talked of Cunegonde, especially at the end of a meal, he still inclined toward the system of Pangloss. "But what do you think of all this, Martin?" said he to the man of letters. "What is your view of moral and physical evil?" "Sir," replied Martin, "my priests accused me of being a Socinian; but the truth is I am a Manichaean." "You are poking fun at me," said Candide, "there are no Manichaeans left in the world." "I am one," said Martin. "I don't know what to do about it, but I am unable to think in any other fashion." "You must be possessed by the devil," said Candide. "He takes so great a share in the affairs of this world," said Martin, "that he might well be in me, as he is everywhere else; but I confess that when I consider this globe, or rather this globule, I think that God has abandoned it to some evil creature—always excepting Eldorado. I have never seen a town which did not desire the ruin of the next town, never a family which did not wish to exterminate some other family. Everywhere the weak loathe the powerful before whom they cower and the powerful treat them like flocks of sheep whose wool and flesh are to be sold. A million drilled assassins go from one end of Europe to the other murdering and robbing with discipline in order to earn their bread, because there is no honester occupation; and in the towns which seem to enjoy peace and where the arts flourish, men are devoured by more envy, troubles, and worries than the afflictions of a besieged town. Secret griefs are even more cruel than public miseries. In a word, I have seen so much and endured so much that I have become a Manichaean." "Yet there is some good," replied Candide. "There may be," said Martin, "but I do not know it." In the midst of this dispute they heard the sound of cannon. The noise increased every moment. Everyone took his telescope. About three miles away they saw two ships engaged in battle; and the wind brought them so near the French ship that they had the pleasure of seeing the fight at their ease. At last one of the two ships fired a broadside so accurately and so low down that the other ship began to sink. Candide and Martin distinctly saw a hundred men on the main deck of the sinking ship; they raised their hands to Heaven and uttered frightful shrieks; in a moment all were engulfed. "Well!" said Martin, "that is how men treat each other." "It is certainly true," said Candide, "that there is something diabolical in this affair." As he was speaking, he saw something of a brilliant red swimming near the ship. They launched a boat to see what it could be; it was one of his sheep. Candide felt more joy at recovering this sheep than grief at losing a hundred all laden with large diamonds from Eldorado. The French captain soon perceived that the captain of the remaining ship was a Spaniard and that the sunken ship was a Dutch pirate; the captain was the very same who had robbed Candide. The immense wealth this scoundrel had stolen was swallowed up with him in the sea and only a sheep was saved. "You see," said Candide to Martin, "that crime is sometimes punished; this scoundrel of a Dutch captain has met the fate he deserved." "Yes," said Martin, "but was it necessary that the other passengers on his ship should perish too? God punished the thief, and the devil punished the others." Meanwhile the French and Spanish ships continued on their way and Candide continued his conversation with Martin. They argued for a fortnight and at the end of the fortnight they had got no further than at the beginning. But after all, they talked, they exchanged ideas, they consoled each other. Candide stroked his sheep. "Since I have found you again," said he, "I may very likely find Cunegonde."

CHAPTER XXI

Candide and Martin Approach the Coast of France and Argue

At last they sighted the coast of France. "Have you ever been to France, Monsieur Martin?" said Candide. "Yes," said Martin, "I have traversed several provinces. In some half the inhabitants are crazy, in others they are too artful, in some they are usually quite gentle and stupid, and in others they think they are clever; in all of them the chief occupation is making love, the second scandal-mongering, and the third talking nonsense." "But, Monsieur Martin, have you seen Paris?" "Yes, I have seen Paris; it is a mixture of all the species; it is a chaos, a throng where everybody hunts for pleasure and hardly anybody finds it, at least so far as I could see. I did not stay there long; when I arrived there I was robbed of everything I had by pickpockets at Saint-Germain's fair; they thought I was a thief and I spent a week in prison; after which I became a printer's reader to earn enough to return to Holland on foot. I met the scribbling rabble, the intriguing rabble, and the fanatical rabble. We hear that there are very polite people in the town; I am glad to think so." "For my part, I have not the least curiosity to see France," said Candide. "You can easily guess that when a man has spent a month in Eldorado he cares to see nothing else in the world but Mademoiselle Cunegonde. I shall go and wait for her at Venice; we will go to Italy by way of France; will you come with me?" "Willingly," said Martin. "They say that Venice is only for the Venetian nobles but that foreigners are nevertheless well received when they have plenty of money; I have none, you have plenty, I will follow you anywhere." "Apropos," said Candide, "do you think the earth was originally a sea, as we are assured by that large book belonging to the captain?" "I don't believe it in the least," said Martin, "any more than all the other whimsies we have been pestered with recently!" "But to what end was this world formed?" said Candide. "To infuriate us," replied Martin. "Are you not very much surprised," continued Candide, "by the love those two girls of the country of the Oreillons had for those two monkeys, whose adventure I told you?" "Not in the least," said Martin. "I see nothing strange in their passion; I have seen so many extraordinary things that nothing seems extraordinary to me." "Do you think," said Candide, "that men have always massacred each other, as they do today? Have they always been liars, cheats, traitors, brigands, weak, flighty, cowardly, envious, gluttonous, drunken, grasping, and vicious, bloody, backbiting, debauched, fanatical, hypocritical and silly?" "Do you think," said Martin, "that sparrow-hawks have always eaten the pigeons they came across?" "Yes, of course," said Candide. "Well," said Martin, "if sparrow-hawks have always possessed the same nature, why should you expect men to change theirs?" "Oh!" said Candide, "there is a great difference; free will . . ." Arguing thus, they arrived at Bordeaux.

CHAPTER XXII

What Happened to Candide and Martin in France

Candide remained in Bordeaux only long enough to sell a few Eldorado pebbles and to provide himself with a two-seated post-chaise, for he could no longer get on without his philosopher Martin; but he was very much grieved at having to part with his sheep, which he left with the Academy of Sciences at Bordeaux. The Academy offered as the subject for a prize that year the cause of the redness of the sheep's fleece; and the prize was awarded to a learned man in the North, who proved by A plus B minus C divided by Z that the sheep must be red and die of the sheep-pox. However all the travelers Candide met in taverns on the way said to him: "We are going to Paris." This general eagerness at length made him wish to see that capital; it was not far out of the road to Venice. He entered by the Faubourg Saint-Marceau and thought he was in the ugliest village of Westphalia. Candide had scarcely reached his inn when he was attacked by a slight illness caused by fatigue. As he wore an enormous diamond on his finger, and a prodigiously heavy strongbox had been observed in his train, he immediately had with him two doctors he had not asked for, several intimate friends who would not leave him and two devotees who kept making him broth. Said Martin: "I remember that I was ill too when I first came to Paris; I was very poor; so I had no friends, no devotees, no doctors, and I got well." However, with the aid of medicine and bloodletting, Candide's illness became serious. An inhabitant of the district came and gently asked him for a note payable to bearer in the next world; Candide would have nothing to do with it. The devotees assured him that it was a new fashion; Candide replied that he was not a fashionable man. Martin wanted to throw the inhabitant out the window; the clerk swore that Candide should not be buried; Martin swore that he would bury the clerk if he continued to annoy them. The quarrel became heated; Martin took him by the shoulders and turned him out roughly; this caused a great scandal, and they made an official report on it. Candide got better; and during his convalescence he had very good company to supper with him. They gambled for high stakes. Candide was vastly surprised that he never drew an ace; and Martin was not surprised at all. Among those who did the honors of the town was a little abbé from Périgord, one of those assiduous people who are always alert, always obliging, impudent, fawning, accommodating, always on the lookout for the arrival of foreigners, ready to tell them all the scandals of the town and to procure them pleasures at any price. This abbé took Candide and Martin to the theater. A new tragedy was being played. Candide was seated near several wits. This did not prevent his weeping at perfectly played scenes. One of the argumentative bores near him said during an interval: "You have no business to weep, this is a very bad actress, the actor playing with her is still worse, the play is still worse than the actors; the author does not know a word of Arabic and yet the scene is in Arabia; moreover, he is a man who does not believe in innate ideas; tomorrow I will bring you twenty articles written against him." "Sir," said Candide to the abbé, "how many plays have you in France?" "Five or six thousand," he replied. "That's a lot," said Candide, "and how many good ones are there?" "Fifteen or sixteen," replied the other. "That's a lot," said Martin. Candide was greatly pleased with an actress who took the part of Queen Elizabeth in a rather dull tragedy which is sometimes played. "This actress," said he to Martin, "pleases me very much; she looks rather like Mademoiselle Cunegonde; I should be very glad to pay her my respects." The abbé offered to introduce him to her. Candide, brought up in Germany, asked what was the etiquette, and how queens of England were treated in France. "There is a distinction," said the abbé, "in the provinces we take them to a tavern; in Paris we respect them when they are beautiful and throw them in the public sewer when they are dead." "Queens in the public sewer!" said Candide. "Yes, indeed," said Martin, "the abbé is right; I was in Paris when Mademoiselle Monime departed, as they say, this life; she was refused what people here call the *honors of burial*—that is to say, the honor of rotting with all the beggars of the district in a horrible cemetery; she was buried by herself at the corner of the Rue de Burgoyne; which must have given her extreme pain, for her mind was very lofty." "That was very impolite," said Candide. "What do you expect?" said Martin. "These people are like that. Imagine all possible contradictions and incompatibilities; you will see them in the government, in the law courts, in the churches and the entertainments of this absurd nation." "Is it true that people are always laughing in Paris?" said Candide. "Yes," said the abbé, "but it is with rage in their hearts, for they complain of everything with roars of laughter and they even commit with laughter the most detestable actions." "Who is that fat pig," said Candide, "who said so much ill of the play I cried at so much and of the actors who gave me so much pleasure?" "He is a living evil," replied the abbé, "who earns his living by abusing all plays and all books; he hates anyone who succeeds, as eunuchs hate those who enjoy; he is one of the serpents of literature who feed on filth and venom; he is a scribbler." "What do you mean by a scribbler?" said Candide. "A scribbler of periodical sheets," said the abbé. "A Fréron." Candide, Martin, and the abbé from Périgord talked in this manner on the stairway as they watched everybody going out after the play. "Although I am most anxious to see Mademoiselle Cunegonde again," said Candide, "I should like to sup with Mademoiselle Clairon, for I thought her admirable." The abbé was not the sort of man to know Mademoiselle Clairon, for she saw only good company. "She is engaged this evening," he said, "but I shall have the honor to take you to the house of a lady of quality, and there you will learn as much of Paris as if you had been here for four years." Candide, who was naturally curious, allowed himself to be taken to the lady's house at the far end of the Faubourg Saint-Honoré; they were playing faro; twelve gloomy punters each held a small hand of cards, the foolish register of their misfortunes. The silence was profound, the punters were pale, the banker was uneasy, and the lady of the house, seated beside this pitiless banker, watched with lynx's eyes every double stake, every seven-and-the-go, with which each player marked his cards; she had them unmarked with severe but polite attention, for fear of losing her customers; the lady called herself Marquise de Parolignac. Her fifteen-year-old daughter was among the punters and winked to her to let her know the tricks of the poor people who attempted to repair the cruelties of fate. The abbé from Périgord, Candide, and Martin entered; nobody rose, nobody greeted them, nobody looked at them; everyone was profoundly occupied with the cards. "Her Ladyship, the Baroness of Thunder-ten-tronckh was more civil," said Candide. However the abbé whispered in the ear of the Marquise, who half rose, honored Candide with a gracious smile and Martin with a most noble nod. Candide was given a seat and a hand of cards, and lost fifty thousand francs in two hands; after which they supped very merrily and everyone was surprised that Candide was not more disturbed by his loss. The lackeys said to each other, in the language of lackeys: "He must be an English Milord." The supper was like most suppers in Paris; first there was a silence and then a noise of indistinguishable words, then jokes, most of which were insipid, false news, false arguments, some politics, and a great deal of scandal; there was even some talk of new books. "Have you seen," said the abbé from Périgord, "the novel by Gauchat, the doctor of theology?" "Yes," replied one of the guests, "but I could not finish it. We have a crowd of silly writings, but all of them together do not approach the silliness of Gauchat, doctor of theology. I am so weary of this immensity of detestable books which inundates us that I have taken to faro." "And what do you say about the *Mélanges* by Archdeacon T.?" said the abbé. "Ah!" said Madame de Parolignac, "the tiresome creature! How carefully he tells you what everybody knows! How heavily he discusses what is not worth the trouble of being lightly mentioned! How witlessly he appropriates other people's wit! How he spoils what he steals! How he disgusts me! But he will not disgust me any more; it is enough to have read a few pages by the Archdeacon." There was a man of learning and taste at table who confirmed what the marchioness had said. They then talked of tragedies; the lady asked why there were tragedies which were sometimes played and yet were unreadable. The man of taste explained very clearly how a play might have some interest and hardly any merit; in a few words he proved that it was not sufficient to bring in one or two of the situations which are found in all novels and which always attract the spectators; but that a writer of tragedies must be original without being bizarre, often sublime and always natural, must know the human heart and be able to give it speech, must be a great poet but not let any character in his play appear to be a poet, must know his language perfectly, speak it with purity, with continual harmony and never allow the sense to be spoilt for the sake of the rhyme. "Anyone," he added, "who does not observe all these rules may produce one or two tragedies applauded in the theater, but he will never be ranked among good writers; there are very few good tragedies; some are idylls in well-written and well-rhymed dialogue; some are political arguments which send one to sleep, or repulsive amplifications; others are the dreams of an enthusiast, in a barbarous style, with broken dialogue, long apostrophes to the gods (because he does not know how to speak to men), false maxims, and turgid commonplaces." Candide listened attentively to these remarks and conceived a great idea of the speaker; and, as the marchioness had been careful to place him beside her, he leaned over to her ear and took the liberty of asking her who was the man who talked so well. "He is a man of letters," said the lady, "who does not play cards and is sometimes brought here to supper by the abbé; he has a perfect knowledge of tragedies and books and he has written a tragedy which was hissed and a book of which only one copy has ever been seen outside his bookseller's shop and that was one he gave me." "The great man!" said Candide. "He is another Pangloss." Then, turning to him, Candide said: "Sir, no doubt you think that all is for the best in the physical world and in the moral, and that nothing could be otherwise than as it is?" "Sir," replied the man of letters, "I do not think anything of the sort. I think everything goes awry with us, that nobody knows his rank or his office, nor what he is doing, nor what he ought to do, and that except at supper, which is quite gay and where there appears to be a certain amount of sociability, all the rest of their time is passed in senseless quarrels: Jansenists with Molinists, lawyers with churchmen, men of letters with men of letters, courtiers with courtiers, financiers with the people, wives with husbands, relatives with relatives—'tis an eternal war." Candide replied: "I have seen worse things; but a wise man, who has since had the misfortune to be hanged, taught me that it is all for the best; these are only the shadows in a fair picture." "Your wise man who was hanged was poking fun at the world," said Martin; "and your shadows are horrible stains." "The stains are made by men," said Candide, "and they cannot avoid them." "Then it is not their fault," said Martin. Most of the gamblers, who had not the slightest understanding of this kind of talk, were drinking; Martin argued with the man of letters and Candide told the hostess some of his adventures. After supper the marchioness took Candide into a side room and made him sit down on a sofa. "Well!" said she, "so you are still madly in love with Mademoiselle Cunegonde of Thunder-ten-tronckh?" "Yes, madame," replied Candide. The marchioness replied with a tender smile: "You answer like a young man from Westphalia. A Frenchman would have said: 'It is true that I was in love with Mademoiselle Cunegonde, but when I see you, madame, I fear lest I should cease to love her.' " "Alas! madame," said Candide, "I will answer as you wish." "Your passion for her," said the marchioness, "began by picking up her handkerchief; I want you to pick up my garter." "With all my heart," said Candide; and he picked it up. "But I want you to put it on again," said the lady; and Candide put it on again. "You see," said the lady, "you are a foreigner; I sometimes make my lovers in Paris languish for a fortnight, but I give myself to you the very first night, because one must do the honors of one's country to a young man from Westphalia." The fair lady, having perceived two enormous diamonds on the young foreigner's hands, praised them so sincerely that they passed from Candide's fingers to the fingers of the marchioness. As Candide went home with his abbé from Périgord, he felt some remorse at having been unfaithful to Mademoiselle Cunegonde. The abbé sympathized with his distress; he had only had a small share in the fifty thousand francs Candide had lost at cards and in the value of the two half-given, half-extorted diamonds. His plan was to profit as much as he could from the advantages which his acquaintance with Candide might procure for him. He talked a lot about Cunegonde and Candide told him that he should ask that fair one's forgiveness for his infidelity when he saw her at Venice. The abbé from Périgord redoubled his politeness and civilities and took a tender interest in all Candide said, in all he did, and in all he wished to do. "Then, sir," said he, "you are to meet her at Venice?" "Yes, sir," said Candide, "without fail I must go and meet Mademoiselle Cunegonde there." Then, carried away by the pleasure of talking about the person he loved, he related, as he was accustomed to do, some of his adventures with that illustrious Westphalian lady. "I suppose," said the abbé, "that Mademoiselle Cunegonde has a great deal of wit and that she writes charming letters." "I have never received any from her," said Candide, "for you must know that when I was expelled from the castle because of my love for her, I could not write to her; soon afterwards I heard she was dead, then I found her again and then I lost her, and now I have sent an express messenger to her two thousand five hundred leagues from here and am expecting her reply." The abbé listened attentively and seemed rather meditative. He soon took leave of the two foreigners, after having embraced them tenderly. The next morning when Candide woke up he received a letter composed as follows: "Sir, my dearest lover, I have been ill for a week in this town; I have just heard that you are here. I should fly to your arms if I could stir. I heard that you had passed through Bordeaux; I left the faithful Cacambo and the old woman there and they will soon follow me. The governor of Buenos Aires took everything, but I still have your heart. Come, your presence will restore me to life or will make me die of pleasure." This charming, this unhoped-for letter, transported Candide with inexpressible joy; and the illness of his dear Cunegonde overwhelmed him with grief. Torn between these two sentiments, he took his gold and his diamonds and drove with Martin to the hotel where Mademoiselle Cunegonde was staying. He entered trembling with emotion, his heart beat, his voice was broken; he wanted to open the bed-curtains and to have a light brought. "Do nothing of the sort," said the waiting-maid. "Light would be the death of her." And she quickly drew the curtains. "My dear Cunegonde," said Candide, weeping, "how do you feel? If you cannot see me, at least speak to me." "She cannot speak," said the maid-servant. The lady then extended a plump hand, which Candide watered with his tears and then filled with diamonds, leaving a bag full of gold in the armchair. In the midst of these transports a police officer arrived, followed by the abbé from Périgord and a squad of policemen. "So these are the two suspicious foreigners?" he said. He had them arrested immediately and ordered his bravoes to hale them off to prison. "This is not the way they treat travelers in Eldorado," said Candide. "I am more of a Manichaean than ever," said Martin. "But, sir, where are you taking us?" said Candide. "To the deepest dungeon," said the police officer. Martin, having recovered his coolness, decided that the lady who pretended to be Cunegonde was a cheat, that the abbé from Périgord was a cheat who had abused Candide's innocence with all possible speed, and that the police officer was another cheat of whom they could easily be rid. Rather than expose himself to judicial proceedings, Candide, enlightened by this advice and impatient to see the real Cunegonde again, offered the police officer three little diamonds worth about three thousand pounds each. "Ah! sir," said the man with the ivory stick, "if you had committed all imaginable crimes you would be the most honest man in the world. Three diamonds! Each worth three thousand pounds each! Sir! I would be killed for your sake, instead of taking you to prison. All strangers are arrested here, but trust to me. I have a brother at Dieppe in Normandy, I will take you there; and if you have any diamonds to give him he will take as much care of you as myself." "And why are all strangers arrested?" said Candide. The abbé from Périgord then spoke and said: "It is because a scoundrel from Atrebatum listened to imbecilities; this alone made him commit a parricide, not like that of May 1610, but like that of December 1594, and like several others committed in other years and in other months by other scoundrels who had listened to imbecilities." The police officer then explained what it was all about. "Ah! the monsters!" cried Candide. "What! Can such horrors be in a nation which dances and sings! Can I not leave at once this country where monkeys torment tigers? I have seen bears in my own country; Eldorado is the only place where I have seen men. In God's name, sir, take me to Venice, where I am to wait for Mademoiselle Cunegonde." "I can only take you to Lower Normandy," said the barigel. Immediately he took off their irons, said there had been a mistake, sent his men away, took Candide and Martin to Dieppe, and left them with his brother. There was a small Dutch vessel in the port. With the help of three other diamonds the Norman became the most obliging of men and embarked Candide and his servants in the ship which was about to sail for Portsmouth in England. It was not the road to Venice; but Candide felt as if he had escaped from Hell, and he had every intention of taking the road to Venice at the first opportunity.

CHAPTER XXIII

Candide and Martin Reach the Coast of England; and What They Saw There

"Ah! Pangloss, Pangloss! Ah! Martin, Martin! Ah! my dear Cunegonde! What sort of a world is this?" said Candide on the Dutch ship. "Something very mad and very abominable," replied Martin. "You know England; are the people there as mad as they are in France?" " 'Tis another sort of madness," said Martin. "You know these two nations are at war for a few acres of snow in Canada, and that they are spending more on this fine war than all Canada is worth. It is beyond my poor capacity to tell you whether there are more madmen in one country than in the other; all I know is that in general the people we are going to visit are extremely melancholic." Talking thus, they arrived at Portsmouth. There were multitudes of people on the shore, looking attentively at a rather fat man with his eyes bandaged who was kneeling down on the deck of one of the ships in the fleet; four soldiers placed opposite this man each shot three bullets into his brain in the calmest manner imaginable; and the whole assembly returned home with great satisfaction. "What is all this?" said Candide. "And what Demon exercises his power everywhere?" He asked who was the fat man who had just been killed so ceremoniously. "An admiral," was the reply. "And why kill the admiral?" "Because," he was told, "he did not kill enough people. He fought a battle with a French admiral and it was held that the English admiral was not close enough to him." "But," said Candide, "the French admiral was just as far from the English admiral!" "That is indisputable," was the answer, "but in this country it is a good thing to kill an admiral from time to time to encourage the others." Candide was so bewildered and so shocked by what he saw and heard that he would not even set foot on shore, but bargained with the Dutch captain (even if he had to pay him as much as the Surinam robber) to take him at once to Venice. The captain was ready in two days. They sailed down the coast of France; and passed in sight of Lisbon, at which Candide shuddered. They entered the Straits and the Mediterranean and at last reached Venice. "Praised be God!" said Candide, embracing Martin, "here I shall see the fair Cunegonde again. I trust Cacambo as I would myself. All is well, all goes well, all goes as well as it possibly could."

CHAPTER XXIV

Paquette and Friar Giroflée

As soon as he reached Venice, he inquired for Cacambo in all the taverns, in all the cafés, and of all the ladies of pleasure; and did not find him. Every day he sent out messengers to all ships and boats; but there was no news of Cacambo. "What!" said he to Martin, "I have had time to sail from Surinam to Bordeaux, to go from Bordeaux to Paris, from Paris to Dieppe, from Dieppe to Portsmouth, to sail along the coasts of Portugal and Spain, to cross the Mediterranean, to spend several months at Venice, and the fair Cunegonde has not yet arrived! Instead of her I have met only a jade and an abbé from Périgord! Cunegonde is certainly dead and the only thing left for me is to die too. Ah! It would have been better to stay in the Paradise of Eldorado instead of returning to this accursed Europe. How right you are, my dear Martin! Everything is illusion and calamity!" He fell into a black melancholy and took no part in the opera *à la mode* or in the other carnival amusements; not a lady caused him the least temptation. Martin said: "You are indeed simple-minded to suppose that a half-breed valet with five or six millions in his pocket will go and look for your mistress at the other end of the world and bring her to you at Venice. If he finds her, he will take her for himself; if he does not find her, he will take another. I advise you to forget your valet Cacambo and your mistress Cunegonde." Martin was not consoling. Candide's melancholy increased, and Martin persisted in proving to him that there was little virtue and small happiness in the world except perhaps in Eldorado where nobody could go. While arguing about this important subject and waiting for Cunegonde, Candide noticed a young Theatine monk in the Piazza San Marco, with a girl on his arm. The Theatine looked fresh, plump, and vigorous; his eyes were bright, his air assured, his countenance firm, and his step lofty. The girl was very pretty and was singing; she gazed amorously at her Theatine and every now and then pinched his fat cheeks. "At least you will admit," said Candide to Martin, "that those people are happy. Hitherto I have only found unfortunates in the whole habitable earth, except in Eldorado; but I wager that this girl and the Theatine are very happy creatures." "I wager they are not," said Martin. "We have only to ask them to dinner," said Candide, "and you will see whether I am wrong." He immediately accosted them, paid his respects to them, and invited them to come to his hotel to eat macaroni, Lombardy partridges, and caviar, and to drink Montepulciano, Lacryma Christi, Cyprus, and Samos wine. The young lady blushed, the Theatine accepted the invitation, and the girl followed, looking at Candide with surprise and confusion in her eyes which were filled with a few tears. Scarcely had they entered Candide's room when she said: "What! Monsieur Candide does not recognize Paquette!" At these words Candide, who had not looked at her very closely because he was occupied entirely by Cunegonde, said to her: "Alas! my poor child, so it was you who put Dr. Pangloss into the fine state I saw him in?" "Alas! sir, it was indeed," said Paquette. "I see you have heard all about it. I have heard of the terrible misfortunes which happened to Her Ladyship the Baroness's whole family and to the fair Cunegonde. I swear to you that my fate has been just as sad. I was very innocent when you knew me. A Franciscan friar who was my confessor easily seduced me. The results were dreadful; I was obliged to leave the castle shortly after His Lordship the Baron expelled you by kicking you hard and frequently in the backside. If a famous doctor had not taken pity on me I should have died. For some time I was the doctor's mistress from gratitude to him. His wife, who was madly jealous, beat me every day relentlessly; she was a fury. The doctor was the ugliest of men, and I was the most unhappy of all living creatures at being continually beaten on account of a man I did not love. You know, sir, how dangerous it is for a shrewish woman to be the wife of a doctor. One day, exasperated by his wife's behavior, he gave her some medicine for a little cold and it was so efficacious that she died two hours afterward in horrible convulsions. The lady's relatives brought a criminal prosecution against the husband; he fled and I was put in prison. My innocence would not have saved me if I had not been rather pretty. The judge set me free on condition that he took the doctor's place. I was soon supplanted by a rival, expelled without a penny, and obliged to continue the abominable occupation which to you men seems so amusing and which to us is nothing but an abyss of misery. I came to Venice to practice this profession. Ah! sir, if you could imagine what it is to be forced to caress impartially an old tradesman, a lawyer, a monk, a gondolier, an abbé; to be exposed to every insult and outrage; to be reduced often to borrow a petticoat in order to go and find some disgusting man who will lift it; to be robbed by one of what one has earned with another, to be despoiled by the police, and to contemplate for the future nothing but a dreadful old age, a hospital and a dunghill, you would conclude that I am one of the most unfortunate creatures in the world." Paquette opened her heart in this way to Candide in a side room, in the presence of Martin, who said to Candide: "You see, I have already won half my wager." Friar Giroflée had remained in the dining room, drinking a glass while he waited for dinner. "But," said Candide to Paquette, "when I met you, you looked so gay, so happy; you were singing, you were caressing the Theatine so naturally; you seemed to me to be as happy as you are unfortunate." "Ah! sir," replied Paquette, "that is one more misery of our profession. Yesterday I was robbed and beaten by an officer, and today I must seem to be in a good humor to please a monk." Candide wanted to hear no more; he admitted that Martin was right. They sat down to table with Paquette and the Theatine. The meal was quite amusing and toward the end they were talking with some confidence. "Father," said Candide to the monk, "you seem to me to enjoy a fate which everybody should envy; the flower of health shines on your cheek, your face is radiant with happiness; you have a very pretty girl for your recreation and you appear to be very well pleased with your state of life as a Theatine." "Faith, Sir," said Friar Giroflée, "I wish all the Theatines were at the bottom of the sea. A hundred times I have been tempted to set fire to the monastery and to go and be a Turk. My parents forced me at the age of fifteen to put on this detestable robe, in order that more money might be left to my cursed elder brother, whom God confound! Jealousy, discord, fury, inhabit the monastery. It is true, I have preached a few bad sermons which bring me in a little money, half of which is stolen from me by the prior; the remainder I spend on girls; but when I go back to the monastery in the evening I feel ready to smash my head against the dormitory walls, and all my colleagues are in the same state." Martin turned to Candide and said with his usual calm: "Well, have I not won the whole wager?" Candide gave two thousand piastres to Paquette and a thousand to Friar Giroflée. "I warrant," said he, "that they will be happy with that." "I don't believe it in the very least," said Martin. "Perhaps you will make them still more unhappy with those piastres." "That may be," said Candide, "but I am consoled by one thing; I see that we often meet people we thought we should never meet again; it may very well be that as I met my red sheep and Paquette, I may also meet Cunegonde again." "I hope," said Martin, "that she will one day make you happy; but I doubt it very much." "You are very hard," said Candide. "That's because I have lived," said Martin. "But look at these gondoliers," said Candide, "they sing all day long." "You do not see them at home, with their wives and their brats of children," said Martin. "The Doge has his troubles, the gondoliers have theirs. True, looking at it all round, a gondolier's lot is preferable to a Doge's; but I think the difference so slight that it is not worth examining." "They talk," said Candide, "about Senator Pococurante who lives in that handsome palace on the Brenta and who is hospitable to foreigners. He is supposed to be a man who has never known a grief." "I should like to meet so rare a specimen," said Martin. Candide immediately sent a request to Lord Pococurante for permission to wait upon him next day.

CHAPTER XXV

Visit to the Noble Venetian, Lord Pococurante

Candide and Martin took a gondola and rowed to the noble Pococurante's palace. The gardens were extensive and ornamented with fine marble statues; the architecture of the palace was handsome. The master of this establishment, a very wealthy man of about sixty, received the two visitors very politely but with very little cordiality, which disconcerted Candide but did not displease Martin. Two pretty and neatly dressed girls served them with very frothy chocolate. Candide could not refrain from praising their beauty, their grace, and their skill. "They are quite good creatures," said Senator Pococurante, "and I sometimes make them sleep in my bed, for I am very tired of the ladies of the town, with their coquetries, their jealousies, their quarrels, their humors, their meanness, their pride, their folly, and the sonnets one must write or have written for them; but, after all, I am getting very tired of these two girls." After this collation, Candide was walking in a long gallery and was surprised by the beauty of the pictures. He asked what master had painted the two first. "They are by Raphael," said the Senator. "Some years ago I bought them at a very high price out of mere vanity; I am told they are the finest in Italy, but they give me no pleasure; the color has gone very dark, the faces are not sufficiently rounded and do not stand out enough; the draperies have not the least resemblance to material; in short, whatever they may say, I do not consider them a true imitation of nature. I shall only like a picture when it makes me think it is nature itself; and there are none of that kind. I have a great many pictures, but I never look at them now." While they waited for dinner, Pococurante gave them a concert. Candide thought the music delicious. "This noise," said Pococurante, "is amusing for half an hour; but if it lasts any longer, it wearies everybody although nobody dares to say so. Music nowadays is merely the art of executing difficulties and in the end that which is only difficult ceases to please. Perhaps I should like the opera more, if they had not made it a monster which revolts me. Those who please may go to see bad tragedies set to music, where the scenes are only composed to bring in clumsily two or three ridiculous songs which show off an actress's voice; those who will or can, may swoon with pleasure when they see a eunuch humming the part of Caesar and Cato as he awkwardly treads the boards; for my part, I long ago abandoned such trivialities, which nowadays are the glory of Italy and for which monarchs pay so dearly." Candide demurred a little, but discreetly. Martin entirely agreed with the Senator. They sat down to table and after an excellent dinner went into the library. Candide saw a magnificently bound Homer and complimented the Illustrissimo on his good taste. "That is the book," said he, "which so much delighted the great Pangloss, the greatest philosopher of Germany." "It does not delight me," said Pococurante coldly; "formerly I was made to believe that I took pleasure in reading it; but this continual repetition of battles which are all alike, these gods who are perpetually active and achieve nothing decisive, this Helen who is the cause of the war and yet scarcely an actor in the piece, this Troy which is always besieged and never taken—all bore me extremely. I have sometimes asked learned men if they were as bored as I am by reading it; all who were sincere confessed that the book fell from their hands, but that it must be in every library, as a monument of antiquity, and like those rusty coins which cannot be put into circulation." "Your Excellency has a different opinion of Virgil?" said Candide. "I admit," said Pococurante, "that the second, fourth and sixth books of his Aeneid are excellent, but as for his pious Aeneas and the strong Cloanthes and the faithful Achates and the little Ascanius and the imbecile king Latinus and the middle-class Amata and the insipid Lavinia, I think there could be nothing more frigid and disagreeable. I prefer Tasso and the fantastic tales of Ariosto." "May I venture to ask you, sir," said Candide, "if you do not take great pleasure in reading Horace?" "He has two maxims," said Pococurante, "which might be useful to a man of the world, and which, being compressed in energetic verses, are more easily impressed upon the memory; but I care very little for his Journey to Brundisium, and his description of a Bad Dinner, and the street brawlers' quarrel between—what is his name?—Rupilius, whose words, he says, were full of pus, and another person whose words were all vinegar. I was extremely disgusted with his gross verses against old women and witches; and I cannot see there is any merit in his telling his friend Maecenas that, if he is placed by him among the lyric poets, he will strike the stars with his lofty brow. Fools admire everything in a celebrated author. I only read to please myself, and I only like what suits me." Candide, who had been taught never to judge anything for himself, was greatly surprised by what he heard; and Martin thought Pococurante's way of thinking quite reasonable. "Oh! There is a Cicero," said Candide. "I suppose you are never tired of reading that great man?" "I never read him," replied the Venetian. "What do I care that he pleaded for Rabirius or Cluentius? I have enough cases to judge myself; I could better have endured his philosophical works; but when I saw that he doubted everything, I concluded I knew as much as he and did not need anybody else in order to be ignorant." "Ah! There are eighty volumes of the Proceedings of an Academy of Sciences," exclaimed Martin, "there might be something good in them." "There would be," said Pococurante, "if a single one of the authors of all that rubbish had invented even the art of making pins; but in all those books there is nothing but vain systems and not a single useful thing." "What a lot of plays I see there," said Candide. "Italian, Spanish, and French!" "Yes," said the Senator, "there are three thousand and not three dozen good ones. As for those collections of sermons, which all together are not worth a page of Seneca, and all those large volumes of theology, you may well suppose that they are never opened by me or anybody else." Martin noticed some shelves filled with English books. "I should think," he said, "that a republican would enjoy most of those works written with so much freedom." "Yes," replied Pococurante, "it is good to write as we think; it is the privilege of man. In all Italy, we only write what we do not think; those who inhabit the country of the Caesars and the Antonines dare not have an idea without the permission of a Dominican monk. I should applaud the liberty which inspires Englishmen of genius if passion and party spirit did not corrupt everything estimable in that precious liberty." Candide, in noticing a Milton, asked him if he did not consider that author to be a very great man. "Who?" said Pococurante. "That barbarian who wrote a long commentary on the first chapter of Genesis in ten books of harsh verses? That gross imitator of the Greeks, who disfigures the Creation, and who, while Moses represents the Eternal Being as producing the world by speech, makes the Messiah take a large compass from the heavenly cupboard in order to trace out his work? Should I esteem the man who spoiled Tasso's hell and devil; who disguises Lucifer sometimes as a toad, sometimes as a pigmy; who makes him repeat the same things a hundred times; makes him argue about theology; and imitates seriously Ariosto's comical invention of firearms by making the devils fire a cannon in Heaven? Neither I nor anyone else in Italy could enjoy such wretched extravagances. The marriage of Sin and Death and the snakes which Sin brings forth nauseate any man of delicate taste, and his long description of a hospital would only please a gravedigger. This obscure, bizarre and disgusting poem was despised at its birth; I treat it today as it was treated by its contemporaries in its own country. But then I say what I think, and care very little whether others think as I do." Candide was distressed by these remarks; he respected Homer and rather liked Milton. "Alas?" he whispered to Martin, "I am afraid this man would have a sovereign contempt for our German poets." "There wouldn't be much harm in that," said Martin. "Oh! What a superior man!" said Candide under his breath. "What a great genius this Pococurante is! Nothing can please him." After they had thus reviewed all his books they went down into the garden. Candide praised all its beauties. "I have never met anything more tasteless," said the owner. "We have nothing but gewgaws; but tomorrow I shall begin to plant one on a more noble plan." When the two visitors had taken farewell of his Excellency, Candide said to Martin:

"Now you will admit that he is the happiest of men, for he is superior to everything he possesses." "Do you not see," said Martin, "that he is disgusted with everything he possesses? Plato said long ago that the best stomachs are not those which refuse all food." "But," said Candide, "is there not pleasure in criticizing, in finding faults where other men think they see beauty?" "That is to say," answered Martin, "that there is pleasure in not being pleased." "Oh! Well," said Candide, "then there is no one happy except me—when I see Mademoiselle Cunegonde again." "It is always good to hope," said Martin. However, the days and weeks went by; Cacambo did not return and Candide was so much plunged in grief that he did not even notice that Paquette and Friar Giroflée had not once come to thank him.

CHAPTER XXVI

How Candide and Martin Supped With Six Strangers and Who They Were

One evening when Candide and Martin were going to sit down to table with the strangers who lodged in the same hotel, a man with a face the color of soot came up to him from behind and, taking him by the arm, said: "Get ready to come with us, and do not fail." He turned round and saw Cacambo. Only the sight of Cunegonde could have surprised and pleased him more. He was almost wild with joy. He embraced his dear friend. "Cunegonde is here, of course? Where is she? Take me to her, let me die of joy with her." "Cunegonde is not here," said Cacambo. "She is in Constantinople." "Heavens! In Constantinople! But, were she in China, I would fly to her; let us start at once." "We will start after supper," replied Cacambo. "I cannot tell you any more; I am a slave, and my master is waiting for me; I must go and serve him at table! Do not say anything; eat your supper, and be in readiness." Candide, torn between joy and grief, charmed to see his faithful agent again, amazed to see him a slave, filled with the idea of seeing his mistress again, with turmoil in his heart, agitation in his mind, sat down to table with Martin (who met every strange occurrence with the same calmness), and with six strangers, who had come to spend the Carnival at Venice. Cacambo, who acted as butler to one of the strangers, bent down to his master's head toward the end of the meal and said: "Sire, your Majesty can leave when you wish, the ship is ready." After saying this, Cacambo withdrew. The guests looked at each other with surprise without saying a word, when another servant came up to his master and said: "Sire, your Majesty's post-chaise is at Padua, and the boat is ready." The master made a sign and the servant departed. Once more all the guests looked at each other, and the general surprise was increased twofold. A third servant went up to the third stranger and said: "Sire, believe me, your Majesty cannot remain here any longer; I will prepare everything." And he immediately disappeared. Candide and Martin had no doubt that this was a Carnival masquerade. A fourth servant said to the fourth master: "Your Majesty can leave when you wish." And he went out like the others. The fifth servant spoke similarly to the fifth master. But the sixth servant spoke differently to the sixth stranger who was next to Candide, and said: "Faith, sire, they will not give your Majesty any more credit nor me either, and we may very likely be jailed tonight, both of us; I am going to look to my own affairs, good-by." When the servants had all gone, the six strangers, Candide and Martin remained in profound silence.

At last it was broken by Candide. "Gentlemen," said he, "this is a curious jest. How is it you are all kings? I confess that neither Martin nor I are kings." Cacambo's master then gravely spoke and said in Italian: "I am not jesting, my name is Achmet III. For several years I was Sultan; I dethroned my brother; my nephew dethroned me; they cut off the heads of my viziers; I am ending my days in the old seraglio; my nephew, Sultan Mahmoud, sometimes allows me to travel for my health, and I have come to spend the Carnival at Venice." A young man who sat next to Achmet spoke after him and said: "My name is Ivan; I was Emperor of all the Russias; I was dethroned in my cradle; my father and mother were imprisoned and I was brought up in prison; I sometimes have permission to travel, accompanied by those who guard me, and I have come to spend the Carnival at Venice." The third said: "I am Charles Edward, King of England; my father gave up his rights to the throne to me and I fought a war to assert them; the hearts of eight hundred of my adherents were torn out and dashed in their faces. I have been in prison; I am going to Rome to visit the King, my father, who is dethroned like my grandfather and me; and I have come to spend the Carnival at Venice." The fourth then spoke and said: "I am the King of Poland; the chance of war deprived me of my hereditary states; my father endured the same reverse of fortune; I am resigned to Providence like the Sultan Achmet, the Emperor Ivan and King Charles Edward, to whom God grant long life; and I have come to spend the Carnival at Venice." The fifth said: "I also am the King of Poland; I have lost my kingdom twice; but Providence has given me another state in which I have been able to do more good than all the kings of the Sarmatians together have been ever able to do on the banks of the Vistula; I also am resigned to Providence and I have come to spend the Carnival at Venice." It was now for the sixth monarch to speak. "Gentlemen," said he, "I am not so eminent as you; but I have been a king like anyone else. I am Theodore; I was elected King of Corsica; I have been called Your Majesty and now I am barely called Sir. I have coined money and do not own a farthing; I have had two Secretaries of State and now have scarcely a valet; I have occupied a throne and for a long time lay on straw in a London prison. I am much afraid I shall be treated in the same way here, although I have come, like your Majesties, to spend the Carnival at Venice." The five other kings listened to this speech with a noble compassion. Each of them gave King Theodore twenty sequins to buy clothes and shirts; Candide presented him with a diamond worth two thousand sequins. "Who is this man," said the five kings, "who is able to give a hundred times as much as any of us, and who gives it?" As they were leaving the table, there came to the same hotel four serene highnesses who had also lost their states in the chance of war, and who had come to spend the rest of the Carnival at Venice; but Candide did not even notice these newcomers, he could think of nothing but of going to Constantinople to find his dear Cunegonde.

CHAPTER XXVII

Candide's Voyage to Constantinople

The faithful Cacambo had already spoken to the Turkish captain who was to take Sultan Achmet back to Constantinople and had obtained permission for Candide and Martin to come on board. They both entered this ship after having prostrated themselves before his miserable Highness. On the way, Candide said to Martin: "So we have just supped with six dethroned kings! And among those six kings there was one to whom I gave charity. Perhaps there are many other princes still more unfortunate. Now, I have only lost a hundred sheep and I am hastening to Cunegonde's arms. My dear Martin, once more, Pangloss was right, all is well." "I hope so," said Martin. "But," said Candide, "this is a very singular experience we have just had at Venice. Nobody has ever seen or heard of six dethroned kings supping together in a tavern." " 'Tis no more extraordinary," said Martin, "than most of the things which have happened to us. It is very common for kings to be dethroned; and as to the honor we have had of supping with them, 'tis a trifle not deserving our attention." Scarcely had Candide entered the ship when he threw his arms round the neck of his old valet, of his friend Cacambo. "Well!" said he, "what is Cunegonde doing? Is she still a marvel of beauty? Does she still love me? How is she? Of course you have bought her a palace in Constantinople?" "My dear master," replied Cacambo, "Cunegonde is washing dishes on the banks of Propontis for a prince who possesses very few dishes; she is a slave in the house of a former sovereign named Ragotsky, who receives in his refuge three crowns a day from the Grand Turk; but what is even more sad is that she has lost her beauty and has become horribly ugly." "Ah! beautiful or ugly," said Candide, "I am a man of honor and my duty is to love her always. But how can she be reduced to so abject a condition with the five or six millions you carried off?" "Ah!" said Cacambo, "did I not have to give two millions to Senor Don Fernando d'Ibaraa y Figueora y Mascarenes y Lampourdos y Souza, Governor of Buenos Aires, for permission to bring away Mademoiselle Cunegonde? And did not a pirate bravely strip us of all the rest? And did not this pirate take us to Cape Matapan, to Milo, to Nicaria, to Samos, to Petra, to the Dardanelles, to Marmora, to Scutari? Cunegonde and the old woman are servants to the prince I mentioned, and I am slave to the dethroned Sultan." "What a chain of terrible calamities!" said Candide. "But after all, I still have a few diamonds; I shall easily deliver Cunegonde. What a pity she has become so ugly." Then, turning to Martin, he said: "Who do you think is the most to be pitied, the Sultan Achmet, the Emperor Ivan, King Charles Edward, or me?" "I do not know at all," said Martin. "I should have to be in your hearts to know." "Ah!" said Candide, "if Pangloss were here he would know and would tell us." "I do not know," said Martin, "what scales your Pangloss would use to weigh the misfortunes of men and to estimate their sufferings. All I presume is that there are millions of men on the earth a hundred times more to be pitied than King Charles Edward, the Emperor Ivan and the Sultan Achmet." "That may very well be," said Candide. In a few days they reached the Black Sea channel. Candide began by paying a high ransom for Cacambo and, without wasting time, he went on board a galley with his companions bound for the shores of Propontis, in order to find Cunegonde however ugly she might be. Among the galley-slaves were two convicts who rowed very badly and from time to time the Levantine captain applied several strokes of a bull's pizzle to their naked shoulders. From a natural feeling of pity Candide watched them more attentively than the other galley-slaves and went up to them. Some features of their disfigured faces appeared to him to have some resemblance to Pangloss and the wretched Jesuit, the Baron, Mademoiselle Cunegonde's brother. This idea disturbed and saddened him. He looked at them still more carefully. "Truly," said he to Cacambo, "if I had not seen Dr.

Pangloss hanged, and if I had not been so unfortunate as to kill the Baron, I should think they were rowing in this galley." At the words Baron and Pangloss, the two convicts gave a loud cry, stopped on their seats and dropped their oars. The Levantine captain ran up to them and the lashes with the bull's pizzle were redoubled. "Stop! Stop, sir!" cried Candide. "I will give you as much money as you want." "What! Is it Candide?" said one of the convicts. "What! Is it Candide?" said the other. "Is it a dream?" said Candide. "Am I awake? Am I in this galley? Is that my Lord the Baron whom I killed? Is that Dr. Pangloss whom I saw hanged?" "It is, it is," they replied. "What! Is that the great philosopher?" said Martin. "Ah! sir," said Candide to the Levantine captain, "how much money do you want for My Lord Thunder-ten-tronckh, one of the first Barons of the empire, and for Dr. Pangloss, the most profound metaphysician of Germany?" "Dog of a Christian," replied the Levantine captain, "since these two dogs of Christian convicts are Barons and metaphysicians, which no doubt is a high rank in their country, you shall pay me fifty thousand sequins." "You shall have them, sir. Row back to Constantinople like lightning and you shall be paid at once. But, no, take me to Mademoiselle Cunegonde." The captain, at Candide's first offer had already turned the bow toward the town, and rowed there more swiftly than a bird cleaves the air. Candide embraced the Baron and Pangloss a hundred times. "How was it I did not kill you, my dear Baron? And, my dear Pangloss, how do you happen to be alive after having been hanged? And why are you both in a Turkish galley?" "Is it really true that my dear sister is in this country?" said the Baron. "Yes," replied Cacambo. "So once more I see my dear Candide!" cried Pangloss. Candide introduced Martin and Cacambo. They all embraced and all talked at the same time. The galley flew; already they were in the harbor. They sent for a Jew, and Candide sold him for fifty thousand sequins a diamond worth a hundred thousand, for which he swore by Abraham he could not give any more. The ransom of the Baron and Pangloss was immediately paid. Pangloss threw himself at the feet of his liberator and bathed them with tears; the other thanked him with a nod and promised to repay the money at the first opportunity. "But is it possible that my sister is in Turkey?" said he. "Nothing is so possible," replied Cacambo, "since she washes up the dishes of a prince of Transylvania." They immediately sent for two Jews; Candide sold some more diamonds; and they all set out in another galley to rescue Cunegonde.

CHAPTER XXVIII

What Happened to Candide, to Cunegonde, to Pangloss, to Martin, Etc.

"Pardon once more," said Candide to the Baron, "pardon me, reverend father, for having thrust my sword through your body." "Let us say no more about it," said the Baron. "I admit I was a little too sharp; but since you wish to know how it was you saw me in a galley, I must tell you that after my wound was healed by the brother apothecary of the college, I was attacked and carried off by a Spanish raiding party; I was imprisoned in Buenos Aires at the time when my sister had just left. I asked to return to the Vicar-General in Rome. I was ordered to Constantinople to act as almoner to the Ambassador of France. A week after I had taken up my office I met toward evening a very handsome young page of the Sultan. It was very hot; the young man wished to bathe; I took the opportunity to bathe also. I did not know that it was a most serious crime for a Christian to be found naked with a young Mohammedan. A cadi sentenced me to a hundred strokes on the soles of my feet and condemned me to the galley. I do not think a more horrible injustice has ever been committed. But I should very much like to know why my sister is in the kitchen of a Transylvanian sovereign living in exile among the Turks." "But, my dear Pangloss," said Candide, "how does it happen that I see you once more?" "It is true," said Pangloss, "that you saw me hanged; and in the natural course of events I should have been burned. But you remember, it poured with rain when they were going to roast me; the storm was so violent that they despaired of lighting the fire; I was hanged because they could do nothing better; a surgeon bought my body, carried me home, and dissected me. He first made a crucial incision in me from the navel to the collar-bone. Nobody could have been worse hanged than I was. The executioner of the holy Inquisition, who was a subdeacon, was marvelously skillful in burning people, but he was not accustomed to hang them; the rope was wet and did not slide easily and it was knotted; in short, I still breathed. The crucial incision caused me to utter so loud a scream that the surgeon fell over backwards and, thinking he was dissecting the devil, fled away in terror and fell down the staircase in his flight. His wife ran in from another room at the noise; she saw me stretched out on the table with my crucial incision; she was still more frightened than her husband, fled, and fell on top of him. When they had recovered themselves a little, I heard the surgeon's wife say to the surgeon: 'My dear, what were you thinking of, to dissect a heretic? Don't you know the devil always possesses them? I will go and get a priest at once to exorcise him.' At this I shuddered and collected the little strength I had left to shout: 'Have pity on me!' At last the Portuguese barber grew bolder; he sewed up my skin; his wife even took care of me, and at the end of a fortnight I was able to walk again. The barber found me a situation and made me lackey to a Knight of Malta who was going to Venice; but, as my master had no money to pay me wages, I entered the service of a Venetian merchant and followed him to Constantinople. One day I took it into my head to enter a mosque; there was nobody there except an old Imam and a very pretty young devotee who was reciting her prayers; her breasts were entirely uncovered; between them she wore a bunch of tulips, roses, anemones, ranunculus, hyacinths, and auriculas; she dropped her bunch of flowers; I picked it up and returned it to her with a most respectful alacrity. I was so long putting them back that the Imam grew angry and, seeing I was a Christian, called for help. I was taken to the cadi, who sentenced me to receive a hundred strokes on the soles of my feet and sent me to the galleys. I was chained on the same seat and in the same galley as My Lord the Baron. In this galley there were four young men from Marseilles, five Neapolitan priests and two monks from Corfu, who assured us that similar accidents occurred every day. His Lordship the Baron claimed that he had suffered a greater injustice than I; and I claimed that it was much more permissible to replace a bunch of flowers between a woman's breasts than to be naked with one of the Sultan's pages. We argued continually, and every day received twenty strokes of the bull's pizzle, when the chain of events of this universe led you to our galley and you ransomed us." "Well! my dear Pangloss," said Candide, "when you were hanged, dissected, stunned with blows and made to row in the galleys, did you always think that everything was for the best in this world?" "I am still of my first opinion," replied Pangloss, "for after all I am a philosopher; and it would be unbecoming for me to recant, since Leibnitz could not be in the wrong and preestablished harmony is the finest thing imaginable like the plenum and subtle matter."

CHAPTER XXIX

How Candide Found Cunegonde and the Old Woman Again

While Candide, the Baron, Pangloss, Martin and Cacambo were relating their adventures, reasoning upon contingent or noncontingent events of the universe, arguing about effects and causes, moral and physical evil, free will and necessity, and the consolations to be found in the Turkish galleys, they came to the house of the Transylvanian prince on the shores of Propontis. The first objects which met their sight were Cunegonde and the old woman hanging out towels to dry on the line. At this sight the Baron grew pale. Candide, that tender lover, seeing his fair Cunegonde sunburned, blear-eyed, flat-breasted, with wrinkles round her eyes and red, chapped arms, recoiled three paces in horror, and then advanced from mere politeness. She embraced Candide and her brother. They embraced the old woman; Candide bought them both. In the neighborhood was a little farm; the old woman suggested that Candide should buy it, until some better fate befell the group. Cunegonde did not know that she had become ugly, for nobody had told her so; she reminded Candide of his promises in so peremptory a tone that the good Candide dared not refuse her. He therefore informed the Baron that he was about to marry his sister. "Never," said the Baron, "will I endure such baseness on her part and such insolence on yours; nobody shall ever reproach me with this infamy; my sister's children could never enter the chapters of Germany. No, my sister shall never marry anyone but a Baron of the Empire." Cunegonde threw herself at his feet and bathed them in tears; but he was inflexible. "Madman," said Candide, "I rescued you from the galleys, I paid your ransom and your sister's; she was washing dishes here, she is ugly, I am so kind as to make her my wife, and you pretend to oppose me! I should kill you again if I listened to my anger." "You may kill me again," said the Baron, "but you shall never marry my sister while I am alive."

CHAPTER XXX

Conclusion

At the bottom of his heart Candide had not the least wish to marry Cunegonde. But the Baron's extreme impertinence determined him to complete the marriage, and Cunegonde urged it so warmly that he could not retract. He consulted Pangloss, Martin and the faithful Cacambo. Pangloss wrote an excellent memorandum by which he proved that the Baron had no rights over his sister and that by all the laws of the empire she could make a left-handed marriage with Candide. Martin advised that the Baron should be thrown into the sea; Cacambo decided that he should be returned to the Levantine captain and sent back to the galleys, after which he would be returned by the first ship to the Vicar-General at Rome. This was thought to be very good advice; the old woman approved it; they said nothing to the sister;

the plan was carried out with the aid of a little money and they had the pleasure of duping a Jesuit and punishing the pride of a German Baron. It would be natural to suppose that when, after so many disasters, Candide was married to his mistress, and living with the philosopher Pangloss, the philosopher Martin, the prudent Cacambo and the old woman, having brought back so many diamonds from the country of the ancient Incas, he would lead the most pleasant life imaginable. But he was so cheated by the Jews that he had nothing left but his little farm; his wife, growing uglier every day, became shrewish and unendurable; the old woman was ailing and even more bad-tempered than Cunegonde. Cacambo, who worked in the garden and then went to Constantinople to sell vegetables, was overworked and cursed his fate. Pangloss was in despair because he did not shine in some German university. As for Martin, he was firmly convinced that people are equally uncomfortable everywhere; he accepted things patiently. Candide, Martin, and Pangloss sometimes argued about metaphysics and morals. From the windows of the farm they often watched the ships going by, filled with effendis, pashas, and cadis, who were being exiled to Lemnos, to Mitylene and Erzerum. They saw other cadis, other pashas, and other effendis coming back to take the place of the exiles and to be exiled in their turn. They saw the neatly impaled heads which were taken to the Sublime Porte. These sights redoubled their discussions; and when they were not arguing, the boredom was so excessive that one day the old woman dared to say to them: "I should like to know which is worse, to be raped a hundred times by Negro pirates, to have a buttock cut off, to run the gauntlet among the Bulgarians, to be whipped and flogged in an *auto-da-fé,* to be dissected, to row in a galley, in short, to endure all the miseries through which we have passed, or to remain here doing nothing?" " 'Tis a great question," said Candide. These remarks led to new reflections, and Martin especially concluded that man was born to live in the convulsions of distress or in the lethargy of boredom. Candide did not agree, but he asserted nothing. Pangloss confessed that he had always suffered horribly; but, having once maintained that everything was for the best, he had continued to maintain it without believing it. One thing confirmed Martin in his detestable principles, made Candide hesitate more than ever, and embarrassed Pangloss. And it was this. One day there came to their farm Paquette and Friar Giroflée, who were in the most extreme misery; they had soon wasted their three thousand piastres, had left each other, made it up, quarreled again, been put in prison, escaped, and finally Friar Giroflée had turned Turk. Paquette continued her occupation everywhere and now earned nothing by it. "I foresaw," said Martin to Candide, "that your gifts would soon be wasted and would only make them the more miserable. You and Cacambo were once bloated with millions of piastres and you are no happier than Friar Giroflée and Paquette." "Ah! Ha!" said Pangloss to Paquette, "so Heaven brings you back to us, my dear child? Do you know that you cost me the end of my nose, an eye, and an ear! What a plight you are in! Ah! What a world this is!" This new occurrence caused them to philosophize more than ever. In the neighborhood there lived a very famous Dervish, who was supposed to be the best philosopher in Turkey; they went to consult him; Pangloss was the spokesman and said: "Master, we have come to beg you to tell us why so strange an animal as man was ever created." "What has it to do with you?" said the Dervish. "Is it your business?" "But, reverend father," said Candide, "there is a horrible amount of evil in the world." "What does it matter," said the Dervish, "whether there is evil or good? When his highness sends a ship to Egypt, does he worry about the comfort or discomfort of the rats in the ship?" "Then what should we do?" said Pangloss. "Hold your tongue," said the Dervish. "I flattered myself," said Pangloss, "that I should discuss with you effects and causes, this best of all possible worlds, the origin of evil, the nature of the soul and pre-established harmony." At these words the Dervish slammed the door in their faces. During this conversation the news went round that at Constantinople two viziers and the mufti had been strangled and several of their friends impaled. This catastrophe made a prodigious noise everywhere for several hours. As Pangloss, Candide, and Martin were returning to their little farm, they came upon an old man who was taking the air under a bower of orange-trees at his door. Pangloss, who was as curious as he was argumentative, asked him what was the name of the mufti who had just been strangled. "I do not know," replied the old man. "I have never known the name of any mufti or of any vizier. I am entirely ignorant of the occurrence you mention; I presume that in general those who meddle with public affairs sometimes perish miserably and that they deserve it; but I never inquire what is going on in Constantinople; I content myself with sending there for sale the produce of the garden I cultivate." Having spoken thus, he took the strangers into his house. His two daughters and his two sons presented them with several kinds of sherbet which they made themselves, caymac flavored with candied citron peel, oranges, lemons, limes, pineapples, dates, pistachios, and Mocha coffee which had not been mixed with the bad coffee of Batavia and the Isles. After which this good Mussulman's two daughters perfumed the beards of Candide, Pangloss, and Martin

"You must have a vast and magnificent estate?" said Candide to the Turk. "I have only twenty acres," replied the Turk. "I cultivate them with my children; and work keeps at bay three great evils: boredom, vice and need." As Candide returned to his farm he reflected deeply on the Turk's remarks. He said to Pangloss and Martin: "That good old man seems to me to have chosen an existence preferable by far to that of the six kings with whom we had the honor to sup." "Exalted rank," said Pangloss, "is very dangerous, according to the testimony of all philosophers; for Eglon, King of the Moabites, was murdered by Ehud; Absalom was hanged by the hair and pierced by three darts; King Nadab, son of Jeroboam, was killed by Baasha; King Elah by Zimri; Ahaziah by Jehu; Athaliah by Jehoiada; the Kings Jehoiakim, Jeconiah, and Zedekiah were made slaves. You know in what manner died Croesus, Astyages, Darius, Denys of Syracuse, Pyrrhus, Perseus, Hannibal, Jugurtha, Ariovistus, Caesar, Pompey, Nero, Otho, Vitellius, Domitian, Richard II of England, Edward II, Henry VI, Richard III, Mary Stuart, Charles I, the three Henrys of France, the Emperor Henry IV. You know . . ." "I also know," said Candide, "that we should cultivate our gardens." "You are right," said Pangloss, "for, when man was placed in the Garden of Eden, he was placed there *ut operaretur eum,* to dress it and to keep it; which proves that man was not born for idleness." "Let us work without theorizing," said Martin; "'tis the only way to make life endurable." The whole small fraternity entered into this praiseworthy plan, and each started to make use of his talents. The little farm yielded well. Cunegonde was indeed very ugly, but she became an excellent pastrycook; Paquette embroidered; the old woman took care of the linen. Even Friar Giroflée performed some service; he was a very good carpenter and even became a man of honor; and Pangloss sometimes said to Candide: "All events are linked up in this best of all possible worlds; for, if you had not been expelled from the noble castle by hard kicks in your backside for love of Mademoiselle Cunegonde, if you had not been clapped into the Inquisition, if you had not wandered about America on foot, if you had not stuck your sword in the Baron, if you had not lost all your sheep from the land of Eldorado, you would not be eating candied citrons and pistachios here." " 'Tis well said," replied Candide, "but we must cultivate our gardens."

Translation by Richard Aldington

Zadig

I. THE ONE-EYED MAN

IN THE reign of King Moabdar there lived in Babylon a young man named Zadig, of naturally charming disposition reinforced by education. Although young and rich, he knew how to control his passions, was unaffected, did not want always to be in the right, and was considerate to human frailty. People were astonished to observe that despite his good sense he never derided the loose, scrappy, noisy tittle-tattle, the reckless backbiting, the ignorant conclusions, the coarse quips, the empty tumult of words, which in Babylon were called "conversation." He had learned in the first book of Zarathustra that self-esteem is a balloon swollen with wind, whence tempests issue when it is pricked. Above all, Zadig did not boast of his scorn for and power over women. He was generous and, in accordance with Zarathustra's great precept—"When thou dost eat, give to eat to the dogs, even though they bite thee"—he did not fear to oblige ingrates. He was as wise as a man can be, for he sought to live with the wise.

Although learned in ancient Chaldean science, he was not ignorant of such physical laws of nature as were then known, and knew of metaphysics what has been known in all ages, that is to say, precious little. Despite the new philosophy of his time, he was strongly persuaded there were three-hundred-and-sixty-five-and-a-quarter days in the year, and that the sun was the center of the world, and when the chief Magi told him with insolent arrogance that he had a sinful heart, that to believe the sun revolved on its own axis and the year had twelve months was to be an enemy of the state, he kept silence without anger or contempt.

With his great wealth (and consequently many friends), his health and pleasant face, his just and modest mind, his sincere and magnanimous nature, Zadig thought he could be happy. He was to be married to Sémire whose birth, beauty and fortune made her the most desirable match in Babylon. For Sémire he had a deep and virtuous attachment, and she loved him passionately. They were nearing the happy moment of their union when, as they walked together toward one of the gates of the city, beneath the palm-trees which adorn the banks of the Euphrates, they saw approaching them some men armed with sabers and arrows. They were retainers of young Orcan, nephew of one of the ministers, who had been led by his uncle's courtiers to believe he could do anything he pleased. He had none of Zadig's graces or charms, but as he thought himself a far finer fellow, he was annoyed at not being deemed more desirable. This jealousy, which was the result solely of his vanity, made Orcan think he was madly in love with Sémire. He was determined to abduct her. His kidnappers seized her and in an outburst of violence wounded her and shed the blood of a person the sight of whom would have melted the hearts of the tigers on Mount Imaus. She pierced the sky with her screams. "Husband! dear husband!" she cried. "They are tearing me from him I adore!" She was not at all troubled by her danger. She thought only of her dear Zadig, who was defending her with all the strength that love and courage give. With only two slaves to help him he routed the kidnappers, and carried Sémire home. She had swooned and was bleeding. On opening her eyes she saw her deliverer. "O Zadig!" she whispered. "I loved you before as my husband; I love you now as the man to whom I owe life and honor!" Never was heart more thrilled than Sémire's; never did a lovelier mouth express more affectionate feelings in words of fire inspired by the sense of the greatest service and the warmest raptures of genuine love.

Her wounds were slight, and she was soon well again. Zadig's hurt was more dangerous. An arrow had hit him near the eye and made a deep wound. Sémire asked nothing of the gods save that her lover should get well. Night and day her eyes were bathed in tears. She lived for the moment when Zadig should be able to delight in her tender looks once more. But an abscess formed on the wounded eye, and made the worst to be feared. The great doctor Hermes was sent for from Memphis, and he came to Babylon with a numerous retinue. He visited the sick man and said he would lose his eye. He even predicted the day and hour when this disastrous accident would happen. "If it had been the right eye," he said, "I should have cured it, but wounds in the left eye are incurable."

All Babylon, while bemoaning Zadig's fate, marveled at Hermes' profound knowledge. Two days later the abscess burst of its own accord, and Zadig was completely cured. Hermes wrote a book in which he proved that Zadig should not have been cured. Zadig did not read the book. As soon as he could go out, he prepared to visit her who was the hope of his happiness in life, and for whom alone he wished to have eyes. Sémire was in the country where she had been for three days past. On his way there, Zadig learned that this beautiful lady had announced her unconquerable aversion to one-eyed men, and had married Orcan that very night. At this news he fainted. His misery brought him to the edge of the grave, and he was ill for a very long time. But reason prevailed at last over his affliction, and the atrocity of what had happened served even to console him.

"Since I have suffered such a cruel caprice," he said, "on the part of a girl brought up at court, I shall have to marry a daughter of the people." He chose Azora, the wisest and best-born girl in the city. He married her and for a month lived in the bliss of the most affectionate union. Only, he noticed in his wife a certain frivolity of temperament and much inclination to think that the best-built young men had necessarily the most virtue and wit.

II. THE NOSE

One day Azora came back from a walk very angry and expostulating loudly.

"What is the matter, dear wife?" asked Zadig. "Who has put you out?"

"Alas!" replied Azora. "You would be as indignant as I am if you had seen what I have seen. I have been to console Cosrou, the young widow, who erected a tomb to her young husband two days ago near the stream which borders this plain. In her anguish she promised the gods to stay by the tomb so long as the stream should flow close to it."

"Well," said Zadig, "she is an estimable woman who really loved her husband."

"Ah!" continued Azora, "if only you knew what she was doing when I called on her!"

"What was she doing, beautiful Azora?"

"She was changing the course of the stream."

Azora indulged in such lengthy protestations, burst into such fierce reproach of the young widow, that Zadig found her display of virtue offensive.

He had a friend named Cador, one of the young men his wife thought better and more honest than the rest. He took him into his confidence and by making him a present of considerable value assured himself, so far as was possible, of his loyalty. Azora had passed two days at the house of one of her friends in the country, and returned home on the third day. The servants in tears announced that her husband had died suddenly that very night, that they had not dared bring her such melancholy news, and that they had just buried him at the end of the garden in the tomb of his fathers.

Azora wept, tore her hair, and swore to kill herself. That night Cador asked permission to speak with her, and they wept together. The next day they wept less and dined together. Cador confided that his friend had left him the greater part of his wealth, and let Azora understand that his happiness would be to share his fortune with her. The lady wept, grew angry, calmed down. The supper was longer than the dinner. They talked to each other with more confidence. Azora sang the praises of the dead man, but admitted he had faults from which Cador was free.

In the middle of the meal Cador complained of a violent pain in his spleen. The lady, anxious and assiduous, sent for all the essences with which she perfumed herself to see if perchance there was one that was good for a pain in the spleen. She was very sorry the great Hermes was no longer in Babylon, and even condescended to touch the place where Cador felt such sharp twinges. "Are you subject to this cruel malady?" she asked tenderly.

"Sometimes I nearly die of it," answered Cador, "and the only thing that relieves me is to apply to the spot the nose of a man twenty-four hours dead."

"What a strange remedy!" said Azora.

"Not stranger than Mr. Arnoult's sachets for apoplexy," replied Cador.

This answer, coupled with the young man's extreme merit, decided the lady. "After all," she said, "when my husband goes over the bridge Tchinavar from the world of yesterday into the world of tomorrow, will the angel Asrael let him pass any the less because his nose will be a little shorter in the second life than it was in the first?"

She took a razor, therefore, went to her husband's tomb, watered it with her tears, and advanced to cut off the nose of Zadig, whom she found stretched out in the grave. Zadig got up, holding his nose with one hand, and checking the razor with the other.

"Madam," he said, "do not cry out any more against young widow Cosrou. The project of cutting off my nose is quite as good as that of changing the course of a stream."

III. THE DOG AND THE HORSE

Zadig found that the first month of marriage, even as it is written in the book of Zend, is the moon of honey, and the second is the moon of wormwood. After a time he had to get rid of Azora, who had become too difficult to live with, and he tried to find his happiness in the study of nature. "No one is happier," said he, "than a philosopher who reads in this great book that God has placed before our eyes. The truths he discovers belong to him. He nourishes and ennobles his soul. He lives in peace, fearing nothing from men, and his dear wife does not come to cut off his nose."

Filled with these ideas, he retired to a house in the country on the banks of the Euphrates. There he did not pass his time calculating how many inches of water flow in one second under the arches of a bridge, or if a cubic line more rain fell in the month of the Mouse than in the month of the Sheep. He did not try to make silk from spiders' webs, or porcelain from broken bottles; but he studied above all the characteristics of animals and plants, and soon acquired a perspicacity which showed him a thousand differences where other men see only uniformity.

While walking one day near a little wood he saw one of the queen's eunuchs hastening toward him, followed by several officers who seemed to be greatly troubled, and ran hither and thither like distracted men seeking something very precious they have lost.

"Young man," cried the Chief Eunuch, "you haven't seen the queen's dog, have you?"

"It's not a dog," answered Zadig modestly, "it's a bitch."

"That's so," said the Chief Eunuch.

"It's a very small spaniel," added Zadig, "which has had puppies recently; her left forefoot is lame, and she has very long ears."

"You have seen her then?" said the Eunuch, quite out of breath.

"Oh, no!" answered Zadig. "I have not seen the animal, and I never knew the queen had a bitch."

Just at this moment, by one of the usual freaks of fortune, the finest horse in the king's stables escaped from a groom's hands and fled into the plains of Babylon. The Master of the King's Hounds and all the other officials rushed after it with as much anxiety as the Chief

Eunuch after the bitch. The Master of the King's Hounds came up to Zadig and asked if he had not seen the king's horse pass by.

"The horse you are looking for is the best galloper in the stable," answered Zadig. "It is fifteen hands high, and has a very small hoof. Its tail is three and a half feet long. The studs on its bit are of twenty-three carat gold, and its shoes of eleven scruple silver."

"Which road did it take?" asked the Master of the King's Hounds. "Where is it?"

"I have not seen the horse," answered Zadig, "and I have never heard speak of it."

The Master of the King's Hounds and the Chief Eunuch had no doubt but that Zadig had stolen the king's horse and the queen's bitch, and they had him taken before the Grand Destur who condemned him to the knout and afterwards to spend the rest of his days in Siberia. Hardly had judgment been pronounced than the horse and the bitch were found. The judges were in the sad necessity of having to rescind their judgment, but they condemned Zadig to pay four hundred ounces of gold for having denied seeing what he had seen. Only after the fine had been paid was Zadig allowed to plead his cause, which he did in the following terms.

"Stars of Justice," he said, "Unfathomable Wells of Knowledge, Mirrors of Truth, that have the solidity of lead, the hardness of iron, the radiance of the diamond, and much affinity with gold, since I am permitted to speak before this august assembly, I swear to you by Ormuzd that I have never seen the queen's honorable bitch or the king of kings' sacred horse. Let me tell you what happened.

"I was walking toward the little wood where I met later the venerable Chief Eunuch and the very illustrious Master of the King's Hounds. I saw an animal's tracks on the sand and I judged without difficulty they were the tracks of a small dog. The long, shallow furrows printed on the little ridges of sand between the tracks of the paws informed me that the animal was a bitch with pendent dugs, who hence had had puppies recently. Other tracks in a different direction, which seemed all the time to have scraped the surface of the sand beside the forepaws, gave me the idea that the bitch had very long ears; and as I remarked that the sand was always less hollowed by one paw than by the three others, I concluded that our august queen's bitch was somewhat lame, if I dare say so.

"As regards the king of kings' horse, you may know that as I walked along the road in this wood I saw the marks of horseshoes, all equal distances apart. That horse, said I, gallops perfectly. The dust on the trees in this narrow road only seven feet wide brushed off a little right and left three and a half feet from the middle of the road. This horse, said I, has a tail three and a half feet long, and its movement right and left has swept away this dust. I saw beneath the trees, which made a cradle five feet high, some leaves newly fallen from the branches, and I recognized that this horse had touched there and was hence fifteen hands high. As regards his bit, it must be of twenty-three carat gold, for he rubbed the studs against a stone which I knew to be a touchstone and tested. From the marks his hoofs made on certain pebbles I knew the horse was shod with eleven scruple silver."

All the judges admired Zadig's profound and subtle perspicacity, news of which came to the ears of the king and queen. In the anterooms, the throne-room, and the closet Zadig was the sole topic of conversation, and although several of the Magi thought he should be burned as a sorcerer, the king ordered the fine of four hundred ounces of gold to which he had been condemned to be returned to him. The clerk of the court, the ushers, the attorneys called on him with great pomp to bring him these four hundred ounces. They retained only three hundred and ninety-eight for judicial costs, and their lackeys demanded largess.

Zadig saw how dangerous it was sometimes to be too knowing, and promised himself, on the first occasion that offered, not to say what he had seen.

The occasion soon presented itself. A state prisoner escaped, and passed beneath the window of Zadig's house. Zadig was questioned, and made no reply. But it was proved he had looked out of the window. For this crime he was condemned to five hundred ounces of gold, and as is the custom in Babylon, he thanked his judges for their indulgence.

"Good God!" he said to himself. "A man who walks in a wood where the queen's bitch or the king's horse have passed is to be pitied! How dangerous it is to look out of the window! How difficult it is to be happy in this life!"

IV. THE ENVIOUS MAN

Zadig resolved to find in philosophy and friendship consolation for the tricks fortune had played him. In a suburb of Babylon he had an elegantly decorated house where he brought together all the arts and pleasures worthy of an honest man. In the morning his library was open to all scholars, at night his table was free to all good fellows. But he soon learned how dangerous scholars are. A great dispute started over one of the laws of Zarathustra which forbade eating the griffon. "How can the griffon be forbidden," asked some, "if this animal does not exist?"

"The griffon must exist," said others, "seeing that Zarathustra does not wish it to be eaten."

Zadig tried to bring the disputants into harmony. "If there are griffons," he said, "do not let us eat them: if there are no griffons, we shall eat still less: anyway we shall all be obeying Zarathustra."

A scholar who had written thirteen books on the characteristics of the griffon, and was moreover a great theurgist, hastened to accuse Zadig before an Archmagus named Yébor, the most stupid of the Chaldeans and, consequently, the most fanatic. This man would have had Zadig impaled for the greater glory of the sun, and for this same glory would have recited Zarathustra's breviary in an even more satisfied voice than usual. Friend Cador (one friend is worth more than a hundred priests) went to see the aged Yébor. "Long live the sun and the griffons!" he cried. "And take good care not to punish Zadig! He is a saint: he has some griffons in his poultry-yard, and he does not eat them at all. His accuser is a heretic who dares assert that although rabbits are cloven-footed they are in no way unclean."

"Well," mumbled Yébor, wagging his bald head, "Zadig must be impaled for thinking wickedly about the griffons, and the other for speaking wickedly about the rabbits."

Cador composed the matter through the agency of a maid of honor whom he had provided with a baby, and who had much influence in the sacred college. No one was impaled, and this made several of the doctors murmur and predict that the omission presaged the fall of Babylon.

"Where, oh! where, is happiness?" cried Zadig. "I am persecuted by everything in the world, and even by things which are not!" He cursed the scholars, and wished thenceforward to live only with good fellows.

He brought together in his house the most honorable men and the most amiable women in Babylon. He gave dainty suppers preceded often by concerts, and enlivened by charming conversation whence he managed to banish the desire to show off one's own wit—which is the surest way both of having none and of spoiling the most brilliant society. Vanity influenced the choice of neither his friends nor his viands, for he preferred in everything to *be* rather than to *appear:* and in this way he won for himself the sincere esteem to which he did not pretend.

Opposite Zadig's house lived Arimaze, a person whose mean soul was depicted on his coarse face. He was corroded with gall and swollen with conceit, and to cap these qualities he had a tedious wit. He slandered the world in revenge for his complete lack of success in it. Although he was rich, he had great difficulty in getting sycophants to come to his house. The carriages which entered Zadig's courtyard each evening annoyed him; the noise of Zadig's renown irritated him still more. Occasionally he went to Zadig's and sat himself at table without being asked. There, he spoiled the company's pleasure, just as harpies are said to defile the meats they touch. When one day he wished to give a party in honor of a lady, she refused his invitation and went to sup with Zadig. On another occasion, while he was talking with Zadig in the palace, they came up with one of the ministers who invited Zadig to supper and did not invite Arimaze. The most implacable hatreds often have no more important cause. This man, whom everyone in Babylon called "Arimaze The Envious," wished to get rid of Zadig because the latter was always called "Zadig The Happy." As Zarathustra says—The opportunity of doing harm presents itself a hundred times a day, and that of doing good once a year.

The Envious went to Zadig's house and found him walking in his gardens with two friends and a lady to whom he often paid compliments without other intention than to be pleasant. The conversation turned to a war which the king had just concluded successfully against his vassal, the King of Hircania. Zadig, who in this short war had shown his courage, praised the king greatly and the lady still more. He took his tablets and wrote four verses which he composed on the spot and gave to this beautiful person to read. His friends begged him to let them hear the verses. Modesty or, rather, a quite understandable vanity, stopped him. He knew that impromptu verses never seem good save to her in whose honor they are composed. He broke in half the tablet on which he had just written, and threw the two pieces into a rosebush, where his friends looked for them in vain. It started to rain a little, and they returned to the house. The Envious stayed in the garden and searched so hard that he found a piece of the tablet. It was broken in such a way that each half of a verse, which filled a line, made sense and even a verse of shorter measure; but by a still stranger chance these little verses made a sense which contained the most horrible insults against the king. This is what they said:

Through prodigies of vice
  Established on his throne,
Amidst the public peace
  He is the foe alone.

For the first time in his life The Envious was happy. He held in his hand the means of getting rid of a good and charming man. Filled with this cruel joy, he arranged for this satire in Zadig's writing to reach the king himself. Zadig was thrown into prison with his two friends and the lady. His trial was soon over without the judges condescending to hear him. When he came up for sentence, The Envious waylaid him and told him at the top of his voice that the verses were worthless. Zadig did not plume himself on being a good poet, but he was in despair at being condemned as guilty of *lèse-majesté,* and at seeing a beautiful woman and two friends kept in jail for a crime they had not committed. He was not allowed to speak because his tablets spoke for him. Such was the law of Babylon. He was made to pass to punishment before a curious crowd of which no member dared sympathize with him, but of which all rushed to look at him to see if he would die with a good grace. Only his relations were distressed, for they inherited nothing. Three quarters of his fortune were confiscated for the king, and the remaining quarter for The Envious.

While Zadig was preparing himself for death, the king's parrot flew from its balcony and swooped down on a rosebush in Zadig's garden. A peach had been carried there from a neighboring tree by the wind, and had fallen on a piece of the writing tablet to which it had stuck. The bird picked up the peach and the tablet, and dropped them in the monarch's lap. The prince, curious, read some words which made no sense and looked like the last syllables of some verses. He liked poetry, and there is always hope for princes who like poetry. His parrot's adventure set him thinking. The queen, remembering what had been written on a piece of Zadig's tablet, had it brought to her. The two pieces were put together, and arranged themselves perfectly. The verses then read as Zadig had written them:

Through prodigies of vice great this earth's troubles are.
  Established on his throne the king brooks no abuse.
Amidst the public peace Love only wages war:
  He is the foe alone who needs stir fear in us.

The king at once ordered Zadig to be brought before him, and his two friends and the beautiful lady to be released. Zadig threw himself on the ground at the feet of the king and queen, and very humbly begged their pardon for having written some bad verse. He spoke with so much grace, wit and sense that the king and queen had a fancy to see him again. He returned, and pleased them still more. They awarded him all the goods of The Envious, who had accused him unjustly. But Zadig gave everything back, and The Envious was touched by nothing but his joy at not losing his belongings.

Day by day the king's esteem for Zadig grew. He made him a participant in all his pleasures, and consulted him in all his affairs. From that time the queen looked on him with a graciousness that might become dangerous for her, for her august husband the king, and for the kingdom. Zadig began to think that it was not so difficult to be happy.

V. THE GENEROUS MAN

The time approached for celebrating the great quinquennial feast. It was the custom in Babylon to proclaim solemnly every five years the citizen who had performed the most generous action. The grandees and the Magi were the judges. The chief satrap, who was charged with the care of the town, announced the finest actions which had taken place during his tenure of office. The vote was put, and then the king pronounced judgment. To this solemn ceremony people came from the ends of the earth. The winner received from the monarch's hands a golden goblet studded with precious stones, and the king said these words to him: "Receive this prize for generosity, and may the gods send me many more subjects like you!"

When the memorable day arrived, the king appeared on his throne surrounded by grandees, Magi, and delegates of all the nations, who came to these games where glory was won not by the fleetness of horses, or physical strength, but by virtue. The chief satrap announced in a loud voice the actions which might earn for their authors this priceless prize. He did not mention the magnanimity with which Zadig had returned to The Envious all his fortune: that was not an action that deserved to compete for the prize.

He presented first of all a judge who, having made a citizen lose an important lawsuit by a mistake for which he was not even responsible, had given him his entire wealth, which was equal in value to what the other had lost.

Then he produced a young man who, in spite of his love for the girl he was going to marry, had ceded her to a friend who was almost dying of love for her, and in addition had even paid her dowry.

His next was a soldier who in the Hircanian war had given an even greater example of generosity. Some enemy soldiers were carrying off his mistress, and he was defending her against them, when he learned that other Hircanians a few steps away were carrying off his mother. In tears, he left his mistress and rushed to deliver his mother. He returned later to his beloved, and found her dying. He wanted to kill himself, but his mother protested that he was her sole support, and he had the courage to endure living.

The judges favored this soldier. The king spoke. "His action," he said, "and these other actions are fine, but they do not astonish me. Yesterday Zadig did something that amazed me. A few days ago I disgraced Coreb, my minister and favorite. I had a bitter complaint against him, and all my courtiers assured me I was too lenient: it was a competition to see who could say the worst of Coreb. I asked Zadig what he thought, and he dared speak well of the man. I have seen in history examples of men who have paid for an error with their wealth, of men who ceded their mistresses, or who have put their mothers before the objects of their adoration, but I have never read of a courtier who spoke well of a disgraced minister who had incurred his king's wrath. I give twenty thousand pieces of gold to each of those whose generous actions have just been told me, but I give the goblet to Zadig."

"Sire," said Zadig, "it is Your Majesty alone deserves the goblet, it is he who has performed the most unheard of action in not letting his royal wrath rise against the slave who opposed his passion."

Both the king and Zadig were accounted splendid. The judge who had given his wealth, the lover who had married his mistress to his friend, the soldier who had preferred his mother's safety to his mistress's, received the king's gifts and saw their names inscribed in the Book of Generosity: Zadig had the goblet. The king acquired the reputation of being a good prince, the which he did not keep long. The day was sanctified by merry-making longer than the law stipulated. The memory of it still remains in Asia.

"At last I am happy!" said Zadig. But he was mistaken.

VI. THE MINISTER

The king had lost his prime minister. He chose Zadig to fill the post. All the beautiful ladies of Babylon applauded this choice, for since the foundation of the empire they had never had so young a minister. All the courtiers were vexed. The Envious had an attack of bloodspitting when he heard the news, and his nose swelled up prodigiously.

Having thanked the king and queen, Zadig went to thank the parrot also. "Beautiful bird," he said, "it is you who have saved my life and made me prime minister. Their majesties' horse and bitch did me much harm, but you have done me good. Behold on what a man's fate depends! But," he added, "so strange a piece of good fortune will perhaps soon disappear."

"Yes," answered the parrot.

This word struck Zadig. As, however, he was a good natural philosopher and did not believe that parrots were prophets, he reassured himself and set about his duties as a minister to the best of his ability.

He made everybody feel the sacred power of the law, and nobody the weight of his importance. He did not muzzle the council of state, and let each vizier have an opinion without being affronted. When he judged a case it was not he who judged, but the law. When, however, the law was too severe he made it more lenient: and when there were no laws, his equity invented such as might have been taken for those of Zarathustra.

It is from him that the nations possess the great principle that it is better to try to save a guilty man than to condemn an innocent. He believed that the laws were made as much to help citizens as to intimidate them. His principal gift was that of deciphering the truth which all men try to obscure, and from the earliest days of his administration he put this great gift to use.

A famous Babylonian merchant had died in the Indies. He had bequeathed his fortune to his two sons equally, after they had given their sister in marriage, and he left a present of thirty thousand pieces of gold to the son who should be judged to love him most. The elder son built his father a tomb, the younger increased his sister's dowry by a part of his own heritage. Everyone said: "The elder loves his father best, the other thinks more of his sister: the elder should have the thirty thousand pieces of gold."

Zadig had them brought before him separately. "Your father is not dead," he said to the elder son. "He has recovered from his last illness, and is returning to Babylon."

"God be praised!" replied the young man, "but there's a tomb which has cost me a pretty penny."

Zadig made the same remark to the second son.

"God be praised!" he answered. "I shall return to my father all I have, but I hope he will leave my sister what I have given her."

"You will return nothing," said Zadig, "and you shall have the thirty thousand pieces of gold. You love your father best."

A very rich girl had promised to marry two Magi, and after being trained by them both for some months, found herself pregnant. They both wished to marry her.

"I will take for my husband," she said, "the one who has put me in the way of giving a citizen to the empire."

"Without question I am the author of this good work," said one.

"Not at all," said the other, "the privilege is mine."

"Well," she conceded, "I recognize as father of my child the man who will give him the better education."

She gave birth to a son. Both the Magi wished to rear him. The case was brought before Zadig. He sent for the two Magi. "What will you teach your ward?" he asked the first.

"I shall teach him," answered the doctor, "the eight parts of speech, logic, astrology, demonology; what is substance and what is quality, the abstract and the concrete, monads and pre-established harmony."

"I," said the second, "shall teach him to be just and worthy of having friends."

"Whether you be the father or not," declared Zadig, "you shall marry the mother."

Every day complaints were received at court against Irax, the Ilimadod-Dowlet of Media. Irax was a great lord who at bottom was not bad but who had been corrupted by vanity and luxurious pleasure. He rarely allowed anyone to speak to him, and never did anyone dare contradict him. The peacocks are not more vain, the doves not more voluptuous, the tortoises less lazy. He thirsted for false glory and false pleasure only, and Zadig undertook to reform him.

He sent in the king's name a bandmaster with twelve singers and twenty-four fiddlers, a steward with six cooks, and four chamberlains, who were not to leave him for a moment. The king's orders were that the following etiquette was to be strictly observed: and this is what happened.

On the first day, as soon as the voluptuary was awake, the bandmaster entered his room followed by the orchestra and choir. They sang a cantata, lasting two hours, the refrain of which, recurring every three minutes, was as follows:

> The merit of my lord is great!
> Ah! what charms! what qualities!
> He must be glad to contemplate
> What a splendid man he is!

After the execution of the cantata a chamberlain harangued him for three-quarters of an hour, praising expressly all the good qualities the voluptuary lacked. The harangue over, he was conducted to table to the sound of instruments. The dinner lasted three hours. As soon as he opened his mouth to speak, the chief chamberlain said: "He's sure to be right." Hardly had he pronounced four words than the second chamberlain said: "He is right." The other two chamberlains laughed loudly at the witticisms which Irax made or ought to have made. After dinner they repeated the cantata.

This first day seemed delightful to him. He thought the king of kings was honoring him according to his merit. The second day was less agreeable. The third was tiresome, the fourth unbearable, the fifth a torture. Finally, incensed at hearing the perpetual cry:

> He must be glad to contemplate
> What a splendid man he is!

at hearing he was always right, and at being harangued every day at the same time, he wrote to the court begging the king to deign to recall his chamberlains, musicians, and steward. He promised thenceforward to be less vain and more industrious. He arranged to have less flattery and fewer feasts, and was all the happier: for, as the Sadder says: Constant pleasure is not pleasure.

VII. DISPUTES AND AUDIENCES

In this wise did Zadig show every day the subtlety of his genius and the goodness of his soul. In spite of being accounted a marvel, he was loved. He passed for the luckiest of men. The whole empire swelled with his name. He was ogled by all the women and praised by all citizens for his fairness. The scholars looked on him as their oracle, and even the priests admitted he knew more than Yébor, the aged Archmagus. They were far from prosecuting him about griffons: they believed only what he thought credible.

For fifteen hundred years there had been in Babylon a great dispute which had split the empire into two stubborn sects. The first claimed that one should always enter the temple of Mithra with the left foot: the other held this custom in abomination, and never entered but with the right foot. They awaited the day of the Festival of the Sacred Fire to see which sect Zadig would favor. The universe had its eyes on his two feet, and the whole city was in a state of agitated suspense. Zadig entered the temple by jumping with his feet together, and proved later in an eloquent speech that the God of heaven and earth, who has no respect of persons, does not esteem the left leg more than the right, or the right more than the left.

The Envious and his wife maintained that there were not enough figures of speech in his discourse, and that he had not made the hills and mountains dance enough. "He is too dry," they said. "He has no genius. When he talks one does not see the ocean take to flight, or the stars fall, or the sun melt like wax. He lacks the good flowery Asiatic style."

Zadig was content to have the style of good sense. Everyone was on his side, not because he was what a man should be, not because he was wise, not because he was lovable, but just because he was grand vizier.

He wound up equally happily the great quarrel between the white Magi and the black Magi. The whites maintained that it was impious, when offering prayer to God, to turn toward the east in winter: the blacks were certain that God held in abomination the prayers of men who turned toward the west in summer. Zadig's order was that people might turn as they pleased.

He learned thus the secret of disposing of particular and general business in the morning: for the rest of the day he occupied himself in improving Babylon. He arranged for tragedies to be presented that made the people cry, and comedies that made them laugh: this had been long out of fashion, and he revived the custom because he was a man of taste. He did not claim to know more about the plays than the players; he rewarded them with favors and distinctions, and did not envy their talents in secret. In the evening he entertained the king and queen very much, particularly the queen. The king spoke of "Our great minister!" The queen of "Our amiable minister!" And both added: "It would have been a great pity if he had been hanged."

Never was a man of high position compelled to give so many audiences to the ladies. Most of them came to talk about affairs of state in which they had no interest so as to have a love-affair with him in which they had much. The wife of The Envious presented herself among the first. She swore to him by Bithra, by the Zend-Avesta, and by the sacred fire, that she had detested her husband's conduct. She then confided that her husband was jealous and brutal to her. She let Zadig understand that the gods were punishing him by refusing him the precious gifts of that sacred fire which alone makes man like the gods. She finished by letting her garter fall. With his usual courtesy Zadig picked it up but did not fasten it on the lady's knee again, and this slight omission—if indeed it be one—was the cause of the most dreadful troubles. Zadig thought no more about it, but the wife of The Envious thought about it a great deal.

Other ladies came every day. The secret annals of Babylon maintain that Zadig succumbed on one occasion, but that he was quite astonished to find himself possessing his paramour without pleasure, and kissing her absent-mindedly. She to whom he gave, almost without perceiving it, the marks of his favor, was one of Queen Astarte's chambermaids. This affectionate Babylonian girl sought to console herself for Zadig's preoccupation by saying to herself: "This man must have a vast number of things in his head seeing that he thinks about them even when he is loving me." At one of those moments when many people are completely silent, and others pronounce only the most sacred words, Zadig, forgetting himself, cried out suddenly: "The queen." The Babylonian girl thought that at last he had come to his senses, and at an appropriate moment, and had said to her: "My queen." But Zadig, still very preoccupied, uttered the name of Astarte. The lady, who at these joyous moments interpreted everything in her own favor, thought he meant—You are more beautiful than Queen Astarte.

She left Zadig's harem with some very fine presents, and went off to narrate her adventure to the wife of The Envious, who was her close friend. The latter was cruelly piqued by Zadig's preference. "He did not even deign," she said, "to put my garter on for me. Here it is: I do not care to wear it any more."

"Oh! oh!" said the lucky girl, "you wear the same garters as the queen! Do you buy them from the same maker?"

The wife of The Envious thought deeply, answered nothing, and went to consult her husband.

And Zadig noticed that when he was giving audiences and when he was judging cases he was always preoccupied. His only trouble was that he did not know to what to attribute his preoccupation.

He had a dream. He seemed at first to be reclining on some dry grasses of which some of the stems pricked and disturbed him. When afterwards he was reposing comfortably on a bed of rose-leaves a snake came out of the flowers and struck him in the heart with its sharp, poisonous tongue. "Alas!" he said. "I rested on these dry and prickly plants for a long time. . . . But who will be the snake?"

VIII. JEALOUSY

Zadig's bad luck was due really to his good luck and, above all, to his merit. Every day he talked with the king and with Astarte, the king's august spouse. The charm of his conversation was heightened by that desire to please which is to the mind what jewels are to beauty. His youth and attractiveness gradually made an impression on Astarte which at first she did not notice. Her passion grew without her in her innocence realizing it. Without fear or scruple Astarte gave herself up to the pleasure of seeing and hearing a young man dear to her husband and to the state. She never ceased praising him to the king; she talked of him to her ladies-in-waiting, who surpassed her in their panegyrics. Everything helped to drive into her heart the arrow she did not feel. She gave Zadig presents in which there was more tender coquetry than she guessed. She thought she spoke to him merely as a queen content with his services, and yet sometimes her utterances were those of a woman sensible to emotion.

Astarte was much more beautiful than that Sémire, who had such a hatred of one-eyed men, and that other woman who had wanted to cut off her husband's nose. Her friendliness; the tenderness with which she spoke, and at which she was beginning to blush; her eyes, which she wanted to turn away but which fixed themselves on his: all lit in Zadig's heart a fire which bewildered him. He fought against it and summoned to his aid that philosophy which hitherto had always aided him; but now he extracted from it only wisdom and no relief. Duty, gratitude, sovereign majesty outraged—all these things appeared before his eyes like avenging gods. He fought and he triumphed, but this victory had to be repeated every moment, and it cost him many groans and tears. No longer did he dare speak to the queen with that easy freedom that had been so charming for them both. His eyes were covered with a mist, his words were stiff and inconsequent. He kept his eyes on the ground and when, in spite of himself, they turned toward Astarte, they found the queen's eyes wet with tears but kindling with passion. They seemed to be saying: "We love each other and we fear to love: we are both burning with a fire we condemn."

Zadig left her bewildered and distracted, his heart weighed down with a burden he could bear no longer. In the violence of his emotion he let his friend Cador penetrate his secret, like a man who after long suffering attacks of sharp pain proclaims his ill by a cry wrenched from him in a moment of more than ordinary agony, and by the cold sweat on his forehead.

"Love shows signs that cannot be mistaken," said Cador. "I have already fathomed the passion you yourself wished to hide. Do you think, my dear Zadig, seeing that I have read your heart, that the king will not discover a sentiment which is an offense against him? His only fault is that he is the most jealous of men. You resist your passion more strongly than the queen because you are a philosopher and because you are Zadig. Astarte is a woman: she lets her face speak with all the more imprudence because she still believes herself to be innocent. Reassured unfortunately as to her freedom from guilt, she neglects necessary appearances. I shall tremble for her so long as she has no reason for self-reproach. If there is an understanding between you, you will know how to gull everyone. A budding passion which is resisted proclaims itself: satisfied love knows how to hide."

Zadig shuddered at the idea of playing the king false, of deceiving his benefactor, and he was never more loyal to his prince than when he was guilty of an involuntary crime against him. The queen, however, pronounced Zadig's name so often, her face flushed so much in pronouncing it when she spoke to him in the king's presence, she was at times so animated and at others so abashed, she fell into such profound reveries after he had gone, that the king was troubled. He considered all he saw, and imagined all he did not see. He noticed particularly that his wife's slippers were blue and that Zadig's slippers were also blue, that her ribbons were yellow and that Zadig's cap was also yellow. These were indeed terrible portents for a prince of delicate sensibilities. In his embittered state of mind suspicion became certainty.

The slaves who serve kings and queens also spy on their hearts. They soon fathomed that Astarte was in love and that Moabdar was jealous. The Envious prevailed on his wife to send the king her garter, which resembled the queen's. As a crowning misfortune this garter was blue. The king thought of nothing but how he should be revenged. He resolved one night to poison the queen, and have Zadig strangled at dawn. The order for Zadig's death was given to a pitiless eunuch, the executor of the king's vengeance. It chanced that there was in the king's room a little dwarf who was dumb but not deaf. He was always allowed to be present, and witnessed the most secret happenings, like a domestic animal. This little dumb fellow was very attached to the queen and Zadig, and he heard with as much surprise as horror the order given for their death. But how to stop this terrible order, which would be executed before so few hours had elapsed? He did not know how to write but he had learned to paint, and knew especially how to draw likenesses. He spent a part of the night penciling what he wanted the queen to understand. His picture showed the king in a fury in one corner, giving orders to the eunuch: a blue cord and a bowl on a table, with blue garters and yellow ribbons: the queen in the middle dying in her women's arms, and Zadig lying strangled at her feet. On the horizon was a rising sun, to show that this horrible execution was to take place at the first sign of day. As soon as he had finished this work, he ran to one of Astarte's women, waked her, and made her understand she must take this picture to the queen at once.

In the middle of the night someone knocked on Zadig's door, waked him and gave him a note from the queen. He wondered if he was dreaming, and opened the letter with trembling hands. What was his surprise, and who could express his consternation and despair, when he read these words: "Fly at once, or your life will be forfeit! Fly, Zadig! In the name of our love and my yellow ribbons I command you. Fly! Up to now I have been innocent, but I feel I shall die guilty."

Zadig had barely the strength to speak. He ordered Cador to be fetched, and without saying a word gave him the note. Cador forced him to obey and take the road to Memphis at once. "If you dare go to find the queen," he said, "you hasten her death. If you speak to the king, you lose her equally. I charge myself with her fate: look after your own. I will spread a rumor that you have taken the road to India. I will soon come to find you and let you know what has happened in Babylon."

Cador gave the order at once to bring two of the fleetest dromedaries to a secret door of the palace. He had Zadig, who was at the point of giving up the ghost, hoisted on to the back of one of them. Only one servant accompanied him, and soon Cador, plunged in grief and amazement, lost his friend from sight.

The illustrious fugitive, reaching the side of a hill whence he could look back on Babylon, turned his eyes to the queen's palace, and fainted. He regained consciousness only to weep and pray for death. At last, after brooding on the calamitous fate of the most lovable of women and the greatest queen in the world, he made an effort to collect himself, and cried—"What, then, is human life? O virtue, how have you served me? Two women have deceived me infamously: the third, who is not guilty at all and is more beautiful than the others, is about to die! All the good in me has never been productive of anything but curses, and I have risen to the height of splendor only to fall into the most terrible abyss of misfortune. If like so many others I had been a miscreant, I should be as happy as they are!"

Worn out by these sad reflections, his eyes veiled with sorrow, the pallor of death on his face, he continued on the road to Egypt.

IX. THE WOMAN WHO WAS FLOGGED

Zadig set his course by the stars. The constellation of Orion and the brilliant star Sirius guided him toward the pole of Canopus. He admired these vast globes of light which to our eyes seem only feeble sparks, whereas the earth which is only an imperceptible point in nature appears to our self-importance something so great and so splendid. He pictured men as they really are, insects devouring each other on a little patch of mud. This image of the truth seemed to annihilate his misfortunes as he reviewed his own complete unimportance and Babylon's. His soul fled into the infinite and, detached from his senses, contemplated the unchanging order of the universe. But when, later, he returned to himself and, probing his heart, thought that perhaps Astarte was dead on his account, the universe disappeared altogether, and in the whole of nature he saw nothing but Astarte dying and Zadig luckless.

Giving himself up to this flux and reflux of sublime philosophy and overwhelming grief, he moved on toward the frontiers of Egypt. His faithful servant was already in the first small town, where he sought lodging, while Zadig wandered toward the gardens on its outskirts. Not far from the high road he saw a woman in distress who called on heaven and earth for help, and a man who was pursuing her in fury. He had already caught up with her, and she was clasping his knees. This man loaded her with reproaches and blows. Zadig judged from the Egyptian's violence and the pardon which the woman repeatedly begged, that she was unfaithful and he jealous; but when he looked more closely at her—she had a pathetic beauty, and resembled Astarte somewhat—he felt himself filled with pity for her and horror for the Egyptian.

"Save me!" she cried to Zadig, sobbing. "Take me away from this savage! Save me! Save me!"

At these cries Zadig rushed to throw himself between her and the savage. He had some knowledge of Egyptian, and spoke in that language. "If you have any humanity in you," he said, "I implore you to respect beauty and weakness. Can you thus defile one of nature's masterpieces who lies at your feet with nothing for her defense but tears?"

"Ho! Ho!" cried the frenzied Egyptian. "So you're in love with her too! You're just the man I'm looking for to get my own back! Ho! Ho!"

With these words he let go of the lady whose hair he held in one hand, and seizing his spear lunged at the stranger. Zadig, who had a cool head, easily escaped the madman's spear, and seized it close to the iron tip. One tried to keep the spear, the other to tear it away, and it snapped in their hands. The Egyptian drew his sword, Zadig did likewise, and they attacked. With a rush the Egyptian struck a hundred blows which Zadig parried easily. The lady, seated on a patch of grass, put her hair straight and watched the fight. The Egyptian was the stronger, but Zadig was more skillful and fought like a man whose hand is guided by his head, whereas the other was like a madman whose blind rage guides his movements by chance. Zadig made a thrust and disarmed him. The Egyptian, madder than ever, tried to throw himself on Zadig. Zadig seized him, crushed him in his arms, and forced him to the ground, his sword at the Egyptian's breast: he then offered to spare his life. The Egyptian, beside himself with rage, drew a dagger and wounded Zadig at the very moment his conqueror was offering him mercy. Exasperated, Zadig plunged his sword into the Egyptian's bosom. The Egyptian died, writhing.

Zadig turned to the lady. "He forced me to kill him," he said humbly. "I have avenged you: you are delivered from the most violent man I have ever seen. What do you desire of me now, Madam?"

"That you die, dog!" she shrieked. "That you die! You have killed my lover. I wish I could tear your heart out, you scoundrel!"

"Really, Madam," replied Zadig, "you had a very strange man for a lover. He beat you as hard as he could, and wanted to kill me because you begged my help."

"I wish he would beat me again!" screamed the lady. "I deserved it, I made him jealous. Oh! God! if only he would beat me! If only you were in his place!"

"Beautiful as you are," said Zadig, more surprised and angry than he had ever been in his life, "you are so preposterous that you deserve a good beating from me in my turn; but I won't take the trouble."

Whereupon he mounted his camel again and set off toward the town. Hardly had he started than he turned again at the noise made by four couriers from Babylon. They came along at full speed. One of them, seeing the woman, cried out: "That's her! She's just like the picture they made for us." They did not bother about the dead man, but seized the woman forthwith. She did not stop crying to Zadig: "Save me once more, generous stranger! I beg your pardon for having been cross with you. Save me, and I am yours till death!"

The desire to do any more fighting for her had left Zadig. "Let someone else save you," he answered. "You won't catch me again." Besides, he was wounded, his blood was flowing, he needed help himself, and the sight of the four Babylonians, sent probably by Moabdar, filled him with disquiet. He moved on to the town with all speed, not guessing why four couriers from Babylon should carry off this Egyptian woman, but still very astonished at the lady's nature.

X. SLAVERY

As he entered the Egyptian town he was surrounded by the townsmen.

"That's the man who carried off beautiful Missouf!" they all cried. "That's the man who has just murdered Clétofis!"

"Gentlemen," said Zadig, "God preserve me from ever carrying off your beautiful Missouf—she is too capricious: and as regards Clétofis, I did not murder him at all; I merely defended myself against him. He wanted to kill me because I had very meekly asked mercy for beautiful Missouf whom he was beating cruelly. I am a stranger seeking asylum in Egypt, and it is unlikely that in coming to ask your protection I should begin by carrying off a woman and murdering a man."

The Egyptian people were at that time humane and just. The townsmen led Zadig to the town hall. They started by dressing his wound, and then questioned him and his servant separately in order to learn the truth. They recognized that Zadig was not in the least a murderer, but he had shed a man's blood. The law condemned him to be a slave. His two camels were sold for the benefit of the town, and all the gold he had brought with him was distributed among the townsmen. His person, with that of his traveling companion, was offered for sale in the marketplace.

An Arab merchant named Sétoc bid for them, but the servant, who was more suited to manual labor, fetched a much better price than the master. The individual qualities of each man were not taken into consideration, and so Zadig was a slave subordinate to his servant. They were tied together with a chain round their feet, and in this state followed the Arab merchant home. On the way Zadig consoled his servant and exhorted him to patience, but as was his habit made some observations on human life.

"I see," he said, "that the misfortunes of my destiny spread themselves over yours. Everything up to now has moved me about in the strangest fashion. I have been condemned to a fine for seeing a bitch pass by; I thought I was going to be impaled for the sake of a griffon; I have been sentenced to death for writing a poem praising the king; I have just missed being strangled because the queen had yellow ribbons, and here I am a slave with you because a brute beat his mistress. Come! let us not lose heart! Maybe there will be an end to all this. Arab merchants must have slaves, and why should not I be a slave like another, seeing that I am a man like another? This merchant will not be pitiless, and he must treat his slaves well if he wishes to get any work out of them." These were the words on his lips, but in his heart he was thinking of the fate of the queen of Babylon.

Sétoc, the merchant, left two days later for Arabia Deserta with his slaves and camels. His tribe dwelt near the desert of Horeb. The road was long and difficult. On the journey Sétoc showed much more esteem for the servant than for the master, because the former looked after the camels well: all the little marks of favor, therefore, were his.

A camel died when they were still two days' journey away from Horeb, and its burden was distributed on the slaves' backs: Zadig had his share. Sétoc started laughing when he saw all his slaves marching with bent backs. Zadig took the liberty of explaining the reason to him, and of teaching him the laws of equilibrium. The astonished merchant began to look at him from a different angle. Zadig, seeing the merchant's curiosity stirred, stimulated it by telling him many things not irrelevant to his business, such as the specific gravities of metals and commodities of equal bulk, the characteristics of various useful animals, the means of making useful such as were not: with result that the merchant thought him a very learned man, and gave him preference over his comrade whom previously he had esteemed so much. He treated Zadig well, and had no cause to repent thereof.

The first thing Sétoc did when he reached his tribe was to ask a Hebrew for the return of five hundred ounces of silver he had lent him in the presence of two witnesses. The two witnesses, however, had died, and the Hebrew, whose guilt could not be proved, appropriated the merchant's money, thanking God for giving him the means of cheating an Arab. Sétoc confided his trouble to Zadig, who had become his adviser.

"In what place," asked Zadig, "did you lend your five hundred ounces to this infidel?"

"On a large stone," replied the merchant, "near Mount Horeb."

"What sort of man is your debtor?" asked Zadig.

"He's a rogue," answered Sétoc.

"But I want to know what sort of man he is. Is he sharp-witted or dull, wary or rash?"

"Of all the slow payers," said Sétoc, "he's the sharpest I've ever met."

"Well," insisted Zadig, "let me plead your cause before the judge."

And so he summoned the Hebrew before the tribunal, and spoke thus to the judge:

"Ear of the Throne of Justice," he said, "I come on behalf of my master to claim from this man the return of five hundred ounces of silver which he will not give up."

"Have you any witnesses?" asked the judge.

"No, they are both dead, but there is still a large stone on which the money was counted, and if it please your Highness to order the stone to be fetched I hope it will bear witness. The Hebrew and I will stay here until the stone arrives. I will have it brought at my master Sétoc's expense."

"Very well," said the judge, and set to disposing of other matters.

At the end of the sitting he turned to Zadig. "Well," he said, "your stone is not here yet?"

"Your Highness might wait until tomorrow," grinned the Hebrew, "and even then the stone would not be here. It is more than six miles away, and it would take fifteen men to move it."

"There!" cried Zadig. "I told you the stone would bear witness. As this man knows where it is, he confesses it is the stone on which the money was paid."

The disconcerted Hebrew was at last constrained to admit everything, and the judge ordered him to be bound to the stone and left without food or drink until he had returned the five hundred ounces of silver. They were soon returned.

The slave Zadig and the stone were held in great esteem throughout Arabia.

XI. THE FUNERAL PYRE

Sétoc was enchanted and made an intimate friend of his slave. He was no more able to do without him than the king of Babylon had been; and Zadig was glad Sétoc had no wife. He found in his master a natural predilection for virtue, much uprightness, and good sense. He was sorry to see that Sétoc worshiped the celestial army

—that is to say, the sun, moon, and stars, in accordance with ancient Arabian custom. At times he spoke to him of it very discreetly. He finished by telling him that they were bodies like the others, and no more deserved his worship than a tree or a rock.

"But," said Sétoc, "they are the Eternal Beings whence we draw all our blessings. They give life to nature and regulate the seasons, and besides, they are so far away one can barely help holding them in veneration."

"You receive more blessings from the waters of the Red Sea," replied Zadig, "on which is borne your merchandise from the Indies. Why should not they be as old as the stars? And if you worship what is distant you should worship the people of the Ganges, which is at the end of the earth."

"No," answered Sétoc, "the stars shine too brightly for me not to worship them."

When night came Zadig lit a large number of tapers in the tent where he was to sup with Sétoc, and as soon as his patron appeared threw himself on his knees before them and cried: "Eternal and Radiant Lights, grant me always your favors!"—after which he sat down to table without looking at Sétoc.

"What are you doing?" asked Sétoc, astonished.

"I do as you do," replied Zadig. "I worship these candles, and neglect their master and mine."

Sétoc grasped the profound meaning of this apologue. His slave's wisdom entered his soul. He no longer burned his incense in honor of things, but worshiped the Eternal Being who had created them.

There was at that time in Arabia a ghastly custom which came originally from Scythia and, having established itself in India on the authority of the Brahmins, threatened to overrun the whole of the Orient. When a married man died and his well-beloved widow wished to be cleansed from sin, she burned herself publicly on her husband's body. It was the solemn ceremony known as "the pyre of widowhood." The tribe in which the most women had been burned was the most esteemed.

An Arab of Sétoc's tribe having died, his widow, Almona by name, a very pious girl, made known the day and the hour when she would throw herself in the fire to the sound of drums and trumpets. Zadig protested to Sétoc how opposed this horrible custom was to the good of the human race. He pointed out that every day young widows were allowed to burn who might otherwise give children to the state, or at least rear those they already had, and he made him agree that such a barbarous habit should, if possible, be abolished.

"But," said Sétoc, "women have had the privilege of burning themselves for more than a thousand years: who among us would dare alter a law thus hallowed by time? Is there anything more worthy of respect than an abuse dating from ancient times?"

"Well," answered Zadig, "reason is more ancient still. Speak to the chiefs of the tribes, and I will go to find the young widow."

He had himself presented to her and, having gained admittance to her mind by praising her beauty and saying what a pity it was to set fire to so many charms, did homage further to her constancy and courage.

"You loved your husband enormously, then?" he asked her.

"Love him!" replied the Arab lady. "Not in the least! He was a jealous brute, an intolerable man! But I am absolutely determined to throw myself on his funeral pyre."

"It seems," said Zadig, "that there is a quite exquisite pleasure in being burned alive."

"Ah!" said the lady, "it makes one's flesh creep, but

one must go through with it. I am a pious woman, my reputation would be lost, and everyone would laugh at me if I did not burn myself."

Zadig got her to agree that she was burning herself out of vanity and for other people, and then spoke to her at length in such a way as to make her love life a little. He even managed to inspire in her some friendliness for the man who was talking to her. "What would you do," he asked her, "if the vanity of burning yourself ceased to possess you?"

"Lack a day!" answered the lady, "I think I should ask you to marry me."

Zadig's heart was too full of Astarte for him not to evade this declaration, but he went at once in search of the chiefs of the tribe, told them what had passed, and counseled them to make a law whereby it would be forbidden for a widow to burn herself unless she had first had a *tête-à-tête* with a young man lasting a complete hour.

From that time forth no lady in Arabia burned herself, and the Arabians were under an obligation to Zadig for having destroyed in a day a cruel custom that had endured for so many centuries. He was therefore the benefactor of Arabia.

XII. THE SUPPER

Sétoc could not part with this man in whom wisdom dwelt, and he took him to the great fair at Bassora, where the chief merchants of the inhabited world were accustomed to congregate. For Zadig it was an evident consolation to see so many men assembled in one place. The universe seemed to him to be a big family, the members of which gathered together at Bassora.

From the second day he found himself eating with an Egyptian, an Indian from the Ganges country, an inhabitant of Cathay, a Greek, a Celt, and several other foreigners who in their frequent travels toward the Arabian Gulf had learned enough Arabic to make themselves understood. The Egyptian seemed very wroth.

"What an accursed place Bassora is!" he said. "No one here will lend me a thousand ounces of gold on a parcel of the finest dry-goods in the world."

"What are the dry-goods," asked Sétoc, "on which you cannot obtain that amount?"

"My aunt's body," replied the Egyptian. "She was the finest woman in Egypt. She always used to accompany me, and now she has died on the road, I've had her made into one of the finest mummies we have. In my own country I could pawn her for as much as I liked. It's very strange that here nobody will give me a paltry thousand ounces of gold on such solid security."

Getting angrier and angrier, he was about to eat some excellent boiled fowl. The Indian took his hand and stopped him. "What are you going to do?" he cried sorrowfully.

"Eat this chicken," said the man with the mummy.

"Take care," continued the man from the Ganges, "take care! Your dead aunt's soul may have passed into this chicken's body, and you do not wish to expose yourself to the possibility of eating your aunt. To cook a chicken is a manifest outrage on nature."

"What are you talking about with your nature and your chickens?" demanded the choleric Egyptian. "We worship a bull, and many a good meal do we make of beef."

"You worship a bull! is it possible?" said the man from the Ganges.

"Nothing more possible," answered the other. "We've

done so for a hundred and thirty-five thousand years, and none of us find anything amiss in it."

"A hundred and thirty-five thousand years?" returned the Indian. "You exaggerate somewhat. Why, India has only been populated eighty thousand, and we're certainly older than you. Brahma forbade us to eat beef before you dreamed of putting the ox on either the altar or the spit."

"A nice booby Brahma to compare with our Apis," sneered the Egyptian. "What did your Brahma do that was so wonderful?"

"It was Brahma taught men to read and write," answered the Brahmin, "and it's to him the world owes the game of chess."

"Not a bit of it," interrupted a Chaldean seated nearby, "we owe such great benefits to the fish Oannes, and it is only fair to render unto him the things that are his. Everyone will tell you he was a divine being, that he had a golden tail and a fine human head, and that he came out of the water to preach on land for three hours each day. He had numerous children who were all kings, as everyone knows. I have his picture at home, and I hold it in veneration, as is my duty. You may eat beef as much as you like, but it is assuredly very great sacrilege to cook fish. And besides, you are both of too recent and too ignoble origin for you to argue with me. The Egyptian nation counts a mere hundred and thirty-five thousand years, the Indians boast of only a palty eighty thousand. *We* have almanacs dating back four thousand centuries. Listen to me, renounce your follies, and I will give each of you a beautiful picture of Oannes!"

The man from Cambalu took up the conversation. "I have a great respect," he said, "for the Egyptians, Chaldeans, Greeks, and Celts, for Brahma, the bull Apis, the beautiful fish Oannes; but maybe Li or Tien, whichever you prefer to call him, is well worth the bulls and the fishes. I will say nothing about my own country: it is as big as the lands of Egypt, Chaldea, and India put together. I do not argue about antiquity because to be happy is sufficient, and to be old precious little, but if you are talking about almanacs let me tell you the whole of Asia accepts ours—and we had some very good ones before they knew arithmetic in Chaldea."

"You're all blockheads!" cried the Greek, "the whole lot of you! Don't you know that Chaos is father of every thing, that Form and Matter have set the world in the state it is?"

This Greek spoke for a long time, but was interrupted at last by the Celt who, having drunk deeply while they were arguing, thought himself wiser than all the others. With an oath on his lips he said that only Teutath and oak-mistletoe were worth talking about, that he for his part always carried a sprig of mistletoe in his pocket, that his ancestors the Scythians were the only people worth anything who had ever existed, that they had indeed sometimes eaten men, but that such a detail was no reason why his race should not be held in great respect. Further, he threatened that if anyone spoke ill of Teutath, he would teach him how to behave.

Thenceforward the quarrel became more heated, and Sétoc saw the moment coming when the table would be running with blood. Zadig, who had kept silence throughout the dispute, rose at last, and as the Celt seemed the maddest addressed him first. He said the Celt was quite right, and asked him for some mistletoe. He congratulated the Greek on his eloquence, and calmed all their heated spirits. To the man from Cathay he said very little, because that worthy had been the most reasonable of them all. "My friends," he wound up, "you are going to quarrel about nothing, for you all hold the same views." At these words all his listeners cried out in protest. "But is it not true," Zadig asked the Celt, "that you worship not the mistletoe but him who made the mistletoe and the oak?"

"That is so," answered the Celt.

"And you, Mr. Egyptian, you worship in a particular bull him who has given you all bulls?"

"Yes," said the Egyptian.

"The fish Oannes," he continued, "must be subject to him who made the sea and the fishes?"

"Agreed," said the Chaldean.

"The Indian," added Zadig, "and the Cathayan recognize a first principle as you do. I did not understand very well the admirable things the Greek said, but I am sure he too admits a superior Being on whom Form and Matter depend."

The Greek, who was much admired, said that Zadig had grasped his meaning very well.

"Well, then," continued Zadig, "you all think the same thing, and consequently there is no reason for quarreling."

Everyone embraced him. Sétoc, having sold his wares at very good prices, took him back to the tribe. On arriving Zadig learned that he had been tried in his absence, and condemned to be burned over a slow fire.

XIII. THE ASSIGNATION

During his journey to Bassora, the priests of the stars had resolved to punish him. The trinkets and precious stones of the young women they sent to the funeral pyre were their perquisites, and it was certainly the least they could do to have Zadig burned for the trick he had played them. They accused him, therefore, of holding unorthodox opinions about the celestial army, and deposed against him on oath that they had heard him say that the stars did not sink into the sea. This appalling blasphemy made the judges shudder. They nearly tore their clothes in anguish when they heard these impious words, and doubtless they would actually have done so had Zadig had the money to pay for new ones. In their exceeding sorrow, however, they contented themselves with condemning him to be burned over a slow fire.

Sétoc, despairing, in vain used all his influence to save his friend: he was soon forced to hold his tongue. Almona, the young widow, who had developed a considerable liking for life (which she owed to Zadig) resolved to get him out of the pyre, with the abuses of which he had acquainted her. She turned her plan over in her head without mentioning it to anyone. Zadig was to be executed on the following day; she had only the night in which to save him. This is how she showed herself a discreet and charitable woman.

Having perfumed herself, she set off her beauty with the richest and most seductive dress she had, and went to beg secret audience of the chief priest of the stars. When she was in the presence of this venerable old man she spoke to him as follows:

"Eldest Son of the Great Bear," she said, "Brother of Taurus, Cousin of the Dog-Star (these were the pontiff's titles), I come to confide to you my twinges of conscience. I fear greatly that I have committed a terrible sin in not burning myself on my dear husband's funeral pyre. What indeed have I saved? Only my mortal flesh, which is already withered." As she said these words she drew from her long silk sleeves two naked arms of beautiful shape and dazzling whiteness. "You see," she continued, "how little it is worth."

The pontiff thought in his heart that it was worth a great deal. His eyes said so, and his mouth confirmed the opinion of his eyes. He swore he had never in his life seen such lovely arms.

"Alas," said the widow, "the arms may be less unlovely than the rest of me, but you will admit the neck is not worthy of my regard." She let him see the most charming bosom nature had ever formed. A rosebud on an ivory apple would have seemed in comparison but a madder-root on a piece of boxwood, and lambs coming from the wash-pen of a brownish-yellow shade. This breast, her great black eyes languishing with a flame of gentle fire in their depths, her ardent cheeks of the most lovely rose mingled with purest milk-white, her nose which was not like the Tower of Lebanon, her lips like two coral reefs enclosing the most beautiful pearls in the Arabian Sea—all together made the old man feel he was but twenty. Stammering, he made a declaration of love. Almona, seeing he was on fire, begged mercy for Zadig.

"Alas, my beautiful lady!" he replied. "My indulgence would be useless alone. You would need the signatures of three of my colleagues as well."

"Anyway," said Almona, "sign for yourself."

"Willingly," returned the priest, "on condition that your favors are the price of my compliance."

"You do me too much honor," answered Almona. "You have but to come to my room when the sun has set, and as soon as the bright star Scheat is on the horizon you will find me on a rose-colored couch which you may make use of as you will with your servant."

Carrying his signature, she left him. The old man was brimming over with love and distrust of his powers. He spent the rest of the day bathing himself, and while he waited impatiently for the star Scheat to appear drank a liqueur composed of Ceylon cinnamon and precious spices from Tidor and Ternate.

Meanwhile, Almona went to find the second pontiff, who assured her that the sun and moon and all the stars of the firmament were but wills o' the wisp compared with her charms. She begged the same mercy, and he asked the same price. She let herself be conquered, and gave to the second pontiff an assignation at the rising of the star Algenib. Thence she went to the third and fourth priests, collecting a signature each time, and making assignations from star to star. After this, she had word sent to the judges asking them to come to her house on important business. They came, and she showed the four signatures, telling the judges the price at which the priests had sold mercy for Zadig. Each priest arrived at his appointed hour, and each was much astonished to find his colleagues there and, still more, the judges, to whom their infamy was manifest.

Sétoc was so charmed with Almona's artfulness that he made her his wife.

XIV. THE DANCE

Sétoc had to go on business to the Isle of Serendib, but the first month of marriage being, as we know, the honeymoon, he could not either leave his wife or think he ever would be able to leave her. He therefore asked his friend Zadig to make the journey for him.

"Alas!" said Zadig, "must I put a still greater distance between myself and beautiful Astarte? However, I cannot refuse to serve my benefactor." After which observation, he wept and set forth.

He was not long in Serendib before he was looked

upon as a remarkable man. He became the arbiter of all the differences between the merchants, the friend of the wise, the adviser of the small number of people who accept advice. The king wished to see and hear him and soon recognized all Zadig's worth. He had confidence in Zadig's wisdom, and made him his friend. The king's intimacy and esteem made Zadig tremble. Night and day he thought of the misfortune Moabdar's goodness had brought him. "I please the king," he said to himself. "Shall I not be lost?" However, he could not escape His Majesty's blandishments, for it must be admitted that Nabussan, King of Serendib, son of Nussanab, son of Nabassun, son of Sanbunas, was one of the finest princes in Asia; and when one spoke to him it was difficult not to like him.

This good prince was praised, deceived, and robbed: it was a competition as to who should despoil him of the most treasure. The Lord High Tax-Collector of the Isle of Serendib always set the example which was faithfully followed by the others. The king was well aware of it. He had changed his comptroller many times, but had not managed to change the established fashion of dividing his revenues into two unequal parts, of which the smaller invariably went to His Majesty and the larger to his administrators.

King Nabussan confided his trouble to Zadig. "You who know so many wonderful things," he said, "do you not know a way of finding me a comptroller who will not rob me?"

"Certainly I do," answered Zadig. "I know an infallible method of finding you a man with clean hands."

The king was delighted and, embracing him, asked how he should set about it.

"All that needs be done," said Zadig, "is to make each man who offers himself for the dignity of comptroller dance: he who dances the most lightly will be infallibly the most honest man."

"You are laughing at me," protested the king. "That would be a nice way to choose a comptroller of my finances. What! you claim that the man who can best do an *entrechat* will make the most upright and competent treasurer!"

"I do not promise he will be the most competent," replied Zadig, "but I do assure you he will undoubtedly be the most honest."

Zadig spoke so confidently that the king thought he had some supernatural secret for recognizing comptrollers.

"I am not fond of the supernatural," said Zadig. "Claimants to magical powers, whether they be men or books, have always displeased me. If Your Majesty will permit me to make the test I propose, you will be quite convinced that my secret is the simplest and easiest thing in the world."

Nabussan, King of Serendib, was far more astonished to learn that the secret was so simple than if he had been told it was a miracle. "Very well then," he said, "do as you think fit."

"Leave it to me," returned Zadig. "By this test you will gain more than you think."

The same day he announced in the king's name that all those who claimed the high office of Comptroller of the Pence of His Gracious Majesty Nabussan, son of Nussanab, were to present themselves, clad in light silk clothes, in the king's antechamber on the first day of the moon of the Crocodile. Sixty-four applicants arrived. Violin-players had been stationed in an apartment nearby, and everything was ready for the ball. The door of this apartment remained closed, however, and to enter it was necessary to pass through a little gallery in semi-obscurity. An usher sought and presented the candidates one after the other. Each was left alone in this passage for a few minutes. The king, who had had the word, had spread all his treasures in this gallery. When all the claimants had passed into the apartment where the fiddlers were, the king commanded them to dance. Never did anyone trip it on the light fantastic toe more heavily or with less grace. All the dancers kept their heads bowed, their backs bent, their hands glued to their sides. "What a lot of rogues!" murmured Zadig under his breath.

Only one of them stepped out nimbly, his head held high, a look of assurance in his eyes, his arms outstretched, body erect, firm on his legs. "Ah! the honest fellow," said Zadig, "the good chap!"

The king embraced this good dancer and declared him comptroller. All the others were punished and taxed with the greatest justice in the world, for each during the time he was in the gallery had filled his pockets, and could scarcely walk. The king was sorry for human nature that out of sixty-four dancers sixty-three were thieves. The dark gallery was called "The Corridor of Temptation." In Persia these sixty-three gentlemen would have been impaled; in some countries a court of justice would have been constituted, which would have absorbed three times the amount of the money stolen and brought nothing back to the king's coffers; in another kingdom the robbers would have vindicated themselves and had such a light dancer disgraced; in Serendib they were condemned merely to add to the public funds, for Nabussan was very lenient.

He was also very grateful, and gave Zadig a greater sum of money than any treasurer had ever stolen from a royal master. Zadig used it to send the fleetest courier to Babylon to obtain information about Astarte's fate. His voice trembled as he gave the order, the blood ebbed in his heart, his eyes clouded, his spirit was near leaving him. The courier set off, Zadig saw him embark, and then returned to the palace seeing nobody, thinking he was in his own room, with the word "love" on his lips.

"Ah! love!" said the king. "That's just the trouble. What a great man you are! You have guessed what's bothering me! I hope you will teach me how to recognize a faithful woman as successfully as you have shown me how to find a disinterested treasurer!"

Zadig came to himself and promised to serve the king in love as he had in finance, although this seemed still more difficult.

XV. BLUE EYES

"My body," said the king to Zadig, "and my heart . . ."

"I'm glad you didn't say 'my heart and my mind,'" broke in Zadig, who could not restrain himself from interrupting his majesty. "Those are the only words one hears in Babylonian conversation, and there's not a book that doesn't deal with the heart and the mind, written by persons who have neither. But I pray you, Sire, continue."

"My body and my heart," resumed Nabussan, "are born to love. The first of these two sovereign powers has every chance of satisfaction for I have at my disposal a hundred wives, all beautiful, complaisant, attentive, voluptuous even—or at least pretending to be so with me. My heart is not anywhere near so happy. I have found only too often that the King of Serendib has most of the kisses, and Nabussan precious few. Not that I think my wives unfaithful, but I want to find a soul to call my own. I would give all the charms I own in my hundred beauties for one such treasure. See if among these hundred sultanesses you can find one who I can be sure will love me."

Zadig answered as he had in the case of the treasurers —"Sire, leave it to me, but first of all let me dispose of what you have spread out in the Gallery of Temptation; I will render you a good account of it, and you shall lose nothing."

The king gave him absolute control. He picked in Serendib thirty-three of the ugliest little hunchbacks he could find, thirty-three of the handsomest pages, and thirty-three of the sturdiest and most eloquent bonzes. He gave all of them liberty to enter the sultanesses' apartments. Each little hunchback had four thousand pieces of gold to bestow, and from the first day all the hunchbacks were lucky. The pages, who had but themselves to offer, triumphed after two or three days only. The bonzes had a little more trouble still, but thirty-three pious ladies finished by yielding to them. The king watched all these tests through blinds which allowed him to see into the apartments, and he was amazed. Of his hundred wives ninety-nine succumbed before his eyes. There remained but one young girl, a new arrival, to whom his majesty had never had access. One, two, three hunchbacks were separated from the rest, and they offered her as much as twenty thousand pieces: she was incorruptible, and could not refrain from laughing at the hunchbacks' idea that money made them a better shape. The two handsomest pages were presented to her, and she said she thought the king more handsome. The most eloquent bonze was left with her, and later, the boldest. She found the first a chatterbox, and did not deign even to suspect the second had any merit.

"The heart is all that counts," she said, "I shall never

give myself to a hunchback's gold, a youth's graces or a bonze's seducements. I shall love Nabussan, son of Nussanab, only, and wait until he deigns to love me."

The king was in transports of delight, astonishment and love. He took back all the money that had made the hunchbacks successful and presented it to beautiful Falide, which was the name of the young person. He gave her his heart, and she was indeed worthy of it. Never was the flower of youth more radiant, never were beauty's charms more entrancing. As this story is true, the fact must not be suppressed that she curtsyed badly, but she danced like the fairies, sang like the sirens, and spoke like the Graces: she brimmed with talents and virtues.

Nabussan, loved at last, adored her. Unfortunately she had blue eyes, and they were the source of the greatest misfortunes. There happened to be a law which forbade kings to love one of those women whom the Greeks have called βοῶπις. The chief bonze had decreed this law more than five thousand years before. It was so that he might get the first king of Serendib's mistress for himself that this chief bonze had incorporated in the constitution of the state a ban on blue eyes. All classes in the empire came to Nabussan to protest. It was said openly that the last days of the kingdom were at hand, that this abomination was the last word, that the whole of nature was threatened by a disastrous event—in short, that Nabussan, son of Nussanab, loved two big blue eyes. The hunchbacks, the treasurers, the bonzes, and the ladies with brown eyes, filled the kingdom with their lamentations.

The savage races which dwelt in the north of Serendib profited by the general discontent. They invaded the country of good Nabussan, who asked his people for supplies. The bonzes owned half the revenues of the state, and they contented themselves with raising their hands to heaven and refusing to put them in their coffers to help the king. They chanted nice tuneful prayers, and left the country a prey to the barbarians.

"O my dear Zadig," sighed Nabussan sadly, "will you help me once more out of my terrible distress?"

"With the greatest of pleasure," answered Zadig. "You shall have as much of the bonzes' money as you want. Abandon the lands where their castles are, and defend only your own."

Nabussan followed this advice, and the bonzes came and fell at his feet begging his help. The king answered them with beautiful songs of which the words were prayers to heaven for the preservation of their lands. In the end the bonzes gave up some money, and the king finished the war happily.

In this way Zadig, by his wise and excellent counsel, attracted to himself the irreconcilable enmity of the most powerful people in the state. The bonzes and the brown-eyed women swore his ruin; the treasurers and the hunchbacks did not spare him: good Nabussan was led to suspect him. As Zarathustra says—Services rendered often remain in the antechamber, while suspicions enter the cabinet. Every day fresh accusations were made against him. The first is repulsed, the second blossoms, the third wounds, the fourth kills.

Zadig was dismayed, and as he had completed his friend Sétoc's business satisfactorily and had forwarded him his money, he thought of nothing but leaving the island. He resolved to go to seek news of Astarte himself, "for," he said, "if I stay in Serendib the bonzes will have me impaled—but where shall I go? I shall be a slave in Egypt, burned alive in Arabia so far as I can tell, strangled in Babylon. However, I must know what has happened to Astarte. Let me away, and see what my sad destiny has in store for me."

XVI. THE BRIGAND

On reaching the frontier which separates Arabia Petraea from Syria, as he was passing near a fairly well fortified castle, some armed Arabs came out. He saw he was surrounded. "All you have belongs to us!" cried his aggressors, "and your person belongs to our master!" In reply, Zadig drew his sword, as did his body-servant who was a brave fellow. They killed the first Arabs who touched them. The number increased, but Zadig and his servant were not taken by surprise. They resolved to die fighting. Two men's struggle against a multitude could not last long. The owner of the castle, seeing Zadig's prodigies of valor from a window, took a liking to him. He came down in haste from his window, dispersed his men, and freed the two travelers.

"Everything that passes over my land," he told them, "belongs to me, as well as everything I find on other people's land; but you seem such a brave chap that I exempt you from the common law." He made Zadig enter his castle, and ordered his men to treat him well. That evening Arbogad had a fancy to sup with Zadig.

The lord of this castle was one of those Arabs whom we call "brigands," but amid the multitude of his bad actions he sometimes did a good one. He robbed with furious rapacity, and gave liberally; fearless in battle, he was pleasant enough in social intercourse; a debauchee at table, and gay in his debauchery; and remarkable for his frankness. Zadig pleased him very much; his conversation grew lively and made the meal draw out.

"Well," said Arbogad at last, "I advise you to enlist in my service. You won't do better! This trade isn't too bad! And one day you may even become what I am."

"May I ask," queried Zadig, "how long you have practiced this noble profession?"

"Ever since I was a boy," answered the chieftain. "I was body-slave to a fairly intelligent Arab, but I found my job unbearable. It made me despair to see that fate had not reserved me my bit of the earth which belongs equally to all men. I confided my troubles to an old Arab who said to me—'My son, do not despair. Once upon a time there was a grain of sand which lamented that it was one unknown speck in the desert. After some years it became a diamond, and now it is the finest jewel in the crown of the Emperor of the Indies.'

"This speech made an impression on me: I was the grain of sand, and I resolved to become a diamond. I started by stealing two horses. I surrounded myself with comrades and prepared to rob small caravans. In this way did I reduce the initial disproportion between myself and other men. I had my share of the good things of this world, I had even usurious compensation. I was much esteemed, I became brigand chief, I acquired this castle by force. The Satrap of Syria wanted to dispossess me of it, but I was already too rich to have anything to fear. I gave money to the satrap, in consideration of which I kept my castle, and I increased my domains. I was even named collector of the tribute which Arabia Petraea paid to the king of kings. I did my work of collection well, and that of payment not at all.

"The Grand Destur of Babylon, in the name of King Moabdar, sent a little satrap here to have me strangled. This man arrived with his troop; I was well-informed about everything and had strangled in his presence the four persons he had brought with him to pull the cord tight: after which I asked him how much he was getting for strangling me. He said his fees might amount to three hundred pieces of gold. I let him see clearly that he would have more to gain with me, and made him under-brigand: today he is one of my best officers and one of the richest. Believe me, you will do as well as he has. The robbing season has never been better, now that Moabdar has been killed and confusion reigns in Babylon."

"Moabdar killed!" exclaimed Zadig. "And what has become of Queen Astarte?"

"I don't know at all," answered Arbogad. "All I know is that Moabdar went mad and was killed, that Babylon is one big nest of cutthroats, that the empire is laid waste, that there are still some nice little jobs to pull off, and that so far as I am concerned I have already done some excellent ones."

"But the queen . . . !" repeated Zadig. "I beg you . . . do you know nothing of the queen's fate?"

"I have heard speak of a Prince of Hyrcania," answered the other. "She's probably become one of his concubines . . . if she wasn't killed in the general riot. But I'm more interested in loot than news. In the course of my raids I've taken plenty of women, but I haven't kept one: I sell 'em dear when they're pretty without even finding out what they are like. Nobody buys rank. An ugly queen wouldn't find a bidder. Maybe I sold Queen Astarte, maybe she's dead, but it's all the same to me, and I don't think you ought to worry about it any more than I do." Talking like this, he drank with so much zeal that he confused all his ideas, and Zadig could get no enlightenment.

He remained dumbfounded, overwhelmed, motionless. Arbogad was drinking all the time, telling stories, repeating over and over again that he was the happiest of men, and exhorting Zadig to be as happy as he was. At last, getting drowsy with the fumes of the wine, he went off to enjoy a peaceful sleep. Zadig passed the night in the most violent agitation. "What!" he cried, "the king has gone mad, has been killed! I cannot help pitying him. The empire is destroyed! . . . and this brigand is happy! O fortune! O destiny! A brigand is happy, and the most lovable creature nature ever made has perhaps died an awful death, or lives in a state worse than death! O Astarte! What has become of you?"

As soon as day broke he questioned all the men he came across in the castle, but they were all busy, and no one answered him. During the night they had made fresh conquests and were dividing the spoils. All he could obtain in the tumult and confusion was permission to depart. He took advantage of the permission without delay, plunged deeper than ever in his sorrowful reflections.

He walked along worried and restless, his mind filled with the thought of unhappy Astarte, of the king, of Babylon and of his faithful Cador, of Arbogad the happy brigand, of that capricious woman whom the Babylonians had carried off on the borders of Egypt, of—in short, of all the mishaps and adversities he had experienced.

XVII. THE FISHERMAN

A few leagues from Arbogad's castle he found himself on the bank of a little river. He was still bewailing his lot and looking on himself as the model of misery. He saw lying on the bank a fisherman who held a net loosely in his listless hand, seeming to let it go while he raised his eyes to the sky.

"I am certainly the most miserable of men," the fisherman was saying. "I was, as everyone acknowledged, the most famous cream-cheese merchant in Babylon, and now I am ruined. I had the prettiest wife a man of my station could have, and she deceived me. I still had a miserable little house, and it was plundered and destroyed. I took refuge in a hut, and now my sole source of livelihood is fishing, and I do not catch any fish. O my net, I will throw thee into the water no more, I will throw myself instead."

As he said these words he stood up and walked toward the water with the bearing of a man who is going to hurl himself into the river and end his life.

"Really!" said Zadig to himself, "so there are other men as unhappy as I am." An eager desire to save the fisherman's life came promptly with this reflection. Zadig ran to him, stopped him and questioned him gently and consolingly. It is claimed that a man is less miserable when he shares his misery with someone else, but according to Zarathustra this is due not to man's malignity but to his need. When one is sad one feels drawn to an unhappy man as to a fellow-creature. The joy of a happy man would be an insult, but two unhappy men are like two young trees which, leaning on each other, brace themselves against the storm.

"Why do you yield to your misfortunes?" Zadig asked the fisherman.

"Because," replied the fisherman, "I see nothing else to do. I was the most highy respected man in the village of Derlback near Babylon, and with my wife's help I made the best cream-cheeses in the whole empire. Queen Astarte and Zadig, the famous minister, adored them. I had supplied them with six hundred cheeses and went to town one day to be paid. On reaching Babylon I learned that Zadig and the queen had disappeared. I ran to the house of my lord Zadig, whom I had never seen, and found there the constables of the Grand Destur: armed with a royal warrant, they were faithfully and methodically ransacking the house. I fled to the queen's kitchens; some of the royal cooks told me she was dead, others that she was in prison, others said she had fled, but all assured me I should not be paid for my cheeses. I went with my wife to my lord Orcan, who was one of my customers, and asked his protection in our affliction. He accorded it to my wife, but refused it to me. She was whiter than the cream-cheeses which started my misfortune, and the glory of Tyrian purple was not more lustrous than the roses that lent life to her whiteness. That is what made Orcan keep her and drive me out of his house. I wrote my dear wife the letter of a man in the depths of despair. She said to the bearer: 'Oh, yes, let me see! I know who wrote this; I have heard speak of him. They say he makes excellent cream-cheeses: let some be brought to me, and let him be paid.'

"In my distress I thought of applying to the courts of justice. I had six ounces of gold left: of these I had to give two to the man of law I consulted, two to the attorney who undertook my case, two to the chief judge's secretary. When that was done my case had not yet started, and I had spent more money than my cheeses and my wife were worth. I went back to my village with the intention of selling my house so that I might have my wife. My house was well worth sixty ounces of gold, but people saw I was poor and eager to sell. The first man I approached offered thirty ounces, the second twenty, and the third ten. So deluded was I that I was about to accept when a Prince of Hyrcania came to Babylon, and laid waste everything on his road. My house was first sacked and then burned.

"Having thus lost my money, my wife, and my house, I retired to this country where you see me now. I have tried to live by plying the fisherman's trade. The fish, like the men, laugh at me. I catch nothing, and am dying of hunger, and if it were not for you, august consoler, I was going to die in the river."

The fisherman did not tell this tale all at once, for at every moment Zadig, overcome with emotion, interrupted him with—"What! you know nothing of the queen's fate?"

"No, my lord," replied the fisherman, "I know nothing of the queen's fate, but I do know that neither she nor Zadig paid for my cream-cheeses, that my wife has been filched from me, and that I am in despair."

"I trust you will not lose all your money," said Zadig. "I have heard speak of this Zadig, he is an honest man, and if he returns to Babylon (as he hopes to) he will give you more than he owes you. As regards your wife, who is not so honest, I counsel you not to try to get her back. Listen to me. Go to Babylon. I shall be there before you because I am on horseback and you are on foot. Go to see the illustrious Cador, tell him you have met his friend. Await me at his house. Go along, perhaps you will not be unhappy always."

"All-powerful Ormuzd!" he continued, "you use me to console this man. Whom will you use to console me?"

Speaking thus he gave the fisherman half of all the money he had brought from Arabia, and the fisherman, overcome with delight, kissed the feet of Cador's friend. "You are my angel deliverer!" he cried.

Zadig, however, went on asking for news, and wept.

"But, lord," said the fisherman, "are you also unfortunate, you who do good?"

"A hundred times more unfortunate than you," answered Zadig.

"But how can it be," pursued the good man, "that he who gives is more to be pitied than he who receives?"

"The reason is that your greatest misfortune was poverty, whereas mine is a trouble of the heart," replied Zadig.

"Did Orcan by chance steal your wife?" asked the fisherman.

This question reminded Zadig of all his adventures. He recited the list of his misfortunes, starting with the queen's bitch right up to his meeting with the brigand Arbogad. "Ah!" he said to the fisherman, "Orcan deserves to be punished, but usually it is just those people who are the favorites of fate. At all events, go to my lord Cador's house and wait for me there."

They parted, the fisherman thanking his fate as he walked, and Zadig cursing his as he rode.

XVIII. THE BASILISK

On reaching a beautiful meadow, Zadig saw a number of women looking for something with much diligence. He took the liberty of approaching one of them and asked if he might have the honor of helping them in their search.

"Do nothing of the sort!" answered the Syrian girl. "What we seek may be touched only by women."

"That is very strange," said Zadig. "Dare I ask what it is that only women may touch?"

"We seek a basilisk," she replied.

"A basilisk, Madam? and why do you seek a basilisk, if you please?"

"It is for Ogul, our lord and master, whose castle you see on the river bank at the edge of this meadow. We are his very humble slaves. My lord Ogul is sick, and his doctor has ordered him to eat a basilisk cooked in rosewater. As this animal is very rare and lets itself be captured only by women, my lord Ogul has promised to choose for his well-beloved wife the girl who brings him a basilisk. Let me go on looking, please; you can see what it would cost me if I were forestalled by my companions."

Zadig left the Syrian girl and her companions to look for their basilisk and continued his walk across the meadow. When he reached the bank of a little stream, he saw lying on the grass another lady who was looking for nothing. She appeared to be of majestic stature, but her face was covered with a veil. She was leaning toward the stream and uttering deep sighs. In her hand she held a little stick with which she was tracing some characters on the fine sand between the grass and the water. Zadig was curious to see what she was writing. He saw the letter Z, then an A: he was surprised: then a D; he started. Never was astonishment greater than his when he saw the last two letters of his own name. For some time he stood motionless. At last, breaking the silence in a halting voice—"Generous lady," he stammered, "forgive a stranger, an unfortunate, daring to ask by what odd chance I find the name of ZADIG traced here by your divine hand."

At this voice, at these words, the lady lifted her veil with trembling hands, looked at Zadig, uttered a cry of affection, surprise, and joy, and succumbing to the variety of emotions that assailed her soul all at once, fell swooning in his arms.

It was Astarte herself, the Queen of Babylon, the woman Zadig adored and whom he reproached himself with adoring. It was the woman for whose fate he had so wept and feared. For a moment he lost the use of his faculties. Then looking at Astarte's eyes, which opened again languidly with a look of mingled love and confusion—"Can it be true?" he cried. "Immortal powers that preside over the destinies of frail mortals, do you give me back Astarte? When, where, in what plight do I see her once more!" He threw himself on his knees before her and fell on his face in the dust at her feet. The Queen of Babylon lifted his head and made him sit beside her on the riverbank: many times did she wipe from her eyes the tears which would not stop flowing. Twenty times did she start and start again telling him things which her lamentations interrupted. She questioned him on the chance which had reunited them, and suddenly forestalled his answers with other questions. She broached the recital of her own misadventures and wanted to hear all about Zadig's. When at last both had calmed the tumult in their souls somewhat, Zadig related briefly by what accident he happened to be in this meadow.

"But, unfortunate and honored queen," he asked, "how is it I find you in this lovely spot clad as a slave and in the company of other slave-women who seek a basilisk to have it cooked in rosewater by doctor's orders?"

"While they are looking for the basilisk," said beautiful Astarte, "I will tell you all I have suffered and all the things I forgive heaven for now that I see you again. You know that the king my husband took it ill that you were the most lovable of men. It was for this reason that he decided one night to have you strangled and me poisoned. You know how heaven allowed my little dwarf to warn me of his sublime majesty's order. Hardly had faithful Cador forced you to obey me and depart, than he dared enter my rooms in the middle of the night by a secret door. He carried me off to the temple of Ormuzd where his brother the Magus shut me up in a huge statue of which the foot touched the temple's foundations, and the head the dome. I was as it were buried, but the Magus looked after me, and I lacked nothing I needed.

"Meanwhile, his majesty's apothecary went at daybreak to my room with a potion of henbane, opium, hemlock, black hellebore and aconite, while another officer went to your rooms with a blue silk cord. They found no one. The better to deceive the king, Cador pretended to betray us: he said you had taken the road to India, and I the road to Memphis. Couriers were sent out after us both.

"The couriers looking for me did not know me by sight. Barely ever had I shown my face to anyone but you, in my husband's presence and by his order. They pursued me on a picture of me made specially for the occasion. A woman of my height, who had greater charms maybe, was noticed by them near the Egyptian frontier. She was wandering about, distraught. They had no doubts as to this being the Queen of Babylon, and brought her to Moabdar. At first their mistake sent the king into a violent rage, but after looking at this woman more closely he discovered she was very beautiful, and was consoled. Her name was Missouf. I have learned since that in Egyptian this name signifies *the capricious beauty*. And indeed she was capricious, but she had as much cunning as caprice. She pleased Moabdar and mastered him to the point of having herself proclaimed his wife. Then her nature displayed itself in its entirety. She gave herself up fearlessly to all the mad whims of her imagination. She had a fancy to force the Chief of the Magi, who was old and gouty, to dance before her, and when he refused she persecuted him with the utmost fury. She ordered her master-of-the-horse to make her a jam tart. The master-of-the-horse pleaded in vain that he was no pastrycook; he had to make the tart, and then Missouf had him dismissed because the tart was burned. She gave the post of master-of-the-horse to her dwarf, and that of chancellor to a page. Everyone missed me.

"The king, who was an honorable enough man up to the time he wished to poison me and strangle you, seemed to have drowned his qualities in the prodigious love he had for the capricious beauty. He came to the temple on the great day of the sacred fire. I heard him pray to the gods for Missouf at the feet of the very statue where I was imprisoned. I raised my voice: 'The gods,' I cried, 'refuse the prayers of a king turned tyrant, who wanted to have his sensible wife killed that he might marry a wild scatterbrain.'

"Moabdar was so dumbfounded by these words that his mind was unhinged. The oracle I had delivered, coupled with Missouf's tyranny, made him lose his reason. In a few days he was quite mad.

"His madness, which seemed a punishment from heaven, was the signal for revolution. The people rose in revolt and ran to arms. Babylon, so long immersed in emasculate indolence, became the theater of terrible civil war. I was taken out of my statue and put at the head of one faction. Cador rushed to Memphis to bring you back to Babylon. The Prince of Hyrcania, learning the disastrous news, returned with his army to make a third faction in Chaldea. He attacked the king, who fled before him with his harebrained Egyptian woman. Moabdar died transpierced. Missouf fell into the hands of the conqueror. My misfortune was to be captured by a party of Hyrcanians and led before the prince at precisely the same moment as Missouf. You will be flattered doubtless to learn that the prince thought me more beautiful than the Egyptian, but you will be sorry to learn that he marked me for his harem. He told me very determinedly that he would come to fetch me when he had completed a military expedition he was about to undertake. You can judge of my sorrow. My bonds with Moabdar being broken, I could belong to Zadig, and I fell into this barbarian's chains. I answered him with the pride my rank and feelings gave me. I had always heard that heaven gave persons of my rank a characteristic majesty which with a word and a glance could drive into the humbleness of deepest respect those who were rash enough to stray beyond it. I spoke as a queen, but I was treated like a chambermaid. The Hyrcanian, without even condescending to speak to me, told his black eunuch I was a saucy wench but he thought me pretty. He ordered him to look after me and put me on the regime of the favorites, so as to refresh my complexion and make me more worthy of his favors when it should be convenient for him to honor me with them. I told him I should kill myself. He laughed, and replied that people did not kill themselves, that he was accustomed to all these little affectations; whereupon he left me, much as a man who has just put a new parrot in his menagerie. What a state of affairs for the first queen in the world and, I will add, for a heart which belonged to Zadig!"

At these words Zadig fell at her knees and bathed them with tears. Tenderly did Astarte lift him up, and continue her story.

"I found myself," she went on, "a barbarian's chattel and the rival of a madwoman with whom I was shut up. She told me the story of her adventure in Egypt. I judged from the description she gave of you, from the time, the dromedary on which you were mounted, from all the details in short, that it was Zadig who had fought for her. I had no doubts as to your being at Memphis, and I resolved to get away there. 'Beautiful Missouf,' I said to her, you are much nicer than I am, you will entertain the Prince of Hyrcania much better than I shall, help me to escape. You will reign alone, and you will make me happy while you relieve yourself of a rival.' Missouf devised with me my plans of escape. I left secretly, therefore, with an Egyptian slave-woman.

"I was already near Arabia when a famous brigand named Arbogad carried me off and sold me to some merchants who brought me to this castle where lives my lord Ogul. He bought me without knowing who I was. He is a voluptuary who thinks nothing but good living, and believes God placed him in the world to eat. He is enormously fat and hence is nearly always at the point of suffocation. His doctor has little influence with him when his digestion is in order, but governs him like a despot when he has overeaten himself. This doctor has persuaded him that a basilisk cooked in rosewater will cure him. Lord Ogul has promised his hand to whichever of his slaves brings him a basilisk. As you can see, I let them flock to merit this honor, and I have never had less desire to find the basilisk than since heaven has let me see you again."

Astarte and Zadig then confided to each other all that long-repressed emotion, misfortune, and love could inspire in the noblest and most passionate hearts; and the genii who rule love carried their words right to the realms of Venus.

The women returned to Ogul's castle without having found anything. Zadig was presented to Ogul, and spoke to him in these terms: 'May immortal health descend from heaven to watch over your days! I am a doctor, and having heard of your illness have hastened to your side, bringing you a basilisk cooked in rosewater. Not that I claim the right to be your wife. All I ask is the freedom of a young Babylonian slave whom you have had only a few days, and should I not be so fortunate as to cure the great lord Ogul, I consent to slavery in her stead."

The offer was accepted, and Astarte left for Babylon with Zadig's servant, having promised to send a courier at once to let him know all that happened. Their farewells were as tender as had been their meeting. The moment of reunion and the moment of parting are the two greatest times in life, as the great book of Zend says. Zadig loved the queen as much as he swore, and the queen loved Zadig more than she said.

While Astarte was on the way to Babylon, Zadig had a talk with Ogul. "My lord," he said, "my basilisk must not be eaten, all its virtues must enter your system by the pores of your skin. I have put it in a little leather bag, which has been well blown out and covered with a fine skin. You must hit this bag with all your strength, and I will send it back to you over and over again. A few days of this treatment will show you the power of my art."

On the first day Ogul was quite out of breath and thought he would have died of weariness. On the second he was less tired and slept better. In a week he had recovered all his health, strength, and agility, and the gaiety of his most blooming years.

"You have played at ball and kept sober," Zadig told him. "Learn that there is no such thing as a basilisk, that with temperance and exercise one is always well. The art of making intemperance and health dwell together is as chimerical as the philosopher's stone, judicial astrology, and the theology of the Magi."

Ogul's chief doctor, seeing how dangerous this man was to the art of medicine, joined forces with the apothecary of the household to send Zadig to look for basilisks in the next world. Thus, having always been punished for doing good, he was about to perish for curing a lordly glutton. He was invited to an excellent dinner. He was to be poisoned during the second course, but during the first he received a messenger from beautiful Astarte. He left the table and the castle.

When one is loved by a beautiful woman, says the great Zarathustra, *one always finds a way out of one's troubles in this world.*

XIX. THE TOURNAMENTS

The queen had been received in Babylon with the delight people always have in a beautiful princess who has been unfortunate. The city seemed quite calm. The Prince of Hyrcania had been killed in a battle. The Babylonian victors declared that Astarte should marry the man they chose as king. They did not wish the first place in the world to be dependent on intrigues and cabals, and they therefore swore to recognize as king the wisest and bravest man. A great arena surrounded by magnificently decorated galleries was built a few leagues from the city. The combatants had to present themselves in full armor. Behind the galleries each had a separate apartment where he was to remain unseen and unknown. Each combatant had to ride against four lances. Those that were fortunate enough to beat four knights would fight afterwards against each other, so that he who finally remained master of the field would be proclaimed winner of the games. The winner had to return four days later with the same arms, and solve riddles propounded by the Magi. If he did not solve the riddles he would not be king, and it would be necessary to joust again until a man was found to win in both contests; for the people insisted on having the bravest man and the wisest. During this time the queen was to be closely guarded, and she could be present at the games only if she were veiled. She was forbidden to speak to any claimant, so that there might be neither favor nor injustice.

This was the news Astarte made known to her lover, in the hope that for her sake he would show greater courage and wit than anybody else. He set out praying that Venus would steel his courage and illumine his mind.

Zadig reached the banks of the Euphrates on the eve of the great day. He wrote down his emblem with those of the other combatants, concealing his name and face as the law commanded, and went to rest himself in the apartment that fate had allotted him. His friend Cador, who had returned to Babylon after searching Egypt for him in vain, arranged for a complete suit of armor from the queen to be sent to his dressing-room. He had sent from her also the most beautiful horse in Persia. Zadig recognized that these presents were from Astarte: his courage and love gathered new hope and strength.

On the morrow, when the queen was seated under her canopy studded with precious stones, and the galleries were crowded with every lady of every class in Babylon, the combatants appeared in the arena. Each placed his armorial shield at the feet of the Grand Magus. The drawing was by lot, and Zadig was drawn last.

The first to advance was a very rich lord named Itobad, a very vain fellow, of little courage, very clumsy and witless. His servants had persuaded him that a man like him ought to be king, and he had replied: "A man like me is born to rule!" Thus had they armed him from head to foot. He wore golden armor enameled green, a green plume, a lance decorated with green ribbons. It was obvious at once from the way Itobad managed his horse that it was not for "a man like him" heaven was reserving the scepter of Babylon. The first knight who rode against him dismounted him; the second knocked him backwards on his horse's crupper, his legs in the air and his arms outstretched. Itobad recovered his seat, but with so bad a grace that everyone in the galleries started laughing. A third did not deign to use his lance, but made a pass, seized him by the right leg, and turning him half-round sent him sprawling on the sand. The stewards ran to him laughing, and put him back in the saddle. The fourth combatant took him by the left leg and made him fall on the other side. He was led back to his room amid hooting. There by law he had to pass the night. And as he picked his painful way back he said: "What an adventure for a man like me!"

The other knights did their duty better. Some of them beat two combatants running, others three even. Only Prince Otame beat four. At last Zadig's turn came. He dismounted four knights one after the other with all the grace in the world. The situation then was—who would win, Otame or Zadig? The former wore blue and gold armor with a similar plume. Zadig's arms were white. The blue knight and the white knight were equal favorites with the crowd. The queen prayed with beating heart that white might win.

The two champions made their thrusts and volts with so much agility, each of them gave such good blows with the lance, each was so firm in his seat, that everyone but the queen hoped there would be two kings in Babylon. At last, their horses being tired and their lances broken, Zadig had resort to this artifice: he passed behind the blue prince, sprang on his horse's crupper, seized the prince by the middle, threw him to the ground, seated himself in the saddle instead, and circled round Otame, who lay stretched on the ground.

"The white knight wins!" cried the whole gallery.

Otame, exasperated, rose and drew his sword. Zadig leaped from his horse with his saber in his hand. There they were both on foot engaging in a new battle in which strength and skill triumphed alternately. The plumes on their casques, the studs on their armlets, the links of their armor, flew far and wide beneath a thousand rapid blows. They strike with the point, with the edge, right and left, on head and on breast. They draw back, they advance, they measure each other, they lock again, they seize each other, twist themselves round each other like snakes, attack like lions. At last, Zadig has a moment to gather his wits, he stops, feints, thrusts, makes Otame fall, and disarms him.

"White knight," cries Otame, " 'tis you shall rule over Babylon."

The queen's joy was unbounded. The blue knight and the white knight, as well as all the others, were led back to their apartments, as laid down by the law. Mutes attended on them and brought them food. As may be guessed, it was the queen's little mute who waited on Zadig. Afterwards they were left to sleep till morning, when the victor had to bring his armorial shield to the Grand Magus for comparison, and to make himself known.

Although Zadig was in love he was so tired that he slept. Itobad, who rested near him, slept not at all. He rose during the night, entered Zadig's room, took Zadig's white armor and armorial shield, and left his own green armor in its place. When day came he went proudly to the Grand Magus and announced that "a man like him" was the victor. His identity caused some surprise, but he was proclaimed victor while Zadig was still asleep. Astarte was bewildered and returned to Babylon with despair in her heart. The galleries were already almost empty when Zadig awoke. He looked for his arms, and found only the green suit. He was forced to put it on as he had nothing else with him. Taken aback and indignant, he dressed in fury and went forward in this apparel.

All the people left in the gallery and the arena received him with hoots. He was surrounded and insulted to his face. Never did man endure such humiliating mortification. He lost patience, and with blows from his saber sent flying the rabble which dared abuse him. But he did not know what action to take. He could not see the queen; he could not claim the white armor she had sent him—that would have meant compromising her. Thus, while he was plunged in sorrow he was steeped in fury and uneasiness.

He went for a walk along the banks of the Euphrates, persuaded that his star destined him to be unfortunate despite all his efforts. He ran over all his afflictions in his mind from the adventure of the woman who hated one-eyed men down to that of his armor. "That is what comes of waking too late," he said. "If I had slept less I should be King of Babylon, I should possess Astarte. Knowledge, morality, courage have therefore ever served only to my undoing." A murmur against Providence escaped him at last, and he was tempted to believe that everything was ordered by a cruel destiny which oppressed the good and made green knights prosper. One of his vexations was that he had to wear the green armor which had called forth so much jeering. A merchant passed, Zadig sold it to him for a song and took from him a robe and a high conical hat. In this apparel he walked along the banks of the Euphrates, filled with despair and secretly reproaching the Providence which persisted in persecuting him.

XX. THE HERMIT

While he was walking along he came across a hermit whose venerable white beard reached to his waist. In his hand he held a book which he was studying intently. Zadig stopped and made a deep bow. The hermit greeted him with a gesture at once so gentle and so dignified that Zadig was curious to talk to him. He asked what book the hermit was reading.

"It is the book of destiny," answered the hermit. "Would you like to read some of it?"

He placed the book in Zadig's hand, and although Zadig was acquainted with several languages he could not decipher one word of the book. This redoubled his curiosity.

"You look very sad," said the good father.

"I have good reason to be, alas!" replied Zadig.

"If you will allow me to accompany you," the old man went on, "perhaps I can be useful to you. I have been able sometimes to bring comfort to the souls of the distressed."

Zadig felt somewhat in awe of the hermit's appearance, of his beard and his book, and he found in his conversation a high wisdom. The hermit spoke of fate, of justice and ethics, of sovereign good and human frailty, of virtue and vice, with such live and moving eloquence that Zadig felt drawn to him irresistibly, and begged the old man not to leave him until they were back in Babylon.

"It is I who ask this favor of you," returned the hermit. "Swear to me by Ormuzd that no matter what I may do you will not leave me for the next few days."

Zadig swore, and they set off together.

That evening the travelers arrived at a magnificent castle. The hermit asked hospitality for himself and the young man with him. The porter, whom one would have taken for a great lord, let them in with a kind of disdainful good-nature. They were presented to a chief servant who showed them the master's splendid apartments. They were allowed to sit at the lower end of the table without the lord of the castle even honoring them with a glance, but they were served like the others with daintiness and profusion of food. After the meal they were given a golden bowl, studded with emeralds and rubies, to wash in. They were taken to a beautiful room to sleep, and on the following morning a servant brought them each a piece of gold, after which he sent them on their way.

"The master of the house," observed Zadig when they were on the road, "seems to be a generous man, although somewhat haughty; his hospitality is indeed liberal." As he spoke he noticed that a sort of pouch the hermit wore seemed to be bulging, and in it he saw the golden bowl studded with gems which the old gentleman had stolen. At first he did not dare mention it, but he was very surprised.

Toward noon the hermit went to the door of a very small house where dwelt a rich miser, and asked hospitality for a few hours. A badly dressed old servant received him rudely, and led Zadig and the hermit to the stable, where they were given a few moldy olives, some musty bread, and stale beer. The hermit ate and drank as contentedly as on the evening before; then, addressing the old servant, who was watching them both to see they stole nothing and hurrying their departure, gave him the two pieces of gold he had received in the morning, and thanked him for all his attention. "Let me speak to your master, please," he added.

The astonished servant showed the two travelers in. "Noble lord," said the hermit, "I can but offer my very humble thanks for the splendid way you have received us. Deign to accept this golden bowl as a small mark of my gratitude." The miser nearly fell over backwards, but the hermit gave him no time to recover from the shock, and with his young companion left the house as quickly as he could.

"Father," said Zadig, "what is all this I see? You seem quite different from other men. You steal a gold bowl studded with precious stones from a nobleman who receives you magnificently, and you give it to a miser who treats you abominably."

"My son," replied the old man, "that lordly man who receives strangers only out of vanity and to have his wealth admired will become wiser: the miser will learn to be more hospitable. Be not surprised at anything, and follow me."

Zadig did not yet know whether he had to do with the maddest or wisest of men, but the hermit spoke with such authority that, bound moreover by his oath, he could not help following.

They arrived that night at a pleasantly, albeit simply, built house, where there was naught of either prodigality or niggardliness. The master of the house was a philosopher who had withdrawn from the world, and peacefully pursued the study of wisdom and virtue: nevertheless, he never felt dull. It had pleased him to build this retreat where he gave strangers a handsome but quite unostentatious reception. He led the way himself for his visitors, whom he first left in a comfortable room to rest themselves. Later, he fetched them himself to invite them to a clean well-ordered meal, during which he spoke discreetly of the recent revolts in Babylon. He seemed to have a sincere attachment for the queen, and wished Zadig had appeared in the lists to fight for the crown. "But men," he added, "do not deserve to have a king like Zadig." At which Zadig blushed and felt his sorrows redouble.

In the course of conversation it was agreed that things in this world did not always accord with the wishes of the wisest men. The hermit maintained that men did not discern the ways of Providence and were wrong to pass judgment on a whole of which they perceived but the smallest part.

They spoke of the passions. "Ah!" said Zadig, "the passions are disastrous things!"

"They are the winds that fill the ship's sails," returned the hermit. "Sometimes they submerge the ship, but without them the ship could not sail. Bile makes a man ill and choleric, but without bile man could not live. Everything here below is dangerous, and everything is necessary."

They spoke of pleasure, and the hermit proved it to be a gift of the gods, "for," said he, "man can give himself neither ideas nor sensations; he receives everything: pleasure and pain come to him as does his being."

Zadig marveled how a man who had done such mad things could reason so well. At last after a talk as instructive as it was agreeable, the host led his guests back to their room, thanking heaven for having sent him two such wise and virtuous men. He offered them money in an easy, big-hearted way which could not offend. The hermit refused it and told him he would take his leave then as he counted on leaving for Babylon before daybreak. Their parting was affectionate, Zadig especially feeling much esteem and liking for so lovable a man.

When the hermit and he were in their room they spoke at length in praise of their host. At dawn the old man waked his comrade. "We must be leaving," he said:

"but while everyone is still sleeping I wish to leave this man a mark of my affection and regard."

With these words he took a taper and set fire to the house. Zadig was horrified and cried out, wishing to stop his committing such a frightful act. The hermit with dominating authority hurried him away. The house was ablaze. The hermit, who with his companion was already far enough off, watched it burn tranquilly.

"Thanks be to God!" he said. "There is my dear host's house completely destroyed! Happy man!"

At these words Zadig was tempted to burst out laughing and at the same time to upbraid him, to beat him, and to flee. But he did nothing of all that, and still dominated by the hermit's power followed the old man in spite of himself to their last lodging.

It was in the house of a charitable and virtuous widow who had a very accomplished nephew, her sole hope. She did the honors of her house as well as she was able. The following day she told her nephew to accompany the travelers as far as a bridge which, having been broken recently, had become dangerous to pass over. The young man assiduously walked ahead of them. When they were on the bridge, the hermit called to the lad. "Come here," he cried, "I must show my gratitude to your aunt." As he spoke, he seized the boy by the hair and threw him into the river. The child fell, reappeared for a moment on the surface of the water, and was then engulfed in the torrent.

"You monster!" cried Zadig. "You most infamous of men!"

"You promised me to be more patient," interrupted the hermit. "Learn that beneath the ruins of the house to which Providence set fire the master has found immense treasure. Learn that this youth whose neck Providence has wrung would have murdered his aunt in a year's time, and you in two."

"Who told you so, savage?" roared Zadig. "Because you have read this event in the book of the decrees of fate, are you permitted to drown a child who has done you no harm?"

While the Babylonian was speaking he noticed suddenly that the old man's beard had gone, that his face was taking on the features of youth. His hermit's habit disappeared. Four beautiful wings covered a mighty body radiant with light. "O envoy from heaven! O divine angel!" cried Zadig, falling on his face. "Have you come from the empyrean to teach a frail mortal how to submit to the commands of eternity?"

"Men," answered the angel Jesrad, "judge of everything without understanding anything. You of all men most merited enlightenment."

Zadig begged permission to speak. "I lack confidence in my own judgment," he said, "dare I beg you to throw light on one of my misgivings: would it not have been better to have corrected this child and to have brought him into the path of virtue than to drown him?"

"If he had been virtuous and if he had lived," replied Jesrad, "his destiny was to have been murdered himself with the woman he was to marry and the child which was to be born to him."

"What then!" said Zadig, "must there be crimes and misfortunes? and must misfortunes fall on good people!"

"The wicked," answered Jesrad, "are always unhappy: they serve to prove the small number of the just scattered over the face of the earth, and there is no evil of which good is not born."

"But supposing," said Zadig, "there were only good, and no evil?"

"In that case," replied Jesrad, "this earth would be another earth, the concatenation of events would belong to another order of wisdom; and that order, which would be perfect, can exist only in the eternal abode of the supreme Being, whom evil cannot approach. He has created millions of worlds, no one of which can resemble another. This vast variety is a symbol of the vastness of his power. On the earth there are no two leaves of a tree like to each other, and in the limitless plains of the heavens no two orbs. All you see on the little atom where you have been born had to be, in its appointed place and time, in accordance with the immutable laws of him who embodies everything. Men think that the child who has just perished fell into the water by chance, that by the same chance this house was burned: but there is no such thing as chance; everything is test, or punishment, or reward, or prevision. Remember the fisherman who thought himself the most unfortunate of men. Ormuzd sent you to change his destiny. Frail mortal! cease contending with that which is to be worshiped."

"But . . ." said Zadig.

As he was saying "but," the angel was already soaring toward the tenth sphere. On his knees Zadig adored Providence, and submitted. From on high the angel called to him: "Go on your way to Babylon."

XXI. THE RIDDLES

Zadig, beside himself and like a man near whom a thunderbolt has fallen, wandered on aimlessly. He entered Babylon on the day when those who had fought in the arena were already gathered in the great hall of the palace to solve the riddles and answer the questions put by the Grand Magus. With the exception of the man in green armor all the knights had arrived. As soon as Zadig appeared in the town the people flocked round him. Their eyes could not see enough of him, their mouths bless him sufficiently, their hearts wish ardently enough that he might be their king. The Envious saw him pass, shuddered and turned away. The people carried him right to the assembly hall. The queen, who was apprised of his arrival, was a prey to a fever of fear and hope. Anxiety consumed her: she could not understand why Zadig was without arms, or how Itobad was wearing the suit of white armor. At sight of Zadig there was a confused murmuring. Everyone was surprised and delighted to see him, but only knights who had fought were allowed to appear at the assembly.

"I have fought as well as anyone else," he said, "but my arms are borne here by another. While awaiting the honor of proving that what I say is true, I ask permission to come forward to solve the riddles." The question was put to the vote: Zadig's reputation for integrity was still so strongly impressed on their minds that they did not hesitate to admit him.

The Grand Magus propounded this question first of all: What of all things in the world is the longest and the shortest, the quickest and the slowest, the most divisible and the most extended, the most neglected and the most regretted, without which nothing can be done, which destroys everything that is small and gives life to everything that is great?

Itobad had to answer. He replied that a man like him knew nothing of riddles, and that it was enough for him that he had conquered with sturdy thrusts from his lance. Some said that the answer to the riddle was Fortune, others the World, others Light. Zadig said it was Time. "Nothing is longer," he added, "since it is the measure of eternity, nothing is shorter since all our schemes lack it; nothing is slower to him who waits, and nothing passes more quickly for him who is happy; on the one hand it extends right up to infinity, and on the other it may be divided and subdivided right down to infinity; all men disregard it, and all men regret losing it; nothing can be done without it; it condemns to oblivion all that is unworthy of posterity, and makes the great things immortal." The assembly agreed that Zadig was right.

The next question was: What is the thing one receives without returning thanks for it, which one enjoys without knowing how, which one gives to others when one has had enough of it, and which one loses without noticing it?

Everyone had his say, but Zadig alone guessed it was Life. He solved all the other riddles with equal ease. Itobad continued to say that nothing was simpler and that he could have succeeded as easily had he wished to give himself the trouble. Questions were put on Justice, the Sovereign Good, the Art of Ruling. Zadig's answers were judged the soundest. "It is a pity," people said, "such a gifted fellow should be so poor a horseman."

"Noble lords," said Zadig, addressing the assembly, "I had the honor of winning in the arena. The white armor belongs to me. Itobad took possession of it while I slept: he evidently thought it would suit him better than the green. I am ready to prove to him, and before you all, with my gown and sword against all that beautiful white armor he has taken from me, that it was I who had the honor of beating brave Otame."

Itobad accepted the challenge with the greatest assurance in the world. He had no doubts but that with his casque, cuirass and armguard he would dispose of a champion in nightcap and dressing-gown. Zadig drew his sword and saluted the queen, who was watching him filled with joy and apprehension. Itobad drew his, and saluted nobody. He advanced on Zadig like a man who had nothing to fear, ready to split his head in two. Zadig parried the blow by opposing what is called the "forte" of his sword to his adversary's "feeble," with result that Itobad's sword snapped. Then Zadig seized his enemy by the body, threw him to the ground and with the point of his sword at a vulnerable spot in Itobad's cuirass, cried to him: "Let yourself be disarmed or I shall kill you!" Itobad, always astonished at the calamities which befell a man like him, let Zadig do as he would, and the latter tranquilly took off his magnificent casque, his splendid cuirass, his beautiful armlets, his bright thigh pieces. These he donned, and then ran to fall at the knees of Astarte. Cador proved easily that the armor belonged to Zadig. He was acknowledged king by consent of all and particularly of Astarte, who tasted after so many adversities the joy of seeing her lover worthy in the world's eyes of being her spouse. Itobad went back to his house to have himself called "my lord." Zadig was king, and was happy. He bore in mind what the angel Jesrad had said. He remembered even the grain of sand that became a diamond. The queen and he worshiped Providence. Zadig let that capricious beauty Missouf travel. He sent to find the brigand Arbogad, to whom he gave honorable rank in his army, with a promise to raise him to the highest rank if he conducted himself as a real warrior, and to hang him if he pursued the profession of brigand.

Sétoc was called from the depths of Arabia, with his beautiful Almona, to be at the head of the commerce of Babylon. A place was found for Cador, and he was cared for as his services entitled him to be: he was the king's friend, and the king was the only monarch on earth who had a friend. The little mute was not forgotten. The fisherman was given a fine house. Orcan was condemned to pay him a large sum, and to give him back his wife: but the fisherman had grown wise, and he accepted the money only.

Beautiful Sémire could not console herself for having thought that Zadig would be a one-eyed man, nor could Azora stop weeping for having wanted to cut off his nose: The Envious died of rage and shame. The empire enjoyed peace, glory, and abundance: it was the finest century on earth, for the government was one of justice and love. Men gave their blessings to Zadig, while he gave his to heaven.

Translation by H. I. Woolf

Micromegas

PHILOSOPHIC STORY

CHAPTER I

Journey of an Inhabitant of the World of the Star Sirius into the Planet Saturn

IN ONE of those planets which revolve round the star named Sirius there was a young man of much wit with whom I had the honor to be acquainted during the last visit he made to our little anthill. He was called Micromegas, a name very well suited to all big men. His height was eight leagues: by eight leagues I mean twenty-four thousand geometrical paces of five feet each.

Some of the mathematicians, persons of unending public utility, will at once seize their pens and discover that, since Mr. Micromegas, inhabitant of the land of Sirius, measures from head to foot twenty-four thousand paces (which make one-hundred-and-twenty thousand royal feet), and since we other citizens of the earth measure barely five feet, and our globe has a circumference of nine thousand leagues—they will discover, I say, that it follows absolutely that the globe which produced Mr. Micromegas must have exactly twenty-one million six hundred thousand times more circumference than our little earth. Nothing in nature is simpler or more ordinary. The states of certain German and Italian sovereigns, round which one may travel completely in half an hour, compared with the empires of Turkey, Muscovy, or China, are but a very feeble example of the prodigious differences which nature contrives everywhere.

His Excellency's stature being as I have stated, all our sculptors and all our painters will agree without difficulty that he is fifty thousand royal feet round the waist; which makes him very nicely proportioned.

As regards his mind, it is one of the most cultured we possess. He knows many things, and has invented a few. He had not yet reached the age of two-hundred-and-fifty, and was studying, according to custom, at the Jesuit college in his planet, when he solved by sheer brain power more than fifty of the problems of Euclid. That is eighteen more than Blaise Pascal who, after solving thirty-two to amuse himself, according to his sister, became a rather mediocre geometer and a very inferior metaphysician.

Toward the age of four hundred and fifty, when his childhood was past, he dissected many of those little insects which, not being a hundred feet across, escape the ordinary microscope. He wrote about them a very singular book which, however, brought him some trouble. The mufti of his country, a hair-splitter of great ignorance, found in it assertions that were suspicious, rash, offensive, unorthodox, and savoring of heresy, and prosecuted him vigorously. The question was whether the bodies of Sirian fleas were made of the same substance as the bodies of Sirian slugs. Micromegas defended himself with spirit, and brought all the women to his way of thinking. The case lasted two hundred and twenty years, and ended by the mufti having the book condemned by some jurists who had not read it, and by the author being banished from the court for eight hundred years.

Micromegas was only moderately distressed at being banished from a court which was such a hotbed of meannesses and vexations. He wrote a very droll song against the mufti, which hardly troubled that dignitary, and set forth on a journey from planet to planet in order to finish forming his heart and mind, as the saying is.

Those who travel only in post-chaise and coach will be astonished, doubtless, at the methods of transport in the world above, for we on our little mud-heap cannot imagine anything outside the range of our ordinary experience. Our traveler had a marvelous knowledge of the laws of gravitation, and of the forces of repulsion and attraction. He made such excellent use of them that sometimes by the good offices of a comet, and at others by the help of a sunbeam, he and his friends went from globe to globe as a bird flutters from branch to branch. He traversed the Milky Way in no time, and I am forced to confess that he never saw through the stars with which it is sown the beautiful paradise that the illustrious and reverend Mr. Derham boasts of having seen at the end of his spyglass. Not that I claim that Mr. Derham's eyesight is bad: God forbid! but Micromegas was on the spot, he is a sound observer, and I do not wish to contradict anyone.

After making a long tour, Micromegas reached the globe of Saturn. Although he was accustomed to see new things, he could not, on beholding the littleness of the globe and its inhabitants, refrain from that superior smile to which even the wisest men are sometimes subject. For Saturn, after all, is hardly more than nine hundred times bigger than the earth, and its citizens are dwarfs only about a thousand fathoms tall. He and his friends laughed at them at first, much as an Italian musician, when he comes to France, laughs at Lulli's music. The Sirian had good brains, however, and understood quickly that a thinking being may very well not be ridiculous merely because his height is only six thousand feet. Having started by amazing the Saturnians, he finished by becoming intimate with them. He engaged in a close friendship with the secretary of the Academy of Saturn, a man of much wit who, although he had indeed invented nothing himself, yet had a very good idea of the inventions of others, and had produced quite passable light verses and weighty computations.

I will record here for the benefit of my readers an odd conversation which Micromegas had with Mr. Secretary.

CHAPTER II

Conversation of the Inhabitant of Sirius with the Inhabitant of Saturn

When his Excellency had laid himself down, and the secretary had drawn near to his face, Micromegas spoke. "It must be admitted," he said, "that there is plenty of variety in nature."

"Yes," agreed the Saturnian, "nature is like a flower bed of which the flowers . . ."

"Enough of your flower bed," said the other.

"Nature," resumed the secretary, "is like a company of fair women and dark women whose apparel . . ."

"What have I to do with your dark women?" said the other.

"Well, then, nature is like a gallery of pictures whose features . . ."

"Oh, no!" said the traveler. "I tell you once more—nature is like nature. Why seek to compare it with anything?"

"To please you," answered the secretary.

"I do not want people to please me," replied the traveler. "I want them to teach me. Begin by telling me how many senses men in your world have."

"We have seventy-two," said the academician, "and we complain every day that we have not more. Our imagination surpasses our needs. We find that with our seventy-two senses, our ring, and our five moons, we are too limited; and despite all our curiosity and the fairly large number of emotions arising from our seventy-two senses, we have plenty of time to be bored."

"That I can quite understand," said Micromegas, "for although in our world we have nearly a thousand senses, we still have an indescribable, vague yearning, an inexpressible restlessness, which warns us incessantly that we are of small account, and that there exist beings far more perfect. I have traveled a little, and I have seen mortals much below our level; I have also seen others far superior: but I have not seen any who have not more appetites than real needs, and more needs than contentment. One day, maybe, I shall reach the country where nobody lacks anything, but up to now no one has given me definite news of that country."

The Saturnian and the Sirian proceeded to tire themselves out with conjectures, but after many very ingenious and very uncertain arguments, they were forced to return to facts.

"How long do you live?" asked the Sirian.

"Ah! a very short time," replied the small man of Saturn.

"Just as with us," said the Sirian. "We are always complaining how short life is. It must be one of the universal laws of nature."

"Alas!" sighed the Saturnian. "We live for only five

hundred complete revolutions of the sun. (That makes fifteen thousand years, or thereabouts, according to our reckoning.) As you can see, that means dying almost as soon as one is born. Our existence is a point, our duration a flash, our globe an atom. Hardly has one started to improve one's self a little than death arrives before one has any experience. For my part, I dare make no plans; I am like a drop of water in an immense ocean. I am ashamed, particularly before you, of the ridiculous figure I cut in this world."

"If you were not a philosopher," returned Micromegas, "I should fear to distress you by telling you that our life is seven hundred times as long as yours, but you know too well that when a man has to return his body to the earth whence it sprang, to bring life again to nature in another form—which is called dying—it is precisely the same thing, when the time for this metamorphosis arrives, whether he has lived a day or an eternity. I have been in countries where the people lived a thousand times longer than my people, and they still grumbled. But everywhere there are persons who know how to accept their fate and thank the author of nature. He has spread over this universe variety in profusion, coupled with a kind of wonderful uniformity. For instance, all thinking beings are different, and yet at bottom all resemble each other in their possession of the gifts of thought and aspiration. Matter is found everywhere, but in each globe it has different properties. How many of these properties do you count your matter as having?"

"If you speak of those properties," said the Saturnian, "without which we believe our globe could not exist in its present form, we count three hundred, such as extension, impenetrability, mobility, gravitation, divisibility, and so on."

"It appears," said the traveler, "that for the Creator's purposes regarding your insignificant abode that small number suffices. I admire His wisdom in everything. I see differences everywhere, but everywhere also I see proportion. Your world is small, and so are its occupants; you have few sensations; your matter has few properties: all that is the work of Providence. Of what color does your sun prove to be if you examine it closely?"

"Of a very yellowish white," said the Saturnian; "and when we split up one of its rays we find it contains seven colors."

"Our sun," remarked the Sirian, "is reddish, and we have thirty-nine primary colors. Of all the suns I have approached there are no two which are alike, just as with you there is no face which does not differ from all the other faces."

After several questions of this kind, he inquired how many essentially different substances they counted in Saturn. He learned that they counted only about thirty, such as God, Space, Matter, substances which have Extension and Feeling, substances which have Extension, Feeling and Thought, substances which have Thought and no Extension; those which are self-conscious, those which are not self-conscious, and the rest. The Sirian, in whose world they counted three hundred, and who had discovered in his travels three thousand others, staggered the philosopher of Saturn. At last, after acquainting each other with a little of what they did know and a great deal of what they did not, after arguing during a complete revolution of the sun, they decided to make together a little philosophical journey.

CHAPTER III

Journey of the Two Inhabitants of Sirius and Saturn

Our two philosophers were ready to set forth into the atmosphere of Saturn, with a nice supply of mathematical instruments, when the Saturnian's mistress, who had heard of their approaching departure, came in tears to protest. She was a pretty little dark girl who stood only six hundred and sixty fathoms; but she made amends for her small stature by many other charms. "Ah! cruel man," she cried, "when after resisting you for fifteen hundred years I was beginning at last to give way, when I have passed barely a hundred years in your arms, you leave me to go on a journey with a giant from another world. Away with you! your intentions are not serious, you are nothing but a philanderer, you have never loved me: if you were a real Saturnian you would be faithful. Where are you going to gad about? What do you seek? Our five moons are less errant than you, our ring is less variable. One thing is certain! I shall never love anyone else."

The philosopher kissed her, wept with her, for all that he was a philosopher, and the lady after having swooned went off to console herself with one of the dandies of the land.

Meanwhile, our two seekers after knowledge departed. First they jumped on the ring; they found it to be fairly flat, as an illustrious inhabitant of our little globe has very well guessed. Thence they journeyed from moon to moon. A comet passed quite close to the last one they visited; with their servants and instruments they hurled themselves on it. When they had covered about a hundred and fifty million leagues they came upon the satellites of Jupiter. They came to Jupiter itself, and stayed there a year, during which time they learned some very wonderful secrets that would now be in the hands of the printers, had not my lords the inquisitors found some of the propositions rather tough. But I read the manuscript in the library of the illustrious archbishop of ——, who with a generosity and kindness which cannot be sufficiently praised, allowed me to see his books.

But let us return to our travelers. When they left Jupiter they crossed a space about a hundred million leagues wide, and passed along the coast of Mars which, as we know, is five times smaller than our little globe. They saw two moons which serve this planet, and which have escaped the attention of our astronomers. I am well aware that Father Castel will decry, even with humor, the existence of these two moons, but I take my stand on those who reason by analogy. Those good philosophers know how difficult it would be for Mars, which is so far from the sun, to do without at least two moons. Whatever the facts are, our friends found Mars so small that they feared they might not have room enough to lay themselves down, and so they continued on their road like two travelers who scorn a miserable village inn, and push on to the nearest town. But the Sirian and his companion soon repented, for they traveled a long while without finding anything. At last they perceived a small glimmer: it was the earth, and it stirred the pity of the people coming from Jupiter. However, fearing that they might have to repent a second time, they decided to land. They passed along the tail of the comet and, finding an aurora borealis handy, climbed on the tail of the comet, and touched land on the northern coast of the Baltic Sea, the fifth of July, seventeen hundred and thirty-seven, new style.

CHAPTER IV

What Happened to Them on Earth

After a short rest, they ate for lunch two mountains which their attendants served up for them quite nicely, and then had a mind to explore the minute country in which they found themselves. They went first from north to south. The usual pace of the Sirian and his people measured about thirty-thousand king's feet. The dwarf from Saturn followed at a distance, panting, for he had to take twelve paces to each of the other's strides. Picture to yourself (if such a comparison be permitted) a very small lap-dog following a captain of the King of Prussia's Guards.

As these foreigners moved rather quickly, they circled the world in thirty-six hours. The sun, or rather the earth, it is true, does a like journey in a day, but it must be remembered that it is easier to travel on one's axis than on one's feet. Here they are, then, returned to the point whence they started. They have seen the puddle, almost imperceptible to them, which we call the "Mediterranean," and that other little pond which under the name of the "Great Ocean," surrounds the molehill. The water had never come above the dwarf's knees, and the other had scarcely wet his heels. Moving above and below, they did their best to discover whether or no this globe was inhabited. They stooped, laid themselves down flat, and sounded everywhere; but as their eyes and their hands were in nowise adapted to the diminutive beings which crawl here, they perceived nothing which might make them suspect that we and our colleagues, the other dwellers on this earth, have the honor to exist.

The dwarf, who sometimes judged a little too hastily, decided at once that there was no one on the earth, his first reason being that he had seen no one. Micromegas politely made him feel that it was a poor enough reason. "With your little eyes," he said, "you do not see certain stars of the fiftieth magnitude, which I perceive very distinctly. Do you conclude from your blindness that these stars do not exist?"

"But," said the dwarf, "I have searched well."

"But," replied the other, "you have seen badly."

"But," said the dwarf, "this globe is so badly constructed and so irregular; it is of a form which to me seems ridiculous! Everything here is in chaos, apparently. Do you see how none of those little brooks run straight? And those ponds which are neither round, square, oval, nor of any regular form? Look at all those little pointed things with which this world is studded; they have taken the skin off my feet! (He referred to the mountains.) Do you not observe the shape of the globe, how flat it is at the poles, and how clumsily it turns round the sun, with result that the polar regions are waste places? What really makes me think there is no one on the earth is that I cannot imagine any sensible people wanting to live here."

"Well, well!" said Micromegas, "perhaps the people who live here are not sensible after all. But anyway there is an indication that the place was not made for nothing. You say that everything here looks irregular, because in Jupiter and Saturn everything is arranged in straight lines. Perhaps it is for that very reason there is something of a jumble here. Have I not told you that in my travels I have always observed variety?"

The Saturnian replied to all these arguments, and the discussion might never have finished, had not Micromegas become excited with talking, and by good luck broken the string of his diamond necklace. The diamonds fell to the ground. They were pretty little stones, but rather unequal; the biggest weighed four hundred pounds, the smallest fifty. The dwarf picked some of them up, and perceived when he put them to his eye that from the way they were cut they made first-rate magnifying-glasses. He took, therefore, one of these small magnifying-glasses, a hundred and sixty feet in diameter, and put it to his eye: Micromegas selected one of two thousand five hundred feet. They were excellent, but at first nothing could be seen by their aid; an adjustment was necessary. After a long time, the inhabitant of Saturn saw something almost imperceptible under water in the Baltic Sea: it was a whale. Very adroitly he picked it up with his little finger and, placing it on his thumbnail, showed it to the Sirian, who started laughing at the extreme smallness of the inhabitants of our globe. The Saturnian, satisfied that our world was inhabited after all, assumed immediately that all the inhabitants were whales, and as he was a great reasoner wished to ascertain how so small an atom moved, if it had ideas, a will, self-direction. Micromegas was very embarrassed by his questions. He examined the animal with great patience, and finished by thinking it impossible that a soul lodged there. The two travelers were disposed to think, therefore, that there was no spirituality in our earthly abode. While they were considering the matter, they noticed with the aid of the magnifying-glass something bigger than a whale floating on the Baltic Sea.

It will be remembered that at that very time a bevy of philosophers were on their way back from the Arctic Circle, where they had gone to make observations of which nobody up to then had taken any notice. The papers said that their ship foundered on the shores of Bothnia, and that the philosophers had a very narrow escape. But in this world one never knows what goes on behind the scenes. What really happened I will relate quite simply and without adding one word of my own. And that is no small effort for a historian.

CHAPTER V

Experiences and Reasonings of the Two Travelers

Micromegas stretched forth his hand very gently toward the spot where the object appeared, and put out two fingers; withdrew them for fear of making a mistake, then opening and closing them, very adroitly took hold of the ship carrying these gentlemen, and placed it on his nail, without squeezing too much for fear of crushing it.

"This animal is quite different from the first one," said the dwarf from Saturn, while the Sirian deposited the supposed animal in the hollow of his hand.

The passengers and the crew, who thought they had been swept up by a cyclone and cast on a kind of rock, started bustling. The sailors took some casks of wine, threw them overboard on Micromegas' hand, and hurled themselves down after them. The geometers took their quadrants, their sectors, and two Lapp girls, and climbed down to the Sirian's fingers. They made such a commotion that finally he felt something tickling him. It was an iron-shod pole which the philosophers were driving a foot deep into his forefinger. From the itching he judged that something had issued from the little animal he held, but at first he did not suspect anything further. The magnifying-glass which could scarcely discern a whale and a ship had perforce no cognizance of such diminutive creatures as men. I do not wish to offend here anyone's vanity, but I feel obliged to ask self-important persons to note with me that, if the average height of a man be taken as five feet, we do not cut a better figure on this earth than would an animal about one six-hundred-thousandth of an inch high on a ball ten feet in circumference. Imagine a being which could hold the earth in its hand and which had organs in proportion to ours—and it is very likely there would be a great number of these beings: then conceive, I ask you, what they would think of those battles which let a conqueror win a village only to lose it in the sequel. I do not doubt that if some captain of giant grenadiers ever reads this work, he will increase by at least two feet the height of his soldiers' forage-caps, but it will be in vain, I warn him: he and his will never be anything but infinitely little.

What marvelous perspicacity would not our Sirian philosopher need, then, to descry the atoms of which I have just spoken? When Leuwenhock and Hartsoeker were the first to see, or think that they saw, the germ of which we are fashioned, they did not, by a long way, make such an astonishing discovery. What pleasure Micromegas experienced in seeing these little machines move, in examining all their tricks, in following all their performances! How he cried out with glee! With what joy did he hand one of his magnifying-glasses to his traveling companion! "I see them!" they exclaimed in concert. "Do you not see them carrying bundles, stooping and standing up again?" As they spoke, their hands trembled, both in delight at seeing such novel objects and in fear of losing them. The Saturnian, passing rapidly from an excess of doubt to an excess of credulousness, thought he observed them to be propagating their species. "Ah!' he said. "I have caught nature redhanded." But he was deceived by appearances—which happens only too often, whether one uses a magnifying-glass or not.

CHAPTER VI

What Befell Them with the Men

Micromegas, who was a much closer observer than his dwarf, saw clearly that the atoms were talking to each other, and drew his companion's attention thereto. The dwarf, ashamed at having been mistaken on the subject of procreation, was not disposed to believe that such species had the power of intercommunication of ideas. With the Sirian he enjoyed the gift of tongues; he had not heard our atoms speak at all, and he assumed they did not speak. Besides, how should such diminutive creatures have organs of speech, and what should they have to talk about? In order to speak, one must think, or very nearly; but if they thought, they would have the equivalent of a soul; attribute to this species the equivalent of a soul? it seemed absurd.

"But," said the Sirian, "you thought just now they were making love to each other; do you think it possible to make love without thinking and without uttering a word, or at least without making one's self understood? Do you suppose, further, that it is more difficult to produce an argument than an infant? To me they both appear great mysteries."

"I dare no longer either believe or disbelieve," said the dwarf. "I cease to have an opinion. We must try to examine these insects: we will argue afterward."

"That is well said," returned Micromegas, and pulled

out a pair of scissors with which he cut his nails. With a paring from his thumbnail he made on the spot a kind of huge speaking-trumpet, like an immense funnel, and placed the small end in his ear. The outer edge of the funnel surrounded the ship and all the crew. The faintest sound entered the circular fibers of the nail, with result that thanks to his ingenuity the philosopher of the world above heard perfectly the buzzing of our insects in this world below. In a very short time he managed to distinguish words, and finally to understand French. As did the dwarf, although with greater difficulty.

The travelers' astonishment increased with each moment. They heard maggots talking tolerably good sense, and this trick of nature seemed inexplicable to them. You can well believe that the Sirian and his dwarf burned with impatience to engage the atoms in conversation. The dwarf feared that the thunder of his voice, and particularly of the voice of Micromegas, might deafen the maggots without their understanding that it was a voice. The strength must be reduced. They put in their mouths a sort of small toothpick of which the very fine end reached close to the ship. The Sirian held the dwarf on his knees and the ship with its crew on one of his nails. He bent his head, and spoke in a low voice. At last, with the help of all these precautions and many others beside, he started to speak; and this is what he said:

"Invisible insects who the Creator has pleased should be born in this abyss of the infinitely little, I thank Him for having deigned to let me discover secrets which seemed unfathomable. At my court, maybe, they would not condescend to look at you, but I despise no one, and I offer you my protection."

If ever anyone was astonished, it was the people who heard these words. They could not imagine whence they came. The ship's chaplain repeated the prayers for casting out devils, the sailors cursed, and the philosophers on board propounded hypotheses; but no matter what hypothesis they propounded they could never guess who was speaking to them. The dwarf from Saturn, whose voice was softer than Micromegas', then told them briefly with what sort of people they had to deal. He related the journey from Saturn, made them aware who Mr. Micromegas was, and, after sympathizing with them for being so small, asked if they had always enjoyed this miserable state so close to complete nonexistence, what their function was in a world which appeared to belong to whales, if they were happy, if they multiplied, if they had souls, and a hundred other questions of a like nature.

One reasoner in the party, bolder than the others, and shocked that anyone should doubt he had a soul, sighted his interlocutor through the eyelet-hole on a quadrant, made two observations, and at the third said: "You assume, sir, that because you measure a thousand fathoms from head to foot you are a—"

"A thousand fathoms!" cried the dwarf. "Holy Heaven! How can he know my height? A thousand fathoms! he is not an inch out! What, this atom has measured me! He is a mathematician, he knows my height! And I who cannot see him at all save through a magnifying-glass, I do not yet know his!"

"Yes, I have measured you," said the physicist, "and what is more I shall measure your big friend too."

The suggestion was accepted, and his Excellency stretched himself out at full length: which was necessary because, if he had remained standing, his head would have been too far above the clouds. Our philosophers planted in him a big tree on a spot which Dr. Swift would specify, but which I refrain from calling by name out of respect for the ladies. Then, by forming a network of triangles they came to the conclusion that what they saw was in reality a young man one hundred and twenty thousand royal feet long.

At this point Micromegas spoke. "I see more than ever," he said, "that nothing must be judged by its apparent size. O God, who has given intelligence to beings which appear so contemptible, the infinitely small costs Thee as little effort as the infinitely great, and if there can possibly be creatures smaller than these, they may still have souls superior to those of the splendid animals I have seen in the sky, whose foot alone would cover the world to which I have come."

One of the philosophers answered him that he might indeed believe that there were intelligent creatures smaller than man, and he related for his benefit not the fables which Virgil told about the bees, but all that Swammerdam discovered and Réaumur dissected. He made him understand in short, that there are animals which to the bee are what the bee is to man, what the Sirian himself was to the prodigious animals he had mentioned, and what these animals are to other things compared with which they seem but atoms.

By degrees the conversation became interesting, and Micromegas spoke as follows:

CHAPTER VII

Conversation with the Men

"O intelligent atoms in whom the Eternal Being has been pleased to manifest His dexterity and His might, the joys you taste on your globe are doubtless very pure, for as you are so immaterial, and seem to be all spirit, your lives must be passed in Love and in Thought: that, indeed, is the true life of spirits. Nowhere yet have I found real happiness, but that you have it here I cannot doubt."

At these words all the philosophers shook their heads and one of them, more frank than the rest, candidly admitted that, apart from a small number of people who were little esteemed, the rest of the inhabitants of the world were a crowd of madmen, miscreants, and unfortunates. "If evil be a property of matter," he said, "we have more matter than is necessary for the doing of much evil, and too much spirit if evil be a property of the spirit. Do you realize, for instance, that at this moment there are a hundred thousand madmen of our species wearing hats killing, or being killed by, a hundred thousand other animals wearing turbans, and that over almost all the face of the earth this has been the custom from time immemorial?"

The Sirian shuddered and asked what could be the ground for these horrible quarrels between such puny beasts.

"The matter at issue," replied the philosopher, "is some mud-heap as large as your heel. It is not that any single man of all these millions who slaughter each other claims one straw on the mud-heap. The point is—shall the mud-heap belong to a certain man called 'Sultan' or to another called, I know not why, 'Caesar'? Neither of them has ever seen or will ever see the little bit of land in dispute, and barely one of these animals which slaughter each other has ever seen the animal for which he is slaughtered."

"Wretch!" cried the Sirian indignantly. "Such a riot of mad fury is inconceivable! I am tempted to take three steps and with three blows of my foot to crush out of existence this anthill of absurd cut-throats."

"Do not trouble," answered the philosopher; "they

wreak their own ruin. Know that after ten years not a hundredth part of these miscreants is ever left. Know that, even when they have not drawn the sword, hunger, exhaustion, or debauchery carries them nearly all off. Besides, it is not they who should be punished, but the stay-at-home barbarians who, after a good meal, order from their remote closets the massacre of a million men, and then have solemn prayers of gratitude for the event offered up to God."

The traveler was stirred with pity for the little human race, in which he discovered such amazing contrasts. "Since you are of the small number of the wise," he said to these gentlemen, "and that apparently you do not kill people for money, tell me, I pray, how you employ yourselves."

"We dissect flies," answered the philosopher, "we measure lines, we gather mathematical data. We agree on the two or three points we understand, and we argue about the two or three thousand we do not."

Immediately a fancy took the Sirian and the Saturnian to question these thinking atoms, in order to find out on what things they were agreed. "What do you reckon to be the distance," asked the latter, "between the Dog-star and Gemini?"

"Thirty-two and a half degrees," they all replied in concert.

"And from here to the moon?"

"In round numbers, sixty times the radius of the earth."

"What does your air weigh?" he continued, thinking to catch them. He did not succeed, however, for they all told him that the air weighs about nine hundred times less than an equal volume of the lightest water, and nineteen thousand times less than ducat gold. The little dwarf from Saturn, astounded at their replies, was tempted to take for sorcerers these same people to whom a quarter of an hour before he had refused a soul.

Finally, Micromegas put in a word. "Since you are so well acquainted with what is outside you," he said, "you doubtless know still better what is inside. Tell me what your soul is, and how you form your ideas."

As before, the philosophers replied in concert—but each held a different opinion. The oldest quoted Aristotle, another pronounced the name of Descartes, a third the name of Malebranche, a fourth that of Leibnitz, a fifth that of Locke. An aged Peripatetic said loudly and confidently: " 'The soul is an entelechy and a proof of its power to be what it is.' That is what Aristotle states expressly, page 653 of the Louvre edition. Ἐντελέχεια ἐστί, etc."

"I do not understand Greek too well," remarked the giant.

"No more do I," said the philosophical maggot.

"Why then," asked the Sirian, "do you quote Aristotle in Greek?"

"Because," replied the scholar, "one should always quote what one does not comprehend at all in the language one understands least."

It was the Cartesian's turn. "The soul," he said, "is a pure spirit which has received in its mother's womb all metaphysical ideas and which, on leaving it, has to go to school to learn over again what it knew so well, and will never know again."

"It was not worth while," observed the animal eight leagues long, "for your soul to be so wise in your mother's womb if it had to become so ignorant by the time your chin could grow a beard. But what do you mean by a spirit?"

"What a question!" said the man of abstractions. "I have not the remotest idea. A spirit, it is said, is not matter."

"But do you know at least what matter is?"

"Very well," replied the man. "For example, this stone is gray, has a certain shape and three dimensions, is heavy and divisible."

"Well," said the Sirian, "this thing which appears to you to be divisible, heavy and gray, will you kindly tell me what it is? You perceive some of its attributes, but do you know what it is fundamentally?"

"No," answered the other.

"Then you do not know at all what matter is."

Mr. Micromegas then asked another of the wise men he held on his thumb what his soul was, and what it did.

"Nothing at all," replied the disciple of Malebranche. "God does everything for me. I see everything in Him, I do everything in Him. It is He who does everything without my interfering."

"It would be as well worth while not to exist," said the sage from Sirius. "And you, my friend," he continued to a Leibnitzian who was there, "what is your soul?"

"My soul," answered the Leibnitzian, "is a hand which points the hours while my body ticks: or, if you prefer it, it is my soul which ticks while my body points the hour: or again, my soul is the mirror of the universe, and my body is the frame of the mirror. That is quite clear."

A humble partisan of Locke stood nearby, and when he was spoken to at last, replied: "I do not know how I think, but I do know that I have never thought save by virtue of my senses. That there are immaterial and intelligent beings I do not doubt: but that it is impossible for God to endow matter with mind I doubt very much. I hold the power of God in veneration: I am not free to set bounds to it: I predicate nothing: I am content to believe that more things are possible than we think."

The animal from Sirius smiled. He did not think the last speaker the least wise. The dwarf from Saturn would have embraced the follower of Locke had it not been for the difference in their proportions.

But, unluckily, there was present a minute animalcule in a clerical hat who interrupted the other animalcule philosophers. He said he understood the whole mystery; that the explanation was to be found in the *Summa* of St. Thomas. He looked the two celestial inhabitants up and down, and asserted that their persons, worlds, suns, and stars were created solely for man.

At this speech the two travelers fell on top of each other, suffocating with that inextinguishable laughter which, according to Homer, is the lot of the gods. Their shoulders and stomachs heaved, and amid these convulsions the ship which the Sirian held on his thumb fell into one of the Saturnian's trousers pockets. These two good people tried to find it for a long time and, having recovered it at last, set everything very nicely in order. The Sirian picked the maggots up again and spoke to them once more with much kindness, although at the bottom of his heart he was rather angry that such infinitely small creatures should be possessed of an arrogance almost infinitely great. He promised to prepare for them a fine volume of philosophy, written very small so that they might be able to read it, and that in the volume they would find an explanation for everything. And to be sure, he did give them this book before he left them. They took it to Paris to the Academy of Science: but when the aged secretary opened it he found nothing but blank pages. "Ah!" said he. "I thought as much."

Translation by H. I. Woolf

Story of a Good Brahmin

ON MY travels I met an old Brahmin, a very wise man, of marked intellect and great learning. Furthermore, he was rich and, consequently, all the wiser, because, lacking nothing, he needed to deceive nobody. His household was very well managed by three handsome women who set themselves out to please him. When he was not amusing himself with his women, he passed the time in philosophizing. Near his house, which was beautifully decorated and had charming gardens attached, there lived a narrow-minded old Indian woman: she was a simpleton, and rather poor.

Said the Brahmin to me one day: "I wish I had never been born!" On my asking why, he answered: "I have been studying forty years, and that is forty years wasted. I teach others and myself am ignorant of everything. Such a state of affairs fills my soul with so much humiliation and disgust that my life is intolerable. I was born in Time, I live in Time, and yet I do not know what Time is. I am at a point between two eternities, as our wise men say, and I have no conception of eternity. I am composed of matter: I think, but I have never been able to learn what produces my thought. I do not know whether or no my understanding is a simple faculty inside me, such as those of walking and digesting, and whether or no I think with my head as I grip with my hands. Not only is the cause of my thought unknown to me; the cause of my actions is equally a mystery. I do not know why I exist, and yet every day people ask me questions on all these points. I have to reply, and as I have nothing really worth saying I talk a great deal, and am ashamed of myself afterward for having talked.

"It is worse still when I am asked if Brahma was born of Vishnu or if they are both eternal. God is my witness that I have not the remotest idea, and my ignorance shows itself in my replies. 'Ah, Holy One,' people say to me, 'tell us why evil pervades the earth.' I am in as great a difficulty as those who ask me this question. Sometimes I tell them that everything is as well as can be, but those who have been ruined and broken in the wars do not believe a word of it—and no more do I. I retire to my home stricken at my own curiosity and ignorance. I read our ancient books, and they double my darkness. I talk to my companions: some answer me that we must enjoy life and make game of mankind; others think they know a lot and lose themselves in a maze of wild ideas. Everything increases my anguish. I am ready sometimes to despair when I think that after all my seeking I do not know whence I came, whither I go, what I am nor what I shall become."

The good man's condition really worried me. Nobody was more rational or more sincere than he. I perceived that his unhappiness increased in proportion as his understanding developed and his insight grew.

The same day I saw the old woman who lived near him. I asked her if she had ever been troubled by the thought that she was ignorant of the nature of her soul. She did not even understand my question. Never in all her life had she reflected for one single moment on one single point of all those which tormented the Brahmin. She believed with all her heart in the metamorphoses of Vishnu and, provided she could obtain a little Ganges water wherewith to wash herself, thought herself the happiest of women.

Struck with this mean creature's happiness, I returned to my wretched philosopher. "Are you not ashamed," said I, "to be unhappy when at your very door there lives an old automaton who thinks about nothing, and yet lives contentedly?"

"You are right," he replied. "I have told myself a hundred times that I should be happy if I were as brainless as my neighbor, and yet I do not desire such happiness."

My Brahmin's answer impressed me more than all the rest. I set to examining myself, and I saw that in truth I would not care to be happy at the price of being a simpleton.

I put the matter before some philosophers, and they were of my opinion. "Nevertheless," said I, "there is a tremendous contradiction in this mode of thought, for, after all, the problem is—how to be happy. What does it matter whether one has brains or not? Further, those who are contented with their lot are certain of their contentment, whereas those who reason are not certain that they reason correctly. It is quite clear, therefore," I continued, "that we must choose not to have common sense, however little common sense may contribute to our discomfort." Everyone agreed with me, but I found nobody, notwithstanding, who was willing to accept the bargain of becoming a simpleton in order to become contented. From which I conclude that if we consider the question of happiness we must consider still more the question of reason.

But on reflection it seems that to prefer reason to felicity is to be very senseless. How can this contradiction be explained? Like all the other contradictions. It is matter for much talk.

Translation by H. I. Woolf

Letters

Letters to Frederick the Great

Paris, 26th August, 1736.

MONSEIGNEUR,

I should indeed be insensitive were I not infinitely touched by the letter with which your Royal Highness has been graciously pleased to honor me. My self-love was but too flattered; but that love of the human race which has always existed in my heart and which I dare to say determines my character, gave me a pleasure a thousand times purer when I saw that the world holds a prince who thinks like a man, a philosophical prince who will make men happy.

Suffer me to tell you that there is no man on the earth who should not return thanks for the care you take in cultivating by sane philosophy a soul born to command. Be certain there have been no truly good kings except those who began like you, by educating themselves, by learning to know men, by loving the truth, by detesting persecution and superstition. Any prince who thinks in this way can bring back the golden age to his dominions. Why do so few kings seek out this advantage? You perceive the reason, Monseigneur; it is because almost all of them think more of royalty than of humanity: you do precisely the opposite. If the tumult of affairs and the malignancy of men do not in time alter so divine a character, you will be adored by your people and admired by the whole world. Philosophers worthy of that name will fly to your dominions; and, as celebrated artists crowd to that country where their art is most favored, men who think will press forward to surround your throne.

The illustrious Queen Christina left her kingdom to seek the arts; reign, Monseigneur, and let the arts come to seek you.

May you never be disgusted from the sciences by the quarrels of learned men! From those circumstances which you were graciously pleased to inform me of, Monseigneur, you see that most of them are men like courtiers themselves. They are sometimes as greedy, as intriguing, as treacherous, as cruel; and the only difference between the pests of the court and the pests of the school is that the latter are the more ridiculous.

It is very sad for humanity that those who term themselves the messengers of Heaven's command, the interpreters of the Divinity, in a word theologians, are sometimes the most dangerous of all; that some of them are as pernicious to society as they are obscure in their ideas and that their souls are inflated with bitterness and pride in proportion as they are empty of truths. For the sake of a sophism they would trouble the earth and would persuade all kings to avenge with fire and steel the honor of an argument *in ferio* or *in barbara.*

Every thinking being not of their opinion is an atheist; and every king who does not favor them will be damned. You know, Monseigneur, that the best one can do is to leave to themselves these pretended teachers and real enemies of the human race. Their words, when unheeded, are lost in the air like wind; but if the weight of authority is lent them, this wind acquires a force which sometimes overthrows the throne itself.

I see, Monseigneur, with the joy of a heart filled with love of the public weal, the immense distance you set between men who seek the truth in peace and those who would make war for words they do not understand. I see that Newton, Leibnitz, Bayle, Locke, those elevated minds, so enlightened, so gentle, have nourished your spirit and that you reject other pretended nourishment which you find poisoned or without substance.

I cannot sufficiently thank your Royal Highness for your kindness in sending me the little book about M. Wolff. I look upon his metaphysical ideas as things which do honor to the human mind. They are flashes in the midst of a dark night; and that, I think, is all we can hope of metaphysics. It seems improbable that the first principles of things will ever be thoroughly known. The mice living in a few little holes of an immense building do not know if the building is eternal, who is the architect, or why the architect built it. They try to preserve their lives, to people their holes, and to escape the destructive animals which pursue them. We are the mice; and the divine architect who built this universe has not yet, so far as I know, told His secret to any of us. If any man can pretend to have guessed accurately, it is M. Wolff. He may be combated, but he must be esteemed; his philosophy is far from being pernicious; is there anything more beautiful and more true than to say, as he does, that men should be just even if they were so unfortunate as to be atheists?

The protection you appear to give, Monseigneur, to this learned man, is a proof of the accuracy of your mind and of the humanity of your sentiments.

You have the kindness, Monseigneur, to promise that you will send me the *Treatise on God, the Soul and the*

World. What a present, Monseigneur, and what an interchange! The heir of a monarchy deigns to send instruction from the heart of his palace to a solitary! Be graciously pleased to send me this present, Monseigneur; my extreme love of truth is the one thing which makes me worthy of it. Most princes fear to listen to the truth, but you will teach it.

As to the verses you speak of—you think as wisely of this art as in everything else. Verses which do not teach men new and moving truths do not deserve to be read. You perceive that there is nothing more contemptible than for a man to spend his life in rhyming worn-out commonplaces which do not deserve the name of thoughts. If there is anything viler it is to be nothing but a satirical poet and to write only to decry others. Such poets are to Parnassus what those doctors, who know nothing but words and intrigue against those who write things, are to the schools.

If *La Henriade* did not displease your Royal Highness I must thank that love of truth, that horror which my poem inspires for the factious, for persecutors, for the superstitious, for tyrants and for rebels. 'Tis the work of an honest man; and should find grace in the eyes of a philosophic prince.

You command me to send you my other work; I shall obey you, Monseigneur; you shall be my judge, you shall stand to me in lieu of the public. I will submit to you what I have attempted in philosophy; your instruction shall be my reward: 'tis a prize which few sovereigns can give. I am certain of your secrecy; your virtue must be equal to your knowledge.

I should consider it a most valuable privilege to wait upon your Royal Highness. We go to Rome to see churches, pictures, ruins, and bas-reliefs. A prince like yourself is far more deserving of a journey; 'tis a more marvelous rarity. But friendship, which holds me in my retreat, does not permit me to leave it. Doubtless you think like Julian, that calumniated great man, who said that friends should always be preferred to kings.

In whatever corner of the world I end my life, be certain, Monseigneur, that I shall constantly wish you well, and in doing so wish the happiness of a nation. My heart will be among your subjects; your fame will ever be dear to me. I shall wish that you may always be like yourself and that other kings may be like you. I am with deep respect, your Royal Highness's most humble, [illegible]

Leiden, January, 1737.

MONSEIGNEUR,

I shed tears of joy on reading the letter of the 9th September with which your Royal Highness honored me; in it I recognized a prince who will be certainly beloved by the human race. In every way I am astonished: you think like Trajan, you write like Pliny, and you use French like our best writers. What difference there is between men! Louis XIV was a great king, I respect his memory; but he did not speak so humanely as you, Monseigneur, and did not express himself in the same way. I have seen his letters; he could not spell his own language. Under your auspices Berlin will be the Athens of Germany and perhaps of Europe. I am now in a town where two private persons, M. Boerhaave on one side, and M. s'Gravesande on the other attract four or five hundred foreigners. A prince like yourself will attract many more; and I confess I shall think myself very unfortunate if I die before I have seen the model of princes and the marvel of Germany.

I would not flatter you, Monseigneur, it would be a

crime. It would be throwing a poisoned breath upon a flower; I am incapable of it; it is my very heart which speaks to your Royal Highness.

On arriving at Amsterdam I found they had begun an edition of my poor works. I shall have the honor to send you the first copy. Meanwhile, I shall be so bold as to send your Royal Highness a manuscript[1] which I should only dare to show to one so free from prejudices, so philosophic, so indulgent as you are, and to a prince who among so many homages deserves that of a boundless confidence. Some time will be needed to revise and to copy it and I shall send it by whatever way you desire.

Indispensable occupations and circumstances beyond my control forbid me to carry myself to your feet that homage I owe you. A time will come perhaps when I shall be more fortunate.

It seems that your Royal Highness likes every sort of literature. A great prince takes care of all ranks in his dominions; a great genius enjoys every sort of study. In my little sphere I have only saluted from afar the frontiers of each science; my time has been shared among a little metaphysics, a little history, some small amount of physics, and a few verses; though weak in all these matters, I offer you at least what I have.

Were I not so interested in the happiness of mankind I should be sorry that you are destined to be a king. I could wish you a private man; I could wish that my soul might freely approach yours; but my wish must yield to the public good. Permit me, Monseigneur, to respect you more as a man than as a prince; permit that, among all your grandeurs, your soul should receive my first homage; and permit me to tell you once more what admiration and hope you give me.

I am, etc.

[1] The *Traité de Métaphysique*.

17th April, 1737.

MONSEIGNEUR,

I do not think there is any demonstration properly so called of the existence of the Supreme Being independent of matter. I remember that in England I did not fail to embarrass the famous Dr. Clarke when I said to him: We cannot call that a demonstration which is only a chain of ideas leaving many difficulties. To say that the square on the hypotenuse of a right-angled triangle is equal to the sum of the squares on the other two sides is a demonstration which, however complicated it may be, leaves no difficulty; but the existence of a Creative Being leaves difficulties insurmountable to the human mind. Therefore this truth cannot be placed among demonstrations properly so called. It is a truth I believe; but I believe it as being the most probable; 'tis a light which strikes me amid a thousand shadows.

Many things might be said on this topic, but it is carrying gold to Peru to fatigue your Royal Highness with philosophical reflections.

All metaphysics, in my opinion, contain two things: The first all that men of good sense know; the second what they will never know.

For example we know what constitutes a simple and a composite idea; we shall never know what the being is which has these ideas. We measure bodies; we shall never know what matter is. We can only judge of this by analogy; 'tis a staff nature has given to the blind and with it we walk and also fall.

Analogy teaches me that animals, being made as I am, having sentiments like me, ideas like me, may well be what I am. When I try to go beyond I find an abyss and I halt on the edge of the precipice. All I know is, whether matter be eternal (which is quite incomprehensible), whether it was created in time (which is subject to great difficulties), whether our soul perishes with us, or enjoys immortality—in these uncertainties you cannot choose a wiser course or one more worthy of yourself than that you take, which is to give your soul, whether it be perishable or not, all the virtues, all the pleasures, all the instruction of which it is capable, to live as a prince, as a man, as a sage, to be happy and to render others happy. I look upon you as a present sent from Heaven to earth. I am amazed that at your age you are not carried away with a taste for pleasure and I congratulate you infinitely that philosophy leaves you the taste for pleasure. We are not born solely to read Plato and Leibnitz, to measure curves and to arrange facts in our heads; we are born with hearts which must be filled, with passions which must be satisfied without our being dominated by them. Monseigneur, I am charmed with your system of morals! My heart feels it was born only to be a subject of yours.

One of the greatest benefits you can confer upon mankind is to trample under foot superstition and fanaticism; not to allow a man in a gown to persecute others who do not think as he does. It is quite certain that philosophers never trouble States. Why then trouble philosophers? What did it matter to Holland that Bayle was right? Why must it be that a fanatical minister like Jurieu had the interest to tear Bayle from his little fortune? Philosophers ask for nothing but tranquillity; they only wish to live in peace under the established government, and there is not a theologian who does not wish to be master of the State. Is it possible that men who have no knowledge save the gift of speaking without understanding themselves or being understood, should have dominated and still do dominate almost everywhere?

The northern countries have this advantage over the south of Europe, that these tyrants of souls have there less power than elsewhere. The princes of the north, therefore, are generally less superstitious and less malevolent than elsewhere. An Italian prince will deal in poison and then go to confession. Protestant Germany does not produce such fools and such monsters; and in general I should have no difficulty in proving that the least superstitious kings have always been the best princes.

You see, worthy heir of the spirit of Marcus Aurelius, with what liberty I dare to speak to you. You are almost the only person in the world who deserves to be spoken to thus.

Cirey, 27th May, 1737.

MONSEIGNEUR,

In the little paradise of Cirey we await impatiently two things which are very rare in France—the portrait of a prince such as you, and M. de Keyserlingk, whom your Royal Highness honors with the name of your intimate friend.

Louis XIV said one day to a man who had rendered important services to Charles II, King of Spain, and who had been one of his familiars: "Then the King of Spain loved you?" "Ah! Sire," replied the poor courtier, "Do kings love anything?"

You, Monseigneur, would have all the virtues which are so uselessly desired in kings and for which they have always been praised so inopportunely; it is not enough to be superior to men in mind as well as in rank, you are so in the heart. You, prince and friend! There are two great titles joined together which hitherto have been thought incompatible.

Yet I have always dared to think that princes could feel pure friendship, for usually private men who pretend to be friends are rivals. We have always something to quarrel about: Fame, position, women, and above all the favors of you masters of the earth, which we struggle for even more than for those of women, who nevertheless are quite as valuable as you are. But it seems to me that a prince, especially a prince like you, has nothing to quarrel over, has no rival to fear, and can feel friendship without embarrassment and at his ease. Happy is he, Monseigneur, who can share the bounties of a heart like yours! Doubtless M. de Keyserlingk has nothing to desire. My only surprise is that he should travel.

Cirey, Monseigneur, is also a little temple dedicated to Friendship. Madame du Châtelet, who I assure you possesses all the virtues of a great man with the graces of her sex, is not unworthy of his visit and will receive him as the Friend of Prince Frederick.

I reproach myself for having said nothing in my letters to your Royal Highness of French literature, in which you deign to take an interest; but I live in a profound solitude near the most estimable lady of this age and the books of the last; in my solitude I have received no novelties which deserve to be sent to Mount Remus.

Our belles-lettres begin to degenerate considerably, either because they lack encouragement or because the French, having found the good in the age of Louis XIV, are always so unfortunate as to seek the best; or because in all countries nature reposes after great efforts, like the fields after an abundant harvest.

That part of philosophy which is the most useful to men—that which treats of the soul—will never be of any value among us so long as we cannot think freely. A certain number of superstitious people here do great damage to every truth. Only the Jesuits are permitted to say anything; and if your Royal Highness has read what they say, I doubt whether you will do them the same honor you have done M. Rollin. History can only be well written in a free country; but most of the French refugees in Holland and in England have corrupted the purity of their language.

Our universities have no merit but their antiquity. The French have no Wolff, no MacLaurin, no Manfredi, no s'Gravesande, no Muschenbroek. Most of our professors of physics are not worthy to study under those I have just named. The Academy of Sciences well sustains the honor of the nation, but 'tis a light insufficiently diffused; each academician is limited to his own particular views. We have neither good physics nor good principles of astronomy for the education of youth and, for this purpose, we are compelled to rely on foreigners.

The Opera keeps up its standard, because music is liked; unfortunately, this music cannot please the taste of other nations, like the Italian. Comedy degenerates completely. A propos Comedy, I am greatly mortified that *L'Enfant Prodigue* should have been sent to your Royal Highness. The copy you have is not my real work; and the true copy is only a sketch I have had neither time nor desire to finish, and is unworthy your attention.

I speak to your Royal Highness with that naturalness which is perhaps too native to my character; I tell you, Monseigneur, what I think of my country without desiring to disparage or to praise it; I think that the French are living in Europe a little on their credit, like a rich man who is imperceptibly ruining himself. Our nation needs for its encouragement the eye of a master; for my part, Monseigneur, I ask nothing more than that

Prince Frederick should continue his supervision. I lack only health; but for that I should work hard to deserve your regard; but feeble genius and ill-health make but a poor man. I am with profound respect, etc.

Cirey, October, 1737.

MONSEIGNEUR,

I have received the last letter with which your Royal Highness honors me, dated the 21st September. I am anxious to know if my last parcel to you and that destined for M. Keyserlingk have reached their address; they were sent off at the beginning of August.

You command me, Monseigneur, to give you some account of my metaphysical doubts; I am taking the liberty of sending you an extract from a chapter On Liberty. Your Royal Highness will at least find good faith in it though you may find ignorance. Would to God all who are ignorant were at least sincere!

Perhaps humanity, the principal of all my thoughts, has seduced me in this work; perhaps my idea that there would be neither vice nor virtue, that neither reward nor punishment would be needed, that society especially among philosophers would be an exchange of malignancy and hypocrisy, if man did not possess full and absolute liberty—perhaps, I say, this opinion carries me too far. But if you find errors in my thoughts, forgive them for the sake of the principle which produced them.

As far as I can I always bring back my metaphysics to morality. I have inquired sincerely and with all the attention of which I am capable whether I can attain any notions of the human soul, and I have seen that the fruit of all my searching is ignorance. I find that this thinking, free, active agent is nearly in the same position as God; my reason tells me that God exists, but this very same reason also tells me that I cannot know what He is. Indeed, how can we know what our soul is, we who can form no conception of light when we have the misfortune to be born blind? Therefore I perceive with anguish that everything which has been written about the soul cannot teach us the least truth.

After groping about this soul to guess its kind, my principal object is to try at least to regulate it; 'tis the works of our clock. All Descartes's fine ideas about elasticity do not tell me the nature of these works; I do not know what is the cause of elasticity; yet I wind up my clock and somehow or other it goes.

I examine man. Whatever materials he may be composed of, we must see whether vice and virtue do in fact exist. This is the important point concerning man, I do not mean concerning a given society living under given laws, but the human race. For you, Monseigneur, who are to reign, for the woodcutter in your forest, for the Chinese doctor, and for the American savage. Locke, the wisest metaphysician I know, seems, by combating (with reason) innate ideas, to think that there is no universal principle of morality. On this point I dare to combat or rather to elucidate that great man's ideas. I agree with him that there is not really any innate idea; it follows obviously that there is no moral proposition innate in our souls; but because we are not born with beards, does it follow that we inhabitants of this Continent are not born to be bearded at a certain age? We are not born with the strength to walk; but whosoever is born with two feet will one day walk. Thus nobody is born with the idea that he must be just; but God has so arranged men's organs that all at a certain age agree upon this truth.

It seems to me obvious that God meant us to live in society, even as He gave bees the instinct and instruments proper to make honey. Since our society could not exist without the ideas of justice and injustice, He gave us the means of acquiring them. Our different customs, it is true, will never allow us to attach the same idea of justice to the same notions. What is a crime in Europe will be a virtue in Asia, just as certain German stews will never please the epicures of France; but God has so constructed Germans and Frenchmen that they all enjoy good cheer. All societies therefore will not have the same laws, but no society will be without laws. Here then the good of society is established by all men from Pekin to Ireland as the immutable rule of virtue; what is useful to society is therefore good in all countries. This single idea at once conciliates all the contradictions which appear in the morality of men. Theft was permitted in Sparta; but why? Because property was there held in common and because to steal from a miser who kept for himself alone what the law gave the public was serving society.

It is said there are savages who eat men and think they do right. I reply that these savages have the same idea of justice and injustice as we have. They make war as we do from madness and passion; we see the same crimes committed everywhere, and eating one's enemies is but an additional ceremony. The wrong is not putting them on the spit but killing them, and I dare to assert that no savage thinks he acts well when he murders his friend. I saw four savages from Louisiana who were brought to France in 1723. Among them was a woman of a very gentle character. I asked through the interpreter if she had ever eaten the flesh of her enemies and if she liked it; she answered: Yes; I then asked if she would willingly have killed or have caused to be killed any of her compatriots in order to eat them; she replied with a shudder and with a visible horror for this crime.

I defy the most determined liar among travelers to dare to assert that there is a tribe, a family, where it is permitted to break one's word. I am justified in believing that since God created certain animals to feed in common, others to see each other only in pairs very seldom, spiders to make webs, every species possesses the instruments necessary for the work it has to do. Man has been given everything needed to live in society; just as he has been given a stomach to digest, eyes to see, a soul to judge.

Place two men on the earth; they will only call that good, virtuous, and just which is good for both of them. Place four, and there will be nothing virtuous except what is suitable to all four; and if one of the four eats another's supper, or beats or kills him, he will assuredly arouse the others. What I say of these four men must be said of the whole universe. That, Monseigneur, is roughly the plan on which I have written this moral metaphysics; but should I speak of virtue in your presence?

Cirey, 18th October, 1738.

I observe with a satisfaction approaching pride, Monseigneur, that the little oppositions I endure in my own country arouse indignation in your Royal Highness's great heart. You cannot doubt but that your approval amply rewards me for all these annoyances; they are common to all who have cultivated the sciences and those men of letters who have most loved the truth have always been the most persecuted.

Calumny attempted the death of Descartes and Bayle; Racine and Boileau would have died of grief had they not found a protector in Louis XIV. We still possess verses made against Virgil. I am far indeed from being able to compare myself with those great men; but I am more fortunate than they; I enjoy repose, I have a fortune sufficient for a private man and greater than a philosopher needs, I live in a delicious solitude beside a most estimable woman whose society ever provides me with new lessons. And then, Monseigneur, you are graciously pleased to love me; the most virtuous, the most amiable prince in Europe deigns to open his heart to me, to confide to me his works and his thoughts and to correct mine. What more do I need? Health alone fails me; but there is not a sick man in the world happier than I.

12th August, 1739.

In Paris they talk of nothing but fêtes and fireworks; they are spending a lot of money on powder and rockets. They used to spend as much on amenities and the things of the mind; when Louis XIV gave fêtes, Corneille, Molière, Quinault, Lulli, Lebrun were concerned in them. I am sorry that a fête should be only a passing fête, a noise, a crowd, a large number of *bourgeois*, a few diamonds and nothing more; I should like it to pass to posterity. Our masters the Romans understood that better than we; the amphitheaters and triumphal arches erected for a day of solemnity still please and instruct us. But we build a scaffold in the Place de Grève where the night before several thieves have been broken on the wheel; and we fire cannons from the Hôtel de Ville. I wish they would use these cannons to destroy the Hôtel de Ville which is in the vilest taste imaginable, and that the money spent on rockets should be used to build a handsome one. A prince who builds necessarily causes the other arts to flourish: Painting, sculpture, engraving follow in the steps of architecture. A fine drawing-room is meant for music, another for comedy. In Paris we have neither comedy nor opera house; and, by a contradiction only too worthy of us, excellent works are played in very ugly theaters. The good plays are in France and the beautiful vessels in Italy.

December, 1740.

SIRE,

I am now like the pilgrims to Mecca who turn their eyes toward that town after they have left it; I turn mine toward your Court. My heart, touched by your Majesty's kindness, feels only the distress of not being able to live near you. I take the liberty to send you a new copy of the tragedy of *Mahomet,* the first sketches of which you desired to see long ago. It is a tribute I pay to the amateur of the arts, to the enlightened judge, above all to the philosopher, far more than to the sovereign.

Your Majesty knows with what spirit I was animated in composing this work; my pen was guided by love of the human race and horror of fanaticism, to virtues which are made to stand beside your throne. I have always thought that tragedy should not be a mere spectacle to touch the heart without reforming it. What does the human race care for the passions and misfortunes of a hero of antiquity, if they do not serve to instruct us? It is admitted that the comedy of *Tartufe,* that masterpiece which no nation has equaled, has done good to men by showing hypocrisy in all its ugliness; may one not attempt to attack in a tragedy that species of imposture which brings into play at once the hypocrisy of some and the fury of others? May we not return to those scoundrels of old, the illustrious founders of superstition and fanaticism, who first took the knife from the altar to make victims of those who refused to be their disciples?

Those who say that the time of these crimes has passed; that we shall never again see a Barcochebas, a Mohammed, a John o' Leiden, etc.; that the flames of religious wars are extinguished; in my opinion do too much honor to human nature. The same poison still exists though less developed; this pest, which appeared to be stamped out, from time to time produces germs which might infect the whole earth. In our own days have we not seen the prophets of the Cevennes kill in the name of God those of their sect who were not sufficiently submissive?

The action I have painted is atrocious; and I do not know whether horror has ever been carried so far on any stage. There is a young man born virtuous, who, seduced by his fanaticism, murders an old man who loves him, and thus with the idea of serving God, unwittingly renders himself guilty of a parricide; there is an imposter who orders this murder and promises the assassin an incest as his reward. I admit that this is setting horror on the stage; and your Majesty is fully persuaded that a tragedy should not consist solely in a declaration of love, a jealousy, and a marriage.

Our historians themselves inform us of actions more atrocious than that I have invented. Séïde at least does not know that the man he murders is his father and, when he has struck the blow, he feels a repentance as great as his crime. But Mézeray relates that at Melun a father killed his son with his own hand on account of his religion, and felt no remorse. We know the incident of the two brothers Diaz, one of whom was at Rome and the other in Germany at the beginning of the disturbances excited by Luther. Barthélemy Diaz, learning at Rome that his brother was inclining to Luther's opinions at Frankfurt, left Rome with the intention of murdering him, arrived there and did murder him. I have read in Herrera, a Spanish author, that "Barthélemy Diaz underwent great perils in this action; but nothing shakes a man of honor conducted by probity." Herrera, with a holy religion completely opposed to cruelty, a religion which teaches us to endure and not to take vengeance, was convinced that probity might lead a man to murder and fratricide; and no one rose up against these infernal maxims!

These are the maxims which placed a dagger in the hand of the monster who deprived France of Henry the Great; set the portrait of Jacques Clément on the altar and his name among the Blessed; cost his life to William Prince of Orange, creator of the liberty and grandeur of the Dutch. Salcède first wounded him in the head with a pistol-shot; and Strada relates that "Salcède (these are his own words) dared not undertake this action until he had purified his soul by confession at the feet of a Dominican and had strengthened it with Heavenly bread." Herrera says something more outrageous and atrocious: "*Estando firme con el exemplo de nuestro Salvadore Jesu-Christo, y de sus Santos.*" Balthazar Gérard who finally deprived that great man of life, had acted in the same way as Salcède.

I observe that all who have committed similar crimes in good faith were young men like Séïde. Balthazar Gérard was about twenty. Four Spaniards, who had taken an oath with him to kill the prince, were of the same age. The monster who killed Henri III was only twenty-three. Poltrot, who murdered the great Duke of Guise, was twenty-five; this is the age of seduction and of fury. In England I almost became an eye-witness of the power of fanaticism upon a weak and youthful imagination. A boy of sixteen named Shepherd undertook to murder your maternal grandfather, King George I. What cause led him to that frenzy? Simply that Shepherd did not hold the same religion as the king. They had pity on his youth, they offered him pardon, they long urged him to repentance; he persisted in saying that it was better to obey God than men and that, if he were free, the first use he would make of his liberty would be to kill his king. And thus they were compelled to send him to execution as a monster they despaired of taming.

I dare to say that anyone who has lived with men may have seen sometimes how ready they are to sacrifice nature to superstition. How many fathers have hated and disinherited their children! How many brothers harried their brothers, from this disastrous principle! I have seen examples in more than one family.

If superstition does not always make itself known by those excesses which are numbered in the history of crime, it causes all the innumerable daily little evils in society that it can. It divides friends; it separates relatives; it persecutes the sage, who is only an honest man, by the hand of the madman, who is an Enthusiast; it does not always give the hemlock to Socrates, but it banished Descartes from a town which should be the refuge of liberty; it gave Jurieu, who played the prophet, sufficient influence to reduce the learned and philosophical Bayle to penury; it banished, it tore the successor of the great Leibnitz from that flower of youth which flocked to his lessons; and to re-establish him Heaven had to send a philosophical king, a real miracle which very seldom happens. In vain does human reason perfect itself by philosophy, which makes such progress in Europe; in vain great prince, do you strive to practice and to inspire this humane philosophy; in this very age, when reason lifts her throne on the one side, we see the most absurd fanaticism still build its altars on the other.

Paris, 15th October, 1749.

SIRE,

I have just made an effort in my present dreadful state of mind to write to M. d'Argens; I will make another to throw myself at your Majesty's feet.

I have lost one who was my friend for twenty-five years, a great man, whose only defect was being a woman, whom all Paris regrets and honors. She did not perhaps receive justice during her life, and you perhaps have not judged her as you would have done, if she had had the honor to be known to your Majesty. But a woman who could translate Newton and Virgil, and who had all the virtues of a man of honor, will no doubt have a share in your regret.

The state I have been in for the last month hardly leaves me a hope of ever seeing you; but I will tell you boldly that if you knew my heart better you might also have the goodness to regret a man who has loved in your Majesty nothing but your person.

Sire, you are a very great king; you dictated peace in Dresden; your name will be great throughout all ages; but all your fame and all your power do not give you the right to distress a heart wholly devoted to you. Were I as well as I am ill, were I but ten leagues from your dominions, I would not stir a foot to visit the court of a great man who did not love me and who only sent for me as a sovereign. But if you knew me, if you had a true kindness for me, I would go to Pekin to throw myself at your feet. I am a man of sensibility, Sire, and nothing but that. I have perhaps only two days left to live, I shall spend them in admiring you but in deploring the injustice you do a soul which was so devoted to yours, and which still loves you as M. de Fénelon loved God—

for his own sake. God should not scorn one who offers so rare an incense.

Continue to believe, if you please, that I have no need of petty vanities and that I seek you alone.

Paris, 10th November, 1749.

SIRE,

I received almost at the same time three letters from your Majesty; one dated the 10th September, via Frankfort, forwarded from Frankfort to Lunéville, sent on to Paris, to Cirey, back to Lunéville and again to Paris, while I was in the country in the most complete retirement; the two others reached me the day before yesterday by the offices of M. Chambrier, who is still I think at Fontainebleau. Alas! Sire, if the first of these letters had reached me in the crisis of my grief, at the time when I ought to have received it, I should only have left that disastrous Lorraine for you; I should have left it to throw myself at your feet; I should have come to hide myself in some corner of Potsdam or Sans Souci; half dead as I was, I should certainly have made this journey; I should have found the strength for it. I should even have had reasons which you may guess, for preferring to die in your dominions rather than in the country where I was born.

What has happened? Your silence made me think that my request had displeased you; that you had really no feeling of kindness toward me; that you took what I proposed as a subterfuge and a determined wish to remain near King Stanislas. His Court, where I saw Mme. du Châtelet die in a way a hundred times more dreadful than you can believe, became for me a horrible dwelling-place, in spite of my tender attachment for that good prince and in spite of his extreme kindness. I therefore returned to Paris; I collected my family about me, I took a house, I found myself the father of a family without having any children. Thus in my grief I have made myself a quiet and honorable establishment, and I am passing the winter in these arrangements and in my business affairs which were mixed up with those of her whom death should not have carried off before me. But, since you are still graciously pleased to love me a little, your Majesty may be very sure that I shall come and throw myself at your feet next summer, if I am still alive. I now need no pretext, I need only the continuation of your kindness. I shall spend a week with King Stanislas, a duty I must fulfill; and the rest shall be for your Majesty.

I beg you will be convinced that I only thought of that black rag because at that time King Stanislas would not have allowed me to leave him. I thought you had conferred that favor upon M. de Maupertuis. I expect new presents from your pen, and I flatter myself that the cargo you will receive immediately from me will bring me one from you. I shall have the honor to continue this little commerce during the winter; and with due respect, Sire, I think that you and I are the only two merchants of that sort in Europe. I shall then come to look over your accounts, to expatiate, to talk of grammar and poetry; I shall bring you Madame du Châtelet's analytical grammar and as much as I can collect of her Virgil; in a word, I shall come with full pockets and I shall find your portfolios well furnished. I have a delicious expectation of these moments; but it is on the express condition that you are graciously pleased to love me a little, for otherwise I shall die at Paris.

Ferney, 11th january, 1771.

Great prophet, you resemble your predecessors sent by the most high; you perform miracles, I owe my life to you. I was dying in the midst of my Swiss snows, when your sacred vision was brought to me. As I read, my head freed itself, my blood circulated, my soul revived; after the second page I regained my strength, and owing to the singular effect of this celestial medicine, it gave me back my appetite and disgusted me with all other food.

The eternal of old ordered your predecessor Ezechial to eat a parchment book; I should gladly have eaten your paper, had I not preferred a hundred times to reread it. Yes, you are the only prophet of Jehovah, since you are the only one who has told the truth and laughed at all his comrades; therefore Jehovah has blessed you by strengthening your throne, sharpening your pen, and illuminating your soul.

Thus spoke the Lord: "This is he whom I announced: He shall make flat the high places and raise them that are low; behold he comes; he shall teach the children of men that a man may be brave and merciful, great and simple, eloquent and a poet; for I have taught him all these things. I illuminated him when he came into the world, so that he should make me known as I am and not as the foolish children of men have painted me. For I take all the spheres of the universe as witness that I, their founder, was never scourged nor hanged in that little globe of the earth; that I never inspired any Jew or crowned any Pope; but in the fullness of time I sent my servant Frederick, who is not called mine anointed, because he was not anointed; but he is my son and my image and I said unto him: 'My son, it is not enough to have made thy enemies thy footstool and to have given laws to thy kingdom, but thou shalt drive superstition forever from this globe.' "

And the great Frederick said unto Jehovah: "The monster of superstition have I driven from my heart and from the hearts of all that are near me; but, Father, you have arranged this world in such a way that I can only do good in my own house and even then with some difficulty. How do you expect me to give common sense to the people of Rome, Naples, and Madrid?"

Then said Jehovah: "Thy lessons and thy examples shall suffice; give them long enough, O my son, and I will cause these germs to grow and to produce fruit in their time."

And the great prophet answered and said: "O Jehovah! You are very powerful, but I defy you to make all men reasonable. Take my advice, and content yourself with a small number of the elect; you will never have more for your share."

13th November, 1772.

Sire,

Yesterday a royal packing-case arrived at my hermitage, and this morning I drank my coffee in a cup such as is not made in the lands of your colleague Kien-Long, the Emperor of China; the tray is of the greatest beauty. I knew that Frederick the Great was a better poet than the good Kien-Long but I did not know that he amused himself by manufacturing in Berlin porcelains superior to those of Kieng-Tsin, Dresden, and Sèvres; this amazing man must then eclipse his rivals in everything he undertakes. However, I will confess that among those who were with me at the opening of the packing-case, there were critics who did not approve the crown of laurel which surrounds the lyre of Apollo on the admirable cover of the prettiest dish imaginable. They said: "How can it happen that a great man, so well known for his scorn of display and false pride, should think of putting his arms on the cover of a dish!" I replied: "It must be a fancy of the workman; kings leave everything to the caprice of artists. Louis XIV did not order a slave to be put at the foot of his statue; he did not order Marshal de la Feuillade to engrave the famous inscription, *To the Immortal Man;* and when we see in a hundred places, *Frederico immortali,* we know that Frederick the Great did not imagine this device and that he let the world talk."

There is also an Amphion carried by a dolphin. I know that once a dolphin, which was no doubt a lover of poetry, saved Amphion from the sea where those who envied him tried to drown him.

And so it is in the north that all the arts flourish today! It is there that the finest porcelain dishes are made, provinces are partitioned by a stroke of the pen, confederations and senates dissolved in two days, and that the confederates and their Notre Dame are most amusingly laughed at.

Sire, we Welches have our merit too; comic-operas have caused Molière to be forgotten, marionettes make Racine fail, as well as financiers wiser than Colbert and generals whom Turenne does not approach.

The one thing that distresses me is that I hear you have caused a renewal of the conferences between Mustapha and my Empress; I should much prefer it if you helped her to drive from the Bosphorus those villainous Turks, those enemies of the fine arts, those extinguishers of beautiful Greece. You might find on the way some province to round off your territory, for after all we must amuse ourselves; we cannot always read, philosophize, make verses and music.

8th November, 1776.

If I do not weep in my cottage, seeing I am too dry, at least I have something to weep for; the gentlemen of Nazareth do not jest like those on the shores of the Baltic, they persecute people secretly and cruelly; they unearth a poor man in his lair and punish him for having laughed at their expense. All the misfortunes which can crush a poor man have fallen on me at once, lawsuits, losses of property, ills of the body, ills of what is called the soul. I am absolutely "the man in his cottage"; but by Heaven, Sire, you are not "the man who weeps on his throne"; many years ago you had some experience of adversity, but with what courage and grandeur of soul did you drink the cup! How much these ordeals contributed to your glory! How much at all times you have been in yourself superior to other men! I dare not lift my eyes to you from the depths of my decrepitude and misery. I do not know where I shall go to die. The reigning Duke of Wurtemburg, uncle to the princess you have just married so well, owes me some money which would have procured me an honorable burial; he does not pay me; which will be a great embarrassment to me when I am dead. If I dared, I would ask you to use your influence with him, but I dare not; I should much prefer to have your Majesty as surety.

Seriously, I do not know where I shall go to die. I am a little Job shrivelled up on my Swiss dunghill; and the difference between Job and me is that Job got well and ended up by being happy. The same thing happened to Tobias, lost like me in a Swiss canton in the country of the Medes; and the amusing part of that affair is that the holy scripture says his grandchildren buried him with rejoicing; apparently they found a good inheritance.

Forgive me, Sire, if now that I am nearly as blind as Tobias, and as miserable as Job, my mind is not sufficiently free to dare to write you a useless letter.

I throw myself at your Majesty's feet. *De profundis.*

Paris, 1st April, 1778.

SIRE,

The French gentleman who will hand this letter to your Majesty and who is considered to be worthy of appearing before you, will be able to tell you that if I have not had the honor of writing to you for a long time the reason is that I have been occupied in avoiding two things which pursued me in Paris—hisses and death.

It is amusing that at eighty-four I have escaped two fatal illnesses. That is the result of being devoted to you; I made use of your name and I was saved.

At the representation of a new tragedy, I saw with surprise and the greatest satisfaction that the public, which thirty years ago looked upon Constantine and Theodosius as the models of princes and even of saints, applauded with unheard-of transports verses which say that Constantine and Theodosius were only superstitious tyrants. I have seen twenty similar proofs of the progress which philosophy has at last made in all ranks. I do not despair of hearing delivered a panegyric of the Emperor Julian in a month's time; and certainly if the Parisians remember that he dispensed justice among them like Cato, and fought for them like Caesar, they owe him eternal gratitude.

It is true, then, Sire, that in the end men become enlightened and that those who think themselves paid to blind them are not always able to thrust out their eyes! Thanks be to your Majesty! You have conquered prejudices like your other enemies. You enjoy all our institutions of every sort. You are the conqueror of superstition, as well as the support of German liberty.

Live longer than I to strengthen all the empires you have founded. May Frederick the Great be Frederick the Immortal! Be graciously pleased to accept the profound respect and inviolable attachment of

VOLTAIRE.

Translations by Richard Aldington

Miscellaneous Letters

TO THE MINISTER FOR THE DEPARTMENT OF PARIS

The Bastille, April, 1726.

M. de Voltaire ventures humbly to point out that an attempt has been made to assassinate him by the brave Chevalier de Rohan (assisted by six cutthroats, behind whom the Chevalier courageously placed himself); and that ever since, M. de Voltaire has tried to repair, not his own honor, but that of the Chevalier—which has proved too difficult. . . . M. de Voltaire demands permission to dine at the table of the Governor of the Bastille and to see his friends. He demands, still more urgently, permission to set out for England. If any doubt is felt as to the reality of his departure for that country, an escort can be sent with him to Calais.

TO M. BERTIN DE ROCHERET

Paris, April 14, 1732.

I received very late, my dear sir, the letter with which you have honored me. I am fully sensible of your goodness in throwing so much light on the *History of Charles XII*. I shall not fail, in future editions, to profit by your observations.

Meanwhile, I have the honor to send you by the coach a copy of the new edition, in which you will find some previous mistakes corrected.

You will still see many printer's errors, but I cannot be responsible for those, and only think of my own. The book has been produced in France with so much haste and secrecy that the proofreader could not go through it. As you yourself, sir, are a writer of history, you will know the difficulty of choosing between absolutely opposite stories. Three officers who were at Poltava have given me three entirely different accounts of that battle. M. de Fierville and M. de Villelongue contradict each other flatly on the subject of the intrigues at the Porte. My greatest difficulty has not been to find Memoirs but to find good ones. There is another drawback inseparable from writing contemporary history: every infantry captain, who has seen ever so little service with the armies of Charles XII, if he happens to have lost his kit on a march, thinks I ought to have mentioned him. If the subalterns grumble at my silence, the generals and ministers complain of my outspokenness. Whoso writes the history of his own time must expect to be attacked for everything he has said, and for everything he has not said: but those little drawbacks should not discourage a man who loves truth and liberty expects nothing, fears nothing, asks nothing, and limits his ambition to the cultivation of letters.

I am highly flattered, sir, that this *métier* of mine has given me the pleasure of your delightful and instructive letter. I sincerely thank you for it, and beg the continuance of your kind interest.

I am, etc.

TO A FIRST COMMISSIONER

June 20, 1733.

As you have it in your power, sir, to do some service to letters, I implore you not to clip the wings of our writers so closely, nor to turn into barndoor fowls those who, allowed a start, might become eagles; reasonable liberty permits the mind to soar—slavery makes it creep.

Had there been a literary censorship in Rome, we should have had today neither Horace, Juvenal, nor the philosophical works of Cicero. If Milton, Dryden, Pope, and Locke had not been free, England would have had neither poets nor philosophers; there is something positively Turkish in proscribing printing; and hampering it *is* proscription. Be content with severely repressing defamatory libels, for they are crimes: but so long as those infamous *calottes* are boldly published, and so many other unworthy and despicable productions, at least allow Bayle to circulate in France, and do not put him, who has been so great an honor to his country, among its contraband.

You say that the magistrates who regulate the literary custom-house complain that there are too many books. That is just the same thing as if the provost of merchants complained there were too many provisions in Paris. People buy what they choose. A great library is like the City of Paris, in which there are about eight hundred thousand persons: you do not live with the whole crowd: you choose a certain society, and change it. So with books: you choose a few friends out of the many. There will be seven or eight thousand controversial books, and fifteen or sixteen thousand novels, which you will not read: a heap of pamphlets, which you will throw into the fire after you have read them. The man of taste will only read what is good; but the statesman will permit both bad and good.

Men's thoughts have become an important article of commerce. The Dutch publishers make a million [francs] a year, because Frenchmen have brains. A feeble novel is, I know, among books what a fool, always striving after wit, is in the world. We laugh at him and tolerate him. Such a novel brings the means of life to the author who wrote it, the publisher who sells it, to the molder, the printer, the papermaker, the binder, the carrier—and finally to the bad wineshop where they all take their money. Further, the book amuses for an hour or two a few women who like novelty in literature as in everything. Thus, despicable though it may be, it will have produced two important things—profit and pleasure.

The theater also deserves attention. I do not consider it a counterattraction to dissipation: that is a notion only worthy of an ignorant curé. There is quite time enough, before and after the performance, for the few minutes given to those passing pleasures which are so soon followed by satiety. Besides, people do not go to the theater every day, and among our vast population there are not more than four thousand who are in the habit of going constantly.

I look on tragedy and comedy as lessons in virtue, good sense, and good behavior. Corneille—the old Roman of the French—has founded a school of Spartan virtue: Molière, a school of ordinary everyday life. These great national geniuses attract foreigners from all parts of Europe, who come to study among us, and thus contribute to the wealth of Paris. Our poor are fed by the production of such works, which bring under our rule the very nations who hate us. In fact, he who condemns the theater is an enemy to his country. A magistrate who, because he has succeeded in buying some judicial post, thinks that it is beneath his dignity to see *Cinna*, shows much pomposity and very little taste.

There are still Goths and Vandals even among our cultivated people: the only Frenchmen I consider worthy of the name are those who love and encourage the arts. It is true that the taste for them is languishing: we are sybarites, weary of our mistresses' favors. We enjoy the fruits of the labors of the great men who have worked for our pleasure and that of the ages to come, just as we receive the fruits of nature as if they were our due . . . nothing will rouse us from this indifference to great things which always goes side by side with our avid interest in small.

Every year we take more pains over snuffboxes and knickknacks than the English took to make themselves masters of the seas. . . . The old Romans raised those marvels of architecture—their amphitheaters—for beasts to fight in: and for a whole century we have not built a single passable place for the representation of the masterpieces of the human mind. A hundredth part of the money spent on cards would be enough to build theaters finer than Pompey's: but what man in Paris has the public welfare at heart? We play, sup, talk scandal, write bad verses, and sleep, like fools, to recommence on the morrow the same round of careless frivolity.

You, sir, who have at least some small opportunity of giving good advice, try and rouse us from this stupid lethargy, and, if you can, do something for literature, which has done so much for France.

TO M. MARTIN KAHLE

1744.

I am very pleased to hear, sir, that you have written a little book against me. You do me too much honor. On page 17 you reject the proof, from final causes, of the existence of God. If you had argued thus at Rome, the reverend father and governor of the Holy Palace would have condemned you to the Inquisition: if you had written thus against a theologian of Paris, he would have had your proposition censured by the sacred faculty: if against a devout person, he would have abused you: but I have the honor to be neither a Jesuit, nor a theologian, nor a devotee. I shall leave you to your opinion, and shall remain of mine. I shall always be convinced that a watch proves a watchmaker, and that the universe proves a God. I hope that you yourself understand what you say concerning space and eternity, the necessity of matter, and preordained harmony: and I recommend you to look once more at what *I* said, finally, in the new edition, where I earnestly endeavored to make myself thoroughly understood—and in metaphysics that is no easy task.

You quote, à propos of space and infinity, the *Medea* of Seneca, the *Philippics* of Cicero, and the *Metamorphoses* of Ovid; also the verses of the Duke of Buckingham, of Gombaud, Regnier, and Rapin. I must tell you, sir, I know at least as much poetry as you do: that I am quite as fond of it: that if it comes to capping verses we shall see some very pretty sport: only I do not think them suitable to shed light on a metaphysical question, be they Lucretius's or the Cardinal de Polignac's.

Furthermore, if ever you understand anything about preordained harmony—if you discover how, under the law of necessity, man is free, you will do me a service if you will pass on the information to me. When you have shown, in verse or otherwise, why so many men cut their throats in the best of all possible worlds, I shall be exceedingly obliged to you.

I await your arguments, your verses, and your abuse: and assure you from the bottom of my heart that neither you nor I know anything about the matter. I have the honor to be, etc.

TO MME. DENIS[1]

Charlottenburg, August 14, 1750.

This is the fact of the matter, my dear child. The King of Prussia is making me his chamberlain, and giving me one of his orders and a pension of twenty thousand francs, and will settle one of four thousand on you for life if you will come and keep house for me in Berlin, as you do in Paris. You had a very pleasant life at Landau with your husband: I promise you that Berlin is worth many Landaus, and has much better operas. Consider the matter: consult your feelings. You may reply that the King of Prussia must be singularly fond of verses. It is true that he is a purely French writer who happened to be born in Berlin. On consideration, he has come to the conclusion that I shall be of more use to him than d'Arnaud. I have forgiven the gay little rhymes

[1] Voltaire's widowed niece, who came to Paris to keep house for him after the death of Mme. du Châtelet.

which his Prussian Majesty wrote for my young pupil, in which he spoke of him as the *rising sun,* extremely brilliant: and of me as the *setting sun,* exceedingly feeble. He still sometimes scratches with one hand, while he caresses with the other: but, so near him, I am not afraid. If you consent, he will have both *rising* and *setting* at his side, and in his *high noon* will be writing prose and verse to his heart's content, now he has no more battles on hand. I have but a short time to live. Perhaps it will be pleasanter to die here at Potsdam, in his fashion, than as an ordinary citizen in Paris. You can go back there afterwards with your four thousand francs pension. If these propositions meet your views, you must pack your boxes in the spring: and, at the end of the autumn, I shall make a pilgrimage to Italy to see St. Peter's at Rome, the Pope, the Venus of Medici, and the buried city. It always lay heavy on my conscience to die without having seen Italy. We will rejoin each other in May. I have four verses by the King of Prussia for His Holiness. It will be very entertaining to take to the Pope four French verses written by a German heretic, and to bring back indulgences to Potsdam. You will see he treats Popes much better than pretty women. He will never write sonnets to you: but you would have excellent company here and a good house. First of all, it is essential that the King, my master, should consent. I believe he will be perfectly indifferent. It matters little to a King of France where the most useless of his twenty-two or twenty-three million of subjects spends his life: but it would be dreadful to live without you.

TO MME. DE FONTAINE[1]

Berlin, September 23, 1750.

When you set about it, my dear niece, you write charming letters, and prove yourself one of the most amiable women in the world. You add to my regrets, and make me feel the extent of my losses. I never lacked delightful society when I was in yours. However, I hope even misfortunes may be turned to account. I can be much more useful to your brother[2] here than in Paris. Perhaps a heretic King will protect a Catholic preacher. All roads lead to Rome, and since *Mahomet* has put me on such good terms with the Pope, I do not despair of a Huguenot doing something for the benefit of a Carmelite.[3]

When I say, my dear niece, that all roads lead to Rome, I do not mean that they will lead *me* there. I was wild to see Rome and our present good Pope: but you and your sister attract me back to France: I sacrifice the Holy Father to you. I wish I could also sacrifice the King of Prussia, but that is impossible. He is as amiable as are you yourselves; he is a king, but his passion for me is of sixteen years' standing: he has turned my head. I had the audacity to think that nature made me for him; I found that there is so remarkable a conformity in our tastes that I forgot he was the lord of half Germany, and that the other half trembled at his name, that he had won five battles, that he was the finest general in Europe, and had about him great monsters of heroes six feet high. All that would, indeed, have made me fly a

[1] Voltaire's younger niece.
[2] Abbé Mignot.
[3] *Mahomet* was dedicated to the Pope.

thousand miles from him: but the philosopher humanized the monarch, and I know him only as a great man, good and kindly. Everybody taunts me with his having written verses for d'Arnaud—which are certainly not among his best: but you must remember that four hundred miles from Paris it is very difficult to judge if a person who has been recommended to you is, or is not, worthy; that, anyhow, verses, ill or well applied, prove that the conqueror of Austria loves literature; and I love him with all my heart. Besides, d'Arnaud is a good sort of person who, now and again, does light on some pretty lines. He has taste: he is improving; and if he does not improve—well, it is no great matter. In a word, that little slight the King of Prussia put on me does not prevent him being the most agreeable and remarkable of men.

The climate here is not so rigorous as people think. You Parisians talk as if I were in Lapland: let me inform you that we have had a summer quite as hot as yours, that we have enjoyed good peaches and grapes, and that you really have no business to give yourself such airs of superiority on the strength of two or three extra degrees of sunshine.

You will see *Mahomet* acted at my house in Paris: but I shall be acting in *Rome Sauvée* at Berlin—the hoarsest old Cicero you ever heard. Further, my dear child, we must look to our digestions: that is the main point. My health is very much as it was in Paris: when I have the colic. I have given up the grand suppers, and am a little the better. I am under a great obligation to the King of Prussia: he sets me an example of temperance. What! said I to myself, here is a king born a gourmand, who sits at table and eats nothing, and yet is excellent company; while I give myself indigestion like a fool! How I pity you, changing your diet of asses' milk for the waters of Forges and pecking like a sparrow, and, with it all, never well! Compensate yourself: there are other pleasures.

Good-bye: my compliments to everyone. I hope to embrace you in November. I am writing to your sister: but please tell her I shall love her all my life, even better than I do my new master.

TO MME. DENIS

Potsdam, October 13, 1750.

Behold us in retreat at Potsdam! The excitement of the fêtes is over, and my soul is relieved. I am not sorry to be here with a king who has neither court nor cabinet. It is true Potsdam is full of the mustaches and helmets of grenadiers: thank God, I do not see them. I work peacefully in my rooms, to the accompaniment of the drum. I have given up the royal dinners: there were too many generals and princes. I could not get used to being always opposite a king in state, and to talking in public. I sup with him, and a very small party. The supper is shorter, gayer, and healthier. I should die at the end of three months of boredom and indigestion if I had to dine every day with a king in state.

I have been handed over, my dear, with all due formalities, to the King of Prussia. The marriage is accomplished: will it be happy? I do not know in the least: yet I cannot prevent myself saying, Yes. After coquetting for so many years, marriage was the necessary end. My heart beat hard even at the altar. I fully intend to come this winter and give you an account of myself, and perhaps bring you back with me. There is no further question of my trip to Italy; I gladly give up for you the Holy Father and the buried city: perhaps I ought also to have sacrificed Potsdam. Who would have guessed, seven or eight months ago, when I was making every arrangement to live with you in Paris, that I should settle three hundred miles away in someone else's house? and that someone else a master. He has solemnly sworn that I shall not repent it: he has included you, my dear child, in a sort of contract he signed which I will bring with me: but do you intend to earn your dowry of four thousand francs?

I am much afraid you will be like Mme. de Rottemberg, who always preferred the operas of Paris to those of Berlin. Oh, destiny! destiny! how you rule all things and dispose of poor humanity.

It is rather amusing that the same literary men in Paris, who longed to exterminate me, are now calling out against my absence—as desertion. They are sorry to have lost their victim. I was indeed wrong to leave you: my heart tells me so daily, more often than you think: but I have done very well to escape those gentry.

Good-bye—with regrets and affection.

TO MME. DENIS

Berlin, September 1, 1751.

I have just time, my dear, to send you a fresh packet of letters. You will find in it one from La Mettrie to the Maréchal de Richelieu, asking his good offices. Reader though he be to the King of Prussia, he is dying to return to France. This cheerful soul, supposed to do nothing but laugh, cries like a child at having to be here. He is imploring me to get M. Richelieu to obtain a permit for him.[1] It is certainly a fact that one must never judge by appearances.

[1] To return from banishment, imposed on him because of his writings.

La Mettrie, in his writings, boasts of his delight at being near a great king, who sometimes reads his verses: in private, he weeps with me. He is ready to go back on foot: but as for me! . . . what am *I* here for? I am going to astonish you.

This La Mettrie is a person of no importance, and chats familiarly with the King after their readings. He tells me much in confidence; and swears that, talking to the King a few days ago of the so-called favor extended to me and the little jealousy it excites, the King replied, "I shall want him a year longer, at the outside: one squeezes the orange and throws away the peel."

I repeated these charming words to myself: I redoubled my questions: La Mettrie redoubled his assertions. Would you believe it? ought I to believe it? is it possible? What! after sixteen years of kindnesses, promises, protestations: after the letter which he desired that you should keep as an inviolable pledge of his word! And at a time, if you please, at a time when I am sacrificing everything to serve him, when I not only correct his works, but write in the margin, à propos of any little faults I detect, reflections on our language which are a lesson in the arts of poesy and rhetoric: having, as my sole aim, to assist his talent, enlighten him and put him in a position to do without my help!

I certainly took both pride and pleasure in cultivating his genius: everything contributed to my illusion. A King who has gained battles and provinces, a King of the North who wrote verses in our language—a King whose favor I did not seek, and who said he was devoted to me: why *should* he have made so many advances? It is beyond me: I cannot understand it. I have done my best not to believe La Mettrie.

All the same—I am not sure. In rereading his verses I came across an Epistle to a painter named Pesne: in which he alludes to the "dear Pesne," whose "brush places him among the gods"; and this Pesne is a man he never looks at. However, this *dear Pesne* is *a god.* He could well say as much of me: it is not to say very much. Perhaps everything he writes is inspired by his mind, and his heart is far from it. Perhaps all those letters wherein he overwhelms me with warm and most touching assurances of kindness really mean nothing at all.

I am giving you terrible weapons to use against me. You will justly blame me for having yielded to his blandishments. You will take me for M. Jourdain, who said, "Can I refuse anything to a court gentleman who calls me his dear friend?" Still, I shall always reply, "He is a most amiable monarch."

You can easily fancy what reflections, what regrets, what difficulties, and, since I must own it, what grief the words of La Mettrie have brought upon me. You will say, Come away! But I am in no position to come away. What I have begun, I must finish—and I have two editions on hand and engagements for several months ahead. I am encompassed on all sides. What is to be done? Ignore that La Mettrie ever told me, confide in you alone, forget all about it, wait? You will most certainly be my consolation. I shall never have to say of you, "She deceived me, vowing she loved me." Were you a queen, you would be true.

Tell me your opinion, I beg you, in detail by the first courier despatched to Lord Tyrconnel.

TO M. BAGIEU[1]

Potsdam, April 10, 1752.

Nothing, my dear sir, has ever so deeply touched me as the letter which you have so kindly and spontaneously written to me, the interest you manifest in a condition of which particulars have not been furnished to you, and the help you tender me with so much good will. The hope of finding in Paris hearts as compassionate as yours and men at once thus worthy of their profession and superior to it quickens my desire to take the journey thither and makes my life of more value to me.

I owe a great deal to Mme. Denis for having claimed your attention on my behalf. Certainly, such thoughtful people are only to be found in France: just as your art attains perfection in France alone. Mine is a small affair. I never set out to do more than amuse people: and some are very far from thanking me. You are busy giving them help in their need. I have always looked on your profession as one of those which did most honor to the age of Louis XIV: and I have spoken of it to that effect in my history of that century: but I have never thought more highly of it than I do now. Mme. de Pimbesche in the *Suitors* learned to plead as a barrister—by pleading—and, in this sense, I have exhaustively studied medicine. I have read Sydenham, Freind, Boerhaave. I know the art must be largely a matter of conjecture, that few temperaments are alike, and that the first aphorism of Hippocrates, *Experientia fallax, judicium difficile,* is the finest and truest of all.

I have come to the conclusion that each man must be his own doctor: that he must live by rule, now and

[1] Surgeon-in-Chief to the King of France's bodyguard.

again assist nature without forcing her: above all, that he must know how to suffer, grow old, and die.

The King of Prussia, who has made peace after his five victories and is now reforming laws and embellishing his country (having finished writing its history), condescends sometimes to very pretty verse, and has addressed an Ode to me on this grim necessity to which we must all submit. This work and your letter have done more for me than all the physicians on earth. I ought not to complain of my fate. I have lived to be fifty-eight years old, with a very feeble body, and have seen the most robust die in the flower of their age. If you had ever met Lord Tyrconnel and La Mettrie you would be astounded that I should survive them: care has saved me. It is true that I have lost all my teeth in consequence of a malady with which I was born: everyone has within him, from the first moment of his life, the cause of his death. We must live with the foe till he kills us. Demouret's remedy does not suit me: it is only of service in cases of pronounced occasional scurvy, and none at all where the blood is affected and the organs have lost their vigor and suppleness. The waters of Brèges, Padua, or Ischia might do me good for a time: but I am far from sure if it is not better to suffer in peace, by one's own fireside, and diet oneself, than to go so far in search of a cure which is both uncertain and short-lived. My manner of life with the King of Prussia is precisely suited to an invalid—perfect liberty, without the slightest constraint, a light and cheerful supper. . . . *Deus nobis haec otia fecit.* He makes me as happy as an invalid can be: and your interest in my well-being adds to the alleviations of my lot. Pray look upon me, sir, as a friend whom you made across four hundred miles of space. I trust this summer to be able to come and assure you personally with what sincere regard I am yours always, etc.

TO MME. DENIS

July 24, 1752.

You and your friends are perfectly right to urge my return, but you have not always done so by special messengers: and what goes through the post is soon known. If this were the only drawback to absence, it would be sufficient to prevent one from ever leaving one's family and friends: but there are so many others! The postal system is all very well for letters of exchange—but not for a communion of hearts: those, when we are parted, we dare open no more.

The greatest of consolations is thus debarred us: I shall only write to you in future, my dear child, through reliable channels: which are few. These are my circumstances: Maupertuis has certainly spread the report that I think the King's writings very bad: he accuses me of conspiring against a very dangerous power—self-love: he gently insinuates that, when the King sent me his verses to correct, I said, "Will he never stop giving me his dirty linen to wash?" He has whispered this extraordinary story in the ears of ten or a dozen people, vowing each of them to secrecy. At last I am beginning to think the King was one of his confidants. I suspect, but cannot prove it. This is not a very pleasant situation: and this is not all.

At the end of last year a young man, named La Beaumelle, arrived here. He is, I think, a Genevan, and was sent back here from Copenhagen, where he was something between a wit and a preacher. He is the author of a book called *My Thoughts*, in which he has given his opinion freely on all the powers in Europe. Maupertuis, with his usual good nature and, of course, not the least maliciously, persuades this young man that I have spoken ill of himself and his book to his Majesty, and have thereby prevented his entering the royal service. So La Beaumelle, to repair the harm I am supposed to have done to his career, has prepared some scandalous *Notes* to my *Century of Louis XIV* which he is about to print —I know not where. Those who have seen these fine notes say they contain as many blunders as words.

As to the quarrel between Maupertuis and Koenig, here are the facts:

Koenig has fallen in love with a geometrical problem, as a paladin with a lady. Last year he traveled from The Hague to Berlin expressly to confer with Maupertuis on an algebraic formula and on a law of nature, which would not interest you in the least. He showed him a couple of letters from an old philosopher of the last century, named Leibnitz, who would interest you no better: and made it clear that Leibnitz, in dealing with this same law, had totally disagreed with Maupertuis. Maupertuis, who is much more engaged in court intrigues—or what he takes to be such—than geometrical truths, did not even read Leibnitz's letters.

The Hague professor demanded permission to ventilate his theories in the Leipzig papers: having it, he refuted therein, with the most exquisite politeness, the opinion of Maupertuis, quoting Leibnitz as his authority and printing passages from his works which bore on the dispute.

Now comes the odd part.

Maupertuis, having looked through and misread the Leipzig papers and the quotations from Leibnitz, gets it into his head that Leibnitz was of *his* opinion, and that Koenig had forged the letters to deprive him (Maupertuis) of the honor and glory of having originated—a blunder.

On these extraordinary grounds, he called together the resident academicians, whose salaries he pays: formally denounced Koenig as a forger, and had sentence passed on him, without taking a vote, and in spite of the opposition of the only geometrician who was present.

He did better still: he did not associate himself with the sentence, but wrote a letter to the Academy to ask pardon for the culprit, who, being at The Hague and so not able to be hanged in Berlin, was merely denounced, with all possible moderation, as a geometrical rogue and forger.

This fine judgment is in print. To crown all, our judicious president writes two letters to the Princess of Orange—Koenig is her librarian—to beg her to insist on the enemy's silence, and so rob him—condemned and branded as he is—of the right to defend his honor.

These details only reached my solitude yesterday.

Every day there is something new under the sun. Never before, surely, was there such a thing as a criminal suit in an academy of sciences! Flight from such a country as this is now proved a necessity.

I am quietly putting my affairs in order. My warmest love to you.

TO MME. DENIS

Potsdam, October 15, 1752.

Here is something unprecedented—inimitable—unique. The King of Prussia, without having read a word of Koenig's reply, without listening to or consulting anybody, has just produced a brochure against Koenig, against me, and against everyone who has tried to prove the innocence of the unjustly condemned professor. He treats all Koenig's friends as fools, envious, dishonest. A singular pamphlet indeed: and a king wrote it!

The German journalists, not suspecting that a monarch who had won battles could be the author of such a work, have spoken of it freely as the effort of a schoolboy, perfectly ignorant of his subject. However, the brochure has been reprinted at Berlin with the Prussian eagle, a crown, and a scepter on the title page. The eagle, the scepter, and the crown are exceedingly surprised to find themselves there. Everybody shrugs their shoulders, casts down their eyes, and is afraid to say anything. Truth is never to be found near a throne: and is never farther from it than when the king turns author. Coquettes, kings, and poets are accustomed to be flattered. Frederick is a combination of all three. How can truth pierce that triple wall of vanity? Maupertuis has not succeeded in being Plato, but he wants his royal master to be Dionysius of Syracuse.

What is most extraordinary in this cruel and ridiculous affair is that the King has no liking for this Maupertuis, for whose benefit he is employing his scepter and his pen. Plato nearly died of mortification at not being invited to certain little suppers, which I attended, and where the King told us a hundred times that this Plato's mad vanity rendered him intolerable.

He has written prose for him now, as he once wrote verses for d'Arnaud—for the pleasure of doing it: and for another motive less worthy of a philosopher—to annoy me. A true author, you see!

But all this is but the most insignificant part of what has happened. I too am unfortunately an author, and in the opposite camp. I have no scepter, but I have a pen: and I have used it[1]—I really do not know how—to turn Plato—with his stipendiaries, his predictions, his dis-

[1] In the *Diatribe of Dr. Akakia*, the famous pamphlet which ridicules Maupertuis.

sections, and his insolent quarrel with Koenig—into ridicule. My raillery is quite innocent, but I did not know when I wrote it I was laughing at the pastimes of the King. The affair is unlucky. I have to deal with conceit and with despotic power—two very dangerous things. I also have reason to believe that my affair with the Duke of Würtemberg has given offense. It was discovered: and I have been made to feel it was discovered. . . .

I am at the moment very wretched and very ill: and, to crown all, I have to sup with the King. Truly, a feast of Damocles! I need to be as philosophical as was the real Plato in the house of Dionysius.

TO MME. DENIS

Berlin, December 18, 1752.

I enclose, my dear, the two contracts from the Duke of Würtemberg: they secure you a little fortune for life. I also enclose my will. Not that your prophecy that the King of Prussia *would worry me to death* is going to be fulfilled. I have no mind to come to such a foolish end: nature afflicts me much more than he can, and it is only prudent that I should always have my valise packed and my foot in the stirrup, ready to start for that world where, happen what may, kings will be of small account.

As I do not possess here below a hundred and fifty thousand soldiers, I cannot pretend to make war. My only plan is to desert honorably, to take care of my health, to see you again, and forget this three years' nightmare. I am very well aware that "the orange has been squeezed": now we must consider how to save the peel. I am compiling, for my instruction, a little Dictionary for the Use of Kings.

"My friend" means "my slave."

"My dear friend" means "you are absolutely nothing to me."

By "I will make you happy" understand "I will bear you as long as I have need of you."

"Sup with me tonight" means "I shall make game of you this evening."

The dictionary might be long: quite an article for the Encyclopedia.

Seriously, all this weighs on my heart. Can what I have seen be true? To take pleasure in making bad blood between those who live together with him! To say to a man's face the kindest things—and then to write brochures upon him—and what brochures! To drag a man away from his own country by the most sacred promises, and then to ill-treat him with the blackest malice! What contradictions! And this is he who wrote so philosophically: whom I believed to be a philosopher! And whom I called the "Solomon of the North!"

You remember that fine letter which never succeeded in reassuring you? "You are a philosopher," said he, "and so am I." On my soul, sir, neither the one nor the other of us!

My dear child, I shall certainly never believe myself to be a philosopher until I am with you and my household gods. The difficulty is to get away from here. You will remember what I told you in my letter of November 1st. I can only ask leave on the plea of my health. It is not possible to say "I am going to Plombières" [1] in December.

There is a man named Pérrard here: a sort of minister of the Gospel and born, like myself, in France: he asked permission to go to Paris on business: the King answered that he knew his affairs better than he did him-

[1] A spa and summer resort.

self, and that there was no need at all for him to go to Paris.

My dear child, when I think over the details of all that is going on here, I come to the conclusion that it cannot be true, that it is impossible, that I must be mistaken—that such a thing must have happened at Syracuse three thousand years ago. What *is* true is that I sincerely love you and that you are my only consolation.

TO MME. DU DEFFAND

Colmar, April 23, 1754.

I feel very guilty, dear madam, at not having answered your last letter. I do not make my bad health an excuse: for, although I cannot write with my own hand, I could at least have dictated the most melancholy things, which, to those who, like you, know all the misfortunes of life and are no longer deceived by its illusions, are not unacceptable.

I remember that I advised you to go on living solely to enrage those who are paying your annuities. As far as I am concerned, it is the only pleasure I have left. When I feel an attack of indigestion coming on, I picture two or three princes as gainers by my death, take courage out of spite, and conspire against them with rhubarb and temperance.

Still, notwithstanding my desire to do them a bad turn by living on, I have been very ill. Add to that, these cursed *Annals of the Empire,* which put an extinguisher on all imagination and take up all my time, and you have the reasons for my idleness. I have been working at these stupid things for a Princess of Saxony—who deserves something livelier from me. She is a most agreeable royalty, and has things much better done than the Duchesse du Maine, while her court allows one much more liberty than did Sceaux, but, unfortunately, the climate is horrible: and just now I care for nothing but the sun. You cannot see it, madam, in the present state of your eyes: but it is good at least to *feel* warm. The horrible winter we have had makes one wretched: and the news that reaches us does not improve matters.

I wish I could send you some trifles to amuse you, but the works I am now engaged on are far from amusing.

In London I was an Englishman: and in Germany a German: with you my chameleon coat would soon take on brighter colors—your lively imagination would fire my drooping wits.

I have been reading the *Memoirs of Lord Bolingbroke.* It seems to me that he talks better than he writes. I declare I find his style as difficult of comprehension as his conduct. He draws a frightful portrait of Lord Oxford —without adducing any proofs. This is the Oxford whom Pope calls:

> "A Soul supreme, in each hard instance try'd,
> Above all Pain, all Passion, and all Pride,
> The rage of Pow'r, the blast of public breath,
> The Lust of Lucre, and the dread of Death."

Bolingbroke would have employed his leisure better if he had written good memoirs on the War of the Succession, the Peace of Utrecht, the character of Queen Anne, the Duke and Duchess of Marlborough, Louis XIV, the Duke of Orléans, and the French and English ministers. If he had been skillful enough to blend his Apologia with these great subjects, he would have made it immortal: instead of which it is completely lost in the abbreviated and confused little book he has left us.

I cannot understand how a man, who appeared to take such wide views, should condescend to such trivialities. His translator is quite mistaken in saying I try to proscribe the study of facts. The reproach I bring against Lord Bolingbroke is that he has given us too few, and that the few he records he smothers in trivialities. However, I think his *Memoirs* will have given you a certain amount of pleasure, and as you read them you must very often have found yourself on familiar ground.

Good-by, madam; let us try to bear our earthly afflictions patiently. Courage is of *some* use: it flatters self-love, it lessens misfortune: but it does not give one back one's sight. I always most sincerely pity you: your fate touches me deeply.

TO MME. DU DEFFAND

Colmar, May 19, 1754.

Do you know Latin, madam? No; that is why you ask me if I prefer Pope to Virgil. All modern languages are dry, poor, and unmusical in comparison with those of our first masters, the Greeks and Romans. We are but the fiddles of a village band. Besides, how can I compare Epistles to an Epic poem, to the loves of Dido, the burning of Troy, to Aeneas' descent into Hades?

I think Pope's *Essay on Man* the finest of didactic and philosophic poems: but nothing is comparable to Virgil. You know him through translations: but it is impossible to translate the poets. Can you translate music? I regret, madam, that you, with your enlightened taste and feeling, cannot read Virgil. I pity you even more if you are reading the *Annals*, short though they are. Germany, even reduced to a miniature, is not likely to please a French imagination such as yours.

As you like epic poems, I would much rather you had the *Pucelle*. It is a little longer than the *Henriade* and the subject is livelier. Imagination has more play—in serious books in France it is generally much too circumscribed. My regard for historical truth and religious prejudice clipped my wings in the *Henriade:* they have grown again in the *Pucelle. Her* annals are much more amusing than those of the Empire.

If M. de Formont is still with you, pray remember me to him: if he has left, remember me to him when you write. I am going to Plombières, not in hopes of recovering my health—those I have quite given up—but because my friends are going there too. I have been six months at Colmar without moving out of my room: and I believe I shall do just the same at Paris unless you are there.

I perceive that, in the long run, there is really nothing worth the trouble of leaving the house for. Illness has great advantages: it spares one society. It is different for you, madam: society is as necessary to you as a violin to Guignon—who is the *King* of the violin.

M. d'Alembert is worthy of you: and much too good for his generation. He has repeatedly honored me far above my deserts, and he can be sure, if I regard him as the first of our philosophers with wit, it is not out of gratitude.

I do not often write to you, madam, although the next best thing to having a letter from you is answering one: but I am overwhelmed with hard work, and divide my time between it and the colic. I have no leisure—I am always either ill or working. That makes life a full one, though not a perfectly happy one: but where is happiness to be found? *I* have not the slightest idea: it is a very nice problem to solve.

TO J. J. ROUSSEAU

Les Délices, August 30, 1755.

I have received, sir, your new book against the human species, and I thank you for it. You will please people by your manner of telling them the truth about themselves, but you will not alter them. The horrors of that human society—from which in our feebleness and ignorance we expect so many consolations—have never been painted in more striking colors: no one has ever been so witty as you are in trying to turn us into brutes: to read your book makes one long to go on all fours. Since, however, it is now some sixty years since I gave up the practice, I feel that it is unfortunately impossible for me to resume it: I leave this natural habit to those more fit for it than are you and I. Nor can I set sail to discover the aborigines of Canada, in the first place because my ill-health ties me to the side of the greatest doctor in Europe,[1] and I should not find the same professional assistance among the Missouris: and secondly because war is going on in that country, and the example of the civilized nations has made the barbarians almost as wicked as we are ourselves. I must confine myself to being a peaceful savage in the retreat I have chosen—close to your country, where you yourself should be.

I agree with you that science and literature have sometimes done a great deal of harm. Tasso's enemies made his life a long series of misfortunes: Galileo's enemies kept him languishing in prison, at seventy years of age, for the crime of understanding the revolution of the earth: and, what is still more shameful, obliged him

[1] Dr. Theodore Tronchin.

to forswear his discovery. Since your friends began the Encyclopedia, their rivals attack them as deists, atheists —even Jansenists.

If I might venture to include myself among those whose works have brought them persecution as their sole recompense, I could tell you of men set on ruining me from the day I produced my tragedy *Oedipe:* of a perfect library of absurd calumnies which have been written against me: of an ex-Jesuit[1] priest whom I saved from utter disgrace rewarding me by defamatory libels: of a man yet more contemptible[2] printing my *Century of Louis XIV* with *Notes* in which crass ignorance gave birth to the most abominable falsehoods: of yet another, who sold to a publisher some chapters of a *Universal History* supposed to be by me: of the publisher avaricious enough to print this shapeless mass of blunders, wrong dates, mutilated facts and names: and, finally, of men sufficiently base and craven to assign the production of this farago to me. I could show you all society poisoned by this class of person—a class unknown to the ancients—who, not being able to find any honest occupation—be it manual labor or service—and unluckily knowing how to read and write, become the brokers of literature, live on our works, steal our manuscripts, falsify them, and sell them. I could tell of some loose sheets of a gay trifle[3] which I wrote thirty years ago (on the same subject that Chapelain was stupid enough to treat seriously) which are in circulation now through the breach of faith and the cupidity of those who added their own grossness to my *badinage* and filled in the gaps with a dullness only equaled by their malice; and who, finally, after twenty years, are selling everywhere

[1] The Abbé Desfontaines.
[2] La Baumelle, who pirated Voltaire's *Louis XIV*.
[3] *La Pucelle*.

a manuscript which, in very truth, is theirs and worthy of them only.

I may add, last of all, that someone has stolen part of the material I amassed in the public archives to use in my History of the War of 1741 when I was historiographer of France; that he sold that result of my labors to a bookseller in Paris; and is as set on getting hold of my property as if I were dead and he could turn it into money by putting it up to auction. I could show you ingratitude, imposture, and rapine pursuing me for forty years to the foot of the Alps and the brink of the grave. But what conclusion ought I to draw from all these misfortunes? This only: that I have no right to complain: Pope, Descartes, Bayle, Camoens—a hundred others—have been subjected to the same, or greater, injustice: and my destiny is that of nearly everyone who has loved letters too well.

Confess, sir, that all these things are, after all, but little personal pinpricks, which society scarcely notices. What matter to humankind that a few drones steal the honey of a few bees? Literary men make a great fuss of their petty quarrels: the rest of the world ignores them, or laughs at them.

They are, perhaps, the least serious of all the ills attendant on human life. The thorns inseparable from literature and a modest degree of fame are flowers in comparison with the other evils which from all time have flooded the world. Neither Cicero, Varron, Lucretius, Virgil, or Horace had any part in the proscriptions of Marius, Scylla, that profligate Antony, or that fool Lepidus; while as for that cowardly tyrant, Octavius Caesar—servilely entitled Augustus—he only became an assassin when he was deprived of the society of men of letters.

Confess that Italy owed none of her troubles to Petrarch or to Boccaccio: that Marot's jests were not responsible for the massacre of St. Bartholomew: or the tragedy of the *Cid* for the wars of the Fronde. Great crimes are always committed by great ignoramuses. What makes, and will always make, this world a vale of tears is the insatiable greediness and the indomitable pride of men, from Thomas Koulikan, who did not know how to read, to a customhouse officer who can just count. Letters support, refine, and comfort the soul: they are serving you, sir, at the very moment you decry them: you are like Achilles declaiming against fame, and Father Malebranche using his brilliant imagination to belittle imagination.

If anyone has a right to complain of letters, I am that person, for in all times and in all places they have led to my being persecuted: still, we must needs love them in spite of the way they are abused—as we cling to society, though the wicked spoil its pleasantness: as we must love our country, though it treats us unjustly: and as we must love and serve the Supreme Being, despite the superstition and fanaticism which too often dishonor His service.

M. Chappus tells me your health is very unsatisfactory: you must come and recover here in your native place, enjoy its freedom, drink (with me) the milk of its cows, and browse on its grass.

I am yours most philosophically and with sincere esteem.

TO M. TRONCHIN OF LYONS

Les Délices, November 24, 1755.

This is indeed a cruel piece of natural philosophy![1] We shall find it difficult to discover how the laws of movement operate in such fearful disasters *in the best of all possible worlds*—where a hundred thousand ants, our neighbors, are crushed in a second on our antheaps, half, dying undoubtedly in inexpressible agonies, beneath débris from which it was impossible to extricate them, families all over Europe reduced to beggary, and the fortunes of a hundred merchants—Swiss, like yourself—swallowed up in the ruins of Lisbon. What a game of chance human life is! What will the preachers say—especially if the Palace of the Inquisition is left standing? I flatter myself that those reverend fathers, the Inquisitors, will have been crushed just like other people. That ought to teach men not to persecute men: for, while a few sanctimonious humbugs are burning a few fanatics, the earth opens and swallows up all alike. I believe it is our mountains which save us from earthquakes.

TO MLLE. ——

Les Délices, June 20, 1756.

I am only an old invalid, mademoiselle, and my not having answered your letter before, and now replying only in prose to your charming verses, prove that my condition is a serious one.

[1] The Lisbon earthquake of 1755 inspired Voltaire's poem *The Lisbon Earthquake* (page 556) and *Candide*. Thirty thousand persons perished in six minutes

You ask me for advice: your own good taste will afford you all you need. Your study of Italian should further improve that taste which was born in you, and which nobody can give you. Tasso and Ariosto will do much more for you than I can, and reading our best poets is better than all lessons; but, since you are so good as to consult me from so far away, my advice to you is—read only such books as have long been sealed with the universal approval of the public and whose reputation is established. They are few: but you will gain much more from reading those few than from all the feeble little works with which we are inundated. Good writers are only witty in the right place, they never strive after smartness: they think sensibly, and express themselves clearly. Now, people appear to write exclusively in enigmas. Everything is affected—nothing simple: nature is ignored, and everyone tries to improve on the masterpieces of our language.

Hold fast, mademoiselle, by everything which delights you in them. The smallest affectation is a vice. The Italians, after Tasso and Ariosto, degenerated because they were always trying to be witty: and it is the same with the French. Observe how naturally Mme. de Sévigné and other ladies write: and compare their style with the confused phrases of our minor romances—I cite writers of your own sex because I am sure you can, and will, resemble them. There are passages of Mme. Deshoulières which are equaled by no writer of the present day. If you wish examples of male authors—look how simply and clearly Racine invariably expresses himself. Every reader of his works feels sure that he could himself say in prose what Racine has said in verse. Believe me, everything that is not equally clear, chaste, and simple is worth absolutely nothing.

Your own reflections, mademoiselle, will tell you all

this a hundred times better than I can say it. You will notice that our good writers—Fénelon, Bossuet, Racine, Despréaux—always use the right word. One gets oneself accustomed to talk well by constantly reading those who have written well: it becomes a habit to express our thoughts simply and nobly, without effort. It is not in the nature of a study: it is no trouble to read what is good, and to read that only: our own pleasure and taste are our only masters.

Forgive this long disquisition; you must please attribute it to my obedience to your commands.

I have the honor to be very respectfully yours.

TO MME. DU DEFFAND

Les Délices, April 12, 1760.

I have not sent you, madam, any of those trifles with which you condescend to while away an idle moment. For more than six weeks I have broken with all humankind: I have buried myself in my own thoughts: then came the usual country employments, and then a fever. Taking all these things into consideration, you have had nothing, and most likely will have nothing, for some time.

You need, however, only write and say to me, "I want to be amused, I am well, in full feather, and a good humor, and I should like some trifles sent along to me," and you shall have a whole postbag—comic, scientific, historical, or poetic, just as pleases you best—on condition you throw it in the fire when read.

You were so enthusiastic over *Clarissa* that I read it as a relaxation from my work when I was ill: the reading made me feverish. It is cruel for a man as impatient as I am to read nine whole volumes containing nothing at all, and serving no purpose whatever but to give a glimpse of Miss Clarissa's love for a profligate like Lovelace. I said to myself: "Were all these people my friends and relatives, I could not take the least interest in them." I see nothing in the author but a cleverish man who knows the invincible curiosity of the human species, and who holds out hopes of gratifying it volume after volume—in order to sell them. When at last I found Clarissa in a house of ill fame, I was greatly touched.

Pierre Corneille's *Théodore* (who wants to get into La Fillons from a Christian motive) does not approach *Clarissa,* either in its situations or in its pathos; but, save that part where the pretty English girl finds herself in that disreputable place, I confess that nothing in the novel gave me the least satisfaction, and I should be sorry to have to read it through again. The only good books, it seems to me, are those which can be reread without weariness.

The only good books of that particular kind are those which set a picture constantly before the imagination, and soothe the ear by their harmony. People want music and painting, with a few little philosophical precepts thrown in now and again with a reasonable discretion. For this reason Horace, Virgil, and Ovid always please —save in the translations, which spoil them.

After *Clarissa* I reread some chapters of Rabelais, such as the fight of brother Jean des Entommeures, and the meeting of the council of Pierochole: I know them almost by heart: but I reread them with the greatest pleasure, for they give a most vivid picture of life.

Not that I compare Rabelais with Horace: but if Horace is the first writer of good epistles, Rabelais, at his best, is the first of buffoons. Two men of this kind in a nation are not needed: but one there must be. I am sorry I once decried him.

But there are pleasures superior to all this sort of thing: those of seeing the grass grow in the fields, and the abundant harvest ripen. That is man's true life: all the rest is vanity.

Forgive me, madam, for speaking to you of a pleasure enjoyed through the eyes: you only know the pleasures of the soul. The way you bear your affliction is wholly admirable: you enjoy, anyhow, all the advantages of society. It is true that that often comes to mean merely giving one's opinion on the news of the day; which, in the long run, seems to me exceedingly insipid. Only our tastes and passions make this world supportable. You replace the passions by philosophy, a poor substitute: while I replace them with the tender and respectful attachment I have always felt for you.

TO M. DAMILAVILLE

Ferney, March 1, 1765.

My dear friend, I have devoured the new *Memoir* of M. de Beaumont on the innocence of the Calas; I have admired and wept over it, but it told me nothing I did not know; I have long been convinced, and it was I who was lucky enough to furnish the first proofs.

You would like to know how this European protest against the judicial murder of the unhappy Calas, broken on the wheel at Toulouse, managed to reach a little unknown corner of the world, between the Alps and the Jura, a hundred miles from the scene of the fearful event.

Nothing more clearly reveals the existence of that imperceptible chain which links all the events of this miserable world.

At the end of March, 1762, a traveler, who had come

through Languedoc and arrived in my little retreat two miles from Geneva, told me of the sacrifice of Calas, and assured me that he was innocent. I answered him that the crime was not a probable one, but that it was still more improbable that Calas' judges should, without any motive, break an innocent man on the wheel.

I heard the next day that one of the children of this unfortunate man had taken refuge in Switzerland, fairly near my cottage. His flight made me presume the guilt of the family. However, I reflected that the father had been condemned to death for having, by himself, assassinated his son on account of his religion, and that, at the time of his death, this father was sixty-nine years old. I never remember to have read of any old man being possessed by so horrible a fanaticism. I have always observed that this mania is usually confined to young people, with weak, heated, and unstable imaginations, inflamed by superstition. The fanatics of the Cevennes were madmen from twenty to thirty years of age, trained to prophesy since childhood. Almost all the convulsionists I had seen in any large numbers in Paris were young girls and boys. Among the monks the old are less carried away and less liable to the fury of the zealot than those just out of their novitiate. The notorious assassins, goaded by religious frenzy, have all been young people, as have all those who have pretended to be possessed—no one ever saw an old man exorcised. This reasoning made me doubt a crime, which was, moreover, unnatural. I was ignorant of its circumstances.

I had young Calas to my house. I expected to find him a religious enthusiast, such as his country has sometimes produced. I found a simple and ingenuous youth, with a gentle and very interesting countenance, who, as he talked to me, made vain efforts to restrain his tears. He told me that he was at Nîmes, apprenticed to a manufacturer, when he heard that his whole family was about to be condemned to death at Toulouse, and that almost all Languedoc believed them guilty. He added that, to escape so fearful a disgrace, he had come to Switzerland to hide himself.

I asked him if his father and mother were of a violent character. He told me that they had never beaten any one of their children, and that never were parents more tender and indulgent.

I confess that no more was needed to give me a strong presumption in favor of the innocence of the family. I gathered fresh information from two merchants of Geneva, of proven honesty, who had lodged at the Calas' house in Toulouse. They confirmed me in my opinion. Far from believing the Calas family to be fanatics and parricides, I thought I saw that it was the fanatics who had accused and ruined them. I had long known of what party spirit and calumny are capable.

But what was my astonishment when, having written to Languedoc on the subject of this extraordinary story, Catholics and Protestants answered that there was no doubt as to the crime of the Calas! I was not disheartened. I took the liberty of writing to those in authority in the province, to the governors of neighboring provinces, and to ministers of state: all unanimously advised me not to mix myself up in such a horrible affair: everybody blamed me: and I persisted: this is what I did.

Calas' widow (from whom, to fill to the brim her cup of misery and insult, her daughters had been forcibly removed) had retired into solitude, where she lived on the bread of tears, and awaited death. I did not enquire if she was, or was not, attached to the Protestant religion, but only if she believed in a God who rewarded virtue and punished crime. I asked her if she would sign a solemn declaration, as before God, that her husband died innocent: she did not hesitate. She had to be persuaded to leave her retirement and to undertake the journey to Paris.

It is then apparent that, if there are great crimes on the earth, there are as many virtues; and that, if superstition produces horrible sufferings, philosophy redresses them.

A lady, whose generosity is as noble as her birth, and who was staying at Geneva to have her daughters inoculated, was the first to succor this unhappy family. French people living in this country seconded her: the traveling English distinguished themselves: there was a beneficent rivalry between the two nations as to which should give the more to virtue so cruelly oppressed.

As to the sequel, who knows it better than you? Who has served innocence with a zeal as faithful and courageous? Who has more generously encouraged the voice of those orators whom all France and Europe paused to hear? The days when Cicero justified, before an assembly of legislators, Amerinus accused of parricide, are with us again. A few people, calling themselves pious, have raised their voices against the Calas: but, for the first time since fanaticism was established, the wise have silenced them.

What great victories reason is winning among us! But would you believe, my dear friend, that the family of the Calas, so efficiently succored and avenged, was not the only one that religion accused of parricide—was not the only one sacrificed to the furies of religious persecution? There is a case yet more pitiable, because, while experiencing the same horrors, it has not had the same consolations: it has not found Mariettes, Beaumonts, and Loiseau.

There appears to be a horrible mania, indigenous to Languedoc, originally sown there by the inquisitors in the train of Simon de Montfort, which, ever since then, from time to time hoists its flag.

A native of Castres, named Sirven, had three daughters. As the religion of the family is the so-called reformed religion, the youngest of the daughters was torn from the arms of her mother. She was put into a convent, where they beat her to help her to learn her catechism: she went mad: and threw herself into a well at a place not far from her parents' house. The bigots thereupon made up their minds that her father, mother, and sisters had drowned the child. The Catholics of the province are absolutely convinced that one of the chief points of the Protestant religion is that the fathers and mothers are bound to hang, strangle, or drown any of their children whom they suspect of any leaning toward the Catholic faith. Precisely at the moment when the Calas were in irons, this fresh scaffold was uplifted.

The story of the drowned girl reached Toulouse at once. Everyone declared it to be a fresh instance of murderous parents. The public fury grew daily: Calas was broken on the wheel: Sirven, his wife, and his daughter were accused. Sirven, terrified, had just time to flee with his delicate family. They went on foot, with no creature to help them, across precipitous mountains, deep in snow. One of the daughters gave birth to an infant among the glaciers: and, herself dying, bore her dying child in her arms: they finally took the road to Switzerland.

The same fate which brought the children of the Calas to me, decided that the Sirvens should also appeal to me. Picture to yourself, my friend, four sheep accused by the butchers of having devoured a lamb: for that is what I saw. I despair of describing to you so much innocence and so much sorrow. What ought I to have done? and what would you have done in my place? Could I rest satisfied with cursing human nature? I took the liberty of writing to the first president of Languedoc, a wise and good man: but he was not at Toulouse. I got one of my friends to present a petition to the vice-chancellor. During this time, near Castres, the father, mother, and two daughters were executed in effigy: their property confiscated and dissipated—to the last sou.

Here was an entire family—honest, innocent, virtuous—left to disgrace and beggary among strangers: some, doubtless, pitied them: but it is hard to be an object of pity to one's grave! I was finally informed that remission of their sentence was a possibility. At first, I believed that it was the judges from whom that pardon must be obtained. You will easily understand that the family would sooner have begged their bread from door to door, or have died of want, than ask a pardon which admitted a crime too horrible to be pardonable. But how could justice be obtained? how could they go back to prison in a country where half the inhabitants still said that Calas' murder was just? Would there be a second appeal to Council? would anyone try to rouse again the public sympathy which, it might well be, the misfortunes of the Calas had exhausted, and which would weary of refuting such accusations, of reinstating the condemned, and of confounding their judges?

Are not these two tragic events, my friend, so rapidly following each other, proofs of the inevitable decrees of fate, to which our miserable species is subject? A terrible truth, so much insisted on in Homer and Sophocles: but a useful truth, since it teaches us to be resigned and to learn how to suffer.

Shall I add that, while the incredible calamities of the Calas and the Sirvens wrung my heart, a man, whose profession you will guess from what he said, reproached me for taking so much interest in two families who were strangers to me? "Why do you mix yourself up in such things?" he asked; "let the dead bury their dead." I answered him, "If I found an Israelite in the desert—an Israelite covered in blood; suffer me to pour a little wine and oil into his wounds: you are the Levite, leave me to play the Samaritan."

It is true that, as a reward for my trouble, I have been treated quite as a Samaritan: a defamatory libel appeared under the titles of *A Pastoral Instruction* and *A Charge:* but it may well be forgotten—a Jesuit wrote it. The wretch did not know then that I was myself giving shelter to a Jesuit! Could I prove more conclusively that we should regard our enemies as our brethren?

Your passions are humanity, a love of truth, and a hatred of calumny. Our friendship is founded on the similarity of our characters. I have spent my life in seeking and publishing the truth which I love. Who else among modern historians has defended the memory of a great prince against the abominable inventions of a writer, whoever he may be, who might well be called the traducer of kings, ministers, and military commanders, and who now has not a single reader?

I have only done in the fearful cases of the Calas and the Sirvens what all men do: I have followed my bent. A philosopher's is not to pity the unhappy—it is to be of use to them.

I know how furiously fanaticism attacks philosophy, whose two daughters, Truth and Tolerance, fanaticism would fain destroy as it destroyed the Calas: while philosophy only wishes to render innocuous the offspring of fanaticism, Falsehood and Persecution.

Those who do not reason try to bring into discredit those who do: they have confused the philosopher with the sophist: and have greatly deceived themselves. The true philosopher can be aroused against the calumny which so often attacks himself: he can overwhelm with everlasting contempt the vile mercenary who twice a month outrages sense, good taste, and morality: he can even expose to ridicule, in passing, those who insult literature in the sanctuary where they should have honored it: but he knows nothing of cabals, underhand dealings, or petty revenge. Like the sage of Montbar, like the sage of Voré, he knows how to make the land fruitful and those who dwell on it happier. The real philosopher clears uncultivated ground, adds to the number of plows and, so, to the number of inhabitants: employs and enriches the poor: encourages marriages and finds a home for the orphan: does not grumble at necessary taxes, and puts the agriculturist in a condition to pay them promptly. He expects nothing from others, and does them all the good he can. He has a horror of hypocrisy, but he pities the superstitious: and, finally, he knows how to be a friend.

I perceive that I am painting your portrait: the resemblance would be perfect, were you so fortunate as to live in the country.

TO LORD CHESTERFIELD

Ferney, September 24, 1771.

Lord Huntington tells me that, of the five senses common to us all, you have only lost one, and that you have a good digestion: that is well worth a pair of ears.

I, rather than you, should be the person to decide whether it is worse to be deaf or blind or to have a weak digestion. I can judge these three conditions from personal experience: only for a long time I have not dared to come to decisions on trifles, much less on subjects so important. I confine myself to the belief that, if you get the sun in the fine house you have built yourself, you will have very bearable moments. That is all that we can hope for at our ages, and, in fact, at any age. Cicero wrote a beautiful treatise on old age, but facts did not confirm his theories, and his last years were very miserable. You have lived longer and more happily than he did. You have not had to deal with perpetual dictators or triumvirs. Your lot has been, and is still, one of the most desirable in this great lottery, where the prizes are so rare, and the biggest one—lasting happiness—has never yet been gained by anybody.

Your philosophy has never been misled by the wild dreams which have confused heads otherwise strong enough. You have never been, in any sort, either an impostor or the dupe of impostors, and I count that as one of the most uncommon advantages of this brief life.

TO M. DE FARGÈS[1]

Ferney, February 25, 1776.

Sir, since thou wouldest enter into judgment with thy servant, permit me to tell you that, if I could leave my bed (being now in my eighty-third year and the victim of many maladies), I should hasten to throw myself at the feet of the Controller General: and this is how I should prose on the subject of our states:

Our little country is worse than Sologne and the miserable land of Champagne, and worse than the worst parts of Bordeaux.

Notwithstanding our wretchedness, eight and twenty parishes sang eight and twenty Te Deums and shouted eight and twenty "Long live the Kings and Long live M. Turgots!" We shall cheerfully pay thirty thousand francs

[1] A Councillor of State.

to the sixty sub-kings—being delighted to die of hunger, on condition of being delivered from seventy-eight rogues who made us die of rage.

We agree with you that near Paris, Milan, and Naples the land can support all the taxes, because the land is productive: but it is not the same with us: in good years the yield is three to one, often two, sometimes nothing, and needs six oxen to plow it. Seeds are fruitful once only in ten years.

You will ask what we live on: I answer, On black bread and potatoes, and principally on the sale of the wood which our peasants cut in the forests and take to Geneva. Even this means of subsistence constantly fails, for the forests are devastated here much more than in the rest of the kingdom.

I may remark, in passing, that timber will soon be scarce in France, and that lately wood for firing is being bought in Prussia.

As I want to be perfectly frank, I own that we make certain cheeses on some of the Jura mountains in June, July, and August.

Our chief means of livelihood is at the end of our fingers. Our peasants, having nothing to live on, have been diligently working at watchmaking for the Genevese—the Genevese making thereat ten millions of francs per annum, and paying the workmen of the province of Gex exceedingly badly.

An old man, who took it into his head to settle between Switzerland and Geneva, has established a watch manufactory in the province of Gex which pays the workmen of the country exceedingly well, which increases the population, and which, if protected by the Government, will supersede the business of wealthy Geneva: but this old man is not much longer for this world.

We exist, then, solely through our industry. But I ask if this watchmaking, which will bring in ten thousand francs a year, which profits by salt much more than do the agriculturists, cannot help these agriculturists with the thirty thousand francs indemnity they must pay for their salt?

I ask if these fat innkeepers, who make even more than the watchmakers, and consume more salt, ought not also to assist the unfortunate proprietors of a wretched soil?

The big manufacturers, the hotelkeepers, the butchers, the bakers, the tradesmen, know so well the miserable condition of the country and the favors of the ministry that they have all offered to help us with a small contribution.

Either permit this contribution, or slightly reduce the exorbitant sum of thirty thousand livres which the sixty deputy-kings demand from us.

One of these sub-kings named Basemont has just died, worth, it is said, eighteen millions [of francs]. Was there any need for that scamp to flay us alive in order that our skin might bring him five hundred livres?

Here, sir, are a few of the grievances which I should lay at the feet of the Controller General: but I say nothing, I leave all to you. If you are moved by my reasonings you will deign to be so good as to present them: if they strike you as bad, you will whistle them down the wind.

If I do wrong to plead thus feebly for my country, I am undoubtedly right in saying that I have the greatest esteem for your enlightenment, the greatest gratitude for your kindnesses, and that I am, with the sincerest respects, yours, sir, etc., etc.

Translation by S. G. Tallentyre

Selections from *The English Letters*

The English Parliament

THE members of the English Parliament are fond of comparing themselves, on all occasions, to the old Romans.

Not long since, Mr. Shippen opened a speech in the House of Commons with these words: "The majesty of the people of England would be wounded." The singularity of this expression occasioned a loud laugh; but this gentleman, far from being disconcerted, repeated the statement with a resolute tone of voice, and the laugh ceased. I must own, I see no resemblance between the majesty of the people of England and that of the Romans, and still less between the two governments. There is in London a senate, some of the members whereof are accused—doubtless very unjustly—of selling their votes, on certain occasions, as was done at Rome; and herein lies the whole resemblance. In other respects, the two nations appear to be quite opposite in character, with regard both to good and to evil. The Romans never knew the terrible madness of religious wars. This abomination was reserved for devout preachers of patience and humility. Marius and Sulla, Caesar and Pompey, Antony and Augustus, did not draw their swords against one another to determine whether the flamen should wear his shirt over his robe, or his robe over his shirt; or whether the sacred chickens should both eat and drink, or eat only, in order to take the augury. The English have formerly destroyed one another, by sword or halter, for disputes of as trifling a nature. The Episcopalians and the Presbyterians quite turned the heads of these gloomy people for a time; but I believe they will hardly be so silly again, as they seem to have grown wiser at their own expense; and I do not perceive the least inclination in them to murder one another any more for mere syllogisms. But who can answer for the follies and prejudices of mankind?

Here follows a more essential difference between Rome and England, which throws the advantage entirely on the side of the latter; namely, that the civil wars of Rome ended in slavery, and those of the English in liberty. The English are the only people on earth who have been able to prescribe limits to the power of kings by resisting them, and who, by a series of struggles, have at length established that wise and happy form of government where the prince is all-powerful to do good, and at the same time is restrained from committing evil; where the nobles are great without insolence or lordly power, and the people share in the government without confusion.

The House of Lords and the House of Commons divide the legislative power under the king; but the Romans had no such balance. Their patricians and plebeians were continually at variance, without any intermediate power to reconcile them. The Roman senate, who were so unjustly, so criminally, formed as to exclude the plebeians from having any share in the affairs of government, could find no other artifice to effect their design than to employ them in foreign wars. They considered the people as wild beasts, whom they were to let loose upon their neighbors, for fear they should turn upon their masters. Thus the greatest defect in the government of the Romans was the means of making them conquerors; and, by being unhappy at home, they became masters of the world, till in the end their divisions sank them into slavery.

The government of England, from its nature, can never attain to so exalted a pitch, nor can it ever have so fatal an end. It has not in view the splendid folly of making conquests, but only the prevention of their neighbors from conquering. The English are jealous not only of their own liberty, but even of that of other nations. The only reason of their quarrels with Louis XIV was on account of his ambition.

It has not been without some difficulty that liberty has been established in England, and the idol of arbitrary power has been drowned in seas of blood; nevertheless, the English do not think they have purchased their laws at too high a price. Other nations have shed as much blood; but then the blood they spilled in defense of their liberty served only to enslave them the more.

That which rises to a revolution in England is no more than a sedition in other countries. A city in Spain, in Barbary, or in Turkey takes up arms in defense of its privileges, when immediately it is stormed by mercenary troops, it is punished by executioners, and the rest of the nation kiss their chains. The French think that the government of this island is more tempestuous than the seas which surround it; in which, indeed, they are not mistaken: but then this happens only when the king raises the storm by attempting to seize the ship, of which he is only the pilot. The civil wars of France lasted longer, were more cruel, and productive of greater evils, than those of England: but none of these civil wars had a wise and becoming liberty for their object.

In the detestable times of Charles IX and Henry III the whole affair was only whether the people should be slaves to the Guises. As to the last war of Paris, it deserves only to be hooted at. It makes us think we see a crowd of schoolboys rising up in arms against their master, and afterward being whipped for it. Cardinal de Retz, who was witty and brave, but employed those talents badly; who was rebellious without cause, factious without design, and the head of a defenseless party, caballed for the sake of caballing, and seemed to foment the civil war for his own amusement and pastime. The parliament did not know what he aimed at, nor what he did not aim at. He levied troops, and the next instant cashiered them; he threatened; he begged pardon; he set a price on Cardinal Mazarin's head, and afterward congratulated him in a public manner. Our civil wars under Charles VI were bloody and cruel, those of the League execrable, and that of the Frondeurs ridiculous.

That for which the French chiefly reproach the English nation is the murder of King Charles I, a prince who merited a better fate, and whom his subjects treated just as he would have treated them, had he been powerful and at ease. After all, consider, on one side, Charles I defeated in a pitched battle, imprisoned, tried, sentenced to die in Westminster Hall, and then beheaded; and, on the other, the emperor Henry VII poisoned by his chaplain in receiving the sacrament; Henry III of France stabbed by a monk; thirty different plots contrived to assassinate Henry IV, several of them put into execution, and the last depriving that great monarch of his life. Weigh, I say, all these wicked attempts, and then judge.

The English Constitution

This mixture of different departments in the government of England; this harmony between the King, Lords, and Commons has not always subsisted. England was for a long time in a state of slavery, having, at different periods, worn the yoke of the Romans, Saxons, Danes, and, last of all, the Normans. William the Conqueror, in particular, governed them with a rod of iron. He disposed of the goods and lives of his new subjects like an eastern tyrant: he forbade, under pain of death, any Englishman to have either fire or light in his house after eight o'clock at night, whether it was that he intended by this edict to prevent their holding any assemblies in the night, or, by so whimsical a prohibition, had a mind to try to what a degree of abjectness men might be subjected by their fellow-creatures. It is, however, certain that the English had parliaments both before and since the time of William the Conqueror; they still boast of them, as if the assemblies which then bore the title of parliaments, and which were composed of the ecclesiastical tyrants and the barons, had been actually the guardians of their liberties, and the preservers of the public felicity.

These barbarians, who poured like a torrent from the shores of the Baltic and overran all the east of Europe, brought the use of these estates or parliaments, which are the subject of so much noise, though very little known, along with them. It is true, kings were not then despotic, which is precisely the reason why the people groaned under so intolerable a yoke. The chiefs of those barbarians who had ravaged France, Italy, Spain, and

England, made themselves monarchs. Their captains divided and shared with them the lands of the conquered: hence those margraves, lairds, barons, with all that gang of petty tyrants who have often disputed with sovereigns who were not firmly fixed on their thrones the spoils and plunder of the people. It was so many birds of prey fighting with an eagle, that they might suck the blood of the doves; and every nation, instead of having one good and indulgent master, which might have been their lot, had a hundred of those bloodsucking monsters. Shortly after, priestcraft began to mingle in civil matters; from earliest antiquity, the fate of the Gauls, Germans, and inhabitants of Great Britain depended on the Druids, and on the heads of their villages, an ancient kind of barons, though a less tyrannical sort than their predecessors. These Druids called themselves mediators between men and the Deity: it was they who made laws, excommunicated, and, lastly, punished criminals with death. The bishops succeeded by imperceptible degrees to their temporal authority in the Gothic and Vandal government. The popes put themselves at their head, and with their briefs, bulls, and their other more mischievous instruments, the monks, made kings tremble on their thrones, deposed or assassinated them at pleasure, and, in a word, drew to themselves all the treasure of Europe. The weak Ina, one of the tyrants of the Saxon heptarchy, was the first who, in a pilgrimage which he made to Rome, submitted to pay "Peter's pence"—about a French crown, or half a crown sterling—for every house in his kingdom. The whole island presently followed this example; England became insensibly a province to the pope; and the holy father sent thither, from time to time, his legates to levy extraordinary impositions. At last John, surnamed Sans Terre, or Lackland, made a formal cession of his kingdom to his holiness, who had excommunicated him. The barons, who were by no means gainers by this proceeding, expelled this wretched prince, and set up in his place Louis VIII, father of St. Louis, king of France; but they were presently disgusted with this new monarch, and compelled him to cross the seas again.

While the barons, with the bishops and popes, were tearing all England to pieces, where each of them would fain have ruled, the people, that is to say, the most numerous, the most useful, and even the most virtuous part of mankind, composed of those who addict themselves to the study of the laws and of the sciences, of merchants, mechanics, and, in a word, of laborers, that first and most despised of all professions; the people, I say, were considered by them as animals of a nature inferior to the rest of the human species. The Commons were then far from enjoying the least share in the government; they were then villeins or slaves, whose labor, and even whose blood, was the property of their masters, who called themselves the nobility. Far the greatest part of the human species were in Europe—as they still are in several parts of the world—the slaves of some lord, and at best but a kind of cattle, which they bought and sold with their lands. It was the work of ages to render justice to humanity, and to find out what a horrible thing it was, that the many should sow while a few did reap: and is it not the greatest happiness for the French, that the authority of those petty tyrants has been extinguished by the lawful authority of our sovereign, and in England by that of the king and nation conjointly?

Happily, in those shocks which the quarrels of kings and great men gave to empires, the chains of nations have been relaxed more or less. Liberty in England has arisen from the quarrels of tyrants. The barons forced John Sans Terre and Henry III to grant that famous charter, the principal scope of which was in fact to make kings dependent on the lords; but, at the same time, the rest of the nation were favored, that they might side with their pretended protectors. This great charter, which is looked upon as the palladium and the consecrated fountain of the public liberty, is itself a proof how little that liberty was understood: the very title shows beyond all doubt that the king thought himself absolute, *de jure;* and that the barons, and even the clergy, forced him to relinquish this pretended right, only because they were stronger than he. It begins in this manner: "We, of our free will, grant the following privileges to the archbishops, bishops, abbots, priors, and barons of our kingdom," etc. In the articles of this charter there is not one word said of the House of Commons; a proof that no such house then existed; or, if it did, that its power was next to nothing. In this the free men of England are specified—a melancholy proof that there were then some who were not so. We see, by the thirty-second article, that those pretended free men owed their lords certain servitude. Such a liberty as this smelled very rank of slavery. By the twenty-first article, the king ordains, that from henceforth officers shall be restrained from forcibly seizing the horses and carriages of free men, except on paying for the same. This regulation was considered by the people as real liberty, because it destroyed a most intolerable kind of tyranny. Henry VII, that fortunate conqueror and politician, who pretended to cherish the barons, whom he both feared and hated, bethought himself of the project of alienating their lands. By this means the villeins, who afterward acquired property by their industry, bought the castles of the great lords, who had ruined themselves by their extravagance; and by degrees nearly all the estates in the kingdom changed masters.

The House of Commons daily became more powerful; the families of the ancient peerage became extinct in time; and as, in the rigor of the law, there is no other nobility in England besides the peers, the whole order would have been annihilated had not the kings created new barons from time to time; and this expedient preserved the body of the peers they had formerly so much dreaded, in order to oppose the House of Commons, now grown too powerful. All the new peers, who form the upper house, receive nothing besides their titles from the crown; scarcely any of them possessing the lands from which those titles are derived. The duke of Dorset, for example, is one of them, though he possesses not a foot of land in Dorsetshire; another may be earl of a village, who hardly knows in what quarter of the island such a village lies. They have only a certain power in parliament, and nowhere out of it, which, with some few privileges, is all they enjoy.

Here is no such thing as the distinction of high, middle, and low justice in France; nor of the right of hunting on the lands of a citizen, who has not the liberty of firing a single shot of a musket on his own estate.

A peer or nobleman in this country pays his share of the taxes as others do, all of which are regulated by the House of Commons; which house, if it is second only in rank, is first in point of credit. The lords and bishops, it is true, may reject any bill of the commons, when it regards the raising of money; but are not entitled to make the smallest amendment in it: they must either pass it or throw it out, without any restriction whatever. When the bill is confirmed by the lords, and approved by the king, then every person is to pay his quota without distinction; and that not according to his rank or quality, which would be absurd, but in proportion to his revenue. Here is no *taille*, or arbitrary poll-tax, but a real tax on lands; all of which underwent an actual valuation under the famous William III. The taxes remain always the same, notwithstanding the fact that the value of lands has risen; so that no one is stripped to the bone, nor can there be any ground of complaint; the feet of the peasant are not tortured with wooden shoes; he eats the best wheaten bread, is well and warmly clothed, and is in no apprehension on account of the increase of his herds and flocks, or terrified into a thatched house, instead of a convenient slated roof, for fear of an augmentation of the *taille* the year following. There are even a number of peasants, or, if you will, farmers, who have from five to six hundred pounds sterling yearly income, and who are not above cultivating those fields which have enriched them, and where they enjoy the greatest of all human blessings, liberty.

English Commerce

Never has any people, since the fall of Carthage, been at the same time powerful by sea and land, till Venice set the example. The Portuguese, from their good fortune in discovering the passage by way of the Cape of Good Hope, have been for some time great lords on the coasts of the East Indies, but have never been very respectable in Europe. Even the United Provinces became warlike, contrary to their natural disposition, and in spite of themselves; and it can in no way be ascribed to their union among themselves, but to their being united with England, that they have contributed to hold the balance in Europe at the beginning of the eighteenth century.

Carthage, Venice, and Amsterdam were undoubtedly powerful; but their conduct has been exactly like that of merchants grown rich by traffic, who afterward purchase lands with the dignity of lordship annexed to them. Neither Carthage, Venice, nor Holland have, from a warlike and even conquering beginning, ended in a commercial nation. The English are the only people existing who have done this; they were a long time warriors before they learned to cast accounts. They were entirely ignorant of numbers when they won the battles of Agincourt, Crécy, and Poitiers, and were also ignorant that it was in their power to become cornfactors and woollen-drapers, two things that would certainly turn to much better account. This science alone has rendered the nation at once populous, wealthy, and powerful. London was a poor countrytown when Edward III conquered one-half of France; and it is wholly owing to this that the English have become merchants; that London exceeds Paris in extent, and number of inhabitants; that they are able to equip and man two hundred sail of ships of war, and keep the kings who are their allies in pay. The Scottish are born warriors, and, from the purity of their air, inherit good sense. Whence comes it then that Scotland, under the name of a union, has become a province of England? It is because Scotland has scarcely any other commodity than coal, and that England has fine tin, excellent wool, and abounds in corn, manufactures, and trading companies.

When Louis XIV made Italy tremble, and his armies, already in possession of Savoy and Piedmont, were on the point of reducing Turin, Prince Eugene was obliged to march from the remotest parts of Germany to the assistance of the duke of Savoy. He was in want of money, without which cities can neither be taken nor defended. He had recourse to the English merchants. In half an hour's time they lent him five millions, with which he effected the deliverance of Turin, beat the French, and wrote this short note to those who had lent him the money: "Gentlemen, I have received your money, and flatter myself I have employed it to your satisfaction." This gives an Englishman a kind of pride, which is extremely well founded, and causes him, not without reason, to compare himself to a citizen of Rome. Thus the younger son of a peer of the realm is not above traffic. Lord Townshend, secretary of state, has a brother who is satisfied with being a merchant in the city. At the time when Lord Oxford ruled all England, his younger brother was a factor at Aleppo, whence he could never be prevailed on to return, and where he died. This custom, which is now unhappily dying out, appears monstrous to a German, whose head is full of the coats of arms and pageants of his family. They can never conceive how it is possible that the son of an English peer should be no more than a rich and powerful citizen, while in Germany they are all princes. I have known more than thirty highnesses of the same name, whose whole fortunes and estate put together amounted to a few coats of arms, and the starving pride they inherited from their ancestors.

In France everybody is a marquis; and a man just come from the obscurity of some remote province, with money in his pocket, and a name that ends with an "*ac*" or an "*ille*," may give himself airs, and usurp such phrases as, "A man of my quality and rank"; and hold merchants in the most sovereign contempt. The merchant again, by dint of hearing his profession despised on all occasions, at last is fool enough to blush at his condition. I will not, however, take upon me to say which is the most useful to his country, and which of the two ought to have the preference; whether the powdered lord, who knows to a minute when the king rises or goes to bed, perhaps to stool, and who gives himself airs of importance in playing the part of a slave in the antechamber of some minister; or the merchant, who enriches his country, and from his counting-house sends his orders into Surat or Cairo, thereby contributing to the happiness and convenience of human nature.

Inoculation

The rest of Europe, that is, the Christian part of it, very gravely assert that the English are fools and madmen; fools, in communicating the contagion of smallpox to their children, in order to hinder them from being subject to that dangerous and loathsome disorder; madmen, in wantonly exposing their children to this pestilence, with the design of preventing a contingent evil. The English, on their side, call the rest of Europe unnatural and cowardly; unnatural, in leaving their children exposed to almost certain death by smallpox; and cowardly, in fearing to give their children a trifling matter of pain for a purpose so noble and so evidently useful. In order to determine which of the two is in the right, I shall now relate the history of this famous practice, which is in France the subject of so much dread.

The women of Circassia have from time immemorial been accustomed to give their children smallpox, even as early as at six months of age, by making an incision in the arm, and afterward inserting in this incision a pustule carefully taken from the body of some other child. This pustule so insinuated produces in the body of the patient the same effect that leaven does in a piece of dough; that is, it ferments in it, and communicates to the mass of blood the qualities with which it is impregnated. The pustules of the child infected in this manner serve to convey the same disease to others. This disorder, therefore, is perpetually circulating through the different parts of Circassia; and when, unluckily, there is no infection of smallpox in the country, it creates the same uneasiness as a dearth or an unhealthy season would have occasioned.

What has given rise to this custom in Circassia, and which is so extraordinary to other nations, is, however, a cause common to all the nations on the face of the earth; that is, the tenderness of mothers, and motives of interest. The Circassians are poor, but have handsome daughters; which, accordingly, are the principal article of their foreign commerce. It is they who furnish beauties for the seraglios of the grand seigneur, the sufi of Persia, and others who are rich enough to purchase and to maintain these precious commodities. These people bring up their children in the nurture and admonition of the Lord; that is, in virtuous and honorable principles, which contain the whole science of wheedling the male part of the creation; the art of dancing, with gestures expressive of uncommon effeminacy and lasciviousness; and lastly, that of rekindling, by the most bewitching artifices, the exhausted appetites of those haughty lords to whom their fates have destined them. These poor creatures repeat their lesson every day with their mothers, in the same manner as our girls do their catechism; that is, without understanding a single syllable of what is taught them. Now it often happened that a father and mother, after having taken an infinite deal of pains in giving their children a good education, suddenly see their hopes frustrated. Smallpox getting into the family, one daughter perhaps died; another lost an eye; a third recovered, but with a disfigured nose; so that here was an honest couple hopelessly ruined. Often, too, an entire stagnation of all kinds of commerce has ensued, and that for several years running, when the disorder happened to be epidemic, to the no small detriment of the seraglios of Turkey and Persia.

A commercial people are always exceedingly vigilant with regard to their interest, and never neglect those items of knowledge that may be of use in the carrying on of their traffic. The Circassians found that, upon computation, in a thousand persons there was hardly one that was ever twice seized with smallpox completely formed; that there had been instances of a person's having had a slight touch of it, or something resembling it, but there never were any two relapses known to be dangerous; in short, that the same person has never been known to have been twice infected with this disorder. They further remark, that when the disease is mild, and the eruption has only to pierce through a thin and delicate skin, it leaves no mark on the face. From these natural observations they concluded, that if a child of six months or a year old was to have a mild kind of smallpox, not only would the child certainly survive, but it would get better without bearing any marks of it, and would assuredly be immune during the remainder of its life. Hence it followed, that their only method would be to communicate the disorder to their children betimes, which they did, by insinuating into the child's body a pustule taken from the body of one infected with smallpox, the most completely formed, and at the same time the most favorable kind that could be found. The experiment could hardly fail. The Turks, a very sensible people, soon adopted this practice; and, at this day, there is scarcely a pasha in Constantinople who does not inoculate his children while they are at the breast.

There are some who pretend that the Circassians formerly learned this custom from the Arabians. We will leave this point in history to be elucidated by some learned Benedictine, who will not fail to compose several volumes in folio upon the subject, together with the necessary vouchers. All I have to say of the matter is that, in the beginning of the reign of George I, Lady Mary Wortley Montagu, one of the most celebrated ladies in England for her strong and solid good sense, happening to be with her husband at Constantinople, resolved to give smallpox to a child she had had in that country. In vain did her chaplain remonstrate that this practice was by no means consistent with Christian principles, and could only be expected to succeed with infidels; my lady Wortley's son recovered, and was presently as well as could be wished. This lady, on her return to London, communicated the experiment she had made to the princess of Wales,[1] now queen of Great Britain. It must be acknowledged that, setting crowns and titles aside, this princess is certainly born for the encouragement of arts, and for the good of the human race, to whom she is a generous benefactor. She is an amiable philosopher seated on a throne, who has improved every opportunity of instruction, and who has never let slip any occasion of showing her innate generosity. It is she who, on hearing that a daughter of Milton was still living, and in extreme misery, immediately sent her a valuable present; she it is who encourages the celebrated father Courayer; in a word, it is she who deigned to become the mediatrix between Dr. Clarke and Mr. Leibnitz. As soon as she heard of inoculation

[1] Queen Caroline. (Footnotes are by Tobias Smollett.)

for smallpox, she caused it to be tried on four criminals under sentence of death, who were thus doubly indebted to her for their lives: for she not only rescued them from the gallows, but, by means of this artificial attack of smallpox, prevented them from having it in the natural way, which they, in all human probability, would have had, and of which they might have died at a more advanced age. The princess, thus assured of the utility of this proof, caused her own children to be inoculated. All England, or rather Britain, followed her example; so that from that time at least six thousand children stand indebted for their lives to Lady Mary Wortley Montagu, as do all the fair of the island for preserving their beauty.

In a hundred persons that come into the world, at least sixty are found to contract smallpox; of these sixty, twenty are known to die, in the most favorable times, and twenty more wear very disagreeable marks of this cruel disorder as long as they live. Here is then a fifth part of the human species assuredly killed, or, at least, horribly disfigured. Among the vast numbers inoculated in Great Britain, or in Turkey, none are ever known to die, except such as were in a very ill state of health, or given over before. No one is marked with it; no one is ever infected a second time, supposing the inoculation to be perfect, that is, to have taken place as it ought. It is, therefore, certain that, had some French lady imported this secret from Constantinople into Paris, she would have rendered an inestimable and everlasting piece of service to the nation. The duke de Villequier, father of the present duke d'Aumont, a nobleman of the most robust constitution, would not have been cut off in the flower of his age; the prince de Soubise, who enjoyed the most remarkable state of good health ever known, would not have been carried off at twenty-five;

nor would the grandfather of Louis XV have been laid in his grave by it in his fiftieth year. The twenty thousand persons who died at Paris in 1723 would have been now alive. What shall we say then? Is it that the French set a lower value upon life? or are the ladies of France less anxious about the preservation of their charms? It is true, and it must be acknowledged, that we are a very odd kind of people! It is possible, that in ten years we may think of adopting this British custom, provided the doctors and curates allow us this indulgence; or, perhaps, the French will inoculate their children, out of mere whim, should those islanders leave it off, from their natural inconstancy.

I learn that the Chinese have practiced this custom for two hundred years; the example of a nation that has the first character in point of natural good sense, as well as of their excellent internal police, is a strong prejudice in its favor. It is true, the Chinese follow a method peculiar to themselves; they make no incision, but take smallpox up the nose in powder, just as we do a pinch of snuff: this method is more pleasant, but amounts to much the same thing, and serves equally to prove that had inoculation been practiced in France, it must assuredly have saved the lives of thousands.

It is some years since a Jesuit missionary having read this chapter, and being in a province of America, where smallpox makes horrible ravages, bethought himself of causing all the Indian children he baptized to be inoculated, so that they are indebted to him not only for this present life, but also for life eternal at the same time; what inestimable gifts for savages!

The bishop of Worcester has lately preached up the doctrine of inoculation at London; he has proved, like a good citizen and patriot, what a vast number of subjects this practice preserves to a nation: a doctrine which he has also enforced by such arguments as might be expected from a pastor and a Christian. They would preach at Paris against this salutary invention, as they wrote twenty years ago against Sir Isaac Newton's philosophy: in short, everything contributes to prove that the English are greater philosophers, and possessed of more courage than we. It will require some time before a true spirit of reason and a particular boldness of sentiment will be able to make their way over the Straits of Dover.

It must not, however, be imagined that no persons are to be met with from the Orkneys to the South Foreland but philosophers; the other species will always form the greater number. Inoculation was at first opposed in London; and a great while before the bishop of Worcester preached this gospel from the pulpit, a certain curate had taken it into his head to declaim against this practice: he told his congregation that Job had certainly been inoculated by the devil. This man spoiled a good Capuchin, for which nature seems to have intended him; he was certainly unworthy the honor of being born in this island. So we see prejudice, as usual, first got possession of the pulpit, and reason could not reach it till long after; this is no more than the common progress of the human mind.

Chancellor Bacon

It is not long since the ridiculous and threadbare question was agitated in a celebrated assembly; who was the greatest man, Caesar or Alexander, Tamerlane or Cromwell? Somebody said that it must undoubtedly be Sir Isaac Newton. This man was certainly in the right; for if true greatness consists in having received from heaven the advantage of a superior genius, with the talent of applying it for the interest of the possessor and of mankind, a man like Newton—and such a one is hardly to be met with in ten centuries—is surely by much the greatest; and those statesmen and conquerors which no age has ever been without, are commonly but so many illustrious villains. It is the man who sways our minds by the prevalence of reason and the native force of truth, not they who reduce mankind to a state of slavery by brutish force and downright violence; the man who by the vigor of his mind, is able to penetrate into the hidden secrets of nature, and whose capacious soul can contain the vast frame of the universe, not those who lay nature waste, and desolate the face of the earth, that claims our reverence and admiration.

Therefore, as you are desirous to be informed of the great men that England has produced, I shall begin with the Bacons, the Lockes, and the Newtons. The generals and ministers will come after them in their turn.

I must begin with the celebrated baron Verulam, known to the rest of Europe by the name of Bacon, who was the son of a certain keeper of the seals, and was for a considerable time chancellor under James I. Notwithstanding the intrigues and bustle of a court, and the occupations incident to his office, which would have required his whole attention, he found means to become a great philosopher, a good historian, and an elegant writer; and what is yet more wonderful is that he lived in an age where the art of writing was totally unknown, and where sound philosophy was still less so. This personage, as is the way among mankind, was more valued after his death than while he lived. His enemies were courtiers residing at London, while his admirers consisted wholly of foreigners. When Marquis d'Effiat brought

Princess Mary, daughter of Henry the Great, over to be married to King Charles, this minister paid Bacon a visit, who being then confined to a sick bed, received him with close curtains. "You are like the angels," said d'Effiat to him; "we hear much talk of them, and while everybody thinks them superior to men, we are never favored with a sight of them."

You have been told in what manner Bacon was accused of a crime which is very far from being the sin of a philosopher,[1] of being corrupted by pecuniary gifts; and how he was sentenced by the house of peers to pay a fine of about four hundred thousand livres of our money, besides losing his office of chancellor, and being degraded from the rank and dignity of a peer. At present the English revere his memory to such a degree that only with great difficulty can one imagine him to have been in the least guilty. Should you ask me what I think of it, I will make use of a saying I heard from Lord Bolingbroke. They happened to be talking of the avarice with which the duke of Marlborough had been taxed, and quoted several instances of it, for the truth of which they appealed to Lord Bolingbroke, who, as being of a contrary party, might, perhaps, without any trespass against the laws of decorum, freely say what he thought. "He was," said he, "so great a man that I do not recollect whether he had any faults or not." I shall, therefore,

[1] Lord Verulam being committed to the Tower, and conscious of that corruption which was laid to his charge, presented a petition to the house of peers, confessing himself guilty, and requesting that he might not be exposed to the shame of a public trial. He was deprived of his office of chancellor; rendered incapable of sitting in the upper house of parliament; fined forty thousand pounds, and condemned to be imprisoned in the Tower during the king's pleasure. James, in consideration of his great genius, remitted his fine, released him from prison, and indulged him with a very considerable pension.

confine myself to those qualities which have acquired Chancellor Bacon the esteem of all Europe.

The most singular, as well as the most excellent, of all his works, is that which is now the least read, and which is at the same time the most useful; I mean his "*Novum Scientiarum Organum.*" This is the scaffold by means of which the edifice of the new philosophy has been reared; so that when the building was completed, the scaffold was no longer of any use. Chancellor Bacon was still unacquainted with nature, but he perfectly knew, and pointed out extraordinarily well, all the paths which lead to her recesses. He had very early despised what those square-capped fools teach in those dungeons called *Colleges,* under the name of philosophy, and did everything in his power that those bodies, instituted for the cultivation and perfection of the human understanding, might cease any longer to mar it, by their "quiddities," their "horrors of a vacuum," their "substantial forms," with the rest of that jargon which ignorance and a nonsensical jumble of religion had consecrated.

This great man is the father of experimental philosophy. It is true, wonderful discoveries had been made even before his time; the mariner's compass, the art of printing, that of engraving, the art of painting in oil, that of making glass, with the remarkably advantageous invention of restoring in some measure sight to the blind; that is, to old men, by means of spectacles; the secret of making gunpowder had, also, been discovered. They had gone in search of, discovered, and conquered a new world in another hemisphere. Who would not have thought that these sublime discoveries had been made by the greatest philosophers, and in times much more enlightened than ours? By no means; for all these astonishing revolutions happened in the ages of scholastic barbarity. Chance alone has brought forth almost all these inventions; it is even pretended that chance has had a great share in the discovery of America; at least, it has been believed that Christopher Columbus undertook this voyage on the faith of a captain of a ship who had been cast by a storm on one of the Caribbee islands. Be this as it will, men had learned to penetrate to the utmost limits of the habitable globe, and to destroy the most impregnable cities with an artificial thunder, much more terrible than the real; but they were still ignorant of the circulation of the blood, the weight and pressure of the air, the laws of motion, the doctrine of light and color, the number of the planets in our system, etc. And a man that was capable to maintain a thesis on the "Categories of Aristotle," the *universale a parte rei,* or such-like nonsense, was considered as a prodigy.

The most wonderful and useful inventions are by no means those which do most honor to the human mind. And it is to a certain mechanical instinct, which exists in almost every man, that we owe far the greater part of the arts, and in no manner whatever to philosophy. The discovery of fire, the arts of making bread, of melting and working metals, of building houses, the invention of the shuttle, are infinitely more useful than printing and the compass; notwithstanding, all these were invented by men who were still in a state of barbarity. What astonishing things have the Greeks and Romans since done in mechanics? Yet men believed, in their time, that the heavens were of crystal, and the stars were so many small lamps, that sometimes fell into the sea; and one of their greatest philosophers, after many researches, had at length discovered that the stars were so many pebbles, that had flown off like sparks from the earth.

In a word, there was not a man who had any idea of

experimental philosophy before Chancellor Bacon; and of an infinity of experiments which have been made since his time, there is hardly a single one which has not been pointed out in his book. He had even made a good number of them himself. He constructed several pneumatic machines, by which he discovered the elasticity of the air; he had long brooded over the discovery of its weight, and was even at times very near to catching it, when it was laid hold of by Torricelli. A short time after, experimental physics began to be cultivated in almost all parts of Europe. This was a hidden treasure, of which Bacon had some glimmerings, and which all the philosophers whom his promises had encouraged made their utmost efforts to lay open. We see in his book mention made in express terms of that new attraction of which Newton passes for the inventor. "We must inquire," said Bacon, "whether there be not a certain magnetic force, which operates reciprocally between the earth and other heavy bodies, between the moon and the ocean, between the planets, etc." In another place he says: "Either heavy bodies are impelled toward the center of the earth, or they are mutually attracted by it; in this latter case it is evident that the nearer falling bodies approach the earth, the more forcibly are they attracted by it. We must try," continues he, "whether the same pendulum clock goes faster on the top of a mountain, or at the bottom of a mine. If the force of the weight diminishes on the mountain, and increases in the mine, it is probable the earth has a real attracting quality."

This precursor in philosophy was also an elegant writer, a historian, and a wit. His moral essays are in high estimation, though they seem rather calculated to instruct than to please; and as they are neither a satire on human nature, like the maxims of Rochefoucauld, nor a school of skepticism, like Montaigne, they are not so much read as these two ingenious books. His life of Henry VII passed for a masterpiece; but how is it possible some people should have been idle enough to compare so small a work with the history of our illustrious M. de Thou? Speaking of that famous impostor Perkin, son of a Jew convert, who assumed so boldly the name of Richard IV, king of England, being encouraged by the duchess of Burgundy, and who disputed the crown with Henry VII, he expresses himself in these terms: "About this time King Henry was beset with evil spirits, by the witchcraft of the duchess of Burgundy, who conjured up from hell the ghost of Edward IV, in order to torment King Henry. When the duchess of Burgundy had instructed Perkin, she began to consider with herself in what region of the heavens she should make this comet shine, and resolved immediately that it should make its appearance in the horizon of Ireland." I think our sage de Thou seldom gives in to this gallimaufry, which used formerly to pass for the sublime, but which at present is known by its proper title, "bombast."

Locke

There surely never was a more solid and more methodical understanding, nor a more acute and accurate logician, than Locke, though he was far from being an excellent mathematician. He never could bring himself to undergo the drudgery of calculation, nor the dryness of mathematical truths, which offer no sensible image to the understanding: and no one has more fully evinced than he has, that a man, without the smallest assistance from geometry, might still possess the most geometrical intellect possible. The great philosophers before his time had made no difficulties in determining the essence or substance of the human soul; but as they were wholly ignorant of the matter, it was but reasonable they should all be of different opinions.

In Greece, which was at one time the cradle of arts and of errors, where the greatness and folly of the human mind were pushed to so great a height, they reasoned on the soul exactly as we do. The divine Anaxagoras, who had altars erected to him for teaching men that the sun was bigger than the Peloponnesus, that snow was black, that the sky was of stone, affirmed that the soul was an aerial spirit, though immortal. Diogenes, a different person from him, who became a cynic from a counterfeiter of money, asserted that the soul was a portion of the substance of God; a notion which had at least something striking. Epicurus maintains the soul is composed of parts, in the same manner as matter. Aristotle, whose works have been interpreted a thousand different ways, because they were in fact absolutely unintelligible, was of opinion, if we may trust some of his disciples, that the understandings of all mankind were but one and the same substance. The divine Plato, master of the divine Aristotle, and the divine Socrates, master of the divine Plato, said that the soul was at the same time corporeal and eternal. The daemon of Socrates had, no doubt, let him into the secret of this matter. There are actually some who pretend that a fellow who boasted of having a familiar was most assuredly either knave or fool; possibly they who say so may be rather too squeamish.

As for our fathers of the Church, several of them, in the first ages were of opinion that the human soul, as well as the angels, and God himself, were all corporeal. The world is every day improving. St. Bernard, as Father Mabillon is forced to own, taught, with respect to the soul, that after death it did not behold God in heaven, but was obliged to rest satisfied with conversing with the humanity of Jesus Christ. Possibly they took it for once on his bare word; though the adventure of the crusade has somewhat lessened the credit of his oracles. Whole drones of schoolmen came after him: there was the irrefragable doctor,[1] the subtile doctor,[2] the angelic doctor,[3] the seraphic doctor,[4] the cherubimical doctor, all of whom made no scruple of saying they were perfectly clear as to the soul's substance, but who have, for all that, spoken of it exactly as if they neither understood one syllable of what they spoke of, and desired that nobody else should. Our Descartes, born to discover the mistakes of antiquity, only that he might substitute his own in their place, and borne down by the stream of system, which hoodwinks the greatest men, imagined he had demonstrated that the soul was the same thing with thought, in the same manner as matter is the same with extension. He firmly maintained that the soul always thinks, and that, at its arrival in the body, it is provided with a whole magazine of metaphysical notions, as of God, space, infinity, and fully supplied with all sorts of abstract ideas, which it unhappily loses the moment it comes forth from its mother's womb. Father Malebranche, of the oratory, in his sublime illusions, admits of no such thing as innate ideas, though he had no doubt of our seeing everything in God; and that God Himself, if it is lawful to speak in this manner, was the very essence of our soul.

After so many speculative gentlemen had formed

[1] Hales.
[2] Duns Scotus
[3] St. Thomas.
[4] Bonaventure.

this romance of the soul, one truly wise man appeared, who has, in the most modest manner imaginable, given us its real history. Mr. Locke has laid open to man the anatomy of his own soul, just as some learned anatomist would have done that of the body. He avails himself throughout of the help of metaphysical lights; and although he is sometimes bold enough to speak in a positive manner, he is on other occasions not afraid to discover doubts. Instead of determining at once what we were entirely ignorant about, he examines, step by step, the objects of human knowledge; he takes a child from the moment of its birth; he accompanies him through all the stages of the human understanding; he views what he possesses in common with the brutes, and in what he is superior to them. Above all, he is solicitous to examine the internal evidence of consciousness. "I leave," says he, "those who are possessed of more knowledge than I am to determine whether our souls exist before or after the organization of the body; but cannot help acknowledging that the soul that has fallen to my share is one of those coarse material kinds of souls which cannot always think; and I am even so unhappy as not to be able to conceive how it should be more indispensably necessary that the soul should always think, than it should be that the body should always be in motion."

For my own part, I am proud of the honor of being every whit as stupid on this point as Mr. Locke. Nobody shall ever persuade me that I always think; and I don't find myself in the least more disposed than he to think that, a few weeks after I was conceived, my soul was very learned, and acquainted with a thousand things that I forgot the moment I came into the world, and that I possessed to very little good purpose in the uterus, so many valuable secrets in philosophy, all of which abandoned me the instant they could have been of any advantage, and which I have never since been able to recover.

Locke, after demolishing the notion of innate ideas; after having renounced the vain opinion that the mind always thinks; having fully established this point, that the origin of all our ideas is from the senses;[1] having examined our simple and compound ideas; having accompanied the mind in all its operations; having shown the imperfection of all the languages spoken by men, and what a gross abuse of terms we are every moment guilty of; Locke, I say, at length proceeds to consider the extent, or rather the nothingness, of human knowledge. This is the chapter in which he has the boldness to advance, though in a modest manner, that "we shall never be able to determine, whether a being, purely material, is capable of thought or not." This sagacious proposition has passed with more than one divine as a scandalous assertion, that the soul is material and mortal. Some English devotees as usual gave the alarm. The superstitious are in society what poltroons are in an army; they infect the rest with their own panics. They cried out that Mr. Locke wanted to turn all religion topsy-turvy: there was, however, not the smallest relation to religion in the affair, the question was purely philosophical, and altogether independent of faith and revelation. They had only to examine, without rancor, whether it were a contradiction to say, that "matter is incapable of thought," and, "God is able to endow matter with thought." But it is too frequent with theologians to begin with pronouncing that God is offended, whenever we are not of their side of the question, or happen not to think as they do: the case is pretty much like that of the bad poets, who

[1] This is expressly the doctrine of Aristotle. The soul has no knowledge but that which it acquires through the canal of the senses.

took it into their heads to imagine Boileau spoke high treason, when he was only laughing at the silliness of their wretched compositions. Doctor Stillingfleet has acquired the character of a moderate divine, only because he has refrained from abuse in his controversy with Mr. Locke. He ventured to enter the lists with him, but was vanquished, because he reasoned too much like a doctor; while Locke, like a true philosopher, fully acquainted with the strength and weakness of human understanding, fought with arms of whose temper he was perfectly well assured.

Suicide

Philip Mordaunt, cousin-german to the famous earl of Peterborough, who was so well known in all the courts of Europe, and who made his boast that he had seen more postilions, and more crowned heads, than any other man in the world; this Philip Mordaunt, I say, was a young man about twenty-seven, handsome, well made, rich, of an illustrious family, and one who might pretend to anything; and, what was more than all the rest, he was passionately beloved by his mistress. However, this man took a distaste to life, discharged all that he owed, wrote to his friends to take leave of them, and even composed some verses upon the occasion, which concluded thus, that "though opium might be some relief to a wise man, if disgusted with the world, yet in his opinion a pistol, and a little resolution, were much more effectual remedies." His behavior was suitable to his principles; and he despatched himself with a pistol, without giving any other reason for it than that his soul was weary of his body, and that when we dislike our house we ought to quit it. One would imagine he chose to die because he was weary of being happy.

One Richard Smith has lately exhibited a most extraordinary instance of this nature to the world. This Smith was tired of being really unhappy; he had been rich, and was reduced to poverty; he had been healthy, and had become infirm; he had a wife, to whom he had nothing to give but a share in his misfortunes; and an infant in the cradle was the only thing he had left. Richard Smith and his wife, Bridget, then, after having affectionately embraced, and given each a formal kiss to their child, first cut the poor little creature's throat, and then hanged themselves at the foot of their bed. I do not remember to have heard anywhere of such a scene of horrors committed in cold blood; but the letter which these unhappy wretches wrote to their cousin, Mr. Brindley, before their death, is as remarkable as the manner of their death. "We are certain," said they, "of meeting with forgiveness from God. . . . We put an end to our lives because we were miserable, without any prospect of relief; and we have done our child that service to put it out of life, for fear it should have been as miserable as ourselves. . . ." It is to be observed that these people, after having murdered their child out of their paternal affection, wrote to a friend, recommending their dog and cat to his care. They thought, probably, that it was easier to make their dog and cat happy in this world than their child, and that keeping them would not be any great expense to their friend.[1]

The earl of Scarborough has lately quitted life with the same indifference as he did his place of master of

[1] Richard Smith was a bookbinder, and a prisoner for debt within the liberty of the King's Bench; and this shocking tragedy was acted in 1732. Smith and his wife had been always industrious and frugal, invincibly honest, and remarkable for conjugal affection.

the horse. Having been told in the house of lords that he sided with the court, on account of the profitable post he held in it, "My lords," said he, "to convince you that my opinion is not influenced by any such consideration, I will instantly resign." He afterward found himself perplexed between a mistress he was fond of, but to whom he was under no engagements, and a woman whom he esteemed, and to whom he had made a promise of marriage. My lord Scarborough, therefore, killed himself to get rid of difficulty.

The many tragical stories of this nature, with which the English newspapers abound, have made the greater part of Europe imagine that the English are fonder of killing themselves than any other people; and yet I question much whether there are not as many madmen at Paris as at London; and if our newspapers were to keep an exact register of those who have either had the folly, or unhappy resolution to destroy themselves, we might in this respect be found to vie with the English. But our compilers of news are more prudent; the adventures of private persons are never set forth to public scandal in any of the papers licensed by the government; however, I believe I may venture to affirm that this rage of suicide will never become epidemic. Nature has sufficiently guarded against it, and hope and fear are the powerful curbs she makes use of to stop the hand of the wretch uplifted to be his own executioner.

I know it may be said, that there have been countries where a council was established to give license to the people to kill themselves, when they could give sufficient reasons for doing it. To this I answer, that either the fact is false, or that such council found very little employment.

There is one thing indeed which may cause some surprise, and which I think deserves to be seriously discussed, which is, that almost all the great heroes among the Romans, during the civil wars, killed themselves when they lost a battle, and that we do not find an instance of a single leader, or great man, in the disputes of the League, the Fronde, or during the troubles of Italy and Germany, who put end to his life with his own hand. It is true, that these latter were Christians, and that there is great difference between a Christian soldier and a Pagan; and yet, how comes it that those very men who were so easily withheld by Christianity, from putting an end to their own lives, should be restrained either by that or any other consideration, when they had a mind to poison, assassinate, or publicly execute a vanquished enemy? Does not the Christian religion forbid this manner of taking away the life of a fellow-creature, if possible more than our own? The advocates for suicide tell us that it is very allowable to quit our house when we are weary of it. Agreed: but most men had rather lie in a bad house than sleep in the open fields.

I one day received a circular letter from an Englishman, in which he proposes a premium to the person who should the most clearly demonstrate that it was allowable for a man to kill himself. I made him no answer, for I had nothing to prove to him, and he had only to examine within himself if he preferred death to life.

But then let us ask why Cato, Brutus, Cassius, Antony, Otho, and so many others gave themselves death with so much resolution, and that our leaders of parties suffered themselves to be taken alive by their enemies, or waste the remains of a wretched old age in a dungeon? Some refined wits pretend to say that the ancients had no real courage; that Cato acted like a coward in putting an end to his own life: and that he would have showed more greatness of soul in crouching beneath the victorious Caesar. This may be very well in an ode, or as a figure in rhetoric; but it is very certain there must be some courage to resign a life coolly by the edge of a sword, some strength of mind thus to overcome the most powerful instinct of nature; in a word, that such an act shows a greater share of ferocity than weakness. When a sick man is in a frenzy, we cannot say he has no strength, though we may say it is the strength of a madman.

Self-murder was forbidden by the Pagan as well as by the Christian religion. There was even a place allotted in hell to those who put an end to their own lives. Witness these lines of the poet.

> Then crowds succeed, who prodigal of breath,
> Themselves anticipate the doom of death;
> Though free from guilt, they cast their lives away,
> And sad and sullen hate the golden day.
> Oh! with what joy the wretches now would bear
> Pain, toil, and woe, to breathe the vital air!
> In vain! by fate forever are they bound
> With dire Avernus, and the lake profound;
> And Styx with nine wide channels roars around.
>
> —PITT.

This was the religion of the heathens; and notwithstanding the torments they were to endure in the other world, it was esteemed an honor to quit this by giving themselves death by their own hands; so contradictory are the manners of men! Is not the custom of duelling still unhappily accounted honorable among us, though prohibited by reason, by religion, and by all laws, divine and human? If Cato and Caesar, Antony and Augustus, did not challenge each other to a duel, it was not that they were less brave than ourselves. If the duke of Montmorency, Marshal Marillac, de Thou, Cinq-Mars, and many others, rather chose to be dragged to execution like the vilest miscreants, than put an end to their own lives like Cato and Brutus, it was not that they had less courage than those Romans; the true reason is, that it was not then the fashion at Paris to kill oneself on such occasions; whereas it was an established custom with the Romans.

The women on the Malabar coast throw themselves alive into the flames, in which the bodies of their dead husbands are burning. Is it because they have more resolution than Cornelia? No; but the custom of the country is for wives to burn themselves.

> Custom and fancy of our fate decide,
> And what is this man's shame is t'other's pride.

Translation by W. F. Fleming

Essay on the Manners and Spirit of Nations

Recapitulation[1]

I HAVE now gone through the immense scene of revolutions that the world has experienced since the time of Charlemagne; and to what have they all tended? To desolation, and the loss of millions of lives! Every great event has been a capital misfortune. History has kept no account of times of peace and tranquillity; it relates only ravages and disasters.

We have beheld our Europe overspread with barbarians after the fall of the Roman Empire; and these barbarians, after becoming Christians, continually at war with the Mohammedans or else destroying each other.

We have seen Italy desolated by perpetual wars between city and city; the Guelphs and Ghibellines mutually destroying each other; whole ages of conspiracies, and successive irruptions of distant nations who have passed the Alps, and driven each other from their settlements by turns, till at length, in all this beautiful and extensive country, there remained only two states of any importance governed by their own natives—Venice and Rome. The others, namely, Naples, Sicily, Milan, Parma,

[1] Footnotes are by Tobias Smollett.

Placentia, and Tuscany, are under the dominion of foreigners.

The other great states of Christendom have suffered equally by wars and intestine commotions; but none of them has been brought under subjection to a neighboring power. The result of these endless disturbances and perpetual jars has been only the separating of some small provinces from one state, to be transferred to another. Flanders, for example, formerly under the suzerainty of France, passed to the house of Burgundy from foreign hands, and from this house to that of Austria; and a small part of this Flanders came again into the hands of the French in the reign of Louis XIV. Several provinces of ancient Gaul were in former times dismembered. Alsace, which was a part of ancient Gaul, became a province of Germany, and is at this day a province of France. Upper Navarre, which should be a demesne of the elder branch of the house of Bourbon, belongs to the younger; and Roussillon, which formerly belonged to the Spaniards, now belongs to the crown of France.

During all these shocks, there have been formed since the time of Charlemagne only two absolutely independent republics—that of Switzerland and that of Holland.

No one great kingdom has been able to subdue another. France, notwithstanding the conquests of Edward III and Henry V; notwithstanding the victories and efforts of Charles V and Philip II, has still preserved its limits, and even extended them; Spain, Germany, Great Britain, Poland, and the northern states are nearly as they were formerly.

What then have been the fruits of the blood of so many millions of men shed in battle, and the sacking of so many cities? Nothing great or considerable. The Christian powers have lost a great deal to the Turks, within these five centuries, and have gained scarcely anything from each other.

All history, then, in short, is little else than a long succession of useless cruelties; and if there happens any great revolution, it will bury the remembrance of all past disputes, wars, and fraudulent treaties, which have produced so many transitory miseries.

In the number of these miseries we may with justice include the disturbances and civil wars on the score of religion. Of these Europe has experienced two kinds, and it is hard to say which of them has proved more fatal to her. The first, as we have already seen, was the dispute of the popes with the emperors and kings: this began in the time of Louis the Feeble, and was not entirely at an end, in Germany, till after the reign of Charles V, in England, till suppressed by the resolution of Queen Elizabeth, and in France, till the submission of Henry IV. The other source of so much bloodshed was the rage of dogmatizing. This has caused the subversion of more than one state, from the time of the massacre of the Albigenses to the thirteenth century, and from the small war of the Cévennois to the beginning of the eighteenth. The field and the scaffold ran with blood on account of theological arguments, sometimes in one century, sometimes in another, for almost five hundred years, without interruption; and the long continuance of this dreadful scourge was owing to the fact that morality was always neglected to indulge a spirit of dogmatizing.

It must once again be acknowledged that history in general is a collection of crimes, follies, and misfortunes, among which we have now and then met with a few virtues, and some happy times; as we sometimes see a few scattered huts in a barren desert.

In those times of darkness and ignorance, which we

distinguish by the name of the Middle Ages, no one perhaps ever deserved so well of mankind as Pope Alexander VIII. It was he who abolished vassalage, in a council which he held in the twelfth century. It was he who triumphed in Venice by his prudence, over the brutal violence of Frederick Barbarossa, and who obliged Henry II of England to ask pardon of God and man for the murder of Thomas à Becket.[1] He restored the rights of the people, and chastized the wickedness of crowned heads. We have had occasion to remark that before this time, all Europe, a very small number of cities excepted, was divided between two ranks of people—the lords or owners of lands, either ecclesiastical or secular, and the villeins, or slaves. The lawyers, who assisted the knights, bailiffs, and stewards of fiefs, in giving their sentences, were in fact, no other than bondmen, or villeins, themselves. And, if mankind at length enjoy their rights, it is to Pope Alexander VIII that they are chiefly indebted for this happy change. It is to him that so many cities owe their present splendor; nevertheless, we know that this liberty was not universally extended. It has never made its way into Poland; the husbandman there is still a slave, and confined to the glebe; it is the same in Bohemia, Suabia, and several other countries of Germany; and even in France, in some of the provinces the most remote from the capital, we still see remains of this slav-

[1] That is to say, he obliged a great prince to do shameful penance, for a murder in which he had no hand; and by what means did he manifest this power? By employing all the villainous arts of priestcraft to alienate the affections of the people from their natural sovereign; by excommunications, interdictions, and absolving the subjects from their oaths of allegiance. As for Becket, whom Alexander allowed to be canonized, we hope there are not three Britons now living who do not detest his character, as that of a pernicious firebrand, whose pride, insolence, and fanaticism kept his sovereign and his country in continual disquiet.

ery. There are some chapters and monks who claim a right to all the goods of the peasants.

In Asia, on the contrary, there are no slaves but those which are purchased with money, or taken prisoners in battle. In the Christian states of Europe they do not buy slaves, neither do they reduce their prisoners of war to a state of servitude. The Asiatics have only a domestic servitude; Christians only a civil one. The peasant in Poland is a bondman in the lands, but not in the house of his lord. We make household slaves only of the Negroes; we are severely reproached for this kind of traffic, but the people who make a trade of selling their children are certainly more blamable than those who purchase them, and this traffic is only a proof of our superiority. He who voluntarily subjects himself to a master is designed by nature for a slave.

We have seen that, from time immemorial, they have tolerated all religions in Asia, much as is at present done in England, Holland, and Germany. We have observed that this toleration was more general in Japan than in any other country whatever, till the fatal affair which rendered that government so inexorable.

We may have observed, in the course of so many revolutions, that several nations almost entirely savage have been formed both in Europe and Asia, in those very countries which were formerly the most civilized. Thus, some of the islands of the Archipelago, which were once so flourishing, are now little better than Indian habitations in America. The country where were formerly the cities of Artaxata, and Tigranocerta, have not now even half the value of some of our petty colonies. There are, in some of the islands, forests, and mountains in the very heart of Europe, a set of people who are in nothing superior to those of Canada, or the Negroes of Africa.

The Turks are more civilized, but we hardly know of one city built by them; they have suffered the most noble and beautiful monuments of antiquity to fall to decay, and reign only over a pile of ruins.

They have nothing in Asia that in the least resembles our European nobility; nor is there to be found throughout the whole East any one order of citizens distinguished from the others by hereditary titles, or particular privileges and indulgences, annexed solely to birth. The Tartars seem to be the only people who have some faint shadow of this institution, in the race of their Mirzas. We meet with nothing, either in Turkey, Persia, the Indies, or China, that bears any similitude to that body of nobility which forms an essential part of every European monarchy. We must go as far as Malabar to meet with any likeness to this sort of constitution; and there again it is very different, and consists in a tribe wholly dedicated to bearing arms, and which never intermixes, by marriage or otherwise, with any of the other tribes or castes, and will not even condescend to hold any commerce with them.

The greatest differences between us and the Orientals is in the manner of treating our women. No female ever reigned in the East, unless that princess of Mingrelia, whom Sir John Chardin tells us of in his voyages, and whom he accuses of robbing him. In France, though the women cannot wear the crown, they may be regents of the kingdom, and have a right to every other throne but that of the empire and Poland.

Another difference in our manner of treating women is the custom of placing about their persons men deprived of their virility, a custom which has always prevailed in Asia and Africa, and has at times been introduced into Europe by the Roman emperors. At present there are not throughout all Christendom two hundred eunuchs employed, either in our churches or theaters, whereas all the Eastern seraglios swarm with them.

In short, we differ in every respect, in religion, policy, government, manners, food, clothing, and even in our manner of writing, expressing, and thinking. That in which we most resemble them is that propensity to war, slaughter, and destruction, which has always depopulated the face of the earth. It must be owned, however, that this rage has taken much less possession of the minds of the people of India and China than of ours. In particular, we have no instance of the Indians or Chinese having made war upon the inhabitants of the North. In this respect they are much better members of society than ourselves; but then, on the other hand, this very virtue, or rather meekness, of theirs has been their ruin; for they have been all enslaved.

In the midst of the ravages and desolations which we have observed during the space of nine hundred years, we perceive a love for order which secretly animates humankind, and has prevented its total ruin. This is one of the springs of nature which always recovers its tone; it is this which has formed the code of all nations, and this inspires a veneration for the laws and the ministers of the laws at Tonkin, and in the island of Formosa, the same as at Rome. Children respect their parents in all countries, and in every country—let others say what they will—the son is his father's heir; for, though in Turkey the son of a Timariot does not inherit his father's dignity, nor, in India, the son of an Omra his lands, the reason is because neither the one nor the other belong to the father himself. A place for life is, in no country of the world, considered as an inheritance; but in Persia, in India, and throughout all Asia, every native, and even every stranger, of whatsoever religion, except in Japan, may purchase lands that are not part of the crown demesnes, and leave them to his family.

In Europe there are still some nations where the law will not suffer a stranger to purchase a field or a burying-place in their territories. The barbarous right of aubaine, by which a stranger beholds his father's estate go to the king's treasury, still exists in all the Christian states, unless where it is otherwise provided by private convention.

We likewise have a notion that in the Eastern countries the women are all slaves, because they are confined to the duties of domestic life. If they were really slaves, they must become beggars at the death of their husbands, which is not the case; the law everywhere provides a stated portion for them, and this portion they obtain in case of a divorce. In every part of the world, we find laws established for the support of families.

In all nations there is a proper curb to arbitrary power, either by law, custom, or manners. The Turkish sultan can neither touch the public treasure, break the janissaries, nor interfere with the inside of the seraglios of any of his subjects. The emperor of China cannot publish a single edict without the sanction of a tribunal. Every state is at times liable to violent oppressions; the grand viziers and the itimadoulets exercise rapine and murder, it is true, but they are no more authorized so to do by the laws than the wild Arabs or wandering Tartars are to plunder the caravans.

Religion teaches the same principles of morality to all nations, without exception; the ceremonies of the Asiatics are ridiculous, their belief absurd, but their precepts are just; the dervish, the fakir, the bonze, and the talapoin, are always crying out: "Be just and beneficent." The common people in China are accused of being great cheats in trade; they are perhaps encouraged to this vice by knowing that they can procure absolution for their crime of their bonzes for a trifling sum of money. The moral precepts taught them are good, the indulgence which is sold them is bad.

We are not to credit those travelers and missionaries, who have represented the Eastern priests to us as persons who preach up iniquity; this is traducing human nature; it is not possible that there should ever exist a religious society instituted for the encouragement or propagation of vice.

We should equally deceive ourselves, were we to believe that the Mohammedan religion owes its establishment wholly to the sword. The Mohammedans have had their missionaries in the Indies and in China; and the sects of Omar and Ali dispute with each other for proselytes, even on the coasts of Coromandel and Malabar.

From all that we have observed in this sketch of universal history, it follows that whatever concerns human nature is the same from one end of the universe to the other, and that what is dependent upon custom differs, or, if there is any resemblance, it is the effect of chance. The dominion of custom is much more extensive than that of nature, and influences all manners and all usages. It diffuses variety over the face of the universe. Nature establishes unity, and everywhere settles a few invariable principles; the soil is still the same, but culture produces various fruits.

As nature has placed in the heart of man interest, pride, and all the passions, it is no wonder that, during a period of about six centuries, we meet with almost a continual succession of crimes and disasters. If we go back to earlier ages, we shall find them no better. Custom has ordered it so that evil has everywhere operated in a different manner.

Translation by W. F. Fleming

The Lisbon Earthquake

Author's Preface

IF THE question concerning physical evil ever deserves the attention of men, it is in those melancholy events which put us in mind of the weakness of our nature; such as plagues, which carry off a fourth of the inhabitants of the known world; the earthquake which swallowed up four hundred thousand of the Chinese in 1699, that of Lima and Callao, and, in the last place, that of Portugal and the kingdom of Fez. The maxim, "whatever is, is right," appears somewhat extraordinary to those who have been eye-witnesses of such calamities. All things are doubtless arranged and set in order by Providence, but it has long been too evident, that its superintending power has not disposed them in such a manner as to promote our temporal happiness.

When the celebrated Pope published his "Essay on Man," and expounded in immortal verse the systems of Leibnitz, Lord Shaftesbury, and Lord Bolingbroke, his system was attacked by a multitude of divines of a variety of different communions. They were shocked at the novelty of the propositions, "whatever is, is right"; and that "man always enjoys that measure of happiness which is suited to his being." There are few writings that may not be condemned, if considered in one light, or approved of, if considered in another. It would be much more reasonable to attend only to the beauties and improving parts of a work, than to endeavor to put an odious construction on it; but it is one of the imperfections of our nature to put a bad interpretation on whatever has a dubious sense, and to run down whatever has been successful.

In a word, it was the opinion of many, that the axiom, "whatever is, is right," was subversive of all our received ideas. If it be true, said they, that whatever is, is right, it follows that human nature is not degenerated. If the general order requires that everything should be as it is, human nature has not been corrupted, and consequently could have had no occasion for a Redeemer. If this world, such as it is, be the best of systems possible, we have no room to hope for a happy future state. If the various evils by which man is overwhelmed, end in general good, all civilized nations have been wrong in endeavoring to trace out the origin of moral and physical evil. If a man devoured by wild beasts, causes the well-being of those beasts, and contributes to promote the orders of the universe; if the misfortunes of individuals are only the consequence of this general and necessary order, we are nothing more than wheels which serve to keep the great machine in motion; we are not more precious in the eyes of God, than the animals by whom we are devoured.

These are the inferences which were drawn from Mr. Pope's poem; and these very conclusions increased the sale and success of the work. But it should have been seen from another point of view. Readers should have considered the reverence for the Deity, the resignation to His supreme will, the useful morality, and the spirit of toleration, which breathe through this excellent poem.

This the public has done, and the work being translated by men equal to the task, has completely triumphed over critics, though it turned on matters of so delicate a nature.

It is the nature of overviolent censurers to give importance to the opinions which they attack. A book is railed at on account of its success, and a thousand errors are imputed to it. What is the consequence of this? Men, disgusted with these invectives, take for truths the very errors which these critics think they have discovered. Cavillers raise phantoms on purpose to combat them, and indignant readers embrace these very phantoms.

Critics have declared that Pope and Leibnitz maintain the doctrine of fatality; the partisans of Leibnitz and Pope have said on the other hand that, if Leibnitz and Pope have taught the doctrine of fatality, they were in the right, and all this invincible fatality we should believe.

Pope had advanced that "whatever is, is right," in a sense that might very well be admitted, and his followers maintain the same proposition in a sense that may very well be contested.

The author of the poem, "The Lisbon Earthquake," does not write against the illustrious Pope, whom he always loved and admired; he agrees with him in almost every particular, but compassionating the misery of man; he declares against the abuse of the new maxim, "whatever is, is right." He maintains that ancient and sad truth acknowledged by all men, that there is evil upon earth; he acknowledges that the words "whatever is, is right," if understood in a positive sense, and without any hopes of a happy future state, only insult us in our present misery.

If, when Lisbon, Moquinxa, Tetuan, and other cities were swallowed up with a great number of their inhabitants in the month of November, 1759, philosophers had cried out to the wretches, who with difficulty escaped from the ruins, "all this is productive of general good; the heirs of those who have perished will increase their fortune; masons will earn money by rebuilding the houses, beasts will feed on the carcasses buried under the ruins; it is the necessary effect of necessary causes; your particular misfortune is nothing, it contributes to universal good," such a harangue would doubtless have been as cruel as the earthquake was fatal, and all that the author of the poem upon the destruction of Lisbon has said amounts only to this.

He acknowledges with all mankind that there is evil as well as good on the earth; he owns that no philosopher has ever been able to explain the nature of moral and physical evil. He asserts that Bayle, the greatest master of the art of reasoning that ever wrote, has only taught to doubt, and that he combats himself; he owns that man's understanding is as weak as his life is miserable. He lays a concise abstract of the several different systems before his readers. He says that Revelation alone can untie the great knot which philosophers have only rendered more puzzling; and that nothing but the hope of our existence being continued in a future state can console us under our present misfortunes; that the goodness of Providence is the only asylum in which man can take refuge in the darkness of reason, and in the calamities to which his weak and frail nature is exposed.

P. S.—Readers should always distinguish between the objections which an author proposes to himself and his answers to those objections, and should not mistake what he refutes for what he adopts.

The Lisbon Earthquake[1]

AN INQUIRY INTO THE MAXIM, "WHATEVER IS, IS RIGHT."

OH WRETCHED man, earth-fated to be cursed;
Abyss of plagues, and miseries the worst!
Horrors on horrors, griefs on griefs must show,
That man's the victim of unceasing woe,
And lamentations which inspire my strain,
Prove that philosophy is false and vain.
Approach in crowds, and meditate awhile
Yon shattered walls, and view each ruined pile,
Women and children heaped up mountain high,
Limbs crushed which under ponderous marble lie;
Wretches unnumbered in the pangs of death,
Who mangled, torn, and panting for their breath,
Buried beneath their sinking roofs expire,
And end their wretched lives in torments dire.
Say, when you hear their piteous, half-formed cries,
Or from their ashes see the smoke arise,
Say, will you then eternal laws maintain,
Which God to cruelties like these constrain?
Whilst you these facts replete with horror view,
Will you maintain death to their crimes was due?
And can you then impute a sinful deed
To babes who on their mothers' bosoms bleed?
Was then more vice in fallen Lisbon found,
Than Paris, where voluptuous joys abound?
Was less debauchery to London known,

[1] (*Note:* All footnotes to *The Lisbon Earthquake* are Tobias Smollett's.) The great earthquake occurred on November 1, 1755. The ruin was instantaneous. Between 30,000 and 40,000 lives were lost in the shock and in the fire.

Where opulence luxurious holds her throne?
Earth Lisbon swallows; the light sons of France
Protract the feast, or lead the sprightly dance.
Spectators who undaunted courage show,
While you behold your dying brethren's woe;
With stoical tranquillity of mind
You seek the causes of these ills to find;
But when like us Fate's rigors you have felt,
Become humane, like us you'll learn to melt.
When the earth gapes my body to entomb,
I justly may complain of such a doom.
Hemmed round on every side by cruel fate,
The snares of death, the wicked's furious hate,
Preyed on by pain and by corroding grief
Suffer me from complaint to find relief.
'Tis pride, you cry, seditious pride that still
Asserts mankind should be exempt from ill.
The awful truth on Tagus' banks explore,
Rummage the ruins on that bloody shore,
Wretches interred alive in direful grave
Ask if pride cries, "Good Heaven, thy creatures save."
If 'tis presumption that makes mortals cry,
"Heav'n, on our sufferings cast a pitying eye."
All's right, you answer, the eternal cause
Rules not by partial, but by general laws.
Say what advantage can result to all,
From wretched Lisbon's lamentable fall?
Are you then sure, the power which could create
The universe and fix the laws of fate,
Could not have found for man a proper place,
But earthquakes must destroy the human race?
Will you thus limit the eternal mind?
Should not our God to mercy be inclined?
Cannot then God direct all nature's course?
Can power almighty be without resource?

Humbly the great Creator I entreat,
This gulf with sulphur and with fire replete,
Might on the deserts spend its raging flame,
God my respect, my love weak mortals claim;
When man groans under such a load of woe,
He is not proud, he only feels the blow.
Would words like these to peace of mind restore
The natives sad of that disastrous shore?
Grieve not, that others' bliss may overflow,
Your sumptuous palaces are laid thus low;
Your toppled towers shall other hands rebuild;
With multitudes your walls one day be filled;
Your ruin on the North shall wealth bestow,
For general good from partial ills must flow;
You seem as abject to the sovereign power,
As worms which shall your carcasses devour.
No comfort could such shocking words impart,
But deeper wound the sad, afflicted heart.
When I lament my present wretched state,
Allege not the unchanging laws of fate;
Urge not the links of the eternal chain,
'Tis false philosophy and wisdom vain.
The God who holds the chain can't be enchained;[1]

[1] The universal chain is not, as some have thought, a regular gradation which connects all beings. There is, in all probability, an immense distance between man and beast, as well as between man and substances of a superior nature; there is likewise an infinity between God and all created beings whatever. There are none of these insensible gradations in the globes which move round our sun in their several periods, whether we consider their mass, their distances, or their satellites.

If we may believe Pope, man is not capable of discovering the reason why the satellites of Jove are less than Jove himself; he is herein mistaken; such an error as this may well be overlooked in so fine a genius. Every smatterer in mathematics could have told Lord Bolingbroke and Mr. Pope, that if the satellites of Jove had equaled him in magnitude, they could not have moved round him; but no mathematician is able to discover the regular gradation in the bodies of the solar system.

By His blest will are all events ordained:
He's just, nor easily to wrath gives way,

It is not true, that the world could not exist if a single atom was taken from it: This was justly observed by Mr. Crousaz, a learned geometrician, in a tract which he wrote against Pope. He seems to have been right in this point, though he was fully refuted by Mr. Warburton and Mr. Silhouette.

The concatenation of events was admitted and defended with the utmost ingenuity by the celebrated philosopher Leibnitz; it is worth explaining. All bodies and all events depend upon other bodies and other events. That cannot be denied; but all bodies are not essential to the support of the universe, and the preservation of its order; neither are all events necessary in the general series of events. A drop of water, a grain of sand more or less, can cause no revolution in the general system. Nature is not confined to any determinate quantity, or any determinate form. No planet moves in a curve completely regular; there is nothing in Nature of a figure exactly mathematical; no fixed quantity is required for any operation: Nature is never very strict or rigid in her method of proceeding. It is, therefore, absurd to advance, that the removal of an atom from the earth might be the cause of its destruction.

This holds, in like manner, with regard to events. The cause of every event is contained in some precedent event; this no philosopher has ever called in question. If Caesar's mother had never gone through the Caesarian operation, Caesar had never subverted the commonwealth; he could never have adopted Octavius, and Octavius could never have chosen Tiberius for his successor in the empire. The marriage of Maximilian with the heiress of Burgundy and the Low Countries, gave rise to a war which lasted two hundred years. But Caesar's spitting on the right or left side, or the Duchess of Burgundy's dressing her head in this manner or in that, could have altered nothing in the general plan of Providence.

It follows, therefore, that there are some events which have consequences and others which have none. Their chain resembles a genealogical tree, some branches of which disappear at the first genertion, whilst the race is continued by others. There are many events which pass away without ever generating others. Thus in every machine there are some effects indispensably necessary toward producing motion, and others which are productive of nothing at all. The wheels of a coach make it go; but whether they raise more or less dust, the journey is finished alike. Such is the general order of the world, that the links of the chain would not be in the least discomposed by a small increase or diminution of the quantity of matter, or by an inconsiderable deviation from regularity.

The chain is not in an absolute *plenum*; it has been demonstrated that the celestial bodies perform their revolutions in an unresisting

Why suffer we beneath so mild a sway:[1]
This is the fatal knot you should untie,
Our evils do you cure when you deny?
Men ever strove into the source to pry,
Of evil, whose existence you deny.
If he whose hand the elements can wield,
To the winds' force makes rocky mountains yield;
If thunder lays oaks level with the plain,
From the bolts' strokes they never suffer pain.
But I can feel, my heart oppressed demands
Aid of that God who formed me with His hands.
Sons of the God supreme to suffer all
Fated alike; we on our Father call.
No vessel of the potter asks, we know,
Why it was made so brittle, vile, and low?
Vessels of speech as well as thought are void;
The urn this moment formed and that destroyed,
The potter never could with sense inspire,
Devoid of thought it nothing can desire.
The moralist still obstinate replies,
Others' enjoyments from your woes arise,
To numerous insects shall my corpse give birth,
When once it mixes with its mother earth:
Small comfort 'tis that when Death's ruthless power

medium. Every space is not filled. It follows then, that there is not a progression of bodies from an atom to the most remote fixed star. There may of consequence be immense intervals between beings imbued with sensation, as well as between those that are not. We cannot then be certain, that man must be placed in one of these links joined to another by an uninterrupted connection. That all things are linked together means only that all things are regularly disposed of in their proper order. God is the cause and the regulator of that order. Homer's Jupiter was the slave of destiny; but, according to more rational philosophy, God is the master of destiny. (See Clarke's Treatise "Upon the Existence of God.")

[1] *Sub Deo justo nemo miser nisi mereatur.*—St. Augustine. The meaning of this *ipse dixit* of the Saint is, no one is miserable under the government of a just God, without deserving to be so.

Closes my life, worms shall my flesh devour.
Remembrances of misery refrain
From consolation, you increase my pain:
Complaint, I see, you have with care repressed,
And proudly hid your sorrows in your breast.
But a small part I no importance claim
In this vast universe, this general frame;
All other beings in this world below
Condemned like me to lead a life of woe,
Subject to laws as rigorous as I,
Like me in anguish live and like me die.
The vulture urged by an insatiate maw,
Its trembling prey tears with relentless claw:
This it finds right, endowed with greater powers
The bird of Jove the vulture's self devours.
Man lifts his tube, he aims the fatal ball
And makes to earth the towering eagle fall;
Man in the field with wounds all covered o'er,
Midst heaps of dead lies weltering in his gore,
While birds of prey the mangled limbs devour,
Of Nature's Lord who boasts his mighty power.
Thus the world's members equal ills sustain,
And perish by each other born to pain:
Yet in this direful chaos you'd compose
A general bliss from individuals' woes?
Oh worthless bliss! in injured reason's sight,
With faltering voice you cry, "What is, is right"?
The universe confutes your boasting vain,
Your heart retracts the error you maintain.
Men, beasts, and elements know no repose
From dire contention; earth's the seat of woes:
We strive in vain its secret source to find.
Is ill the gift of our Creator kind?
Do then fell Typhon's cursed laws ordain
Our ill, or Arimanius doom to pain?

Shocked at such dire chimeras, I reject
Monsters which fear could into gods erect.
But how conceive a God, the source of love,
Who on man lavished blessings from above,
Then would the race with various plagues confound
Can mortals penetrate His views profound?
Ill could not from a perfect being spring,
Nor from another, since God's sovereign king;
And yet, sad truth! in this our world 'tis found,
What contradictions here my soul confound!
A God once dwelt on earth amongst mankind,
Yet vices still lay waste the human mind;
He could not do it, this proud sophist cries,
He could, but he declined it, that replies;
He surely will, ere these disputes have end,
Lisbon's foundations hidden thunders rend,
And thirty cities' shattered remnants fly,
With ruin and combustion through the sky,
From dismal Tagus' ensanguined shore,
To where of Cadiz' sea the billows roar.
Or man's a sinful creature from his birth,
And God to woe condemns the sons of earth;
Or else the God who being rules and space,
Untouched with pity for the human race,
Indifferent, both from love and anger free,
Still acts consistent to His first decree:
Or matter has defects which still oppose
God's will, and thence all human evil flows;
Or else this transient world by mortals trod,
Is but a passage that conducts to God.
Our transient sufferings here shall soon be o'er,
And death will land us on a happier shore.
But when we rise from this accursed abyss,
Who by his merit can lay claim to bliss?
Dangers and difficulties man surround,

Doubts and perplexities his mind confound.
To nature we apply for truth in vain,
God should His will to human kind explain.
He only can illume the human soul,
Instruct the wise man, and the weak console.
Without Him man of error still the sport,
Thinks from each broken reed to find support.
Leibnitz can't tell me from what secret cause
In a world governed by the wisest laws,
Lasting disorders, woes that never end
With our vain pleasures real sufferings blend;
Why ill the virtuous with the vicious shares?
Why neither good nor bad misfortunes spares?
I can't conceive that "what is, ought to be,"
In this each doctor knows as much as me.
We're told by Plato, that man, in times of yore,
Wings gorgeous to his glorious body wore,
That all attacks he could unhurt sustain,
By death ne'er conquered, ne'er approached by pain.
Alas, how changed from such a brilliant state!
He crawls 'twixt heaven and earth, then yields to fate.
Look round this sublunary world, you'll find
That nature to destruction is consigned.
Our system weak which nerves and bone compose,
Cannot the shock of elements oppose;
This mass of fluids mixed with tempered clay,
To dissolution quickly must give way.
Their quick sensations can't unhurt sustain
The attacks of death and of tormenting pain,
This is the nature of the human frame,
Plato and Epicurus I disclaim.
Nature was more to Bayle than either known:
What do I learn from Bayle, to doubt alone?
Bayle, great and wise, all systems overthrows,
Then his own tenets labors to oppose.

Like the blind slave to Delilah's commands,
Crushed by the pile demolished by his hands.
Mysteries like these can no man penetrate,
Hid from his view remains the book of fate.
Man his own nature never yet could sound,
He knows not whence he is, nor whither bound.[1]
Atoms tormented on this earthly ball,
The sport of fate, by death soon swallowed all,
But thinking atoms, who with piercing eyes
Have measured the whole circuit of the skies;
We rise in thought up to the heavenly throne,
But our own nature still remains unknown.
This world which error and o'erweening pride,
Rulers accursed between them still divide,
Where wretches overwhelmed with lasting woe,
Talk of a happiness they never know,
Is with complaining filled, all are forlorn
In seeking bliss; none would again be born.
If in a life midst sorrows past and fears,
With pleasure's hand we wipe away our tears,
Pleasure his light wings spreads, and quickly flies,
Losses on losses, griefs on griefs arise.

[1] It is self-evident, that man cannot acquire this knowledge without assistance. The human mind derives all its knowledge from experience; no experience can give us an insight into what preceded our existence, into what is to follow it, nor into what supports it at present. In what manner have we received life? What is the spring upon which it depends? How is our brain capable of ideas and memory? In what manner do our limbs obey every motion of the will? Of all this we are entirely ignorant. Is our globe the only one that is inhabited? Was it created after other globes, or at the same instant? Does every particular species of plants proceed from a first plant? Is every species of animals produced by two first animals? The most profound philosophers are no more able to solve these questions than the most ignorant of men. All these questions may be reduced to the vulgar proverb: Was the hen before the egg, or the egg before the hen? The proverb is rather low, but it confounds the utmost penetration of human wisdom, which is utterly at a loss with regard to the first principles of things without supernatural assistance.

The mind from sad remembrance of the past,
Is with black melancholy overcast;
Sad is the present if no future state,
No blissful retribution mortals wait,
If fate's decrees the thinking being doom
To lose existence in the silent tomb.
All may be well; that hope can man sustain,
All now is well; 'tis an illusion vain.
The sages held me forth delusive light,
Divine instructions only can be right.
Humbly I sigh, submissive suffer pain,
Nor more the ways of Providence arraign.
In youthful prime I sung in strains more gay,
Soft pleasure's laws which lead mankind astray.
But times change manners; taught by age and care
Whilst I mistaken mortals' weakness share,
The light of truth I seek in this dark state,
And without murmuring submit to fate.
A caliph once when his last hour drew nigh,
Prayed in such terms as these to the most high:
"Being supreme, whose greatness knows no bound,
I bring thee all that can't in Thee be found;
Defects and sorrows, ignorance and woe."
Hope he omitted, man's sole bliss below.

Translation by Tobias Smollett and others